Dear Reader,

As many of you know, I've long been interested in futuristic and time-travel stories. In this special 2-in-1 volume, Silhouette has brought together two of my early books dealing with men of the future: *Time Was* and *Times Change*.

Imagine what you would feel like if you encountered, practically in your own backyard, a man who came from a world that was more than two centuries ahead of your own! That's exactly what happens to sisers Liberty and Sunny Stone in these two novels.

In *Time Was*, Liberty is standing on the porch of her remote mountain cabin when time traveler Caleb Hornblower literally drops out of the sky and into her world. There is nothing rational about falling in love with this hunk from the future. And yet, as both Liberty and Caleb discover, not even time can stop the pull of love.

Times Change features Caleb's brother, Jacob, who has followed his brother across time in order to bring Caleb home. But after spending some time with Liberty's sexy sister, Sunny, Jacob realizes his only home is in Sunny's arms.

I hope you enjoy these two books. In February 2002, look for my 100th book for Silhouette, *Cordina's Crown Jewel*, available from Silhouette Special Edition.

All the best,

Nora Roberts

NORA ROBERTS

TIME AND AGAIN

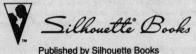
Silhouette Books

Published by Silhouette Books

America's Publisher of Contemporary Romance

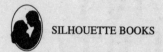 SILHOUETTE BOOKS

TIME AND AGAIN

Copyright © 2001 by Harlequin Books S.A.

ISBN 0-373-48441-0

The publisher acknowledges the copyright holder
of the individual works as follows:

TIME WAS
Copyright © 1989 by Nora Roberts

TIMES CHANGE
Copyright © 1990 by Nora Roberts

Visit Silhouette at www.eHarlequin.com

Printed in U.S.A.

CONTENTS

TIME WAS   9

TIMES CHANGE   259

TIME WAS

For Joan and Tom
Just for fun

Chapter 1

He was going down. The instrument panel was a maze of wildly flashing numbers and lights, and the cockpit was spinning like a merry-go-round gone mad. He didn't need the scream of warning bells to tell him he was in trouble. He didn't need the insistent red blip on his computer screen to tell him the trouble was big. He'd known that the moment he'd seen the void.

Swearing, clamping down on his panic, he struggled with the controls, using one hand to shove the lever forward for full power. The vehicle bucked and shuddered, fighting the gravitational pull. The G's hit him like a wall. All around him metal screamed against metal.

"Hold together, baby," he managed to say as his lips stretched back over his teeth. The floor near his feet ripped open in a jagged line three inches long. "Hold together, you son of a—"

He jammed hard due east, swearing again when it seemed that no matter how cleverly he maneuvered he and his ship would be sucked into the hole.

The cockpit lights went out, leaving only the whirl of kaleidoscopic colors from the instrument panel. His ship went into a spiral, tumbling end over end like a stone fired from a slingshot. Now the light was white, hot and brilliant. Instinctively he threw up an arm to shield his eyes. The sudden crushing pressure on his chest left him helpless to do more than gasp for breath.

Briefly, before he lost consciousness, he remembered that his mother had wanted him to be a lawyer. But he'd just had to fly.

When he came to he was no longer spiraling—he was in a screaming free-fall. A glance at his instruments showed him only that they were damaged, the numbers racing backward. A new force had him plastered back against his seat, but he could see the curve of the earth.

Knowing he could pass out again at any moment, he lunged forward to knock the throttle back and turn the ship over to the computer. It would, he knew, scan for an unpopulated area, and if God was in His heaven the crash control in the old bucket would still be functional.

Maybe, just maybe, he'd live to see another sunrise. And how bad could practicing law be?

He watched the world rush toward him, blue and green and beautiful. The hell with it, he thought. Flying a desk would never be like this.

Libby stood on the porch of the cabin and watched the night sky boil. The wicked slices of lightning and the blowing curtain of rain were the best show in town. Even though she was standing under the overhang, her hair and her face were wet. Behind her, the lights in the cabin glowed a warm, cozy yellow. The next boom of thunder made her grateful she'd set out candles and kerosene lamps.

But the light and warmth didn't lure her back. Tonight she preferred the chill and the crashing power that was barreling through the mountains.

If the storm kept up much longer, it would be weeks before the north pass through the mountains was negotiable. It didn't matter, she thought as another spear of lightning split the sky. She had weeks. In fact, she thought with a grin, hugging herself against the brisk wind, she had all the time in the world.

The best decision she'd ever made had been to pack up and dig in at her family's hideaway cabin. She'd always had an affection for mountains. The Klamaths of southwestern Oregon had everything she wanted. A spectacular view, high, rugged peaks, pure air and solitude. If it took six months to write her dissertation on the effects of modernizing influences on the Kolbari Islanders, then so be it. She'd spent five years studying cultural anthropology, three of them in extensive field work. She hadn't let up on herself since her eighteenth birthday, and she certainly hadn't given herself any time alone, away from family, studies and other scientists. The dissertation was important to her—too important, she could sometimes admit. Coming here to work alone, giving herself a little time for self-study, was an excellent compromise.

She'd been born in the squat two-story cabin behind her, and she'd spent the first five years of her life here in these mountains, living as free and unfettered as a deer.

It made her smile to remember how she and her younger sister had run barefoot, how they had believed the world began and ended with them and their counterculture parents.

She could still picture her mother weaving mats and rugs and her father digging happily in his garden. At night there had been music and long, fascinating stories. The four of them had been happily self-sufficient, seeing other people only on their monthly trips to Brookings for supplies.

They might have continued just that way, but the sixties had become the seventies. An art dealer had discovered one of Libby's mother's wall hangings. Almost simultaneously her father had found that a certain mixture of his homegrown herbs brewed into a soothing and delicious tea. Before Libby's eighth birthday her mother had become a respected artist and her father a successful young entrepreneur. The cabin had become a vacation hideaway when the family had moved into the Portland mainstream.

Perhaps it was Libby's own culture shock that had steered her toward anthropology. Her fascination with it, with society's structures and the effects of outside influences, had often dominated her life. Sometimes she nearly forgot the times she was living in with her avid quest for answers. Whenever that happened she came back here or took a few days to visit her family. That was all it took to ground her in the present.

Starting tomorrow, she decided, if the storm was over, she would turn her computer on and get to work.

But only for four hours a day. For the past eighteen months she had too often worked triple that.

Everything in its time—that was what her mother had always said. Well, this time she was going to get back a little of the freedom she'd experienced during the first five years of her life.

Peaceful. Libby let the wind rush through her hair and listened to the hammering of rain on rock and earth. Despite the storm and the rocketing thunder, she felt serene. In all her life she had never known a more peaceful spot.

She saw the light race across the sky, and for a moment she was fooled into thinking it might be ball lightning, or perhaps a meteor. But when the sky lit up she caught a vague outline and a quick flash of metal. She stepped forward, into the rain, instinctively narrowing her eyes. As the object rushed closer, she raised her hand to her throat.

A plane? Even as she watched, it seemed to skim the tops of the firs just to the west of the cabin. The crash echoed through the woods, leaving her frozen to the spot. Then she was running back into the cabin for her slicker and her first-aid kit.

Moments later, with the thunder rolling overhead, she clambered into her Land Rover. She'd noted the spot where she'd seen the plane go down, and she could only hope her sense of direction was as keen as it had always been.

It took her almost thirty minutes of fighting both the blinding storm and the rain-rutted roads and logging trails. She gritted her teeth as the Land Rover plunged through a swollen stream. She knew all too well the dangers of flash floods in the mountains. Still, she kept her speed just above the point of safety, negotiating the twists and turns as much from instinct as from memory. As it happened, she almost ran over him.

Libby hit the brakes hard when her headlights beamed over a figure crumpled at the side of the narrow trail. The Land Rover skidded, spitting mud, before the wheels grabbed hold. Grabbing her flashlight, she scrambled out to kneel beside him.

Alive. She felt a surge of relief when she pressed her fingers against the pulse in his throat. He was dressed all in black, and he was already soaked to the skin. Automatically she tossed the blanket she was carrying over him and began to probe for broken bones.

He was young and lean and well muscled. As she examined him she prayed that those facts would work in his favor. Ignoring the lightning racing across the sky, she played her flashlight over his face.

The gash on his forehead concerned her. Even in the driving rain she could see that it was bleeding badly, but the possibility of a broken back or neck made her reluctant to shift him. Moving quickly, she went back for the first-aid kit. She was applying a butterfly bandage to his wound when he opened his eyes.

Thank God. That single thought ran through her mind as she instinctively took his hand to soothe him. "You're going to be all right. Don't worry. Are you alone?"

He stared at her but saw only a vague outline. "What?"

"Was there anyone with you? Is anyone else hurt?"

"No." He struggled to sit up. The world spun

again as he grabbed at her for support. His hands slid
off her wet slicker. "I'm alone," he managed before
he blacked out again.

He had no idea just how alone.

Libby slept in snatches most of the night. She'd
been able to get him inside the cabin and as far as
the couch. She'd stripped him, dried him and tended
his wounds before she'd fallen into a half doze in the
big armchair by the fire. Periodically, she rose to
check his pulse and pupils.

He was in shock, and she'd decided he undoubtedly
had a concussion, but the rest of his wounds were
relatively minor. Some bruised ribs and a few nasty
scratches. A very lucky man, she mused as she sipped
her tea and studied him in the firelight. Most fools
were. Who else but a fool would have been flying
through the mountains in a storm like this?

It was still raging outside the cabin. She set the cup
aside to throw another log on the fire. The light grew,
sending towering shadows throughout the room. A
very attractive fool, she added with a smile as she
arched her sore back. He was an inch or two over six
feet, and well built. She considered it good luck for
both of them that she was strong, accustomed to carrying heavy packs and equipment. Leaning against the
mantle, she watched him.

Definitely attractive, she thought again. He'd be
even more so when his color returned. Though he was
pale now, his face had good bone structure. Celtic,
she thought, with those lean, high cheekbones and
that full, sculpted mouth. It was a face that hadn't
seen a razor for a day or two. That and the bandage
on his forehead gave him a rakish, almost dangerous

look. His eyes were blue, she remembered, a particularly dark, intense blue.

Definitely Celtic origins, she thought again as she picked up her tea. His hair was black, coal black, and it waved slightly even when it was dry. He wore it too long to be military, she reflected, frowning as she remembered the clothes she'd taken off him. The black jumpsuit had a decidedly military look to it, and there had been some sort of insignia over the breast pocket. Perhaps he was in some elite section of the air force.

She shrugged and settled into the chair. Then again, he'd worn old, scuffed high-top sneakers, as well. Sneakers, and a very expensive-looking watch—one with a half-dozen tiny dials. The only thing she'd been able to figure out on it after a brief look was that it wasn't keeping the right time. Apparently both the watch and its owner had been damaged in the crash.

"I don't know about the watch," she told him over a yawn, "but I think you're going to be all right." With that she dozed off again.

He woke once with a splitting headache and blurred vision. There was firelight, or a first-class simulation. He could smell the woodsmoke…and rain, he thought. He had a misty memory of having stumbled through the rain. The most he could concentrate on was the fact that he was alive. And warm. He remembered being cold and wet and disoriented, afraid at first that he had crashed into an ocean. There had been…someone. A woman. Low, quiet voice…soft, gentle hands… He tried to think, but the drumming in his head made the effort too painful.

He saw her sitting in an old chair with a colorful blanket over her lap. A hallucination? Maybe, but it was certainly a pleasant one. Her hair was dark, and the firelight was glinting off it. It appeared to be chin-length and very full and was now tousled appealingly around her face. She was sleeping. He could see the quiet rise and fall of her breasts. In this light her skin seemed to glow gold. Her features were sharp, almost exotic, set off by a wide mouth that was soft and relaxed in sleep.

As hallucinations went, you couldn't do much better.

Closing his eyes again, he slept until sunrise.

She was gone when he surfaced the second time. The fire was still crackling, and the dim light coming through the window was watery. The pain in his head hadn't dulled, but it was bearable. With cautious fingertips he probed the bandage on his forehead. He realized he might have been unconscious for hours or for days. Even as he tried to struggle upright, he discovered that his body was weak and rubbery.

So was his mind, obviously, he decided as he used what strength he had to take in his surroundings. The small, dimly lit room appeared to be fashioned out of stone and wood. He'd seen some carefully preserved relics that had been built of such primitive materials. His family had once taken a vacation west that had included tours of parks and monuments. He turned his head enough so that he could watch the flames eat at the logs. The heat was dry, and the scent was smoke. But it was hardly likely that he would have been given shelter and care in a museum or a historical park.

The worst part was that he didn't have a clue where he was.

"Oh, you're awake." Libby paused in the doorway with a cup of tea in her hand. When her patient just stared at her, she smiled reassuringly and crossed to the couch. He looked so helpless that the shyness she had battled all her life was easily overcome. "I've been worried about you." She sat on the edge of the couch and took his pulse.

He could see her more clearly now. Her hair was no longer tousled, but was combed sleekly from a side part. It was a warm shade of brown. *Exotic* was exactly the right word to describe her, he decided, with her long-lidded eyes, slender nose and full mouth. In profile she reminded him of a drawing he'd once seen of the ancient Egyptian queen Cleopatra. The fingers that lay lightly on his wrist were cool.

"Who are you?"

Steady, she thought with a nod as she continued to monitor his pulse. And stronger. "I'm not Florence Nightingale, but I'm all you've got." She smiled again and, holding each of his eyelids up in turn, peered closely at his pupils. "How many of me do you see?"

"How many should I see?"

With a chuckle, she arranged a pillow behind his back. "Just one, but since you're concussed, you may be seeing twins."

"I only see one." Smiling, he reached up to touch her subtly pointed chin. "One beautiful one."

Color rushed into her cheeks even as she jerked her head back. She wasn't used to being called beautiful, only competent. "Try some of this. My father's secret blend. It isn't even on the market yet."

Before he could decline, she was holding the cup to his lips. "Thanks." Oddly, the flavor brought back a foggy memory of childhood. "What am I doing here?"

"Recovering. You crashed your plane in the mountains a few miles from here."

"My plane?"

"Don't you remember?" A frown came and went in her eyes. Gold eyes. Big, tawny gold eyes. "It'll come back after a bit, I imagine. You took a bad hit on the head." She urged more tea on him and resisted a foolish urge to brush the hair back from his forehead. "I was watching the storm, or I might not have seen you go down. It's fortunate you're not hurt more than you are. There's no phone in the cabin, and the two-way's in being repaired, so I can't even call for a doctor."

"Two-way?"

"The radio," she said gently. "Do you think you could eat?"

"Maybe. Your name?"

"Liberty Stone." She set the tea aside, then laid a hand on his brow to check for fever. She considered it a minor miracle that he hadn't caught a chill. "My parents were in the first wave of sixties counterculture. So I'm Liberty, which is better than my sister, who got stuck with Sunbeam." Noting his confusion, she laughed. "Just call me Libby. How about you?"

"I don't—" The hand on his brow was cool and real. So she had to be real, he reasoned. But what in the hell was she talking about?

"What's your name? I usually like to know who it is I've saved from plane wrecks."

He opened his mouth to tell her—and his mind was

blank. Panic skidded along his spine. She saw it whiten his face and glaze his eyes before his fingers clamped hard over her wrist. "I can't—I can't remember."

"Don't push it." She swore silently, thinking of the radio she had so conscientiously taken for repairs on her trip in for supplies. "You're disoriented. I want you to rest, try to relax, and I'll fix you something to eat."

When he closed his eyes, she got directly to her feet and started back into the kitchen. He'd had no identification, Libby remembered as she began to prepare an omelet. No wallet, no papers, no permits. He could be anyone. A criminal, a psychopath... No. Laughing to herself, she grated some cheese over the egg mixture. Her imagination had always been fruitful. Hadn't the ability to picture primitive and ancient cultures as real people—families, lovers, children—pushed her forward in her career?

But, imagination aside, she had also always been a good judge of character. That, too, probably came from her fascination with people and their habits. And, she admitted ruefully, from the fact that she had always been more comfortable observing people than interacting with them.

The man who was wrestling with his own demons in her living room wasn't a threat to her. Whoever he was, he was harmless. She flipped the omelet expertly, then turned to reach for a plate. With a shriek, she dropped the pan, eggs and all. Her harmless patient was standing, gloriously naked, in her kitchen doorway.

"Hornblower," he managed as he started to slide down the jamb. "Caleb Hornblower."

Dimly he heard her swearing at him. Shaking off his giddiness, he surfaced to find her face close to his. Her arms were around him, and she was struggling to drag him up. In an attempt to help her, he reached out and sent them both sprawling.

Winded, Libby lay flat on her back, pinned under his body. "You'd better still be disoriented."

"Sorry." He had time to register that she was tall and very firm. "Did I knock you down?"

"Yes." Her arms were still around him, her hands splayed over a ridge of muscle along his back. She snatched them away, blaming her breathlessness on her fall. "Now, if you don't mind, you're a little heavy."

He managed to brace one hand on the floor and push himself up a couple of inches. He was dazed, he admitted to himself, but he wasn't dead. And she felt like heaven beneath him. "Maybe I'm too weak to move."

Was that amusement? Yes, Libby decided, that was definitely amusement in his eyes. That ageless and particularly infuriating male amusement. "Hornblower, if you don't move, you're going to be a whole lot weaker." She caught the quick flash of his grin before she squirmed out from under him. She made a halfhearted attempt to keep her eyes on his face— and only his face—as she helped him up. "If you're going to walk around, you're going to have to wait until you can manage it on your own." She slipped a supporting hand around his waist and instantly felt a strong, uncomfortable reaction. "And until I dig through my father's things and find you some pants."

"Right." He sank gratefully onto the couch.

"This time stay put until I come back."

He didn't argue. He couldn't. The walk to the kitchen doorway and back had sapped what strength he'd had left. It was an odd and unwelcome feeling, this weakness. He couldn't remember having been sick a day in his adult life. True, he'd bashed himself up pretty good in that aircycle wreck, but he'd been, what—eighteen?

Damn it, if he could remember that, why couldn't he remember how he'd gotten here? Closing his eyes, he sat back and tried to think above the throbbing in his head.

He'd wrecked his plane. That was what she—Libby—had said. He certainly felt as though he'd wrecked something. It would come back, just as his name had come back to him after that initial terrifying blankness.

She walked back in carrying a plate. "Lucky for you I just laid in supplies." When he opened his eyes, she hesitated and nearly bobbled the eggs a second time. The way he looked, she told herself, half-naked, with only a blanket tossed over his lap and the glow of the fire dancing over his skin, was enough to make any woman's hands unsteady. Then he smiled.

"It smells good."

"My specialty." She let out a long, quiet breath, then sat beside him. "Can you manage it?"

"Yeah. I only get dizzy when I stand up." He took the plate and let his hunger hold sway. After the first bite, he sent her a surprised glance. "Are these real?"

"Real? Of course they're real."

With a little laugh, he took another forkful. "I haven't had real eggs in—I don't remember."

She thought she'd read somewhere that the military used egg substitutes. "These are real eggs from real

hickens.'' The way he plowed his way through them
made her smile. ''You can have more.''

''This should hold me.'' He looked back to see her
smiling as she sipped her ever-present cup of tea. ''I
guess I haven't thanked you for helping me out.''

''I just happened to be in the right place at the right
time.''

''Why are you here?'' He took another look around
the cabin. ''In this place?''

''I suppose you could say I'm on sabbatical. I'm a
cultural anthropologist, and I've just finished several
months of field research. I'm working on my dissertation.''

''Here?''

It pleased her that he hadn't made the usual com-
ment about her being too young to be a scientist.
'Why not?'' She took his empty plate and set it aside.
'It's quiet—except for the occasional plane crash.
How are your ribs? Hurt?''

He looked down, noticing the bruises for the first
time. ''No, not really. Just sore.''

''You know, you're very lucky. Except for the head
wound, you got out of that with cuts and bruises. The
way you were coming down, I didn't expect to find
anyone alive.''

''The crash control…'' He got a misty image of
himself pushing switches. Lights, flashing lights. The
echo of warning bells. He tried to focus, to concentrate, but it broke apart.

''Are you a test pilot?''

''What? No… No, I don't think so.''

She put a comforting hand on his. Then, unnerved
by the depth of her reaction, cautiously removed it
again.

"I don't like puzzles," he muttered.

"I'm crazy about them. So I'll help you put thi one together."

He turned his head until their eyes met. "Mayb you won't like the solution."

A ripple of unease ran through her. He'd be strong When his injuries healed, his body would be as stron as she sensed his mind was. And they were alone…a completely alone as any two people could be. Sh shook off the feeling and busied herself drinking tea What was she supposed to do, toss him and his con cussion out into the rain?

"We won't know until we find it," she said a length. "If the storm lets up, I should be able to ge you to a doctor in a day or two. In the meantime you'll have to trust me."

He did. He couldn't have said why, but from th moment he'd seen her dozing in the chair he'd know she was someone he could count on. The problem was, he didn't know if he could trust himself—or i she could.

"Libby…" She turned toward him again, and th moment she did he lost what he'd wanted to say "You have a nice face," he murmured, and watched her tawny eyes turn wary. He wanted to touch her felt compelled to. But the moment he lifted his hand she was up and out of reach.

"I think you should get some more rest. There's spare bedroom upstairs." She was speaking quickly now, her words fast and edgy. "I couldn't get you up there last night, but you'd be more comfortable."

He studied her for a moment. He wasn't used to women backing away from him. Cal mused over tha impression until he was certain it was a true one. No when there was attraction between a man and a woman, the rest was easy. Maybe all his circuits weren't working, but he knew there was attraction on both sides.

"Are you matched?"

Libby's brows lifted into her fringe of bangs. "Am I what?"

"Matched? Do you have a mate?"

She had to laugh. "That's a quaint way of putting it. No, not at the moment. Let me help you upstairs." She held up a hand before he could push himself up. "I'd really appreciate it if you'd keep that blanket on."

"It's not cold," he said. Then, with a shrug, he hooked the material around his hips.

"Here, lean on me." She draped his arm over her shoulder, then slipped her own around his waist. "Steady?"

"Almost." When they started forward, he found that he was only slightly dizzy. He was almost sure he could have made it on his own, but he liked the idea of starting up the stairs with his arm wrapped around her. "I've never been in a place like this before."

Her heart was beating a little too quickly. Since he was putting almost none of his weight on her, she couldn't blame it on exertion. Proximity, however, was a different matter. "I suppose it's rustic by most standards, but I've always loved it."

Rustic was a mild word for it, he mused, but he didn't want to offend her. "Always?"

"Yes, I was born here."

He started to speak again, but when he turned his

head he caught a whiff of her hair. When his body tightened, he became aware of his bruises.

"Right in here. Sit at the foot of the bed while I turn it down." He did as she asked, then ran his hand over one of the bedposts, amazed. It was wood, he was certain it was wood, but it didn't seem to be more than twenty or thirty years old. And that was ridiculous.

"This bed…"

"It's comfortable, really. Dad made it, so it's a little wobbly, but the mattress is good."

Cal's fingers tightened on the post. "Your father made this? It's wood?"

"Solid oak, and heavy as a truck. Believe it or not, I was born in it, since at that time my parents didn't believe in doctors for something as basic and personal as childbirth. I still find it hard to picture my father with his hair in a ponytail and wearing love beads." She straightened and caught Cal staring at her. "Is something wrong?"

He just shook his head. He must need rest—a lot more rest. "Was this—" He made a weak gesture to indicate the cabin. "Was this some kind of experiment?"

Her eyes softened, showing a combination of amusement and affection. "You could call it that." She went to a rickety bureau her father had built. After rummaging through it, she came up with a pair of sweatpants. "You can wear these. Dad always leaves some clothes out here, and you're pretty much the same size."

"Sure." He took her hand before she could leave the room. "Where did you say we were?"

He looked so concerned that she covered his hand

with hers. "Oregon, southwest Oregon, just over the California border in the Klamath mountains."

"Oregon." The tension in his fingers relaxed slightly. "U.S.A.?"

"The last time I looked." Concerned, she checked for fever again.

He took her wrist, concentrating on keeping his grip light. "What planet?"

Her eyes flew to his. If she hadn't known better, she would have sworn the man was serious. "Earth. You know, the third from the sun," she said, humoring him. "Get some rest, Hornblower. You're just rattled."

"Yeah." He let out a long breath. "I guess you're right."

"Just yell if you need something."

He sat where he was when she left him. He had a feeling, a bad one. But she was probably right—he was rattled. If he was in Oregon, in the northern hemisphere of his own planet, he wasn't that far off course. Off course, he repeated as his head began to pound. What course had he been on?

He looked down at the watch on his wrist and frowned at the dials. In a gesture that came from instinct rather than thought, he pressed the small stem on the side. The dials faded, and a series of red numbers blinked on the black face.

Los Angeles. A wave of relief washed over him as he recognized the coordinates. He'd been returning to base in L.A. after…after what, damn it?

He lay down slowly and discovered that Libby had been right. The bed was surprisingly comfortable. Maybe if he just went to sleep, clocked out for a few hours, he would remember the rest. Because it seemed important to her, Cal tugged on the sweats.

What had she gotten herself into? Libby wondered. She sat in front of her computer and stared at the blank screen. She had a sick man on her hands—an incredibly good-looking sick man. One with a concussion, partial amnesia…and eyes to die for. She sighed and propped her chin on her hands. The concussion she could handle. She'd considered learning extensive first aid as important as studying the tribal habits of Western man. Fieldwork often took scientists to remote places where doctors and hospitals didn't exist.

But her training didn't help her with the amnesia. And it certainly didn't help her with his eyes. Her knowledge of man came straight out of books and usually dealt with his cultural and sociopolitical habits. Any one-on-one had been purely scientific research.

She could put up a good front when it was necessary. Her battle with a crushing shyness had been long and hard. Ambition had pushed her through, driving her to ask questions when she would have preferred to have melded with the background and been ignored. It had given her the strength to travel, to work with strangers, to make a select few trusted friends.

But when it came to a personal man-woman relationship…

For the most part, the men she saw socially were easily dissuaded. The majority of them were intimidated by her mind, which she admitted was usually one-track. Then there was her family. Thinking of them made her smile. Her mother was still the dreamy artist who had once woven blankets on a handmade loom. And her father... Libby shook her head as she thought of him. William Stone might have made a fortune with Herbal Delights, but he would never be a three-piece-suit executive.

Bob Dylan music and board meetings. Lost causes and profit margins.

The one man she'd brought home to a family dinner had left confused and unnerved—and undoubtedly hungry, Libby remembered with a laugh. He hadn't been able to do more than stare at her mother's zucchini-and-soybean soufflé.

Libby was a combination of her parents' idealism, scientific practicality and dreamy romanticism. She believed in causes, in mathematical equations and in fairy tales. A quick mind and a thirst for knowledge had locked her far too tightly to her work to leave room for real romance. And the truth was that real romance, when applied to her, scared the devil out of her.

So she sought it in the past, in the study of human relationships.

She was twenty-three and, as Caleb Hornblower had put it, unmatched.

She liked the phrase, found it accurate and concise on the one hand and highly romantic on the other. To be matched, she mused, was the perfect way to describe a relationship. She corrected herself. A true relationship, like her parents'. Perhaps the reason she was more at ease with her studies than with men was that she had yet to meet her match.

Satisfied with her analysis, she slipped on her glasses and went to work.

Chapter 2

The rain had slowed when he woke. It was only a hiss and patter against the windows. It was as soothing as a sleep tape. Cal lay still for a moment, reminding himself where he was and struggling to remember why.

He'd dreamed...something about flashing lights and a huge black void. The dreams had brought a clammy sweat to his skin and had accelerated his heartbeat. He made a conscious effort to level it.

Pilots had to have a strong and thorough control over their bodies and their emotions. Decisions often had to be made instantly, even instinctively. And the rigors of flight required a disciplined, healthy body.

He was a pilot. He kept his eyes closed and concentrated on that. He'd always wanted to fly. He'd been trained. His mouth went dry as he fought to remember...anything, any small piece.

The ISF. He closed his hands into fists until his

pulse leveled again. He'd been with the ISF and earned a captaincy. Captain Hornblower. That was right, he was sure of it. Captain Caleb Hornblower. Cal. Everyone called him Cal except his mother. A tall, striking woman with a quick temper and an easy laugh.

A new flood of emotion struck him. He could see her. Somehow that, more than anything else, gave him a sense of identity. He had family—not a mate, of that he was sure, but parents and a brother. His father was a quiet man, steady, dependable. His brother…Jacob. Cal let out a quiet breath as the name and the image formed in his mind. Jacob was brilliant, impulsive, stubborn.

Because his head was pounding again, he let it go. It was enough.

His eyes opened slowly and he thought of Libby. Who was she? Not just a beautiful woman with warm brown hair and eyes like a cat. Being beautiful was easy, even ordinary. She didn't strike him as ordinary. Perhaps it was the place. He frowned at the log walls and the gleaming glass windows. Nothing was ordinary here. And certainly no woman he had ever known would have chosen to live here, like this. Alone.

Had she really been born in the bed he was now in, or had she been joking? It occurred to Cal that a great deal of her behavior was odd, and perhaps there was a joke somewhere, and he'd missed the punch line.

A cultural anthropologist, he mused. That might explain it. It was possible he'd dropped down in the middle of some kind of field experiment, a simulation. For her own reasons, Liberty Stone was living in the fashion of the era she studied. It was odd, certainly, but as far as he was concerned most scientists were a bit odd. He could certainly understand looking toward the future, but why anyone would want to dig back into the past was beyond him. The past was done and couldn't be changed or fixed, so why study it?

Her business, he supposed.

He owed her. From what he could piece together, he might well have died if she hadn't come along. He'd have to pay her back as soon as he was working on all thrusters again. It pleased him to know that he was a man who settled debts.

Liberty Stone. Libby. He turned her name over in his mind and smiled. He liked the sound of her name, the soft sound of it. Soft, like her eyes. It was one thing to be beautiful; it was another to have gorgeous velvet eyes. You could change the color of them, the shape, but never the expression. Maybe it was that that made her so appealing. Everything she felt seemed to leap right into her eyes.

He'd managed to stir a variety of feelings in her, Cal thought as he pushed himself up in bed. Concern, fear, humor, desire. And she had stirred him. Even through his confusion he'd felt a strong, healthy response, a man-woman response.

He dropped his head into his hands as the room spun. His system might be churning for Libby Stone, but he was far from ready to do anything about it. More than a little disgusted, he settled back on the pillows. A little more rest, he decided. A day or two of letting his body heal should snap his mind and his memory back. He knew who he was and where he was. The rest would come.

A book on the table beside the bed caught his eye.

He'd always liked to read, almost as much as he'd liked to fly. He preferred the written word to tapes or disks. That was another good and solid memory. Pleased with it, Cal picked up the book.

The title puzzled him. *Journey to Andromeda* seemed a particularly foolish name for a book, especially when it was touted as science fiction. Anyone with a free weekend could journey to Andromeda— if he liked being bored into a coma. With a small frown, he started to leaf through the book. Then his eyes fell on the copyright page.

That was wrong. The clammy sweat was back. That was ridiculous. The book he was holding was new. The back hadn't been broken, and the pages looked as though they'd never been turned. Some stupid clerical error, he told himself, but his mouth was bone-dry. It had to be an error. How else could he be holding a book that had been published nearly three centuries ago?

Absorbed in her work, Libby ignored the small circle of pain at the center of her back. She knew very well that posture was important when she was writing for several hours at a stretch, but once she lost herself in ancient or primitive civilizations she always forgot everything else.

She hadn't eaten since breakfast, and the tea she'd carried up with her was stone-cold. Her notes and reference books were scattered everywhere, along with clothes she hadn't yet put away and the stack of newspapers she'd picked up at the store. She'd toed off her shoes and had her stockinged feet curled around the legs of her chair. Occasionally she stopped hammering at the keyboard to push her round, black framed glasses back on her nose.

It cannot be argued that the addition of modern implements has a strong and not always positive effect on an isolated culture such as the Kolbari. The islanders have remained, in the latter years of the twentieth century, at a folk level and do not, as has been implied in the human relations area files, seek integration with the modern industrial societies. What may be seen by certain factions as offering the convenience of progress, medically, industrially, educationally, is most often—

"Libby."

"What?" The word came out in a hiss of annoyance before she turned. "Oh." She spotted Cal, pale and shaky, with one hand braced on the doorframe and the other wrapped around a paperback. "What are you doing up, Hornblower? I told you to call if you needed anything." Annoyed with him and with the interruption, she rose to help him to a chair. The moment she touched his arm, he jerked away.

"What are you wearing on your face?"

The tone of his voice had her moistening her lips. It was fury, with a touch of fear. A dangerous combination. "Glasses. Reading glasses."

"I know what they are, damn it. Why are you wearing them?"

Go slow, she warned herself. She took his arm gently and spoke as if she were soothing a wounded lion. "I need them to work."

"Why haven't you had them fixed?"

"My glasses?"

He gritted his teeth. "Your eyes. Why haven't you had your eyes fixed?"

Cautious, she took the glasses off and held them behind her back. "Why don't you sit down?"

He only shook his head. "I want to know the meaning of this."

Libby looked at the book in his hand, the one he was shaking in her face. She cleared her throat. "I don't know the meaning, since I haven't read it. I imagine my father left it here. He's into science fiction."

"That's not what I—" Patience, he told himself. He had never had an abundance of it, and now was the time to use all he could find. "Open it up to the copyright page."

"All right. I will if you'll sit. You're not looking well."

He reached the chair in two rocky strides. "Open it. Read the date."

Head injuries could often cause erratic behavior, Libby thought. She didn't believe he was dangerous, but all the same she decided it was best to humor him and read the year out loud, then she tried an easy smile. "Hot off the presses," she added.

"Is that supposed to be a joke?"

"I'm not sure." He was furious, she realized. And terrified. "Caleb." She said his name quietly as she crouched beside him.

"Does that book have something to do with your work?"

"My work?" The question threw her off enough to have her frowning at him, then at the computer behind her. "I'm an anthropologist. That means I study—"

"I know what it means." Patience be damned, he thought. Incensed, he snatched the book from her. "I want to know what this means."

"It's just a book. If I know my father, it's second-rate science fiction about invasions from the planet Kriswold. You know, mutants and ray guns and space warriors. That kind of thing." She eased it from his hand. "Let me get you back to bed. I'll make you some soup."

He looked at her, saw the soft eyes overflowing with concern, the encouraging half smile. And the nerves. His gaze shifted to where her hand lay almost protectively over his, despite the fact that he had obviously frightened her. There was a link there. It was absurd to believe that, almost as absurd as it was to believe the date in the book.

"Maybe I'm losing my mind."

"No." Her fear forgotten, she lifted her free hand to his face, soothing him as she would have anyone who seemed so utterly lost. "You're hurt."

He closed surprisingly strong fingers over her wrist. "Jolted the memory banks? Yeah, maybe. Libby..." His eyes were suddenly intense, almost desperate. "What's the date today?"

"It's May the 24th or 25th. I lose track."

"No, the whole thing." He fought to keep the urgency out of his voice. "Please."

"Okay, it's probably Tuesday, the 25th." Then she repeated the year. "How's that?"

"Fine." He pulled out every ounce of control and managed to smile at her. One of them was crazy, and he dearly hoped it was Libby. "You got anything to drink around here besides that tea?"

She frowned for a moment. Then her face cleared. "Brandy. There's always some downstairs. Hold on a minute."

"Yeah, thanks."

He waited until he heard her moving down the stairs. Then, cautiously, he rose and pulled open the first drawer that came to hand. There had to be something in this ridiculous place to tell him what was going on.

He found lingerie, neatly stacked despite the chaos of the rest of the room. He frowned a moment over the styles and materials. She'd said she wasn't matched, yet it was obvious that she wore things to please a man. Apparently she preferred the romance of past eras even when it came to her underwear. Far from comfortable with the ease with which he could picture Libby in this little chocolate-brown swatch with the white lace, he shoved the drawer shut again.

The next drawer was just as tidy and held jeans and sturdy hiking pants. He puzzled for a moment over a zipper, ran it slowly up and down, then shoved the jeans back into place. Annoyed, he turned and started toward her desk, where her computer continued to hum. He had time to think it was a noisy, archaic machine before he stumbled over the pile of newspapers. He didn't scan the headlines or study the picture. His eyes were drawn to the date.

He was unarguably in the twentieth century.

His stomach clenched. Ignoring the sudden buzzing in his ears, he bent to snatch up the paper. Words danced in front of his eyes. Something about arms talks—nuclear arms, he noted with a kind of dull horror—and hail damage in the Midwest. There was a tease about the Mariners trouncing the Braves. Very slowly, knowing his legs would give out in a moment, he lowered himself back into the chair.

It was too bad, he thought dully. It was too damn bad, but it wasn't Libby Stone who was going crazy.

"Caleb?" The moment she saw his face, Libby rushed into the room with brandy sloshing in a snifter. "You're white as a sheet."

"It's nothing." He had to be careful now, very careful. "I guess I stood up too fast."

"I think you really could use some of this." She held the snifter until she was certain he had both hands on it. "Take it slow," she began, but he'd already drained it. Sitting back on her heels, she frowned at him. "That should cure you or knock you out again."

The brandy was the genuine article and no hallucination, he decided. It was velvet fire coursing down his throat. He closed his eyes and let the fire spread. "I'm still a little disoriented. How long have I been here?"

"Since last night." The color was coming back, she noted. His voice sounded calmer, more controlled. It wasn't until her muscles relaxed that she realized how tightly they'd been tensed. "I guess I saw you crash about midnight."

"You saw it?"

"Well, I saw the lights and heard you hit." She smiled, continuing to monitor his pulse, when he opened his eyes again. "For a minute I thought I was seeing a meteor or a UFO or something."

"A—a UFO?" he repeated, dazed.

"Not that I believe in extraterrestrials or spaceships

or anything, but my father's always been fascinated by that kind of thing. I realized it was a plane.'' He was staring at her again, she thought, but there was curiosity rather than anger in his eyes. ''Feeling better?''

He couldn't have begun to tell her how and what he was feeling. Cal had an idea that that was all for the best: He needed to think before he said too much. ''Some.'' Still hoping it was all some bizarre mistake, he rattled the paper in his hand. ''Where'd you get this?''

''I drove into Brookings a couple of days ago. That's about seventy miles from here. I picked up supplies and a few newspapers.'' She glanced absently at the one in his hand. ''I haven't gotten around to reading any of them yet, so they're already old news.''

''Yeah.'' He looked at the papers that were still on the floor. ''Old news.''

With a laugh, she rose and began to make an effort to tidy the room. ''I always feel so cut off here, more so than when I'm in the field hundreds of miles away. I imagine we could establish a colony on Mars and I wouldn't hear about it until it was all over.''

''A colony on Mars,'' he murmured, feeling his stomach sink as he glanced at the paper again. ''I think you've got about a hundred years to go.''

''Sorry I'll miss it.'' With a sigh, she looked out the window. ''Rain's starting up again. Maybe we can catch the weather on the early news.'' After stepping over books, she flicked on a small portable television. After a moment, a snowy picture blinked on. She dragged a hand through her hair and decided to watch without her glasses. ''The weather should be on in a—Caleb?'' She tilted her head to one side, fascinated by his dumbstruck expression. ''I'd swear you'd never seen a television in your life.''

''What?'' He brought himself back, wishing he had another brandy. A television. He'd heard of them, of course, in the same way Libby had heard of covered wagons. ''I didn't realize you had one.''

''We're rustic,'' she told him, ''not primitive.'' She narrowed her eyes when he gave a choked laugh. ''Maybe you should lie down again.''

''Yeah.'' And when he woke up again, this would all have been a dream. ''Mind if I take these papers?''

She stood to help him up. ''I don't know if you should be reading.''

''I think that's the least of my worries.'' He discovered that the room didn't spin this time, but it was still a comfort to drape his arm around her shoulders. Strong shoulders, he thought. And a soft scent. ''Libby, if I wake up and find out this has all been an illusion, I want you to know you've been the best part of it.''

''That's nice.''

''I mean it.'' The brandy and his own weakened system were taking over. Because his mind felt as if it had been fried in a solar blast, he didn't fight it. She had little trouble easing him into bed. But his arm stayed around her shoulders long enough to keep her close, just close enough to brush his lips over hers. ''The very best.''

She jerked back like a spring. He was asleep, and her blood was pounding.

Who was Caleb Hornblower? The question interrupted Libby's work throughout the evening. Her interest in the Kolbari Islanders didn't even come close to her growing fascination with her unexpected and confusing guest.

Who was he, and what was she going to do about him? The trouble was, she had a whole list of unanswered questions that applied to her odd patient, Caleb Hornblower. Libby was a great listmaker, and a woman who knew herself well enough to be aware that all her organizational talents were eaten up by her work.

Who was he? Why had he been flying through a storm at midnight? Where did he come from and where had he been going? Why had a simple paperback novel sent him into a panic? Why had he kissed her?

Libby pulled herself up short there. That particular question wasn't important—it wasn't even relevant. He hadn't really kissed her, she reminded herself. And whether he had or hadn't wasn't the issue. It was gratitude, she decided, and began to nibble on her thumbnail. He'd only been trying to show her that he was grateful to her. Libby certainly understood that a kiss was—could be—a very casual gesture. It was part of Western culture. Over the centuries it had become as unimportant as a smile or a handshake. It was a sign of friendship, affection, sympathy, gratitude. And desire. She bit down harder on her nail.

Not all societies used the kiss, of course. Many tribal cultures… She was lecturing again, Libby thought in disgust. She looked down at her hands. And she was biting her nails. That was a bad sign.

What she needed was to get her mind off Hornblower for a while and fill her stomach. Pressing a hand to it, Libby rose. She wasn't going to get any work done this way, so she might as well eat.

Since Caleb's room was dark, she passed it by, telling herself she'd check on him when she came back up. Sleep was undoubtedly more essential to his recovery than another meal.

There was a low rumble of thunder as she descended the stairs. Another bad sign, she thought. At this rate it would be days before she could get him down the mountain.

Perhaps someone was already looking for him. Friends, family, business associates. A wife or a lover. Everyone had someone.

She groped for the kitchen light as the sky cracked with the first bolt of lightning. It was going to be another boomer, she decided as she opened the refrigerator door. Finding nothing that appealed to her, she rummaged through the cupboards. A night like this called for a nice bowl of soup and a seat by the fire.

Alone.

She sighed a little as she opened the can. Recently she'd begun to think about being alone. As a scientist she knew the reason. She lived in a culture of couples. Single—unmatched, she remembered with a quick smile—single men and women often found themselves dissatisfied and depressed in their own company. The entertainment media subtly—and not so subtly—drilled into them the pleasures of relationships. Families added pressure for the single to marry and continue the family line. Good-natured friends offered help and advice, generally unwanted, on finding a mate. The human being was programmed, almost from birth, to search for and find a companion of the opposite sex.

Maybe that was why she'd resisted. An interesting analysis, Libby mused as she stirred the soup. The desire for individuality and self-sufficiency had been ingrained in her from birth. It would take a very special person to tempt her to share. She had dated only rarely in high school. The same pattern had held true in college. She'd had no interest.

That wasn't precisely true, she thought. She had had interest—the trouble was, it had usually been scientific. She'd never met a man who dazzled her enough to stop her from making lists and forming hypotheses. Professor Stone, they'd called her in high school. And it still rankled. In college she'd been considered a professional virgin. She'd detested that, had struggled to ignore it, pouring her energy into her studies. The appeal of her personality had made her friends, both male and female. But intimate relationships were another matter.

When all the data had been analyzed, there had never been one who had made her...well, yearn, Libby decided. That was the appropriate term.

She supposed there wasn't a man on the planet who could make her yearn.

Wooden spoon in hand, she turned to take out a bowl. For the second time she saw Cal framed in the doorway. She gave a muffled shriek, and the spoon went flying. A flash of lightning lit up the room. Then it was plunged into darkness.

"Libby?"

"Damn it, Hornblower, I wish you wouldn't do that." Her voice was breathless as she rummaged through drawers for a candle. "You scared the life out of me."

"Did you think I was one of the mutants from Andromeda?" There was a dry tone to the words that had her wrinkling her nose.

"I told you I don't read that stuff." She closed a drawer on her thumb, swore, then wrenched open another. "Where are the stupid matches?" She turned and bumped solidly into his chest in the dark. Lightning flashed again, illuminating his face. It took only that instant for her mouth to go dry. He'd looked stunning, strong and dangerous.

"You're shaking." His voice had gentled almost imperceptibly, but the hands on her shoulders stayed firm. "Are you really frightened?"

"No, I..." She wasn't a woman to be scared of the dark. Certainly she wasn't a woman to be afraid of a man—intellectually speaking. But she was shaking. The hands that had reached up to his bare chest trembled—and intellect had nothing to do with it. "I need to find the matches."

"Why did you turn the lights off?" She smelled wonderful. In the cool, unrelieved darkness he could concentrate on her scent. It was light and almost sinfully feminine.

"I didn't. The storm knocked out the power." His fingers tightened on her arms, hard enough to make her gasp. "Caleb?"

"Cal." Lightning flashed again, and she saw that his eyes had darkened. He was staring out the window into the storm now. "People call me Cal."

His grip had eased. Though she ordered herself to relax, the crash of the thunder made her jolt. "I like Caleb," she said, hoping her voice was pleasant and casual. "We'll have to save it for special occasions. You have to let me go."

He slid his hands down to her wrists, then back. "Why?"

Her mind went blank. Beneath her palms she could feel the strong, steady beating of his heart. Slowly his fingers skimmed down to her elbows, where his thumbs traced lazy, erotic circles on the sensitive inner skin. She could no longer see him, but she could taste the warm flutter of his breath on her parted lips.

"I..." She felt each separate muscle in her body go lax. "Don't." The word nearly strangled her as she jerked back. "I need to find the matches."

"So you said."

Leaning weakly against the counter, she began to search the drawer again. Even after she found a pack, it took her a full minute to light the match. Thoughtful, his hands plunged deep in the pockets of the sweats, Cal watched the little flame dance and flicker. She lit two tapers, keeping her back to him.

"I was heating soup. Would you like some?"

"All right."

It helped to keep her hands busy. "You must be feeling better."

His mouth twisted into a humorless smile when he thought of the hours he'd lain in the dark willing his memory to return completely. "I must be."

"Headache?"

"Not much of one."

She poured the water she'd already boiled for tea, then arranged everything meticulously on a tray. "I was going to sit by the fire."

"Okay." He picked up the two candles and led the way.

The storm helped, Cal thought. It made everything he was seeing, everything he was doing, seem that much more unreal. Perhaps by the time the rain stopped he'd know what he had to do.

"Did the storm wake you?"

"Yeah." It wouldn't be the last lie he told her. Though he was sorry for the necessity of it, Cal smiled and settled in a chair by the fire. There was something charming about being in a place where a simple rainstorm could leave you in the dark, dependent on candles and firelight. No computer could have set a better scene. "How long do you think it'll be before you regain power?"

"An hour." She tasted the soup. It nearly calmed her. "A day." She laughed and shook her head. "Dad always talked about hooking up a generator, but it was one of those things he never got around to. When we were kids, we'd sometimes have to cook over the fire for days in the winter. And we'd sleep all curled up here on the floor while my parents took turns making sure the fire didn't die out."

"You liked it." Cal knew people who went into preserved areas and camped. He'd always thought they were strange. But the way Libby spoke of it, it seemed homey.

"I loved it. I guess those first five years helped me handle the more primitive parts of digs and fieldwork."

She was relaxed again. He could see it in her eyes, hear it in her voice. Though a nervous Libby held a definite appeal for him, he wanted her relaxed now. The more at ease she was, the more information he might glean.

"What era do you study?"

"No specific era. I'm hung up on tribal life, mainly isolated cultures and the effects of modern tools and machines. Things like how electricity changes the sociopolitical mores of the traditional man. I've toyed around with extinct cultures, Aztecs, Incas." This was easy, she decided. The more she talked about her work, the less she would think about that jolting moment in the kitchen and her own inexplicable reaction to it. "I'm planning on going to Peru in the fall."

"How'd you get started?"

"I think it was a trip to the Yucatan when I was a kid, and all those wonderful Mayan ruins. Have you ever been to Mexico?"

Looking back, he remembered a particularly wild night in Acapulco. "Yes. About ten years ago." Or a couple of centuries from now, he thought, and frowned into his bowl.

"Bad time?"

"What? No. This tea…" He took another sip. "It's familiar."

Grinning, she tucked her legs up under her. "My father will be glad to hear that. Herbal Delight—that's his company. He started it right here in this cabin."

Cal looked down into his cup, then laid his head back and laughed. "I thought that was a myth."

"No." With a half smile forming, she studied him. "I don't get the joke."

"It's hard to explain." Should he tell her that over two centuries from now Herbal Delight would be one of the ten biggest and most powerful companies on Earth and its colonies? Should he tell her that it made not only tea but organic fuel and God knew what else? Here was Cal Hornblower, he thought, sitting cozily in a chair in the cabin where it all began. He noted that she was staring at him as if she were going to check his pulse again.

"My mother used to give me this," he told her. "When I had—" He wasn't sure what childhood illness he could name, but he was certain it wasn't red dust fever. "Whenever I wasn't feeling well."

"A cure for all ills. You're remembering more."

"Patches, pieces," he said, still cautious. "It's easier to remember childhood than last night."

"I don't think that's unusual. Are you married?" Where had that come from? she wondered, and immediately turned her attention to the fire.

He was glad she wasn't looking at him when the grin split his face. "No. It wouldn't be wise for me to want you if I were."

Her mouth dropped open, and she twisted around to look at him. Quickly she rose and began stacking the dishes on the tray. "I should take these back in."

"Would you rather I didn't tell you?"

She had to swallow once, hard, before she could speak at all. "Tell me what?"

"That I want you." He closed his hand over her wrist to keep her still. It amazed and aroused him to feel her pulse hammering. His word-by-word perusal of the newspaper hadn't given him an inkling of how men and women interacted in the here and now, but he didn't believe it could be so different.

"Yes— No."

Smiling, he took the tray out of her hands. "Which?"

"I don't think it's a good idea." When he stood up, she stepped back and felt the heat from the fire on her legs. "Caleb..."

"Is this a special occasion?" He traced a fingertip

across her jaw and watched her eyes go as hot as the flames behind her.

"Don't." It was ridiculous. He couldn't make her tremble with just a touch. But all he had done was touch her. And she was trembling.

"When I woke up and saw you sleeping in the chair in the firelight I thought you were an illusion." He rubbed his thumb gently over her bottom lip. "You look like one now."

She didn't feel like one. She felt real, shatteringly real, and terrified. "I have to bank the fire for the night, and you should go back to bed."

"We can bank the fire for the night. Then we can go to bed."

She squared her shoulders, furious at the realization that her palms were sweating. She would not stammer, she promised herself. She would not act the inexperienced fool. She would handle him the way a strong, independent woman would, a woman who knew her own mind. "I'm not going to sleep with you. I don't know you."

So that was a condition, Cal mused. After thinking it over, he found it rather sweet and not completely unreasonable. "All right. How long do you need?"

She stared at him. At length she dragged both hands through her hair. "I can't figure out if you're joking or not, but I do know you're the oddest man I've ever met."

"You don't know the half of it." He watched her bank the fire carefully. Competent hands, he thought, an athletic body, and the most vulnerable eyes he'd ever seen. "We'll get to know each other tomorrow. Then we'll sleep together."

She straightened so quickly that she rapped her

head on the mantel. Swearing and rubbing her head, she turned to him. "Not necessarily. In fact it's very unlikely."

He took the screen and placed it in front of the fire, exactly as he had seen her do earlier. "Why?"

"Because…" Flustered, she fumbled for words for a moment. "I don't do that kind of thing."

She recognized genuine astonishment when she saw it. It was staring at her now out of Cal's dark blue eyes. "At all?"

"Really, Hornblower, that's none of your business." Dignity helped, but not a great deal. As she swept up the tray, the bowls slid dangerously, and they would have crashed to the floor if he hadn't caught the end of the tray and balanced it.

"Why are you angry? I only want to make love with you."

"Listen." She took a deep breath. "I've had enough of all this. I did you a favor, and I don't appreciate you insinuating that I should hop into bed with you just because you've—you've got an itch. I don't find it flattering—in fact, I find it very insulting—that you think I'd make love with a perfect stranger just because it's convenient."

He tilted his head, trying to take it all in. "Is inconvenient better?"

She could only grit her teeth. "Listen, Hornblower, I'll drop you off at the nearest singles bar the minute we can get out of here. Until then, keep your distance."

With that, she stormed out of the room. He could hear the dishes crash in the kitchen.

He dug his hands in his pockets again as he started upstairs. Twentieth-century women were very difficult to understand. Fascinating, he admitted, but difficult.

And what in the hell was a singles bar?

Chapter 3

He felt almost normal in the morning. Normal, Cal thought, if you considered he hadn't even been born yet. It was a bizarre situation, highly improbable according to most of the current scientific theories, and deep down he clung to the faint hope that he was having some kind of long, involved dream.

If he was lucky, he was in a hospital suffering from shock and a little brain damage. But from the looks of things he'd been snapped back over two centuries into the primitive, often violent twentieth century.

The last thing he could remember before waking up on Libby's couch was flying his ship. No, that wasn't quite accurate. He'd been fighting to fly his ship. Something had happened.... He couldn't quite bring that into focus yet. Whatever it had been, it had been big.

His name was Caleb Hornblower. He'd been born in the year 2222. That made two his lucky number, he remembered with a half laugh. He was thirty, un-matched, the older of two sons, and a former member of the International Space Force. He'd been a captain, and for the last eighteen months he'd been an inde-pendent. He'd made a routine supply delivery to the Brigston Colony on Mars and had veered off from his normal route on the return trip home because of a meteor shower. Then it had happened. Whatever *it* was.

Now he had to accept the fact that something had shot him back in time. He had crashed, not only through Earth's atmosphere, but through about two and a half centuries. He was a healthy, intelligent flier who was stuck in a time when people considered in-terplanetary travel the stuff of science fiction and were, incredibly, playing around with nuclear fission.

The good part was that the experience hadn't killed him and he'd landed in an isolated area in the hands of a gorgeous brunette.

It could, he supposed, be worse.

His problem at the moment was figuring out how he could get back to his own time. Alive.

He adjusted his pillow, scratched at the stubble on his chin and wondered what Libby's reaction would be if he went downstairs and calmly related his story.

He'd probably find himself out the door, wearing no more than her father's sweats. Or she'd call the authorities and have him hauled off to whatever passed for rest-and-rehabilitation clinics at this point in time. He didn't imagine they were luxury resorts.

What annoyed him at the moment was that he'd been a poor history student. What he knew about the twentieth century would barely fill a computer screen. But he imagined they would have a pretty primitive way of dealing with a man who claimed he'd crashed his F27 into a mountain after making a routine run to Mars.

Until he could find a way out, he was going to have to keep his problem to himself. In order to do so, he'd have to be more careful about what he said. And what he did.

He'd obviously made a misstep the night before. In more ways than one. He grimaced as he recalled Libby's reaction to his simple suggestion that they spend the night together. Things were obviously done differently then—no, now, he corrected. It was a pity he hadn't paid more attention to those old romances his mother liked to read.

In any case, his problems ran a lot deeper than having been rejected by a beautiful woman. He had to get back to his ship, had to try to reconstruct what had happened in his head. Then he had to make it happen in reality. As far as he could see, that was the only way to get home again.

She had a computer, he remembered. As archaic as it was, between that and the mini on his wrist he might be able to calculate a trajectory.

Right now he wanted a shower, a shave and some more of Libby's eggs. He opened his door and nearly walked into her.

The cup of coffee she held was steaming, and she nearly splashed it all over his bare chest. Libby righted it, though she thought a little scalding was just what he deserved.

''I thought you might like some coffee.''

''Thanks.'' He noted that her voice was frigid, her back stiff. Unless he missed his guess, women hadn't changed that much. The cold shoulder never went out of style. "I want to apologize," he began, offering her his best smile. "I know I veered out of orbit last night."

"That's one way of putting it."

"What I mean is…you were right and I was wrong." If that didn't do the trick, he knew nothing about the nature of women.

"All right." Nothing made her more uncomfortable than holding a grudge. "We'll forget it."

"Is it okay if I think you have beautiful eyes?" He saw her blush and was utterly charmed.

"I suppose." The corners of her mouth turned up. She'd been right about the Celtic blood, she reflected. If the man didn't have Irish ancestors, she'd have to go into a different line of work. "If you can't help it."

He held out a hand. "Friends?"

"Friends." The moment she put her hand in his she wondered why it felt as though she'd made a mistake. Or jumped off a bridge. He had a way of using only the barest brush of his fingertips to send her pulse scrambling. Slowly, wishing he wasn't so obviously aware of her reaction, she drew her hand away. "I'm going to fix breakfast."

"Is it all right if I have a shower?"

"Sure. I'll show you where everything is." More comfortable with something practical to do, she led the way down the hall. "Clean towels in the closet." She opened a narrow louvered door. "Here's a razor if you want to shave." She offered him a disposable safety razor and a can of shaving cream. "Something wrong?" He was staring at the items she offered as though they were instruments of torture. "I guess you're used to an electric,'' she said, ''but I don't have one.''

''No.'' He managed a weak smile, hoping he wouldn't slit his throat. ''This is fine.''

''Toothbrush.'' Trying not to stare at him, she handed him a spare that was still in its box. ''We don't have an electric one of these, either.''

''I'll, ah, rough it.''

''Fine. Take whatever looks like it will fit out of the bedroom. There should be jeans and sweaters. I'll have something ready in a half hour. Time enough?''

''Sure.''

Cal was still staring at the toiletries in his hands when she shut the door.

Fascinating. Now that he was over the panic, the fear and the disbelief, he was finding the whole episode fascinating. He studied the cardboard box and toothbrush with a grin, like a boy who'd found a fabulous puzzle under the Christmas tree.

They were supposed to use these things three times a day, he remembered. He'd read all about it. They had different flavors of paste that they scrubbed all over their teeth. Sounded revolting. Cal squirted a dab of the shaving cream on his finger. Gamely he touched it to his tongue. It was revolting. How had anyone tolerated it? Of course, that had all been in the days before tooth and gum diseases had been eradicated by fluoratyne.

After opening the box, he ran a thumb over the bristles. Interesting. He grimaced into the mirror, studying his strong white teeth. Maybe he shouldn't take any chances.

Setting everything on the sink, he turned to look at the bathroom. It was like something out of those old videos, he thought. The clunky oval tub, with its single awkward-looking shower head sticking out of the wall. He would start filing it all away. Who could tell, maybe he'd write a book when he got home.

Of more immediate importance was figuring out how to operate the shower. Above the lip of the tub were three round white knobs. One was marked *H*, another *C*, and the middle was graced with an arrow. Cal scowled at them. He could certainly figure out that they meant Hot and Cold, but it was a far cry from the individual temperature settings he was accustomed to. There would be no stepping inside and telling the computerized unit he wanted ninety-eight degrees at a mist. It was fend-for-yourself.

He scalded himself first, then froze, then scalded himself again before he and the shower began to understand each other. Once it was running smoothly he could appreciate the feel of hot water beating down on his skin. He found a bottle marked Shampoo, took a moment to be amused by the packaging, then dumped some in his hand.

It smelled like Libby.

Almost immediately his stomach muscles tightened, and a wave of desire flowed over him, as hot as the water on his back. That was odd. Baffled, he continued to stare down at the pool of shampoo. Attraction had always been easy—simple, basic. But this was painful. He pressed a hand to his stomach and waited for it to pass. But it persisted.

It probably had to do with the accident. That was what he told himself, and what he preferred to believe. When he got back home he'd have to check into a rest center for a full workup. But he'd lost his pleasure in the shower. He toweled off quickly. The

scent of soap and shampoo—and Libby—was everywhere.

The jeans were a little loose in the waist, but he
liked them. Natural cotton was so outrageously expensive that no one but the very rich could afford it.
The black roll-necked sweater had a hole in the cuff
and made him feel at home. He'd always preferred
casual, comfortable clothes. One of the reasons he'd
left the ISF was that they had a penchant for uniforms
and polish. Barefoot and pleased with himself, he followed the scents of cooking into the kitchen.

She looked great. Her baggy pants accentuated her
slenderness and made a man imagine all the curves
and angles beneath the material. He liked the way
she'd pushed the sleeves of the bulky red sweater up
past her elbows. She had very sensitive elbows, he
recalled, and felt his stomach knot again.

He wasn't going to think of her that way. He'd
promised himself.

"Hi."

This time she was expecting him, and she didn't
jump. "Hi. Sit down. You can eat before I check your
bandage. I hope you like French toast." She turned,
holding a plate heaped with it. When their eyes met,
her fingers curled tight around the edges. She recognized the sweater, but it didn't remind her of her father when it was tugged over Cal's long, limber torso.
"You didn't shave."

"I forgot." He didn't want to admit he'd been
afraid to try his skill at it. "It stopped raining."

"I know. The sun's supposed to come out this afternoon." She set the platter down, then tried not to
react when he leaned over her to sniff at the food.

''Did you really make that?''

''Breakfast is my best meal.'' She sat down, breathing a little sigh of relief when he took the seat across from her.

''I could get used to this.''

''Eating?''

He took his first bite and let his eyes close with a sigh of pure pleasure. ''Eating like this.''

She watched him plow through the first stack. ''How did you eat before?''

''Packaged stuff, mostly.'' He'd seen ads for complete meals in packages in the newspaper. At least there was some hope for civilization.

''I live like that myself most of the time. When I come here I get the urge to cook, stack wood, grow herbs. The kind of things we did when I was a kid.'' And though she'd come here for solitude, she'd discovered she enjoyed his company. He seemed safe this morning, despite her initial reaction to the way he looked in the black sweater and trim jeans. She could almost believe she'd imagined the tense and unexpected little scene by the fire the night before.

''What do you do when you're not crashing planes?''

''I fly.'' He'd already thought his answer through and had decided it was best to stick as close to the truth as possible.

''Then you *are* in the service.''

''Not anymore.'' He picked up his coffee and smoothly changed the subject. ''I don't know if I've really thanked you properly for everything you've done. I'd like to pay you back for all this, Libby. Do you need anything done around here?''

"I don't think you're up to manual labor at this point."

"If I stay in bed all day again I'll go crazy."

She took a good look at his face, trying not to be distracted by the shape of his mouth. It was impossible to forget how close she'd come to feeling it on hers. "Your color's good. No dizziness?"

"No."

"You can help me wash the dishes."

"Sure." He took his first good look at the kitchen. Like the bath, it distracted and fascinated him. The west wall was stone, with a little hearth cut into it. There was a hammered copper urn on the ledge stuffed with tall dried flowers and weeds. The wide window over the sink opened onto a view of mountains and pine. The sky was gray and clear of traffic. He identified the refrigerator and the stove, both a glossy white. The wide planked-wood floor shone with a polished luster. It felt cool and smooth under his bare feet.

"Looking for something?"

With a little shake of his head, he glanced back at her. "Sorry?"

"The way you were staring out the window, it seemed you were expecting to see something that wasn't there."

"Just, ah…taking in the view."

Satisfied, she gestured toward his plate. "Are you finished?"

"Yeah. This is a great room."

"I've always liked it. Of course, it's a lot more convenient with the new range. You wouldn't believe the old museum piece we used to cook on."

He couldn't keep from grinning. ''I'm sure I wouldn't.''

''Why do I get the feeling there's a joke and it's two inches above my head?''

''I couldn't say.'' After picking up his plate, he moved to the sink and began to open cupboards.

''If you're looking for a dishwasher, you're out of luck.'' Libby stacked the rest of the breakfast dishes in the sink. ''My parents would never bend their sixties values that far. No dishwasher, no microwave, no satellite dish.'' She plugged the sink, then reached in front of Caleb for the bottle of dish detergent. ''You want to wash or dry?''

''I'll dry.''

He watched, delighted, as she filled the sink with hot, soapy water and began to scrub. Even the smell was nice, he thought, resisting the urge to bend down and sniff at the lemony bubbles.

Libby rubbed an itch on her nose with her shoulder. ''Come on, Hornblower, haven't you ever seen a woman wash dishes before?''

He decided to test her reaction. ''No. Actually, I think I did in a movie once.''

With a bubbling laugh, she handed him a plate. ''Progress steals all these charming duties from us. In another hundred years we'll probably have robots that will stack the dishes inside themselves and sterilize them.''

''More like a hundred and fifty. What do you want me to do with this?'' He turned the plate in his hand.

''Dry it.''

''How?''

She lifted a brow and nodded toward a neatly folded cloth. ''You might try that.''

"Right." He dried the plate and picked up another. "I was hoping to go take a look of what's left of my sh—my plane."

"I can almost guarantee the logging trail's washed out. The Land Rover might make it, but I'd really like to give it another day."

He bit down on his impatience. "You'll point me in the right direction?"

"No, but I'll take you."

"You've already done enough."

"Maybe, but I'm not handing you the key to my car, and you can hardly walk that distance on those roads." She took the corner of his cloth and dried her hands while he tried to formulate a reasonable excuse. "Why wouldn't you want me to see your plane, Hornblower? Even if you'd stolen it, I wouldn't know."

"I didn't steal it."

His tone was just abrupt enough, just annoyed enough, to make her believe him. "Well, then, I'll help you find the wreckage as soon as the trail's safe. For now, have a seat and let me look at that cut."

Automatically he lifted his fingers to the bandage. "It's all right."

"You're having pain. I can see it in your eyes."

He shifted his gaze to meet hers. There was sympathy there, a quiet, comforting sympathy that made him want to rest his cheek on her hair and tell her everything. "It comes and goes."

"Then I'll check it out, give you a couple of aspirin and see if we can make it go again. Come on, Cal." She took the cloth from him and led him to a chair. "Be a good boy."

He sat down, flicking her a glance of amused exasperation. "You sound like my mother."

She patted his cheek in reply before taking fresh bandages and antiseptic from a cupboard. "Just sit still." She uncovered the wound, frowning over it in a way that made him shift uncomfortably in his chair. "Sit still," she murmured. It was a nasty cut, jagged and deep. Bruises the color of storm clouds bloomed around it. "It looks better. At least there doesn't seem to be any infection. You'll have a scar."

Appalled, he lifted his fingers to the wound. "A scar?"

So he was vain, she thought, more than a little amused. "Don't worry, it'll look dashing. I'd be happier if you'd had a few stitches, but I think that's more than my Sears and Roebuck degree can handle."

"Your what?"

"Just a joke. This'll sting some."

He swore, loudly and richly, when she cleaned the wound. Before she was half finished, he grabbed her wrist. "Sting? Some?"

"Toughen up, Hornblower. Think about something else."

He set his teeth and concentrated on her face. The burning pushed his breath out in a hiss. Her eyes reflected both determination and understanding as she went competently about cleaning, treating and bandaging the wound.

She really was beautiful, he realized as he studied her in the watery early sunlight. It wasn't cosmetics, and it was highly unlikely that there had been any restructuring. This was the face she'd been born with. Strong, sharp, and with a natural elegance that made him long to stroke her cheek again. Her skin had been soft, he remembered, baby-smooth. And color had rushed in and out of it as her emotions had shifted.

Perhaps, just perhaps, she was an ordinary woman of her time. But to him she was unique and almost unbearably desirable.

That was why she made him ache, Cal told himself as he felt the muscles in his stomach knot and stretch. That was why she made him want her more than he'd ever wanted anything before, more than it was possible for him to want now. She was real, he reminded himself. But it was he who was the illusion. A man who had never been born, yet one who felt as though he had never been more alive.

"Do you do this often?" he asked her.

She hated knowing she was causing him pain, and she answered absently, "Do what often?"

"Rescue men."

He watched her lips curve and could almost taste them. "You're my first."

"Good."

"There, that should do."

"Aren't you going to kiss it and make it better?" His mother had always done so, as he imagined mothers had done for all time. When she laughed, he felt his heart lurch in his chest.

"Since you were brave." She leaned down and brushed her lips just above the bandage.

"It still hurts." He took her hand before she could move away. "Why don't you try again?"

"I'll get the aspirin." Her hand flexed in his. She would have backed away when he rose, but something in his eyes told her it would do no good. "Caleb…"

"I make you nervous." His thumb caressed her knuckles. "It's very stimulating."

"I'm not trying to stimulate you."

"Apparently you don't have to try." She was nervous, he thought again, but not frightened. He would have stopped if he'd seen fear. Instead, he brought her hand to his lips, then turned the palm upward. "You have wonderful hands, Libby. Gentle hands." He saw the emotions flickering in her eyes—confusion, unease, desire. He concentrated on the desire and drew her closer.

"Stop." She was appalled by the lack of conviction in her own voice. "I told you, I…" He brushed his lips against her temple, and her knees turned to water. "I'm not going to bed with you."

With a quiet murmur of agreement, he ran his hand up her back until her body was fitted against his. It amazed him how much he'd wanted to hold her like this. Her head nestled perfectly against his shoulder, as if they had been made to dance together. He had a moment's regret that there wasn't music, something low and pulsing. The thought made him smile. None of the women in his life had ever wanted to have the stage set. Nor had he ever had the urge to set one before.

"Relax," he murmured, and slid his hand up to the back of her neck. "I'm not going to make love with you. I'm only going to kiss you."

Panic had her straining away. "No, I don't…"

The fingers at the back of her neck shifted, tightened, held firm. Later, when she could think, she would tell herself that he had inadvertently touched some nerve, some secret vulnerability. An unspeakable pleasure sprang into her, and her head fell back in submission. On the heels of that flash of sensation he brought his lips to hers.

She went rigid, though not from fear, not from anger, and certainly not in resistance. It was shock, wave after wave of it. A live wire, she thought dimly. Somehow she had closed her hand over a live wire, and the voltage was deadly.

His lips barely touched hers, teasing, titillating, tormenting. It was a caress, mouth against mouth, unbearably erotic. Then it was a nibble, an almost playful nibble. And a caress again, sweet and light and compelling. His lips were warm and smooth as they rubbed a whispering trail over hers. In arousing contrast, the stubble of his beard scraped roughly over her cheek as he turned his head to trace the outline of her lips with his tongue.

It was intimate, impossibly so, the way he tasted her, toyed with her. His tongue dipped to hers, savoring dark new flavors, before he changed the mood again and caught her bottom lip between his teeth, nipping, stopping unerringly at a point between pleasure and pain.

It was seduction, the kind she had never dreamed of. Slow, soft-edged, inescapable seduction. She could hear the low, helpless sound that caught in her throat as he closed his teeth lightly over her chin.

The hand that had tensed against his chest began to tremble. She felt the solid cabin floor sway under her feet. Her rigidity melted degree by degree until she was shuddering with the heat and pliant in his arms.

He'd never experienced anything, anyone, like her. It was as though she had melted against him, quietly, completely. Her taste was fresh, like the air that wafted through the open window. He heard the soft, yielding sound of her sigh.

Then her arms were around him, clinging. She plunged her fingers deep into his hair as she strained against him. In a heartbeat, her mouth went from submissive to avid, pressing hungrily, possessively, desperately, against his. Rocked by the force, he dived into the kiss and let passion rule.

She wanted…too much. Why hadn't she known she'd been starving? Just the taste of him made her ravenous. Her body felt as though it would explode as dozens of new sensations arrowed into it, each of them sharp, separate and stunning. A muffled cry escaped her when his arms tightened painfully around her. She was no longer trembling—but he was.

What was she doing to him? He couldn't catch his breath. He couldn't think. But he could feel—too much, too quickly. The loss of control was more dangerous to a pilot than an uncharted meteor storm. He'd only meant to give and take a moment of pleasure, to satisfy a simple need. But this was more than pleasure, and it was far from simple. He needed to pull back before he was sucked into something he didn't yet understand.

He drew her away with unsteady hands. It helped—a little—that her breathing was as ragged as his. Her eyes were wide and stunned. Yes, stunned was the word, he decided. He felt as though he'd flown into the side of a building.

What had he done? Confused, she lifted a hand to her lips. What had she done? She could almost feel her blood bubbling through her veins. Libby took a step back, wanting to find solid ground again, and easy answers.

"Wait." He couldn't resist. He might curse himself for it later, but he couldn't resist. Before the first shock waves had passed, he hauled her against him a second time.

Not again. The single thought echoed in both their minds as they went under. The pull was just as strong, the need just as gripping. She felt herself seesaw between limp surrender and furious demand before she managed to yank herself free.

She nearly stumbled, and caught the back of a kitchen chair to steady herself. Her knuckles went white on the wood as she stared at him, dragging air into her lungs. She knew nothing about him, yet she had given him more than she had ever given anyone. Her mind was trained to ask questions, but at the moment it was her heart, fragile and irrational, that held sway.

"If you're going to stay here, in this house, I don't want you to touch me again."

It was fear he saw in her eyes now. He understood it, as he felt a trace of it himself. "I didn't expect that any more than you did. I'm not sure I like it any more than you do."

"Then we shouldn't have any trouble avoiding anything like this in the future."

He tucked his hands in his pockets and rocked back on his heels, not bothering to analyze why he was suddenly so angry. "Listen, babe, that was just as much your doing as mine."

"You grabbed me."

"No, I kissed you. You did the grabbing." It gave him little satisfaction to see her color rise. "I didn't force myself on you, Libby, and we both know it. But if you want to pretend you've got ice in your veins, that's fine with me.''

The embarrassed flush fled from her face, leaving it very white and very still. In contrast, her eyes went dark and wide. The stunned hurt that glazed them had him cursing himself and stepping forward.

''I'm sorry.''

She shifted behind the chair and managed to speak calmly. ''I don't want or expect an apology from you, but I do expect cooperation.''

His eyes narrowed. ''You'll get both.''

''I have a lot of work to do. You're welcome to take the television into your room, and there are books on the shelf by the fireplace. I'd appreciate it if you'd stay out of my way for the rest of the day.''

He dug his hands into his pockets. If she wanted to be stubborn, he could match her. ''Fine.''

She waited, her arms crossed over her chest, until he strode out of the room. She wanted to throw something, preferably something breakable. He had no right to say that to her after what he'd made her feel.

Ice in her veins? No, her problem had always been that she felt too much, wanted too much. Except when it came to personal, physical, one-to-one relationships with men. Miserable, she yanked out the chair and dropped onto it. She was a devoted daughter, a loving sister, a faithful friend. But no one's lover. She'd never experienced the driving need for intimacy. At times she'd been certain there was something lacking in her.

With one kiss, Cal had made her want things she'd almost convinced herself weren't important. At least not for her. She had her work, she was ambitious, and she knew she would make her mark. She had her family, her friends, her associates. Damn it, she was happy. She didn't need some hotshot pilot who couldn't keep his plane in the air to come along and make her feel restless—and alive, she mused, running a fingertip over her bottom lip. She hadn't known just how alive she could feel until he'd kissed her.

It was ridiculous. More unnerved than annoyed, she sprang up to pour another cup of coffee. He'd simply reminded her of something she forgot from time to time. She was a young, normal, healthy woman. A woman, she remembered, who had just spent several months on a remote island in the South Pacific. What she needed was to finish her dissertation and get back to Portland. Socialize, take in some movies, go to a few parties. What she needed, she decided with a nod, was to get Caleb Hornblower on his way, back to wherever the devil he came from.

Taking the coffee, she started upstairs. For all she knew, he might have dropped down from the moon.

She passed his room and couldn't prevent a quick snicker when she heard the frantic sounds of a television game show. The man, she thought as she slipped behind her own door, was easily entertained.

Chapter 4

It was an education. Cal spent several hours engrossed in a sea of daytime television. Every ten or fifteen minutes he switched channels, moving from game show to soap opera, from talk show to commercial. He found the commercials particularly entertaining, with their bright, often startling, intensity.

He preferred the musical ones, with their jumpy tunes and contagious cheer. But others made him wonder about the people who lived in this time, in this place.

Some selections showcased frazzled women fighting things like grease stains and dull wax buildup. He couldn't imagine his mother—or any other woman, for that matter—worrying about which detergent made whites whiter. But the commercials were delightful entertainment.

There were others that had attractive men and women solving their problems by drinking carbonated beverages or coffee. It seemed everyone worked, many outside, in sweaty jobs, so that they could go to a bar with friends at the end of the day and drink beer. He thought their costumes were wonderful.

On a daytime drama he watched a woman have a brief, intense conversation with a man about the possibility of her being pregnant. Either a woman was pregnant or she wasn't, Cal mused, switching over to see a paunchy man in a checked jacket win a week's vacation in Hawaii. From the winner's reaction, Cal figured that must be a pretty big deal in the twentieth century.

He wondered, as he caught snippets of *The News At Noon*, how humanity had ever made it to the twenty-first century and beyond. Murder was obviously a popular sport. As were discussions on arms limitations and treaties. Politicians apparently hadn't changed much, he thought as he snacked on a box of cookies he'd found in Libby's kitchen, his legs folded under him. They were still long-winded, they still danced around the truth, and they still smiled a great deal. But to imagine that world leaders had actually negotiated over how many nuclear weapons each would build and maintain was ludicrous. How many had they thought they needed?

No matter, he decided, and switched back to a soap. They had come to their senses eventually.

He liked the soaps the best. Though the picture was wavy and the sound occasionally jumped, he enjoyed watching the people react, agonizing about their problems, contemplating marriages, divorces and love affairs. Relationships had apparently been among the top ten problems of this century.

As he watched, a curvy blonde with tears in her

eyes and a tough-looking bare-chested man fell into each other's arms for a long, deep, passionate kiss. The music swelled until fade-out. Kissing was obviously an accepted habit of the time, Cal reflected. So why had Libby been so upset by one?

Restless, he rose and walked to the window. He hadn't exactly reacted in an expected fashion himself. The kiss had left him feeling angry, uneasy and vulnerable. None of those reactions had ever occurred before. And none of them, he admitted now, had lessened his desire for her in the least.

He wanted to know everything there was to know about Liberty Stone. What she thought, what she felt, what she wanted most, what she liked the least. There were dozens of questions he wanted to ask her, dozens of ways he wanted to touch her, and he knew that when he did her eyes would become dark and confused and depthless. He could imagine, with only the slightest effort, what her skin would feel like on the back of her knee, at the small of her back.

It was impossible. There was only one thing he should be thinking about now. Going home.

The time with Libby was only an interlude. Knowing as little as he did about women of this time didn't prevent him from being certain that Liberty Stone was not a woman a man could love and leave with any comfort. One look in her eyes and you saw not only passion but home fires burning.

He was a man who had no intention of settling down anytime soon. True, his parents had matched early and had married fairly young, at thirty. But he had no desire to be matched, mated or married yet. And when he did, Cal reminded himself it would be on his own ground. He would think of Libby only as a distraction, however pleasant, in a tense and delicate situation.

He needed to be gone. He pressed his palms against the cool glass of the window as if it were a prison he could easily escape. This was an experience some men might have craved, but he preferred breaking the boundaries of his own world—and his own time.

True, he'd learned things by reading the newspapers and watching the television. In the twentieth century the world was a long way from reaching peace, people worried a great deal about what to have for dinner and weapons were owned and used with reckless abandon. A dozen farm-fresh eggs could be had for about a dollar—which was the current U.S. currency—and everyone was on a diet.

It was all very interesting, but he didn't think any of this information was going to help. He had to concentrate on taking his mind back to what had happened on board his ship.

But he wanted to think about Libby, about what it had felt like to hold her against him. He wanted to remember how she had heated, about the way her lips had softened when his had met them.

When her arms had come around him, he had trembled. That had never happened to him before. He had what he considered a normal, healthy track record with women. He enjoyed them, both for company and for mutual physical pleasure. Since he believed in giving as much as he took, most of his lovers had remained his friends. But none of them had ever made his system churn as it had during one kiss with Libby.

All at once she'd taken him beyond what he knew and into some wild, gut-wrenching spin. Even now he could remember what it had felt like when her lips had gone hot and urgent against his. His balance had tilted. He'd almost believed he saw lights whirling behind his eyes. It had been like being pulled toward something of enormous, limitless force.

His legs turned to water under him. Slowly he lifted a hand to brace himself against the wall. The dizziness passed, leaving a hollow throbbing at the base of his skull. And suddenly he remembered. He remembered the lights. The flashing, blinking lights in the cockpit. Navigational system failed. Shields inoperative. Automatic distress signal engaged.

The void. He could see it, and even now the sweat pearled cold on his brow. A black hole, wide and dark and thirsty. It hadn't been on the charts. He would never have wandered so close if it had been on the charts. It had just been there, and his ship had been dragged toward it.

He hadn't gone in. The fact that he was alive and undoubtedly on Earth made him certain of that. It was possible that he had somehow skimmed the edge of it, then shot like a rubber band through space and time. The scientists of his era would question that idea. Time travel was only a theory, and one that was usually laughed at.

But he'd done it.

Shaken, he sat on the edge of the bed. He'd survived what no one in recorded history had survived. Lifting his hands, he turned the palms upward and stared at them. He was whole, and relatively undamaged. And he was lost. He fought back a fresh wave of panic, balling his hands into fists. No, not lost—he wouldn't accept that. If he had been shot one way, it was only logical that he could be shot another. Back home.

He had his mind, and his skill. He glanced at his wrist unit. He could work some basic computations on it. It wouldn't be enough, it wouldn't be nearly enough, but when he got back to his ship... If there was anything left of his ship.

Refusing to consider the fact that it might be completely destroyed, he began to pace. It was possible that he could interface his mini with Libby's machine. He had to try.

He could hear her downstairs. It sounded as though she were in the kitchen again, but he doubted she would fix him another meal. The regret came, too quickly to block, and the image of her sitting across the table from him flashed through his mind. He couldn't afford regrets, Cal reminded himself. And, if there was any choice, he wouldn't hurt her.

He'd apologize again, he decided. In fact, if he was successful with her computer, he would get out of her life as smoothly and painlessly as possible.

He moved quickly, quietly, into her room. He could only hope she would stay occupied until he made a few preliminary calculations. He'd have to be satisfied with those until he could find his ship and employ his own computer. Though impatience pushed at him, he hesitated for another moment, listening at the doorway. She was definitely in the kitchen, and, judging by the banging going on, she was still in a temper.

The computer, with its awkward box screen and its quaint keyboard, sat on the desk, surrounded by books and papers. Cal sat in Libby's chair and grinned at it.

"Engage."

The screen remained blank.

"Computer, engage." Impatient with himself, Cal

remembered the keyboard. He tapped in a command and waited. Nothing.

Sitting back, he drummed his fingers on the desk and considered. Libby, for reasons Cal couldn't fathom, had shut the machine down. That was easily remedied. He pushed through a few papers and picked up a letter opener. He turned the keyboard over, preparing to pry off the face. Then he saw the switch.

Idiot, he said to himself. They had switches for everything here. Calling on his remaining patience, he turned on the keyboard, then searched for more switches on the unit. When it began to hum, he had to muffle a cry of triumph.

"Now we're getting somewhere. Computer—" He caught himself with a shake of the head and began to type.

Computer, evaluate and conclude time warp factor—

He stopped himself again, swore, then pried off the plastic cover to reveal the memory board. His impatience was making him sloppy. And—worse—stupid. You couldn't get anything out of a machine that hadn't been put in. It was delicate, time-consuming work, but he forced himself not to rush. When he was finished, it was jury-rigged at best, but his wrist unit was interfaced with Libby's computer.

He took a deep breath and crossed the fingers on both hands. "Hello, computer."

Hello, Cal. The tinny words beeped from his wrist unit as the letters flashed across Libby's screen.

"Oh, baby, it's good to hear from you."

Affirmative.

"Computer, relay known data on theory of time travel through force of gravity and acceleration."

Untested theory, first proposed by Dr. Linward Bowers, 2110. Bowers hypothesized—

"No." Cal dragged a hand through his hair. In his hurry, he was getting ahead of himself. "I don't have time for all of that now. Evaluate and conclude. Time travel and survival probability on encounter with black hole."

Working… Insufficient data.

"Damn it, it happened. Analyze necessary acceleration and trajectory. Stop." He heard Libby coming up the stairs and had time only to shut down the unit before she stepped inside.

"What are you doing?"

Trying for a look of innocence, Cal smiled and swung out of the chair. "I was looking for you."

"If you've messed with my machine…"

"I couldn't help glancing at your papers. Fascinating stuff."

"I think so." She frowned at her desk. Everything seemed in order. "I could have sworn I heard you talking to someone."

"No one here but you and me." He smiled again. If he could distract her for a few minutes, he could disengage his unit and wait for a safer time. "I was probably mumbling to myself. Libby…" He took a step toward her, but she thrust a tray at him.

"I made you a sandwich."

He took the tray and set it on the bed. Her simple kindness left him feeling as guilty as sin. "You're a very nice woman."

"Just because you annoy me doesn't mean I'd starve you."

"I don't want to annoy you." He stepped over quickly when she wandered toward the computer. "I don't seem to be able to avoid it. I'm sorry you didn't like what happened before.''

She cast him a quick, uneasy glance. ''That's better forgotten.''

''No, it's not.'' Needing the contact, he closed a hand over hers. ''Whatever happens, it's something I won't forget. You touched something in me, Libby, something that hasn't been touched before.''

She knew what he meant, exactly, precisely. And it frightened her. ''I have to get back to work.''

''Do all women find it difficult to be honest?''

''I'm not used to this,'' she blurted out. ''I don't know how to deal with it. I'm not comfortable around men. I'm just not passionate.''

When he laughed, she spun away, furious and embarrassed.

''That's the most ridiculous thing I've ever heard. You're overloaded with passion.''

She felt something shift inside her, strain for freedom. ''For my work,'' she said, spacing her words carefully. ''For my family. But not in the way you mean.''

She believed it, Cal decided as he studied her. Or she had made herself believe it. In the past two days he'd learned what it was like to doubt yourself. If he could repay her in no other way, perhaps he could show her what kind of woman she held trapped inside.

''Would you like to take a walk?''

She blinked at him. ''What?''

''A walk.''

''Why?''

He tried not to smile. She was a woman who would

require reasons. "It's a nice day, and I'd like to see a little of where I am. You could show me."

She untangled the fingers she'd twisted together. Hadn't she promised herself she would take time to enjoy herself? He was right. It was a nice day, and her work could certainly wait.

"You'll need your shoes," she told him.

There was a scent to the cool, slightly moist air. Pine, he realized after several moments' mental debate. The scent was pine, like Christmas. But it came from the genuine article, not a scent disk or a simulator. The ground was thick with trees, and the breeze, though it was light, sounded through them like a sea. The clear pale-blue sky was marred only by the gray-edged clouds due north. There was birdsong.

But for the cabin behind them and a dilapidated shed, there were no man-made structures—just mountain, sky and forest.

"This is incredible."

"Yes, I know." She smiled, wishing it didn't please her quite so much that he appreciated and understood. "Whenever I come here, I'm tempted to stay."

He walked beside her, matching her pace, as they entered the sun-dappled forest. It didn't feel odd being alone with her now. It felt right. "Why don't you?"

"My work, primarily. The university wouldn't pay me to walk in the woods."

"What do they pay you for?"

"To research."

"When you don't research, how do you live?"

"How?" She tilted her head. "Quietly, I suppose.

I have an apartment in Portland. I study, lecture, read."

The path was steeper now. "For entertainment?"

"Movies." She shrugged. "Music."

"Television?"

"Yes." She had to laugh. "Sometimes too often. What about you? Do you remember what you like to do?"

"Fly." His grin was quick and charming. She hardly noticed when he took her hand. "There's nothing else like it, not for me. I'd like to take you up and show you."

Her expression was bland as she glanced at the bandage on his head. "I'll pass."

"I'm a good pilot."

Amused, she reached down to pick a wildflower. "Possibly."

"Absolutely." In a move that was both smooth and natural, he took the flower from her and slipped it into her hair. "I had some trouble with my instruments, or I wouldn't be here."

Because the gesture threw her off, she stared at him for a moment before she began to walk again. "Where were you going?" She slowed her pace as Cal dallied, picking wildflowers along the trail.

"Los Angeles."

"You had a long way to go."

He opened his mouth, fooled for a moment into thinking she was making a joke. "Yes," he finally managed. "Longer than I anticipated."

Hesitantly she touched the blossom in her hair. "Will someone be looking for you?"

"Not for a while." He turned his face to the sky.

"If we find my...plane tomorrow, I can assess the damage and go on from there."

"We should be able to drive into town in another day or two." She wanted to smooth away the worry line that had formed between his brows. "You can see a doctor, make some phone calls."

"Phone calls?"

His baffled look had her worrying about his head injury again. "To your family or friends, or your employer."

"Right." He took her hand again, absently sniffing at the clutch of flowers he held. "Can you give me the bearing and distance from here to where you found me?"

"Bearing and distance?" Laughing, she sat on the bank of a narrow, fast-running creek. "How about if I tell you it was that way?" She pointed toward the southeast. "Ten miles as the crow flies, double that by the road."

He dropped down beside her. Her scent was as fresh as the wildflowers, and more alluring. "I thought you were a scientist."

"That doesn't mean I can give you longitude and latitude or whatever. Ask me about the mudmen of New Guinea and I'll be brilliant."

"Ten miles." Eyes narrowed, he scanned the fringe of fir. Where it thinned, he could see a towering, rough-edged mountain, blue in the sunlight. "And there's nothing between here and there? No city? No settlement?"

"No. This area is still remote. We get a few hikers now and again."

Then it was unlikely that anyone had come across his ship. That was one concern he could push to the back of his mind. His main problem now was how to locate his ship without Libby. The easiest way, he supposed, would be to leave at first light, in her vehicle.

But that was tomorrow. He was coming to understand that time was too precious, and too capricious, to waste.

"I like it here." It was true. He enjoyed sitting on the cool grass, listening to the water. It made him wonder what it would be like to come back to this same spot two centuries later. What would he find?

The mountain would be there, and possibly part of the forest that closed in around them. This same creek might still rush over these same stones. But there would be no Libby. The ache came again, dull and gnawing.

"When I'm home again," he said very slowly, "I'll think of you here."

Would he? She stared at the water, at the play of sunlight over it, and wished it didn't matter. "Maybe you'll come back sometime."

"Sometime." He toyed with her fingers. She would be a ghost to him then, a woman who had existed only in a flash of time, a woman who had made him wish for the impossible. "Will you miss me?"

"I don't know." But she didn't draw her hand away, because she realized she would miss him, more than was reasonable.

"I think you will." He forgot his ship, his questions, his future, and concentrated on her. He began to weave the flowers he'd picked through her hair. "They name stars and moons and galaxies for goddesses," he murmured. "Because they were strong and beautiful and mysterious. Man, mortal man, could never quite conquer them.''

''Most cultures have some historical belief in mythology.'' She cleared her throat and began to pleat the baggy material of her slacks. ''Ancient astronomers...'' He turned her face to his with a fingertip.

''I wasn't talking about myths. Though you look like one with flowers in your hair.'' Gently he touched a petal near her cheek. '' ''There be none of Beauty's daughters/ With a magic like thee;/ And like music on the waters/ Is thy sweet voice to me.'' ''

It was a dangerous man, she knew instinctively, who could smile like the devil and quote poetry in a voice like silk. His eyes were the color of the sky just before dusk, a deep, dreamy blue. She'd never thought she was the kind of woman who could go weak just looking into a man's eyes. She didn't want to be.

''I should go back. I have a lot of work to do.''

''You work too much.'' His brow rose when she turned her head aside and frowned. ''What button did I push?''

Restless, more annoyed with herself than with him, she shrugged. ''Someone always seems to be saying that to me. Sometimes I even say it to myself.''

''It isn't a crime, is it?''

She laughed because his question seemed so sincere. ''Not yet, anyway.''

''It's not a crime to take a day off?''

''No, but—''

''No's enough. Why don't we say 'It's Miller Time?' '' At her baffled look, he spread his hands. ''You know, like on the commercials.''

''Yes, I know.'' Hooking an arm around one upraised knee, she studied him. Poetry one moment, beer commercials the next. "Every now and again, Hornblower, I wonder if you're for real."

"Oh, I'm real." He stretched out to watch the sky. The grass was cool and soft beneath him, and the wind played lazily through the trees. "What do you see? Up there?"

She tilted her head back. "The sky. A blue one, thank goodness, with a few clouds that should clear by evening."

"Don't you ever wonder what's beyond it?"

"Beyond what?"

"The blue." With his eyes half-closed, he imagined…the endless sweep of stars, the pure black of space, the beautiful symmetry of orbiting moons and planets. "Don't you ever think about the worlds up there, just out of reach?"

"No." She saw only the arc of blue, speared through by mountains. "I suppose it's because I think more about worlds that were. My work usually keeps my feet, and my eyes, on the ground."

"If there's going to be a world tomorrow, you have to look to the stars." He caught himself. It seemed foolish to pine for something that might be lost. How odd it was that he was thinking so much of the future, and Libby so much of the past, when they had the here and now.

"What movies and music?" he asked abruptly. Libby shook her head. There seemed to be no order to his thought patterns. "Before, you said you liked movies and music for fun. Which ones?"

"All sorts. Good or bad. I'm easily entertained."

"Tell me your favorite movie."

"That's difficult." But his eyes were so intense, so

earnest, that she picked one at random from her list of favorites. *"Casablanca."*

He liked the sound of it, the way she said it. "What's it about?"

"Come on, Hornblower, everyone knows what it's about."

"I missed it." He gave her a quick, guileless smile that no woman should have trusted. "I must have been busy when it came out."

She laughed again, with a quick shake of her head, a brightening of her eyes. "Sure. Both of us must have had pretty full schedules in the forties."

He let that pass. "What was the story?" He didn't care about the plot. He only wanted to hear her talk, to watch her as she did.

To humor him, and because it was easy to sit by the water and daydream, she began. He listened, enjoying the way she told the tale of lost love, heroism and sacrifice. Even more, he enjoyed the way she gestured with her hands, the way her voice ebbed and flowed with her feelings. And the way her eyes mirrored them, darkening, softening, when she spoke of lovers reunited, then pulled apart, by destiny.

"No happy ending," Cal murmured.

"No, but I always felt that Rick found her again, years later, after the war."

"Why?"

She had settled back, pillowing her head on her folded arms. "Because they belonged together. When people do, they find each other, no matter what." She was smiling when she turned her head, but the smile faded slowly when she saw the way he was looking at her. As if they were alone, she thought. Not just alone in the mountains, but totally, completely alone, as Adam and Eve had been.

She yearned. For the first time in her life, she yearned—body, mind and heart.

"Don't." He said the word quietly as she started to scramble to her feet. The lightest touch of his hand on her shoulder kept her still. "I wish you weren't afraid of me."

"I'm not." But she was breathless, as if she'd already been running.

"Of what, then?"

"Of nothing." His voice could be so gentle, she thought. So terrifyingly gentle.

"But you're tense." With his long, limber fingers, he began to rub at the tight muscles of her shoulders. He shifted, and his lips skimmed over her temple, as cool and stirring as the breeze. "Tell me what you're afraid of."

"Of this." She lifted her hands to push against his chest. "I don't know how to fight what I'm feeling."

"Why do you have to?" He skimmed a hand down the side of her body, astonished by the grinding need in his own.

"It's too soon." But she was no longer pushing him away. Her resolve was melting in a flood of hot, hammering need.

"Soon?" His laugh was strained as he buried his face against her throat. "It's already been centuries."

"Caleb, please." There was an urgency in her voice, a plea that was at once weak and unarguable. He knew as he felt her body vibrate beneath his that he could have her. Just as he knew as he looked down at the clouded confusion in her eyes that once he had she might not forgive him.

Need jerked inside him. It was a new and frustrating sensation. He rolled to one side and stood, and with his back to her he watched the water ripple.

"Do you drive all men crazy?"

She brought her knees up tight against her breasts. "No, of course not."

"Then I'm just lucky, I guess." He lifted his eyes to the sky. He wanted to be back there, spearing through space. Alone. Free. He heard the grass rustle as she stood and wondered if he would ever truly be free again. "I want you, Libby."

She didn't speak. She couldn't. No man had ever said those three simple words to her before. If thousands had, it wouldn't have mattered. No one would ever have spoken them in just that way.

Pushed to the brink by her silence, he whirled around. He wasn't her amiable, slightly odd patient now, but a furious, healthy and obviously dangerous man.

"Damn it, Libby, am I supposed to say nothing, to feel nothing? Are those the rules here? Well, the hell with it. I want you, and if I stay near you much longer, I'm going to have you."

"Have me?" She'd been certain her system was too weak and warm for anger. But it filled her with a flash that had her body straightening like an arrow. "What? Like a shiny car on a showroom floor? You can want anything you like, Cal, but when those wants concern me I've got some say in it."

She was magnificent…unbearably vivid, with fury in her eyes and flowers clinging to her hair. He would remember her like this, always. He knew it, and he knew the memory would be bittersweet, and yet his temper pushed him forward.

"You can have all the say you like." Taking both her arms, he pulled her against him. "But I'll have something before I go."

This time she struggled. It was pride, pride and anger, that had her jerking free. Then his arms came around her, twin vises that clamped her body unerringly to his. She would have sworn at him, but his mouth closed hard over hers.

It was nothing like the first time. Then he had seduced, persuaded, tempted. Now he possessed, not as if he had the right, but simply taking it. Her muffled protest went unheeded, her struggles ignored. Panic skidded up her spine, then slid down again, overwhelmed by pure desire.

She didn't want to be forced. She didn't want to be left without choice. That was her mind talking. It was right; it was reasonable. But her body leaped forward, leaving intellect far behind. She reveled in the strength, in the tension, even in the temper. She met power with power.

She came alive in his arms, making him forget who and why and where. When he could taste her, hot and potent on his lips, no other world, no other time, existed. For him it was as new, as exciting, as frightening as it was for her. Irresistible. The thought didn't come to him. No thought could. But she was as irresistible as the gravity that held their feet on the ground, as compelling as the need that sent their pulses racing.

He dragged her head back and plunged into the velvet moistness of her waiting mouth.

The world was spinning. With a moan, she ran her hands up his back, until she was clinging desperately to his shoulders. She wanted it to go on spinning,

whirling madly, until she was dizzy and breathless
and limp. She could hear the murmur of the water,
the whisper of the breeze through the pines. There
was a strong shaft of sunlight on her back. She knew
that in reality her feet were still on solid ground. But
the world was spinning.

And she was in love.

The sound that came from deep in her throat was
one of surrender. To him. To herself.

He murmured her name. A searing ache arrowed
through him as desire veered painfully toward a new,
uncharted emotion. The hand that had been roaming
through her hair clenched reflexively. He felt the petals of a flower crush. The scent, sweet and dying, rose
on the air.

He jerked away, appalled. The flower was in his
hand, fragile and mangled. His gaze was drawn to her
lips, still warm and swollen from his. His muscles
trembled. A wave of self-disgust rose up inside him.
Never, never had he forced himself on a woman. The
idea itself was abhorrent to him, the most shameful
of sins. The reality was unforgivable—most unforgivable because she mattered as no one else ever had.

"Did I hurt you?" he managed.

Libby shook her head quickly, too quickly. Hurt?
she thought. That was nothing. Devastated. With one
kiss he had devastated her, showed her that her will
could be crumbled and her heart lost.

He wouldn't apologize. Cal turned away until he
was certain he was under control enough to speak
rationally. But he would not apologize for wanting,
or for taking. He would have nothing else of her when
he left.

"I can't promise that won't happen again, but I'll

do my best to see that it doesn't. You should go back inside now.''

And that was all? Libby wondered. After he had stripped her emotions to the bone he could calmly tell her to go back inside? She opened her mouth to protest, and she nearly took a step toward him before she stopped herself.

He was right, of course. What had happened should never happen again. They were strangers, whatever her heart told her to the contrary. Without a word, she turned and left him alone by the creek.

Later, when the sun and shadows had shifted, he opened his hand to let the wounded flower fall into the water. He watched it drift away.

Chapter 5

She couldn't concentrate. Libby stared at her computer screen, trying to work up some interest in the words she'd already written. The Kolbari Islanders and their traditional moon dance no longer fascinated her. She'd been certain work was the answer—an immersion in it. No one had ever distracted her from her studies before. In college she'd completed a thesis while her roommates threw an open-door pizza party. That single-minded concentration had followed her into her professional life. She'd written papers in tents by lamplight, read notes on the back of a jogging mule and prepared lectures in the jungle. Once a project was begun, nothing broke the flow.

As she read a single paragraph through for the third time, all she could think of was Cal.

It was a pity she hadn't had a greater interest in chemistry, she thought, pulling off her glasses to rub at her eyes. If she had, perhaps she would understand more clearly her reaction to him. Surely there was a book somewhere that would give her the information so that she could analyze it. She didn't want to feel without being able to list logical reasons why. Daydreaming about love and romance was one thing. Experiencing it was something else altogether.

This wasn't like her.

With a long sigh, she pushed away from the desk and folded her legs under her. Her eyes still on the screen, she propped her elbows on her knees and braced her chin on her fisted hands. She wasn't in love, she told herself. It had been a knee-jerk reaction to the intensity of the moment. People didn't really fall in love that quickly. They could be attracted, of course, even strongly attracted. For love, though, other factors had to be mixed in.

Common ground and common interests, Libby decided. That made good, solid sense to her. How could she be in love with Cal when the only interest he had that she knew about was flying? And eating, she added with a reluctant smile.

An understanding of each other's feelings, goals, temperaments. Surely that was vital to love. How could she be in love when she didn't understand Caleb Hornblower in the least? His feelings were a mystery to her, his goals had never been discussed, and his temperament seemed to change by the hour.

He was troubled. A frown brought her brows together when she thought of the look that she so often saw in his eyes. Sometimes he made her think of a man who had taken a wrong turn on the freeway and ended up in a strange, foreign land.

Troubled, yes, but he was also just plain trouble, she reminded herself, trying to keep her compassion

from outweighing her common sense. His personality
was too strong, his charm too smooth, his confidence
too high. She didn't have room in her neatly ordered
life for a man like Cal. He would, simply by existing,
cause chaos.

She heard him come in the kitchen door, and her
body braced automatically. Just as her pulse speeded
up and her blood ran faster. Automatically.

Disgusted with herself, she scooted her chair back
to her desk. She was going to work. In fact, she was
going to work straight through to midnight, and she
wasn't going to give Cal another thought. She caught
herself gnawing on her thumbnail again.

"Damn it, who is Caleb Hornblower?"

The last thing she'd expected from her muttered
question was an answer. The tinny, disembodied
voice had her jolting. She grabbed the edge of her
desk to keep from spilling out of her chair, then
stared, openmouthed, at her computer screen.

Hornblower, Caleb, Captain ISF, retired.

"Oh, my God." With a hand to her throat, she
shook her head. "Now just hold on," she whispered.

Holding.

It wasn't possible, Libby told herself as she pressed
an unsteady hand to her mouth. She had to be hallucinating. That was it. Emotional stress, overwork
and the lack of a good night's sleep were causing her
to hallucinate. Closing her eyes, she took three deep
breaths. But when she opened them again, the words
were still on the screen.

"What the devil is going on here?"

*Information requested and relayed. Is additional
data required?*

With an unsteady hand, she pushed aside some of

the papers on her desk and uncovered Cal's watch. She would have sworn the voice she had heard had come from it. No, it just wasn't possible. Using a fingertip, she traced a thread-slim transparent wire that ran from his watch to the computer's drive.

"What kind of game is he playing?"

"Five hundred twenty games are available on this unit. Which would you prefer?

"Libby?" Caleb stood just inside the doorway, thinking fast. There was no use berating himself for being careless. In fact, he wondered if subconsciously he'd wanted to put himself in a position where he would be forced to tell her the truth. But now, when she turned, he wasn't certain that would be good for either of them. She wasn't just frightened, she was furious.

"All right, Hornblower, I want you to tell me exactly what's going on here."

He tried an easy, cooperative smile. "Where?"

"Right here, damn it." She jabbed a finger at the machine.

"You'd know more about that than I would. It's your work."

"I want an explanation, and I want it now."

He crossed to her. A quick scan of the screen had a smile tugging at his mouth. So she'd wanted to know who he was. There was some comfort in knowing she was as confused by him as he was by her—and as interested.

"No, you don't."

He said it quietly, and he would have taken her hand if she hadn't batted his away.

"I not only want one, I insist on one. You... you..." On a sound of frustration, she took another breath. He wasn't going to make her stutter. "You come in here and plug your watch into my machine, and—"

"Interface," he said. "If you're going to work on a computer, you should know the language."

She snapped her teeth together. "Suppose you tell me how you can interface a watch with a PC."

"A what?"

She couldn't prevent the smirk. "Personal computer. You'd better brush up on the language yourself. Now—answers."

He put a hand on each of her shoulders. "You'd never believe me."

"You'd better make me believe. Is that watch some kind of miniature computer?"

"Yes." He started to reach for it, but she slapped a hand down on his wrist.

"Leave it. I've never heard of any miniature computer that answers voice commands, interfaces with a PC and claims to play over five hundred games."

"No." He looked down at her angry eyes. "You wouldn't have."

"Why don't you tell me how to get one, Hornblower? I'll buy my father one for Christmas."

Pure good humor tilted the corner of his mouth. "Actually, I don't think that model's going to be on the market for a little while yet. Can I interest you in something else?"

She kept her eyes level with his. "You can interest me in the truth."

Stalling seemed to be the best approach. He turned her hand over and linked his fingers with hers. "The whole truth, or the simple parts?"

"Are you a spy?"

The last thing she'd expected was laughter. After his first chuckle it rolled out of him, warm and delighted. He kissed her, once on each cheek, before she could stop him.

"You didn't answer my question." She wiggled out of his hold. "Are you an agent?"

"What makes you think so?"

"A wild guess," she said, throwing up her hands and spinning around the room. "You crash down in the middle of a storm no sensible person would have been driving in, much less flying. You have no ID. You claim you're not in the military, but you were wearing some kind of weird uniform. Your shoes were nearly falling apart, but you have a watch that makes a Rolex look like a Tinkertoy. A watch that talks back." Even as she said it, it seemed so preposterous that she looked at the screen to make certain she hadn't imagined it all. "Look, I know intelligence agencies have some pretty advanced equipment. It might not be James Bond, but—"

"Who's James Bond?" Cal asked.

Bond, James. Code name 007. Fictional character created by twentieth-century writer Ian Fleming. Novels include—

"Disengage," Cal ordered, dragging a frustrated hand through his hair. One look at Libby's face told him he was in deep. "Maybe you should sit down."

With a weak nod, she sat on the edge of the bed.

Though it was a bit late for precautions, Cal unhooked the wire and slipped it and his unit into his pocket. "You want an explanation."

She wasn't so sure anymore. Calling herself a coward, she gave a quick, jerky nod. "Yes."

"Okay, but you're not going to like it." He sat in

her chair and crossed his ankles. "I was making a routine run from the Brigston colony."

"Excuse me?"

"The Brigston colony," Cal repeated. Then he took the plunge. "On Mars."

Libby closed her eyes and rubbed a hand over her face. "Give me a break, Hornblower."

"I told you you wouldn't like it."

"You want me to believe you're a Martian."

"Don't be ridiculous."

She dropped her hand into her lap. "I'm ridiculous? You sit there and try to feed me some story about coming from Mars and *I'm* ridiculous?" For lack of anything better to do, she tossed a pillow across the room, then rose and began to pace. "Look, it's not as though I'm prying into your personal life, or even that I expect some kind of humble gratitude for dragging you in out of that storm, but I think some mutual respect is in order here. You're in my home, Hornblower, and I deserve the truth."

"Yes, I think you do. I'm trying to give it to you."

"Fine." Temper wasn't going to help, she thought. She dropped back on the bed and spread her arms. "So you're from Mars."

"No, I'm from Philadelphia."

"Ah." She let out a long, relieved breath. "Now we're getting somewhere. You were on your way to Los Angeles when you crashed your plane."

"My ship."

Her face remained calm and impassive. "That would be your spaceship."

"You'd call it that." He leaned forward. "I had to reroute because of a meteor shower. I was off course...farther, I realize, than I had first thought, because my instruments were unstable. I ran into a black hole, an uncharted one.''

''A black hole.'' She no longer felt like laughing. His eyes were absolutely sincere. He believed it, she realized as she folded her hands tightly in her lap. His concussion was obviously much more serious than she had originally thought.

''That's a compressed star. Very dense, very powerful. Its gravity sucks up everything—stellar dust, gas, even light.''

''Yes, I know what a black hole is.'' She had to keep him calm, Libby reasoned. She would humor him, express a friendly interest in his story, then get him back into bed. ''So you were flying your spaceship, ran into a black hole and crashed.''

''In simple terms. I'm not sure exactly what happened. That's why I hooked my wrist unit up to your computer. I need more information before I can calculate how to get back.''

''To Mars?''

''No, damn it. To the twenty-third century.''

The small, polite smile froze on her face. ''I see.''

''No, you don't.'' He rose to prowl the room. Patience, he told himself. He could hardly expect her to accept in a moment what he still had trouble believing himself. ''There have been theories about time travel for centuries. It's generally accepted that if a ship could get up the needed speed and slingshot around the sun it could pass through time. It's only theory at this point, because no one's sure how to keep the ship from being sucked into the sun's gravity and frying. The same holds true for a black hole. If I'd been pulled in, the power and radiation would have ripped the ship apart. It had to be blind luck, but somehow

I hit on the right trajectory—the precise speed, distance, angle. Instead of being pulled in, I bounced off.'' He flicked the curtain aside to look out at the darkening sky. ''And landed here, over two and a half centuries back in the past.''

Libby rose to lay a hesitant hand on his shoulder. ''You should lie down.''

He didn't look back at her, didn't need to. ''You don't believe me.''

She opened her mouth, but she couldn't bring herself to lie to him. ''You believe it.''

He turned then. There was sympathy in her eyes, the warm golden glow of it. ''How would you explain it?'' He reached in his pocket for his unit. ''How would you explain this?''

''There's no need for explanations now. I'm sorry I pressured you, Caleb. You're tired.''

''You have no explanation. For this—'' he dropped the unit in his pocket again ''—or for me.''

''All right. My theory is that you're part of an intelligence operation, perhaps some elite section of the CIA. You were probably burned out—stress, tension, overwork. When you crashed, the shock and trauma of your head injury pushed you over the edge. You don't want to be a part of what you were, so you've chosen to give yourself a different time, a different history.''

''So you think I'm crazy.''

''No.'' The compassion was back, in her eyes, in her voice. She touched her hand to the side of his face in a comforting gesture. ''I think you're confused and you need rest and attention.''

He started to swear, but he caught himself. If he continued to insist, he would only frighten her. He'd already caused her a great deal of trouble that she didn't deserve.

"You're probably right. I'm still shaky from the crash. I should get some rest."

"That's a good idea." She waited until he reached the door. "Caleb, don't worry. It's going to be all right."

He turned back, thinking this would be the last time he saw her. Purple twilight filled the window at her back, and she seemed to be standing at the edge of a mist. Her eyes were dark and full of compassion. He remembered how rich and sweet the flavor of her lips was. Regret struck him like a fist.

"You are," he said quietly, "the most beautiful woman I've ever seen."

She stared, speechless, at the door he closed behind him.

He didn't sleep. As he lay in the dark he could only think of her. He switched on the television and watched the figures move like ghosts over the screen. They were, he realized, more real than he.

She hadn't believed him. There was little surprise in that. But she had tried to comfort him. He wondered if she knew how unique she was, in this age or any other. A woman who was strong enough to live on her own yet fragile enough to tremble in a man's arms. His arms.

He wanted her. In the pearly-gray light of early dawn he wanted her almost more than he could stand. Just to hold her would be enough. To lie beside her with her head settled on his shoulder. In silence. He could think of no other woman he would be content to spend hours of silence with. If he had a choice...

But he had no choice.

He was lying across the bed fully dressed. Now he rose. He had nothing to take with him, and nothing to leave behind. Moving quietly downstairs, he slipped out of the house.

The Land Rover was parked near the porch steps, where she had left it the night she'd brought him home. He crossed to it, casting a final glance at Libby's window. He hated to leave her stranded. Later he'd break into a radio frequency and broadcast her location. Someone would come for her.

She'd be mad. The idea made him smile a little as he climbed into the driver's seat. She would curse him, hate him. And she wouldn't forget him.

Cal took a moment to be charmed by the old-fashioned instruments and controls. The birds were singing as he tested the steering wheel and pumped the gas pedal curiously.

There was a lever between the seats marked with numbers running from one to four in an H pattern. Gears clanked when he shoved the lever forward. Confident he had the skill to operate such a simple vehicle, he turned knobs. When he got no response he jiggled the gearshift while depressing the floor pedals. Through trial and error, he found the clutch and shifted smoothly into first gear.

A beginning, he decided, and wondered where the hell the designer had put the ignition.

"You're going to have a hard time starting it without this." Libby stood on the porch, one hand in a fist on her hip, the other aloft, with the ignition key dangling from her fingers.

She was mad, all right, Cal thought. But he didn't

feel like smiling. "I was just…thinking about taking a ride."

"Were you?" She tugged her hastily donned sweater farther over her hips before she walked down the steps. "It's your bad luck I didn't leave the keys in the car."

So it took a key. He should have known. "Did I wake you?"

She jabbed a fist hard at his shoulder. "You've got nerve, Hornblower. Feeding me all that garbage last night so I'd feel sorry for you, then trying to steal my car. What were you going to do, hot-wire it and leave me stranded? I'd have thought a hotshot pilot like you would be able to do it faster, and quieter."

"I was just borrowing it," he said, though he doubted the difference would matter to her. "I thought you'd be better off if I drove out to where I wrecked by myself."

She'd trusted him, she thought, calling herself ten kinds of a fool. She'd felt sorry for him. She'd wanted to help him. Betrayal and fury had her clenching her fist until the key bit into her palm. She'd help him, all right.

"Well, you can stop thinking. Move over."

"I'm sorry?"

"I said move over. You want to go to the wreck, I'll take you to the wreck."

"Libby—"

"Move over, Hornblower, or that hole in your head's going to have company."

"Fine." Giving up, he eased himself over the gearshift and dropped into the passenger seat. "Don't say I didn't warn you."

"To think I was feeling sorry for you."

He watched, intrigued, as she pushed the key into a slot and turned. The engine roared to life. The radio blared, the windshield wipers swished, and the heater blasted.

"You really are a case," she muttered, switching knobs.

Before he could comment, she popped the clutch, rammed down on the gas and sent them speeding onto the narrow dirt road.

"Libby." He cleared his throat, then pitched his voice above the noise of the engine. "I was doing what I thought was best for you. I didn't want to involve you any more than I already have."

"That's swell." She yanked the gearshift back and sent stones flying. "Just who do you work for, Hornblower?"

"I'm an independent."

"Oh, I see." Her mouth tightened into a grim line. "You sell to the highest bidder?"

The renewed anger in her tone puzzled him. "Sure. Doesn't everyone?"

"Some people don't put a price on their loyalty to their country."

Cal pressed his fingers to his eyes. He hadn't realized they were back to that. "Libby, I am not a spy. I don't work for the CAI—"

"CIA."

"Whatever. I'm a pilot. I run supplies, people, equipment. I deliver to spaceports, colonies, labs."

"So you're playing that tune again." She gritted her teeth as she sent the Land Rover over a sloping bank and across a stream. Water gushed up the sides. "What are you claiming to be this time—an intergalactic truck driver?"

He lifted his hands, then let them fall. "Close enough."

"I'm not buying it anymore, Cal. I don't think you're crazy. I don't think you're deluded. So cut it."

"Cut what?" When she only hissed at him, he decided to try again, once more, calmly. "Libby, everything I told you is true."

"Stop it." If she hadn't needed both hands on the wheel, she might have slapped him. "I wish I'd never seen you. You literally fall into my life and make me care about you, make me feel things I've never felt before, and all you do is lie."

He saw only one option. On impulse, he reached out and turned off the key. The Land Rover bumped to a stop. "Now listen to me." With his free hand, he grabbed her sweater and yanked her around. "Damn it." The oath came out as a murmur when he saw her face. "Don't cry. I can't stand it."

"I'm not crying." She wiped angry tears away with the backs of her hands. "Give me back the key."

"In a minute." He released her, holding his hand palm out in a gesture of truce. "I wasn't lying when I said I was leaving this morning because I thought it was best for you."

She believed him. And she hated herself because he could so easily make her believe. "Will you tell me what kind of trouble you're in?"

"Yes." Because he couldn't resist, he trailed a fingertip across her damp cheek. "After we've found the—where I went down—I'll tell you anything you want to know."

"No more evasions or ridiculous stories?"

"I'll tell you everything." He lifted her hand, then pressed his palm to hers. "You have my word.

Libby…'' He linked his fingers with hers. ''What do I make you feel?''

She drew her hand away to grip the wheel. ''I don't know, and I don't want to think about it.''

''I'd like you to know that I've never had the same feelings for another woman as I have for you. I wish things could be different.''

He was already saying goodbye, she realized. A rippling ache spread in her chest. ''Don't. Let's just concentrate on what needs to be done.'' While she stared straight ahead, he slipped the key back into the ignition. ''You were right up there,'' she told him as she switched it on. ''At the curve. The best I could say is that you were coming from that direction. I got the impression when I saw you crash that you went down along that ridge somewhere.'' With a frown, she lifted a hand to shield her eyes. ''Strange…it looks like there's a break in that bank of trees up there.''

Not strange, Cal thought, when you considered that a ship over seventy meters long and thirty across had come down in them. ''Why don't we take a look?''

Libby turned off the road and started up the rocky slope. The part of her that was still annoyed hoped the jostling ride gave Cal the willies. But when she glanced at him, he was grinning.

''This is great!'' he shouted. ''I haven't done anything like this since I was a kid.''

''Glad you're having fun.'' She turned her attention back to driving and didn't notice when Cal pushed a series of buttons on his watch. Excitement began to drum in him as he studied the directional beam on one of the dials.

''Twenty-five degrees north.''

"What?"

"That way." He used his other hand to gesture with. "It's that way. Two point five kilometers."

"How do you know?"

He sent her a brilliant smile. "Trust me."

They climbed the ridge to where the line of pines thickened. The scattered dogwoods were budded but not yet ready to bloom. Libby shivered once in the cool air before she shut the engine off. "I can't drive through this. We'll have to walk."

"It's not far." He was already out and offering an impatient hand. "A few hundred meters."

She kept her hand at her side as she stared at his watch. It was sending out a low, regular beep. "Why is it doing that?"

"It's scanning. It only has a range of ten kilometers, but it's fairly accurate." Holding his wrist out, he moved in a slow circle. "Since I doubt there's anything metallic as big as my ship around here, I'd say we've found it."

"Don't start that again." Libby pushed her hands into her pockets and started to walk.

"You're supposed to be a scientist," Cal reminded her as he fell into step beside her.

"I am a scientist," she muttered, "which is why I know that men do not bounce off black holes and drop into the Klamath Mountains on the way back from Mars."

He slung a friendly arm around her shoulders. "You're looking behind you, Libby, not ahead. You've never seen anyone who lived two centuries ago, but you know they existed. Why is it so difficult to believe that they exist two centuries in the future?"

"I hope they will, but I don't expect to offer them

coffee." He wasn't crazy, she decided, but he was clever. "You told me you'd tell me the truth—all of the truth—when we found your plane. I'm holding you to that." She tossed up her head, then froze. "Oh, my God."

Less than twenty feet ahead she saw a gap in the trees, the break she had spotted from beneath the ridge. Up close it looked as though a huge sickle had sliced through the forest, hewing down a swath of evergreen and undergrowth more than thirty feet wide.

"But there was no fire." She had to quicken her pace to keep up with Cal. "What could have done all this?"

"That." When they reached the break, Cal pointed. There, nestling on the rocky, needle-strewn ground, was his ship. Trees, some of them thirty feet high, lay like pickup sticks around it. "Don't go any closer until I check for radiation," Cal warned, but he needn't have bothered. Libby couldn't have moved if she'd wanted to.

Using his wrist unit, he checked the level and gave a quick nod. "It's well within normal limits. The time warp must have neutralized any excess." He slipped an arm around her shoulders again. "Come on inside. I'll show you my etchings."

Dazed, silent, she went with him. It was huge, as big as a house, and like no plane she had ever seen. A military secret, she told herself. That was why Cal had been so evasive. But surely one man couldn't fly something so large.

The front was its narrowest point, blunted, somewhat bullet-shaped, before it curved out into the body. There were no wings. That thought caused an uneasy lurch in her stomach. It's shape reminded her of a stingray that scuttled across the ocean floor.

An experiment, she told herself as she climbed over a fallen pine.

The body was a dull metallic color not glitzy enough to be called silver. There were scrapes and dents and dust all over it. Like an old, reliable family car, she thought giddily.

The damage had happened in the accident, she decided, but it worried her more than a little that several of the dents looked old. The Pentagon or NASA or whoever had built it would certainly have taken better care of something that had to be worth millions of taxpayer dollars.

"You came in this thing by yourself," Libby managed when he leaped down the slight slope to run his hand over the side of the ship.

"Sure." His fingers moved over the metal in an unmistakable caress. "She handles like a dream."

"Who does it belong to?"

"It's mine." There was both pleasure and excitement in his eyes when he held up a hand to help her down. "I told you I didn't steal it."

As a wave of relief passed over him, he spun her in a circle, then kissed her hard on the mouth. Finding the taste alluring, he kept her feet an inch off the ground and lingered over a second kiss.

"Caleb—" Breathless, dizzy, she pushed away from him.

"Kissing you's become a habit, Libby." He circled her waist with his hand. "I've always had a hard time breaking habits."

He was just trying to distract her, she thought. And he was doing an excellent job of it. "Pull yourself together," she ordered. "Now we've found this...thing. You promised me an explanation. We both know very well that nothing like this is owned by a private citizen. Spill it, Hornblower."

"It is mine," he told her, still grinning. "Or it will be after ten more payments." He pressed a button to open the hatch. Libby's mouth dropped open as a door lifted up silently. "Come on, I'll show you the registration."

Unable to resist, she walked up the two steps and into the cabin. It was as large as her living room and was dominated by a control panel. There were hundreds of colored buttons and levers in front of two high-backed black seats shaped like scoops.

"Have a seat," he said.

Staying close to the open hatch, she rubbed her arms to ward off a sudden chill. "It's, ah...dark in here."

"Oh, yeah." Crossing to a panel, he touched a switch. Libby let out a muffled shriek as the front of the craft opened. "I must have hit the shields when I started down."

She could only stare. Before her were the forest, the distant mountains and the sky. Strong sunlight poured through. You could hardly call it a windshield when it spanned twenty feet.

"I don't understand." Because she needed to, she moved quickly to one of the chairs and sat. "I don't understand any of this."

"I felt the same way a couple of days ago." Cal opened a compartment, scanned through some material, then took out a small, shiny card. "This is my pilot's license, Libby. After you read it, take a nice long breath. It might help."

His picture was in the corner. His grin was as attractive and disarming as it was in the flesh. The ID claimed that he was a United States citizen and licensed to pilot all A to F model ships. It listed his height as 185.4 cm, his weight as 70.3 kg. Hair black, eyes blue. And his birth date was…2222.

"Oh, my God," Libby whispered.

"You forgot to take that breath." He closed a hand over hers on the card. "Libby, I'm thirty. When I left L.A. two months ago it was February, 2252."

"That's crazy."

"Maybe, but it happened."

"This is a trick." She pushed the card back into his hand and sprang up. Her heart was racing so hard and fast that she could feel it vibrating between her temples. "I don't know why you're doing this, but it's all some kind of elaborate trick. I'm going home."

She rushed toward the hatch just as the door closed. "Sit down, Libby. Please." He saw the wild, trapped look in her eyes and forced himself not to step toward her. "I'm not going to hurt you. You know that. Just sit down, and listen."

Because she was angry that she had tried to run, she walked stiffly back and sat down. "So?"

He sat opposite her, steepled his fingers and thought it all through. There were times, he supposed, when it was best to treat an abnormal situation as if it were normal. "You didn't have any breakfast," he said abruptly. Pleased with the inspiration, he opened a small door and took out a glossy silver pouch. "How about ham and eggs?" Without waiting for an answer, he swiveled, opened another door and tossed the pouch inside. He pushed a button, then sat smiling at her until a buzzer sounded. Taking a plate out of another compartment, he opened the door and scooped out a heap of steaming eggs loaded with chunks of ham.

Libby locked her icy hands in her lap. "You're full of tricks."

"No trick. Irradiation. Come on, taste." He held the plate under her nose. "They're not as good as yours, but they'll do in a pinch. Libby, you have to believe what's in front of your eyes."

"No." Very slowly, she shook her head from side to side. "I don't think I do."

"Not hungry?"

She shook her head again, more firmly this time. With a shrug, Cal plucked a fork from a drawer and dug in.

"I know how you feel."

"No, you don't." She took his advice, belatedly, and sucked in three long breaths. "You're not sitting in what looks like a spaceship having a conversation with a man who claims to be from the twenty-third century."

"No, but I'm sitting in my ship talking to a woman who's a couple of centuries older than I am."

She blinked at that, then found laughter—only slightly hysterical—bubbling out. "This is ludicrous."

"Oh, yeah."

"I'm not saying I believe it."

"Give it time."

Her hand was no longer cold, but it was still unsteady when she pressed it to her head. "I need to think."

''Fine.''

With a sigh, she sat back and studied him. ''I'll take that breakfast now.''

Chapter 6

The eggs were bland, but they were certainly hot. Irradiated, Libby thought as she took a second bite. She'd heard of the controversial process for preserving food. Still, it was a far cry from a microwave TV dinner.

Somehow she'd woken up in the middle of a science-fiction movie.

"I keep telling myself there has to be another explanation."

Cal polished off his eggs. "Let me know if you find one."

Dissatisfied, she set her plate aside. "If all this is real, you seem to be taking it very calmly."

"I've had some time to get used to it. Are you going to eat the rest of that?"

She shook her head, then turned to stare through the clear shield. She saw a pair of elk meander into the trees about a hundred yards away. A beautiful sight, she mused. Beautiful, and normal here in the mountains of Oregon. If the elk had wandered down Fifth Avenue in Manhattan they would still have been beautiful, and they would still have been real. But, for reasons of basic geography, they wouldn't have been normal.

There was no denying that Cal was real. Was it possible that he and his incredible vehicle were a perfectly normal sight in another place? In another time?

If it were true...if she allowed herself for just one moment to believe it... How must he feel? She looked at the elk again. They were standing in a patch of sunlight. Mustn't he be feeling as confused and displaced as any animal taken out of its natural habitat and tossed into a strange world?

She remembered the panic she had seen on his face the day he'd come to her with a paperback novel. A novel published this year, Libby reflected. She'd dismissed his pallor, his dazed confusion, as the effects of his head injury. She'd discounted his odd questions and remarks the same way.

Now there was the ship—and no matter how far she stretched it she couldn't call the vehicle à plane. If she accepted that it was real and not part of some strange, vivid dream, then she had to accept Cal's story.

"'There are more things in heaven and earth, Horatio,/ than are dreamt of in your philosophy.'"

"Hamlet." He grinned at her quick, suspicious look. "We still read Shakespeare. Want some coffee?"

She shook her head. Dream or not, she needed answers. "You say you...bounced off a black hole?"

He smiled, immeasurably relieved. She believed

him. Perhaps she didn't fully realize it herself, but she believed him. "That's right, or at least that's what I think. I'm going to need my computer. My instruments went berserk when we hit the gravitational field, so I went to manual and managed to bank east. I remember the force. It must be what a fly feels like when someone gives it a good solid bat. I passed out. When I came to, I was free-falling toward Earth. I switched back to computer and thought my troubles were over."

"That doesn't explain how you ended up here—or should I say now."

"There are a lot of theories. The one I lean toward deals with the space-time continuum. It's like a curved bowl." He cupped his palm to demonstrate. "Mathematically, the bowl isn't space and it isn't time. It's a combination of both. Everything in it moves through space and time. Gravity's the curve of the bowl, drawing everything down. Around the Earth it's not much of a curve. You don't really feel it unless you, say, fall off a cliff. But around the sun, and around a black hole..." He deepened the cup of his palm.

"And you're saying you were caught in that curve?"

"Like a marble being spun around the lip of the bowl. And somewhere, somehow, along the spin, I was flicked off. The speed, the trajectory, sent me tunneling not just through space but through time."

"It sounds almost plausible when you say it."

"It's the only theory I've got. Maybe if we look at it, it'll sound more plausible." Leaning forward, he turned a dial. "Computer."

Yes, Cal.

Libby lifted a brow at the soft, sultry voice. "Since when do they make computers tall, blond and busty?"

He just grinned. "Intergalactic runs can be lonely. Computer, play back log date 02-05. On screen."

Cal swiveled in his chair and leaned forward as a small viewing screen rose out of the console. Sound filled the cockpit. Impassive, he watched his own image flicker on. From her chair, Libby stared mesmerized, as the playback progressed. She could see him sitting precisely where he was sitting now. But there were lights flashing, buzzers sounding. While the cockpit vibrated, he reached up to secure a safety strap. She could see the sweat beading on his face as he fought the controls of the bucking ship.

"Widen image," Cal commanded.

Then Libby saw what he had seen through the shield. There was the vastness of space, seductive and compelling. There were stars, clusters of them, and what was surely a distant planet. There was a blackness, an absolute blackness, that spread for miles. The ship seemed to be hurtling toward it.

She heard Cal swearing—or rather the image of Cal was swearing as he pulled on a lever. There was a sound, a screaming rip of metal that seemed to vibrate all around her. The cockpit began to roll, end over end, with sickening speed. And then the screen went blank.

"Damn it. Computer, continue playback."

Memory banks damaged. No further playback possible.

"Terrific." He started to command an analysis, but then he caught a glimpse of Libby. She was sitting limply in the chair beside his, her cheeks a dead white, her eyes glassy. "Hey." He was up quickly and leaning over her. "Take it easy." Cupping her face in his hands, he pressed his thumbs lightly on either side of her throat.

"It was like I was there."

He cursed himself and took her icy hand in his to warm it. He had known better, Cal thought in disgust. But he had only been thinking of himself and his need to see what had happened. "I know. I'm sorry."

"It was horrible." Whatever doubts she had harbored had vanished completely during the playback. Her fingers tightened convulsively on his as she looked up at him. "It's all been horrible for you."

"No." He combed his fingers through her hair. "Not all." Softly, gently, he touched his lips to hers, then skimmed them over her jaw. She reached a hand to his face, letting it linger while she gave and took the comfort.

"What are you going to do?"

"I'm going to find a way back."

She felt a pain, sharp and sudden. Of course he couldn't stay. Carefully she laid her hand back in her lap. "When will you go?"

"It's going to take a little time." He straightened and glanced around the cabin. "I need to do some repairs on the body of the ship. There are a lot of calculations that have to be done."

"I'd like to help you." She made a helpless gesture with her hands. "I don't know how."

"I'd like you to stay while I'm working. I know you've got a lot to do, but if you could spare a few hours?"

"Sure." She dug up a smile. "I don't get many offers to spend the day in a spaceship." But she couldn't sit beside him at that moment. If he looked at her too closely he might see what she had just discovered: when he left he would break her heart. "Can I look around?"

"All you want." She was still pale, he noted, but her voice was strong. Perhaps, like him, she needed some time alone. "I'd like to get the computer started on some calculations."

She left him to it, trying not to jolt when automatic doors whispered open at her approach. She entered what seemed to be a small lounge. A pair of couches were built into the walls, curving back, then out, with bright orange cushions. A table of what appeared to be Lucite was bolted to the floor. There were a few glossy informational sheets tossed around. The future's version of *Car and Driver*, she thought with a nervous laugh as she chose one. She tapped it absently against her thigh as she wandered around the room.

She was a sensible woman, Libby told herself. A sensible woman accepted what couldn't be denied. But—

There were no buts. She was a scientist. One who studied man. For the time being, she would study what man would be rather than what he had been.

For an hour she walked through the ship, observing, absorbing. There was a narrow, untidy room she took to be the galley. There was no stove, only a wall unit that resembled a microwave. A refrigerator of sorts held a few bottles. The labels were a familiar red, white and blue and carried the name of a popular brand of American beer.

Man hadn't changed that much, Libby decided. She chose an equally familiar brand of soft drink and twisted off the cap. She took a first experimental sip.

Amazing, she thought as she took another. She might have found the bottle in her own refrigerator. Taking the bottle and its comforting familiarity with her, she wandered on.

She found herself in an enormous bay area. It was empty except for a huddle of boxes strapped into a corner.

He'd said he'd just made a supply run, she remembered. To Mars. When her stomach fluttered, she took another sip from the bottle.

So man had conquered Mars. Even in the twentieth century, scientists had been making plans to do so. She would have to ask Cal when the first colony had been built and how the colonists had been chosen. Slowly she rubbed her fingers against her temple. Perhaps in a day or two this would all seem less fantastic. Then she would begin to think logically and ask appropriate questions.

She continued through the ship. There was a second level that seemed to be comprised almost completely of bedrooms. Cabins, Libby corrected automatically. On ships they were called cabins.

The furniture was streamlined, and most of it was built directly into the wall. Smooth formed plastic and bright colors were the style.

She found Cal's almost by accident. She didn't want to admit she'd been looking. There was little difference between his and the other cabins, other than its homey untidiness. She saw a jumpsuit, similar to the one he'd been wearing when she'd found him, tossed in a corner. The bed was unmade. On the wall was a picture, eerily three-dimensional, of Cal standing with a group of people.

The dwelling behind them was multileveled and

almost entirely glass. There were white terraces jutting out at all angles, and there were tall, shady trees on a green lawn.

This was his home, she thought, certain of it. And his family. She studied them again. The woman was tall and striking and appeared much too young to be his mother. A sister? she wondered, but then she remembered that he had spoken of only one brother.

They were all laughing. Cal had his arm slung around the shoulder of another man. The height and build were similar, and there was enough facial resemblance to make her certain that this was Cal's brother. His eyes were green, and even in the photograph they were uneasily piercing. A tough customer, she decided and shifted her attention to the third man in the photo.

He seemed slightly befuddled. His face wasn't as blatantly handsome, but there was kindness in it.

Trapped in time, she mused. That was what a photograph did. It trapped people in time. Just as Cal was trapped now. She lifted a hand, but she caught herself just before she stroked the image of his face.

It was important to remember that he was only here until he could break free. He had another life, in another world. What she was feeling about him, for him, was impossible. Just as impossible, she thought as she pressed the cool bottle to her brow, as the fact that she was standing in a vehicle designed to travel through space.

Abruptly weary, she sat down on the bed. It was crazy, all of it. And the craziest part of all was that she had fallen in love for the first time in her life. And the man she loved would soon be far beyond her

reach. With a sigh, she stretched out on the slick, cool
sheets. Perhaps it was all a dream after all.

He found her there more than an hour later, curled
up on his bed. She was sleeping, as she had been the
first time he remembered seeing her. It brought him
an odd, unsettling feeling to watch her now.

She was lovely, but it was no longer her beauty
that drew him. There was a sweetness about her, a
combination of compassion and shyness. She had
strength and passion. And innocence—an incredibly
alluring innocence. He wanted to go to her now, to
gather her up and make love with her in the softest,
gentlest way he knew.

But she wasn't for him. He wished it could be like
a fairy tale, wished she could go on sleeping for a
hundred years, for two hundred and more, until he
awakened her and claimed her for his own.

He wasn't a prince, he reminded himself. He was
just an ordinary man caught in an extraordinary situation.

Moving quietly, he crossed to the bed to draw the
sheet over her. She stirred, murmured. Unable to resist, he reached down to stroke her cheek. Her eyes
fluttered open.

"Cal. I had the strangest dream." Then she was
awake and pushing herself up to stare around the
cabin. "Not a dream."

"No." He sat beside her. No matter how much he
lectured himself, he couldn't deny the pleasure it gave
him to share his bed with her, if only as a friend.
"How do you feel?"

"Still a little rattled." She combed both hands
through her hair, holding it away from her face for a
moment before she let it fall. "I'm sorry, I didn't

realize I'd fallen asleep. I guess my mind needed to shut off for a while.''

"It's a little much to take in all at once. Libby?''

"Yes?'' She glanced distractedly around the cabin, trying to let it all settle in.

"I'm sorry. I have to.'' He closed his lips over hers and savored. She was warm and soft from sleep. He couldn't have explained to her how badly he needed that yielding texture. Reflexively she lifted a hand to his shoulder. But there it relaxed.

It took all his willpower not to touch her and, with the need raw in his gut, to draw away.

"I lied,'' he murmured as his gaze dipped down to her mouth. "I'm not sorry.'' But he rose and moved away from the bed. She stood up and tried to keep her nervous fingers from fiddling with the hem of her sweater.

"Is that your family?''

"Yeah.'' He'd been staring at the picture, wishing life could be as simple as it had been at that moment. "My brother Jacob and my parents.''

The love, somewhat wistful in his voice, was unmistakable. Moved by it, she laid a hand on his arm. "This is Jacob?'' she asked, indicating his brother. "But they don't look old enough to be your parents.''

"It isn't difficult to look young.'' He shrugged. "Well, it won't be.''

"And that's your home?''

"I grew up there. It's about twenty kilometers outside the city limits.''

"You'll get back to them.'' She buried her own yearnings. Love, no matter how suddenly it came or how deep it reached, was selfless. "Think of the story you'll have to tell.''

"If I remember."

"But you couldn't forget." The possibility struck her painfully. She couldn't bear it if he forgot her, if even her memory no longer existed. "I'll write it down for you."

He shook off his black mood and turned to her. "I'd appreciate that. Will you let me go back with you?"

She felt a flutter of hope. "Go back?"

"To the cabin. I've done about all I can for now. I can start the repairs on the ship tomorrow. I was hoping you'd let me stay until it's all ready."

"Of course." It was foolish, and selfish, to hope that he would stay any longer than necessary. She put on a bright smile as they started from the room. "I have dozens of questions to ask you. I don't even know where to begin."

Still, she asked him nothing on the drive back. He seemed distracted, moody, and her own mind was crowded with impressions and contradictions. It would be best, she decided, if they pretended a kind of normality for a few hours. Then, with a thud, inspiration hit.

"How would you like to have lunch in town?"

"What?"

"Try to stay tuned, Hornblower. Would you like to drive into town? You haven't seen anything but this little slice. If I suddenly found myself back in, say, the 1700s, I'd want to explore a little, watch people. It only takes a couple of hours. What do you say?"

The moodiness left his eyes, and he smiled. "Can I drive?"

"Not on your life." She laughed and tossed her

hair back. "We'll stop back at the cabin for my purse."

It took more than thirty minutes to get to the highway through a narrow pass where the Land Rover had powered its way through the mud. When they reached the highway Cal saw the vehicles that had fascinated him on television. They rumbled noisily along. He shook his head as Libby jockeyed aggressively for position.

"I could teach you to fly a jet buggy in an hour."

The wind felt wonderful on her face. They had today, and perhaps a day or two more. She wasn't going to lose a moment of it.

"Is that a compliment?"

"Yeah. You're still using what—gasoline?"

"That's right."

"Amazing."

"Being smug and superior suits you—especially since you didn't even know how to turn my car on."

"I'd've figured it out." He reached out to touch the flying strands of her hair. "If I were home I'd fly you to Paris for lunch. Have you ever been there?"

"No." She tried not to think too deeply about the romance of it. "We'll have to settle for pizza in Oregon."

"Sounds great to me. You know, the strangest thing is the sky. There's nothing in it." A car whizzed by, muffler coughing, radio blaring. "What was that?"

"A car."

"That's debatable, but I meant what was the noise?"

"Music. Hard rock." She reached over to turn on the radio. "That's not as hard, but it's still rock."

"It's good." With the music playing in his head, he watched the buildings they passed. Neat single-family homes, chunky apartment complexes and a spreading single-level shopping center. The traffic thickened as they came closer to the city. He could see the high rectangular forms of office buildings and condos. It was a cluttered and, to his eyes, awkward skyline, but it was oddly compelling. Here were people, here life continued.

Libby eased down the curving ramp and headed downtown. "There's a nice Italian place, very traditional. Red checked tablecloths, candles in bottles, hand-tossed pizza."

Cal gave an absent nod. There were people walking the sidewalk, some old, some young, some plain, some pretty. There was noise from car engines, and the occasional bad-tempered blare of a horn. The air was warmer here and smelled slightly of exhaust. For him it was a picture out of an old book come to life.

Libby pulled into a graveled lot next to a squat white-and-green building. The neon sign across the front window said Rocky's.

"Well, it's not Paris."

"It's fine," he murmured, but he continued to twist his head and stare.

"It must feel like stepping through the looking glass."

"Hmm. Oh." He remembered the book, one he'd read as a teenager. "Something like that. More like something from H. G. Wells."

"It's nice to know literature has survived. Are you hungry?"

"I was born hungry." Once again he fought off a darkening mood. She was trying, and so could he.

The restaurant was dim, nearly empty, and the air simmered with spices. In the corner was a jukebox pumping out a current Top 40 hit. After a glance at a sign that read Please Seat Yourself, Libby led Cal to a corner booth. "The pizza's really wonderful here. Have you had pizza before?"

He flicked a finger at the hardened candle wax on the bottle in the center of the table. "Some things transcend time. Pizza's one of them."

The waitress toddled over, a plump young woman in a bright red bib apron that had Rocky's and a few splashes of tomato sauce dashed across the front. She placed two paper napkins beside place mats decorated with maps of Italy.

"One large," Libby said, taking Cal's appetite into account. "Extra cheese and pepperoni. Would you like a beer?"

"Yeah." He tore a corner from the napkin and rolled it thoughtfully between his thumb and forefinger.

"One beer and one diet cola."

"Why is everyone here on a diet?" Cal asked before the waitress was out of earshot. "Most of the ads deal with losing weight, quenching thirst and getting clean."

Libby ignored the quick curious look the waitress shot over her shoulder. "Sociologically our culture is obsessed with health, nutrition and physique. We count calories, pump iron and eat a lot of yogurt. And pizza," she added with a grin. "Advertising reflects current trends."

"I like your physique."

Libby cleared her throat. "Thanks."

"And your face," he added, smiling. "And the way your voice sounds when you're embarrassed."

She let out a long, windy sigh. "Why don't you listen to the music?"

"The music stopped."

"We can put more on."

"On what?"

"The jukebox." Enjoying herself, Libby rose and extended a hand to him. "Come on, you can pick a song."

Cal stood over the colorful machine, scanning the titles. "This one," he decided. "And this one. And this one. How does it work?"

"First you need some change."

"I've had enough change for a while, thanks."

"No, I mean change. Quarters." Chuckling, she dug into her purse. "Don't they use coins in the twenty-third century?"

"No." He plucked the quarter from her palm and examined it. "But I've heard of them."

"We use them around here, often with reckless abandon." Taking the quarter back, she dropped it and two more into the slot. "An eclectic selection, Hornblower." The music drifted out, slow and romantic.

"Which is this?"

"'The Rose.' It's a ballad—a standard, I suppose, even today."

"Do you like to dance?"

"Yes. I don't often, but..." Her words trailed away as he gathered her close. "Cal—"

"Shh." He rubbed his cheek against her hair. "I want to hear the words."

They danced—swayed, really—as the music drifted

through the speakers. A mother with two squabbling children rested her elbow on her table and watched them with pleasure and envy. In the glassed-in kitchen a man with a bushy mustache tossed pizza dough in quick, high twirls.

"It's sad."

"No." She could dream like this, with her head cushioned on his shoulder and her body moving to their inner rhythm. "It's about how love survives."

The words floated away. Her eyes were shut, her arms still around him when the next selection blasted out with a primeval scream and a thundering drum roll.

"What about this one?"

"It's about being young." She drew away, embarrassed, when she saw the smiles and stares of the other patrons. "We should sit down."

"I want to dance with you again."

"Some other time. People don't usually dance in pizza parlors."

"Okay." Obligingly he walked back across the room to their table. Their drinks were waiting. As Libby had with the drink in his galley, Cal found enormous comfort in the familiar taste of American beer. "Just like home."

"I'm sorry I didn't believe you at first."

"Babe, *I* didn't believe me at first." In a natural gesture he reached across the table to take her hand. "Tell me, what do people do here on a date?"

"Well, they…" His thumb was skimming over her knuckles in a way that made her pulse unsteady. "They go to movies or restaurants."

"I want to kiss you again."

Her eyes darted up to his. "I don't really think—"

"Don't you want me to kiss you?"

"If she doesn't," the waitress said as she plopped their pizza in front of them, "I get off at five."

Grinning, Cal slipped a slice of pizza onto a paper plate. "She's very friendly," he commented to Libby, "but I like you better."

"Terrific." She took a bite. "Are you always obnoxious?"

"Mostly. But I do like you, a lot." He waited a beat. "Now you're supposed to say you like me, too."

Libby took another bite and chewed it thoroughly. "I'm thinking about it." Taking her napkin, she dabbed at her mouth. "I like you better than anyone I've met from the twenty-third century."

"Good. Are you going to take me to the movies?"

"I suppose I could."

"Like a date." He took her hand again.

"No." Carefully she removed it. "Like an experiment. We'll consider it part of your education."

His smile spread, slow, easy and undoubtedly dangerous. "I'm still going to kiss you good-night."

It was dark when they returned to the cabin. More than a little frazzled, Libby pushed open the door and tossed her purse aside.

"I did not make a scene," Cal insisted.

"I don't know what they call being asked to leave a theater where you come from, but around here we call it making a scene."

"I simply made some small, practical comments about the film. Haven't you heard about freedom of speech?"

"Hornblower—" Stopping herself she held up a

hand and turned to the cupboard to get the brandy. "Talking throughout the picture about it being a crock of space waste is not exercising the Bill of Rights. It's being rude."

With a shrug, he plopped down on the couch and propped his feet on the coffee table. "Come on, Libby, all that bull about creatures from Galactica invading Earth. I have a cousin on Galactica, and he doesn't have a face full of suction cups."

"I should have known better than to take you to a science-fiction movie." She sipped the brandy. Then, because she decided it was as much her fault as his, she poured another snifter. "It was fiction, Hornblower. Fantasy."

"Rot."

"All right." She passed him the snifter. "But there were people in the theater who had paid to watch it."

"How about that nonsense with the creatures sucking all the water out of the human body? Then there was the way that space jockey zipped around the galaxy shooting lasers. Do you have any idea how crowded that sector is?"

"No, I don't." She sampled more brandy. "Tell you what, next time we'll try a Western. Remind me not to let you turn on *Star Trek*."

"*Star Trek*'s a classic," he said, and sent her into a fit of giggles.

"Never mind. You know, I almost think I'm losing my grip. I spent the morning in a spaceship and the afternoon eating pizza and not watching a movie. I don't seem to be able to make sense of it all."

"It'll come clear." He touched his glass to hers before settling his arm around her shoulders. It was comforting, the glow of the lamplight, the warmth of the brandy, the scent of the woman. His woman, Cal thought, if for only a moment. "I like this better than the movies. Tell me about Liberty Stone."

"There's not much."

"Tell me, so I can take it with me."

"I was born here, as I told you before."

"In the bed I sleep in."

"Yes." She sipped her brandy, wondering if it was that, or the image of him in the old bed, that warmed her. "My mother used to weave. Blankets, wall hangings, rugs. She would sell them to supplement what my father grew in the garden."

"They were poor?"

"No, they were children of the sixties."

"I don't understand."

"It's difficult to explain. They wanted to be closer to the land, closer to themselves. It was their part of a revolution against material power, world violence, the entire social structure of the time. So we lived here and my mother bartered and sold her work in the surrounding towns. One day an art buyer on a camping trip with his family came across one of her tapestries." She smiled into her brandy. "The rest, as they say, is history."

"Caroline Stone," he said abruptly.

"Why, yes."

With a laugh, he downed the brandy and reached for the bottle in one smooth motion. "Your mother's work is in museums." Bemused, he picked up the corner of the blanket beside them. "I've seen it in the Smithsonian." He poured more brandy in her glass while she gaped at him.

"This gets stranger and stranger." She drank again, letting the brandy influence her sense of unreality.

"It's you we need to talk about, you I need to understand. All these questions." Unable to sit any longer, she cupped the snifter in both hands and started to pace. "The oddest ones pop into my mind. I keep remembering you spoke of Philadelphia and Paris. Do you know what that means?"

"What?"

"We made it." She lifted the snifter in a toast, then recklessly drained it. "It's still there, all of it. Somehow, no matter how close we came to blowing everything, we survived. There's a Philadelphia in the future, Hornblower, and that's the most wonderful thing I can imagine."

Still laughing, she spun in a circle. "All these years I've been studying the past, trying to understand human nature, and now I've had a glimpse of tomorrow. I don't know how to thank you."

Just looking at her left his stomach in a knot. Her cheeks were flushed with excitement. Her body was long and slim and wonderfully graceful as she moved. Wanting her was no longer an urge, it was an obsession.

He drew a long, careful breath. "Glad I could help."

"I want to know everything, absolutely everything. How people live, how they feel. How they court and make love and marry. What games do the children play?" She leaned over to pour another inch of brandy in her glass. "Are hot dogs still the best bet at a baseball game? Are Mondays still the hardest day of the week?"

"You'll have to make a list," he told her. He wanted to keep her talking, moving, laughing. Watching her now, animated, bursting with enthusiasm and humor, was as arousing as being in her arms. "What I can't answer, the computer can."

"A list. Of course. I make terrific lists." Her eyes glowed as she laughed at him. "I know there are more important things for me to ask. Nuclear disarmament, world peace, a cure for cancer and the common cold. But I want to know it all, from the inconsequential to the shattering." Impatiently she pushed her hair back from her face. Her words couldn't seem to keep up with her thoughts. "Every second I think of something new. Do people still have Sunday picnics? Have we beaten world hunger and homelessness? Do all men in your time kiss the way you do?"

The snifter paused halfway to his lips. Very slowly, very deliberately, he set it down. "I can't answer that, because I've only practiced on women."

"I don't know where that came from." She, too, set the snifter aside, then rubbed her suddenly damp palms on the thighs of her jeans. "I suppose I'm a bit wired."

"Excuse me?"

"Nervous, excited. Confused." She pushed her hands through her hair. "Oh, God, Caleb, you confuse me. Even before...before all this."

"We're even there, Libby."

She stared at him. He hadn't moved, but she saw that he had tensed. "That's odd," she murmured. "I don't usually confuse anyone. Nothing seems to be exactly the way I expect it to be with you. I guess I'm a coward, because every time you come near me I want to run." She closed her eyes. "That's not true. You asked me once if I was afraid of you, and I said I wasn't. That's not true, either. I am afraid. Of you, of me, and most of all of thinking I might never feel this way again with anyone else.'' She began to roam the room again, picking up a pillow, tossing it aside, shifting a lamp. ''I wish I knew what to do, what to say. I don't have any experience with this kind of thing. And, damn it, I wish you'd kiss me again and shut me up.''

He thought he could feel each separate nerve in his body stretch. ''Libby, you know I want you. I haven't kept it to myself. But under the circumstances...the fact that I'll be gone in a few days...''

''That's just it.'' Suddenly, she wanted to weep. ''You will be gone. I don't want to wonder what it might have been like. I want to know. I feel...oh, I don't know how I feel. The only thing I'm sure of is that I want you to make love with me tonight.''

She stopped, shocked that she had said it aloud, stunned that it was perhaps the truest thing she'd ever said. Then the nerves were gone, and the shock with them. She was absolutely calm, and absolutely certain.

''Caleb, I want to be with you tonight.''

He rose. The hands he tucked in his pockets were two tense fists. ''A few days ago it would have been easy. Things have changed, Libby. I care about you.''

''You care, so you don't want to love me?''

''I want to so badly I can taste it.'' When his gaze whipped to hers, she could see that he spoke nothing less than the truth. ''I also know that you've had a little too much to drink and more than too much to deal with tonight.'' He didn't dare touch her, but his voice was like a caress. ''There are rules, Libby.''

She took what she knew might be the biggest step

in her life when she moved to him and held out both
hands.

"Break them."

Chapter 7

He could hear his own heart beating, could feel the blood pumping to and from it. In the shadowy light she looked mysterious, impossibly erotic in a baggy sweater and worn corduroy. Her hair was mussed, from the drive and from her own restless fingers. He could imagine, all too clearly, what it would be like to smooth it himself. How it would be to slip off all those layers of oversize clothing and find her slim and warm underneath. He took a long, careful breath and tried to think clearly.

"Libby…" He ran a hand over his roughened chin. "I'm trying to think like a man you'd understand, one from your time. I don't seem to be doing a good job of it."

"I'd rather you'd think like yourself." She wanted to be calm and confident. This was a decision she'd waited years to make. She was sure. But still there were nerves, brought on by excitement, anticipation and deep-rooted doubts about her own capabilities as a woman. "Time doesn't change everything, Caleb."

"No." He was certain men had felt this stirring since the first dawn. But when he looked at her he was afraid that what he was feeling was far more complicated than basic attraction. His throat was dry, his palms were damp. The harder he tried to think rationally, the less clear his thoughts became. "Maybe we should talk about it."

She resisted the urge to stare at her feet and kept her eyes on his. "Don't you want me?"

"I've imagined making love with you a dozen times."

She felt the thrill, and the fear, tangle in a race up her spine. "When you imagined, where were we?"

"Here. Or in the forest. Or thousands of miles away in space. There's a pond near my house, with water as clear as glass and a bank of flowers my father planted. I've seen you there with me."

It hurt, more than a little, knowing he would go back to that pond, to a place where she couldn't follow. But they had now. The present was all that mattered, all she would let matter. She crossed to him, knowing that they both needed for her to take the first step.

"Here's a good start." She lifted a hand to his cheek. "Kiss me again, Caleb."

How could he resist her? He was certain no man could. Her eyes were huge and dark, her lips were parted. Waiting. Slowly he lowered his, just brushing, testing. Her soft, yielding sigh seemed to fill him. Need did, a wild, urgent need. Shaken by the scope of it, he put his hands on her shoulders to draw her away.

"Libby—"

"Don't make me seduce you," she murmured. "I don't know how."

With a strangled laugh, he pulled her hard against him, burying his face in her hair. "Too late. You already have."

"Have I?" Her arms were around him, holding tight to what she told herself she would release without regret when the time came. A shudder had her gripping harder when he caught her earlobe between his teeth. "I don't know what to do next."

Cal plucked her up into his arms. "Enjoy," he told her before he carried her up the stairs.

He wanted her in the bed where he'd dreamed of her. In the pale light of the rising moon he laid her down. Whatever he had he would give her. What she had he would take. He understood pleasure, the degrees, the depths, the layers. Soon, very soon, so would she.

Slowly he undressed her, drawing out the process for his own enjoyment and for the simple wonder of it. Every inch he uncovered delighted him, the slender ankles, the smooth calves, the curving shoulders. He watched her eyes widen and cloud with confused passions when he touched her, palms skimming, fingers trailing.

Taking her hand, he brought it to his mouth to taste and savor. "I've seen you like this," he murmured. "Even when I tried not to."

She'd thought she would feel awkward, even foolish. She lay naked in the splash of moonlight and felt only beautiful as he looked his fill. "I've wanted to be here with you, even when I tried not to." She was smiling when she lifted her hands to undress him.

He was determined to be patient, to be thorough, to be very, very gentle. He knew, as he understood she did not, that there were hundreds of varied paths to fulfillment. This time, her first time, it would be sweet. Then her inexperienced hands made his blood leap under his skin. Seduction, unplanned, was potent. Once he covered her hands with his and bit back a moan.

Her fingers tightened under his, and her body tensed. "Am I doing something wrong?"

"No." He let out his breath on a quick laugh and forced himself to relax. "A little too right. This time." Shifting away, he slipped out of the rest of his clothes. "Remind me to ask you to undress me like that again later." He brushed her hair back from her face and began to kiss her. "This first time I have things to show you, places to take you." He nipped lightly at her chin. "Trust me."

"I do." But she was already trembling. The brush of his body against hers, warmth to warmth, was like some strange, exciting dream. His hands roamed over her, whisper-soft, limber as a violinist's, and a knot of heat built from her center out to her fingertips before she could do more than wrap her arms around him. She melted into the kiss, into the long, luxurious depth of it. Then those clever fingers found a point, some pulse that beat under the skin near the base of her spine, and sent her reeling.

His mouth muffled her cry of stunned release as her body arched, then went as fluid as water beneath his. Almost experimentally, he eased her up and over again, his own body vibrating from her pleasure.

"Incredible," he murmured before she dragged his mouth back to hers.

Her response had his blood pounding. She was like a fast fuse, and he held the still-smoking match. He knew that if he had taken her that instant she would have welcomed him, just as he knew desire was only the root of the flower. He wanted to give her the blossom.

Delving deep, he found the control that he needed to prolong passion rather than be commanded by it. She seemed so fragile now, her taste, her scent, the liquid movements she made under him. Like the moonbeams that washed the room, she was pale and beautiful. With his lips against her throat, he could feel her pulse thunder, echoing his own.

No fantasy he had ever indulged in, no woman he had ever pleasured, had been as glorious as the woman who held him now. He linked a hand with hers, knowing he would never find the words to explain to either of them what this night with her meant to him.

But he could show her. He would show her.

One moment she was floating, the next racing. Then she was flying. Love with him was a myriad of tastes and textures, a storm of sensations, a symphony of sounds. His hands were almost unbearably gentle, and the scrape of his beard against her skin was an arousing contrast. As she gave herself the liberty of touching him, of stroking him, she discovered that his body was wire-taut and his muscles were trembling.

She wanted to think, to analyze each moment, but it was possible only to experience.

Soft, so incredibly soft…she was almost afraid it was an illusion, his touch, the words he murmured, the glow that seemed to surround her. Then there was heat, stunningly real. She was steeped in it. In him.

He lifted her so that they were kneeling in the center of the bed, wrapped close. Flickers of urgency came through…a roughened caress, a quickened breath. A skim of fingers, a press of pulse to pulse, and he had her gasping, her head thrown back, her body curved against his. He groaned and crushed his hungry mouth to her throat.

Her nails bit into his skin. Even that aroused him. Here was passion, wilder, freer than any he had ever imagined. She was open for him, only him. He was half-mad with the knowledge that she would give to him what she had given to no one else.

But gently. Dragging himself back, he eased his possessive grip into a caress. When he lowered his mouth to her breast, the sound of pleasure came from both of them. He used his tongue to tease, his teeth to torment. He could feel her skin hum under his hands and lips.

She was small, delicate. It helped to bring out the tenderness he wanted to show her. But when he laid her back there was a strength and demand in the hands that pressed him against her.

So long. The thought raced in and out of her mind as he did things to her, for her, things she had never imagined. She had waited so long for this. For him. Her response came freely and fully, her loving of him totally instinctive. There was no way for her to know as she spun in the world he had opened for her what she brought to him.

He was skilled, and he used his skill to take her beyond those first flashes of pleasure into the velvet space reserved for lovers. She was innocent, yet, just as truly, just as easily, she took him. He slipped into her. She closed around him.

It was a merging of bodies, and of hearts, and of time.

Clouds. Dark, silver-edged clouds. Libby was floating on one. She wanted to go on drifting forever. Her arms had slid from around him, limp, to lie on the rumpled sheets. She couldn't find the strength to lift them and encircle him again. Nor could she find her voice. She wanted to tell him not to move—not ever to move. With her eyes closed and his body fitted so perfectly against hers, she counted each beat of his heart.

Silk. Her skin was like hot, fragrant silk. He was certain he could never get enough of it. With his face buried in her hair, he felt his system drift back to earth like a feather on the breeze. How could he tell her that no one had ever moved him as she did? How could he explain that at this moment he was more at home than he had ever been in his own world, or in the sky he loved so much? How could he accept that he had found his match in a place, and in a time, where he was a stranger?

He wouldn't think of it. Cal turned his lips into her neck. For as long as it was possible, he would live from minute to minute.

"You are so lovely." He propped himself on an elbow so that he could see her face, the paleness of it in the moonlight. It was flushed from the afterglow of lovemaking. Her eyes were clouded with the last dregs of spent passion. "Very lovely," he murmured, and kissed her. "Your skin's still warm." He began to nibble, as though she were a delicacy he couldn't resist.

"I don't think I'll ever be cold again." Fresh desire

began to tingle within her. "Caleb—" Her breath caught on a fast, hot shudder. "You make me feel…"

"How?" With his tongue, he traced her parted lips. "Tell me how I make you feel."

"Magical." Her fingers curled into the sheets. "Helpless." And went lax. "Strong." She gripped his forearms, rocked by a dazzling array of new sensations. "I don't know."

"I'm going to love you again, Libby." He crushed his mouth to hers in a soul-wrenching kiss that left them both breathless. "And again, and again. Each time I do, it'll be different."

There was a power building in him. It might have frightened her if she hadn't felt its twin growing in her. Her eyes stayed open and on his as she lifted her arms and rose to meet him.

Limbs entwined, they lay together in the deepest part of the night and listened to the wind rising through the trees. He was right, Libby thought. Each time was different, excitingly different, yet beautifully the same. She could, she hoped, live out her life on the memories of this one night.

"Are you asleep?"

She settled her head more comfortably in the curve of his shoulder. "No."

"I might enjoy waking you." He slid his hand up to cup her breast. "In fact, I'm sure I would." He nestled his leg cozily between her thighs. "Libby?"

"Yes?"

"Something's missing."

"What?"

"Food."

She smothered a yawn against his shoulder. "You're hungry? Now?"

"I've got to keep up my strength."

A quick, wicked grin curved her lips. "You've been doing pretty well so far."

"Pretty well?" When she chuckled, he pulled her on top of him. "But I'm not finished yet. Why don't I watch while you fix me a sandwich?"

She traced lazy patterns on his chest with her fingertip. "So, male chauvinism survives in the twenty-third century."

"I fixed you breakfast this morning."

She remembered the little silver bag. "More or less."

Had it only been that morning? Could a life change so unalterably in just a few short hours? Hers had. She wondered if that should frighten her, but all she felt was gratitude.

"All right." She started to push away, but then he gripped her hips and shifted her.

"First things first," he murmured, and sent her soaring again.

Later, Libby struggled into a robe, wondering if her mind could handle the simple task of slapping some meat between two slices of bread. He'd drained her and filled her, aroused her and soothed her, until her limbs were weak and her mind was mush.

He switched on the bedside light as he rose out of the bed, unabashedly naked. "Got any cookies to go with that sandwich?"

"Probably." She didn't want to stare at him. Yes, she did. Though she knew it was foolish, her color rose as she lowered her eyes to watch her fingers fumble with the belt of her robe. When he walked toward the door, she looked up quickly. "You're not going downstairs like that."

"Like what?"

"Without… You need to put something on."

He leaned a hand against the doorjamb and grinned. Watching her blush delighted him. "Why? You should know how I'm built by now."

"That's not the point."

"What is the point?"

Giving up, she gestured to the pile of clothes. "Put something on."

"Okay. I'll put on the sweater."

"Very funny, Hornblower."

"You're shy." A glint came into his eyes, one she recognized very well by now. Even as he took the first step toward her, she snatched up the jeans and tossed them at him.

"If you want me to fix you a sandwich, you'll have to cover up some of your…attributes."

Still grinning, he struggled into the jeans. If he put them on, she'd just have to take them off him later. Enjoying the idea, he followed her downstairs.

"Why don't you fill the teakettle?" she suggested as she opened the refrigerator.

"With what?"

"Water," she said with a sigh. "Just water. Put it on the front burner of the stove and turn the little knob under it." She pulled out some packaged ham, some cheese and a hothouse tomato. "Mustard?"

"Hmm?" He was studying the stove. "Sure."

People now had to be very patient, he decided as he watched the electric coil of the burner slowly glow red with heat. Still, there were advantages. Libby's cooking was a far cry from the quick packs he was accustomed to. Then there were the living arrangements. Though he had always loved the home he'd grown up in and was more than comfortable in his quarters aboard his ship, he liked the feel of real wood under his bare feet, and the smell of it burning when she had a fire going in the main room.

Then there was Libby herself. He wasn't certain it was proper to call her an advantage. She was distinct, unique, and everything he'd ever wanted in a woman. His mouth fell open an instant before the heat from the burner singed his finger. With a quick yelp, he jumped back.

"What is it?"

For a moment he just stared at her. Her hair was tousled around her face, and her eyes were heavy from lack of sleep. The robe she wore seemed to swallow her up.

"Nothing," he managed, nearly overwhelmed by an emotion that he prayed was only desire. "I burned my finger."

"Don't play with the stove," she said mildly, then went back to making the sandwiches.

Everything he wanted in a woman? That wasn't possible. He didn't know what he wanted in a woman, and he was a long way from making up his mind. Or had been.

That thought put the fear of God into him. That, and the uncomfortable suspicion that his mind had been made up for him the moment he'd opened his eyes and seen her dozing in the chair. Ridiculous. He hadn't even known her then.

But he knew her now.

He couldn't be in love with her. He watched as she tossed her hair back from her face with a flick of her hand, and his stomach tied itself into knots. Attraction, however outrageous, was acceptable. It wasn't possible that he was in love. He could love being with her, love making love with her, laughing with her. He could care for her, find her fascinating and arousing, but as for love, that wasn't an option.

Love, here and in his time, meant things neither of them could ever have together. A home, a family. Years.

As the kettle began to sputter, he let out a long breath. He was simply magnifying the situation. She was special to him, and always would be. The days he spent with her would be a precious part of his life. But it was essential for him to remember, for both their sakes, that his life began two hundred years after Libby no longer existed.

"Is something wrong?"

He glanced over to see her holding two plates, her head cocked a bit to the side, as it did whenever she was trying to work out a problem.

"No." He smiled and took the plates from her. "My mind was wandering."

"Eat, Hornblower." She patted his cheek. "You'll feel better."

Because he wanted to believe it could be that simple, he sat down and dug in while she fixed the tea.

It seemed natural, Libby thought, for them to share tea and sandwiches in the middle of the night—just the two of them sitting in the cozy kitchen, with an owl hooting somewhere in the forest and the moonlight fading. The awkwardness she had felt—foolishly, she believed—before she'd tugged on her robe, was gone.

"Better?" she asked him when he'd downed half of his sandwich.

"Yes." The tension that had slammed into him so unexpectedly had nearly dissipated. He stretched out his legs so that the arch of his foot rubbed over her ankle. There was something soothing in the contact, like a long nap on a rainy afternoon. She looked so pretty with her hair mussed and her eyes heavy. "How is it," he murmured, "that I'm the first man to have you?"

She nearly choked before she managed to swallow the tea that was halfway down her throat. "I don't..." She coughed a little, then tugged the lapels of her robe closer. "I don't know how to answer that."

"Do you consider that an odd question?" Charmed again, he smiled, leaning closer so that he could touch her hair. "You're so sensitive, so attractive. Other men must have wanted you."

"No...that is, I can't say. I haven't really paid much attention."

"Does it embarrass you for me to tell you you're attractive?"

"No." But when she picked up her teacup with both hands she was flushed. "A little, perhaps."

"I can't be the first to have told you how lovely you are. How warm." He pried one of her hands from the cup to soothe her fingers. "How exciting."

"Yes, you can." Almost unbearably aroused, she let out a long, shaky breath. "I haven't had a lot of...social experience with men. My studies." Her breath snagged as he kissed her fingers. "My work."

He released her hand before he went with his impulse to make love with her again. "But you study men."

"Studying and interacting are different things." He didn't have to touch her to stir her, Libby realized. He only had to look, as he was looking now. "I'm not very outgoing unless I concentrate on it."

He started to laugh, then realized she believed it. "I think you underestimate Liberty Stone. You took me in and cared for me, and I was a stranger."

"I could hardly have left you out in the rain."

"You couldn't. Others could. History may not be my strong suit, Libby, but I doubt human nature has changed that much. You went out in the storm to find me, brought me into your home, let me stay even when I annoyed you. If I get back to my own time and place it will be because of you."

She rose then to fix more tea she didn't want. She didn't want to think about his leaving, though she knew she would have to. It was wrong to pretend, even for a few hours, that he would stay with her and forget the life he'd left behind.

"I don't think giving you a bed and some scrambled eggs constitutes a real debt." She made herself smile as she turned toward him again. "But if you want to be grateful I won't argue with you."

He'd said something wrong. Though he couldn't put his finger on it, Cal could tell from the way her eyes had changed. She was smiling at him, but her eyes were dark and sad. "I don't want to hurt you, Libby."

Her eyes softened now, and he was relieved. "No, I know that." She sat down again and poured each of them another full cup. "What do you plan to do? About getting back, I mean."

"How much do you know about physics?"

"Next to nothing."

"Then let's just say I'll put the ship's computer to work. The damage was pretty minimal, so that shouldn't be a problem. I'll have to ask you to drive me out to the ship again."

"Of course." She felt a bubble of panic and struggled to get past it. "I suppose you'll want to stay on the ship now, while you work out your calculations and make your repairs."

It would be more practical, and it would certainly be more convenient. Cal gave it no more than a moment's consideration. "I was hoping I could stay here. I've got my aircycle on board, so I can get back and forth easily enough. If you don't mind the company."

"No, of course not." She said it quickly, too quickly, flustering herself. Then she stopped and backed up. "Your aircycle?"

"If it wasn't damaged in the crash," he mused. Then he tossed the possibility aside. "We'll have a look tomorrow. Are you going to eat the rest of that?"

"What? Oh, no." She passed him the second half of her sandwich. It was ridiculous, she supposed, but every now and then he said something that made her wonder if she was dreaming again. "Cal," she began slowly, "it occurs to me that I can never tell anyone about you, or any of this."

"I'd rather you'd wait until I'd gone." He finished off the sandwich. "But I don't mind if you tell anyone."

"That's big of you." She gave him a bland look. "Tell me, do they have padded cells in the twenty-third century?"

"Padded cells?" He took a moment to imagine one. "Is that a joke?"

"Only on me," she told him as she rose to clear the plates.

"It may be one on me, too. I've wondered if, once I get back, anyone will believe me."

A thought struck her that was both absurd and fascinating. "Maybe I could do a time capsule. I could write everything down, put in a few interesting or pertinent items and seal it up. We could bury it—I don't know, down by the stream, perhaps. When you got back you could dig it all up."

"A time capsule." The idea appealed to him, not just scientifically, but personally. Wouldn't it mean he would still have something of her, even when they were separated by centuries? He would need that, he realized, the solid proof of not only where he had been but that she had existed. "I can run it through the computer, make sure we don't put it somewhere that's going to be covered by a building or a landslide or some such thing."

"Good." She picked up a pad from the counter and began to scribble.

"What are you doing?"

"Making notes." She squinted at her own writing and wished she had her glasses. "We'll need to write everything down, of course, starting with you and your ship. What else should we put in it?" she wondered, tapping the pencil against the pad. "A newspaper, I think, and a picture would be good. We may have to drive back into town and find one of those little booths that take pictures. No, I'll buy a Polaroid camera." She scribbled faster. "That way we can take pictures here, in the house or right outside. Then we'll need some personal things…" She fingered the thin gold chain at her throat. "Maybe some basic household items."

"You're being a scientist." He took her by the waist and drew her slowly, unerringly, against him. "I find that very exciting."

"That's silly."

But it didn't seem silly at all when he lowered his head and began to nibble at her neck. She felt the floor tilt beneath her feet.

"Cal…"

"Hmm?" He journeyed up to a small, vulnerable spot just behind her ear.

"I wanted to…" The pad slipped out of her hand and landed on the floor at their feet.

"To what?" Quick and clever, his fingers loosened the knot at her waist. "Tonight you can have anything you want."

"You." She sighed as her robe slid off her shoulders. "Just you."

"That's the easy part." More than willing to oblige, he braced her against the counter. A hundred erotic ideas swam through his mind. He was going to see to it that neither of them thought the same way about this cozy little kitchen again. The streaks of pink along her skin stopped him.

"What's all this?" Curious, he ran a finger over the swell of her breast, then shifted his hand to his chin. "I've scratched you."

"What?" She was already floating an inch off the floor, and she was less than willing to touch down.

"I haven't shaved in days." Annoyed with himself, he bent to lightly kiss the skin he'd irritated earlier. "You're so soft."

"I didn't feel a thing." She reached for him again, but he only kissed her hair.

"There's only one thing to do."

"I know." She ran her hands up his muscled back.

With a laugh, he hugged her tighter. "That's two things." He scooped her up again for no other reason than that it felt wonderful.

"You don't have to carry me." But she nuzzled into his shoulder. "I can walk to bed."

"Maybe, but we'd better use the bathroom for this."

"The bathroom?"

"I'm going to have to deal with that nasty-looking device," he told her as he started up the stairs. "And you're going to walk me through it so I don't cut my throat."

Nasty-looking device? She tried to put it all together as he carried her upstairs. "Don't you know how to use a razor?"

"We're civilized where I come from. All instruments of torture have been outlawed."

"Is that so?" She waited until he set her down again. "I suppose that means women don't wear high heels or control-top panty hose. Never mind," she said when he opened his mouth. "I think this could become a very philosophical discussion, and it's much too late." Opening the linen closet, she took out the razor and the shaving cream. "Here you go."

"Right." He looked at the tools in his hand with a kind of resigned dread. What a man did for his woman. "Just how do I go about this?"

"This is all secondhand, as I've never shaved my face before, but I believe you spread on the shaving cream, then slide the edge of the razor over your beard.''

''Shaving cream.'' He squirted some into his hand, then ran his tongue over his teeth. ''Not toothpaste.''

''No, I…'' It didn't take her long to get the picture. Leaning back against the sink, she covered her mouth with her hand and tried, unsuccessfully, not to giggle. ''Oh, Hornblower, you poor thing.''

Cal studied the can in his hand. As he saw it, he really had no choice. While Libby was bent nearly double, he turned, aimed and fired.

Chapter 8

She awakened slowly, muttering a bit when the sunlight intruded on her dreams. She shifted, or tried to, but she was weighed down by an arm around her waist and a leg hooked possessively over hers. Content with that, she snuggled closer and had the pleasure of feeling her sleep-warmed skin rub against Cal's.

She didn't know what time it was, and for perhaps the first time in her life it didn't matter. Morning or afternoon, she was happy to lie curled in bed, dozing the day away, as long as he was with her.

Drifting, nearly dreaming again, she stroked a hand over him. Solid, she thought. He was solid and real and, for the moment, hers. Even with her eyes closed she could see him, every feature of his face, every line of his body. There had never been anyone she had felt belonged so completely to her before. Even her parents, for all their love, all their understanding, had belonged to each other initially. She would always think of them as a unit, first and last. And Sunny… Libby smiled a little as she thought of her sister. Even though she was younger by nearly two years, Sunny had always been independent and her own person—argumentative and daring in ways Libby could never try to emulate.

But Cal… It was true that he had only just appeared in her life, would disappear again all too quickly, but he was hers. His laughter, his temper, his passion…they all belonged to her now. She would keep them, treasure them, long after he was gone.

To love as she did, Libby mused, when every emotion, every word, every look, had to be squeezed into a matter of hours, was both precious and heartbreaking.

He thought he'd been dreaming, but the shape, the texture, the scent of a woman's body were very, very real. Libby's body. Her name was there, his first waking thought. She was pressed against him, a perfect fit even in sleep. The slow, gentle stroke of her hand aroused him in the most exquisite way.

He'd lost count of the times they had moved together during the night, but he knew dawn had been breaking the last time she'd cried out his name. The light had been dim and pearly. He would never forget it. She was like a fantasy, all soft curves, agile limbs and tireless passions. Somewhere along the line he had stopped being the teacher and had been taught.

There was more to loving than the uncountable physical pleasures a man and a woman could offer each other. There was trust and patience, generosity and joy. There was the drugging contentment of falling asleep knowing your partner would be there when you awoke.

Partner. The word floated through his mind. His match. Was it fate or fancy that he had had to travel through time to meet his match?

He didn't want to think of it. Refused to. All he wanted now was to make love with Libby in the sunlight.

He shifted, and before either of them was fully awake, slipped into her. Her soft moan mingled with his own as their lips met. Acceptance. Affection. Arousal. Slowly, drawing out the lazy delight, they moved together, their hands beginning a quiet exploration, the kiss deepening.

"I love you."

He heard her words, a caressing whisper in his mind, and answered them like an echo as his lips began to trace her face.

The admissions shocked neither of them, as they were too dazed by the tumultuous sensations and emotions running through them. She had never spoken those words to another man, nor he to another woman. Before the impact hit home, need had them clinging closer.

Gracefully, gloriously, they took each other to the pinnacle.

Later, he nuzzled down between her breasts, but he was no longer sleeping. Had she said she loved him? And had he told her he loved her? What disturbed him most was that he couldn't be sure if it had happened, or if it had been his imagination, something wished for while his mind was vulnerable with sleep and pleasure.

And he couldn't ask her. Didn't dare. Any answer

she would give would hurt. If she didn't love him, it would be like losing part of his heart, of his soul. If she did, it would make leaving her something akin to dying.

It was best, for both of them, to take what they had. He wanted to make her laugh, to see both passion and humor in her eyes, to hear them in her voice. And he would remember. Cal closed his eyes tight. Whatever happened to him, he would always remember.

So would she. He needed to be certain of his place in her memories.

"Come with me." Sliding off the bed, he dragged her with him.

"Where?"

"To the bathroom."

"Again?" Laughing, she tried to snag her robe, but he pulled her into the hall without it. "You don't need another shave."

"Good thing."

"You only cut yourself three or four times. And it's your own fault you used up most of the shaving cream beforehand."

He sent her a wicked grin. "I liked rubbing it all over you better."

"If you're getting ideas about the toothpaste…"

"Maybe later." He lifted her up and into the tub. "For now I'll settle for a shower."

She let out a quick shriek when the cold water hit her. Before she could retaliate or form even a token protest he had joined her, wrapping one arm around her while he adjusted the water temperature with his free hand. He thought he was getting rather good at it.

She took a stream of water in the face, sputtered, started to swear, then found herself caught in a hot, wet, endless kiss.

She'd never experienced anything like it. Steamy air, slick skin, soapy hands. Her knees were weak by the time he shut the spray off and wrapped her in a towel. As dizzy as she, he rested a forehead on hers.

"I think if we're going to get anything done—anything else, that is—we'd better get out of the house."

"Right."

"After we eat."

She was amazed she had the energy to laugh. "Naturally."

It was late afternoon when they stood by Cal's ship again. Clouds had moved in from the north, bringing a chill. Libby told herself that was the reason she felt cold. She hugged the short jacket tighter, but the cold came from inside.

"I'm standing here, looking at it, knowing it's real, but I still can't understand it."

Cal nodded. His contented, relaxed mood had fled, and he wasn't entirely sure why. "I get the same sensation whenever I look at your cabin." There was a headache building behind his eyes, the kind he knew came from tension. "Look, I know you've got work of your own, and I don't want to hold you up, but would you mind waiting a few minutes while I check the cycle?"

"No." She'd been hoping he'd ask her to stay all day. Masking her disappointment, she smiled at him. "Actually, I'd like to see it."

"I'll be right back."

He opened the hatch and disappeared inside.

He would do that again soon, and for the last time, Libby thought. She had to be prepared for it. Strange, but she'd imagined he'd told her he loved her that morning. It was a nice, soothing thought, though she understood he didn't really. He couldn't. He cared for her, more than anyone had ever cared for her, but he hadn't fallen deeply, completely in love with her, as she had with him.

Because she loved him, she was going to do everything she could to help him, starting with accepting limitations. It was a beautiful day, after the most beautiful night of her life. Smiling, really smiling, she looked up at the cloudy sky. The rain would come by evening, and it would be welcome.

She glanced back at the ship when she heard a low, metallic hum. Another door opened—the cargo door, she assumed because of its size and location. Her mouth dropped open as Cal, on the back of a small, streamlined bike, raced out, six inches above the ground.

It made a sound that was something like a purr, not catlike or motorlike, more like the sound of air parting. It was shaped something like a motorcycle, but without the bulk. There were two wheels for ground transportation, and a narrow, padded seat to accommodate riders. The body itself was a long, curving cylinder that forked into two slender handlebars.

He drove—or flew—it over to her, then sat grinning on the seat like a ten-year-old showing off his first twelve-speed.

"It runs great." He made some small movement with his hand on the handgrips that had the purr deepening. "Want a ride?"

Frowning, she eyed the little gauges and buttons on

the stock beneath the handlebars. It looked like a toy.
"I don't know."

"Come on, Libby." Wanting to share his pleasure,
he held out a hand. "You'll like it. I won't let anything happen to you."

She looked at him, and at the bike, hovering just
above the pine needles that were strewn on the forest
floor. It was a small machine—if indeed that was the
proper term—but there was room enough for two on
the narrow black seat. The body was painted a metallic blue that glistened with deeper shades in the
sunlight. It looked harmless, she decided after a moment, and she doubted if anything so small could hold
much power. With a shrug, she slid on the seat behind
him.

"Better hold on," he told her, mostly because he
wanted to feel her body curve against his.

The strength of the vibration beneath her shocked
her, though she knew it was foolish. Cal had looked
harmless, too, she remembered. "Hornblower,
shouldn't we have helmets or—" The words whipped
away as he accelerated.

She might have screamed, but instead she squeezed
her eyes shut and gripped Cal so tightly that he
choked on a laugh. He could feel her heart beating
against him, as fast and heavy as it had through the
night. With an innate skill honed finer by practice, he
steered once around the ship, then up the slope.

Speed. He'd always been addicted to it. He felt the
air slap his face, stream through his hair, and pressed
for more. The sky beckoned, his first and most constant lover, but he resisted, aware that Libby would
be more frightened than thrilled if he took her too
high too quickly. Instead he breezed through the for-

est, winding around trees, skimming over rock and water. A bird burst off a branch just above their heads and went wheeling away, chattering bad-temperedly at the competition. He could feel her grip relax a fraction, then a little more. Her face was no longer pressed between his shoulder blades.

"What do you think?"

She could nearly breathe again. It seemed her stomach had decided to stay in place. At least for the moment. She opened one eye for a cautious look. And swallowed hard.

"I think I'm going to murder you the minute we're on the ground again."

"Relax." The cycle tilted thirty degrees right, then left, as he danced through the trees.

Easy for him to say, she thought. Another look showed her that they were more than ten feet above the ground. She gasped, nearly managed to squeal out a demand to be set down, but then it hit her. She was flying. Not enclosed in some huge, bulky plane thousands of feet up, but freely, lightly. She could feel the wind on her face, in her hair, could taste the promise of spring on it. There was no loud roar of engine noise to disturb the sensation. They were skimming through the forest as playfully as birds.

He stopped in the center of the clearing his ship had created. While the bike hovered, he turned to look at her.

"Want me to go down?"

"No. Up." She laughed and tossed her head back. She had already felt the pull of the sky.

He was grinning when he leaned back to kiss her. "How high?"

"What's the limit?"

"I don't know, but I don't think we ought to chance it. If we go up above the trees, somebody might spot us."

He was right, of course. Libby pushed her hair out of her face, wondering why she seemed to have so little sense when she was around him. "To the tree-tops, then. Just once."

Delighted with her, he turned around. He felt her arms hook firmly around him, and then they were flying again.

He'd never forget. However many times he had taken to sky and space, however many times he would yet take to them, he would never forget this one playful flight with Libby. She was laughing, and the sound of it caressed his ear as her body pressed companionably against his. Her fingers were linked loosely at his waist. His only regret was that he couldn't watch her face as they rose up and up. Making love with her was like this, as clean and clear as cutting through the air. As mystifying and seductive as defying gravity.

He resisted the temptation to crest the trees, contenting himself, and her, with gliding around the thick branches at a hundred feet. Below they could see a thin stream that cut through the rock, and a waterfall, driven by the spring rain and the snowmelt that danced down the ridge and fell into space. The sun pushed through the clouds so that they could watch the pattern of shadows shift on the ground below.

For a moment they both turned their faces to the sky and wished.

He slowed for their descent, and they seemed to drift downward, weightless, soundless. Libby felt her hair lift off her neck, teased by the air currents. She thought pleasantly of Peter Pan and fairy dust before they touched down lightly beside the ship.

"Okay?"

When he turned to look over his shoulder, Libby noticed that the faint hum had stopped. The chill had vanished. "It was wonderful. I could have stayed up all day."

"Flying's habit-forming." No one knew that better than he. He swung off, then took her hand. "I'm glad you liked it."

It was over, Libby told herself when she felt her feet on solid ground again. But she had one more memory to store away. "I loved it. I'm not going to ask you how it works. I doubt I'd understand anyway, and it might spoil the fun." With her hand still caught in his, she looked at the ship. Her feelings about it were as confused as the rest of her emotions. It had brought him to her, and it would take him away. "I'll let you get to work."

Cal was dealing with the same tug-of-war himself. "I'll be back around nightfall."

"All right." She took her hand from his, then stuck it restlessly in her pocket. "You won't have any trouble finding your way?"

"I'm a good navigator."

"Of course." The birds they had frightened away with their ride were beginning to sing again. Time was slipping by. "Well, I'd better go."

He knew she was stalling, but then, so was he. It was stupid, Cal told himself. He would be with her again in a matter of hours. "You could come in with me, but I don't think I'd get a lot done."

It was tempting. She could go inside, distract him, keep him away from the computer and the answers for a few more hours. But it wouldn't be right. Libby looked up at him again as all the love and the longing welled up inside her.

"I haven't gotten any work done the last couple of days, either."

"All right." Leaning over, he kissed her. "See you tonight."

He stood by the open hatch as she started up the slope. But when she reached the top of the ridge she didn't look back.

Libby spent most of the day drafting an account of the series of events that had occurred over the last week. She used Cal's words, his theory, to explain how he had come to be with her, coloring them with her own impressions. Then she listed, in the orderly fashion that was second nature to her, everything that had happened, from the time she had seen the flash in the sky until she had left Cal beside the ship.

That was the simple part, setting down the facts. Her memory was faultless. She knew that would be both a blessing and a curse when she was alone again. But for now she pulled together her objectivity and gave the story as much skill and dedication as she had her dissertation.

Once done, she read the entire story over twice, refining or enlarging where she saw fit. She was trained to report, she mused as she studied the computer screen. When Cal presented his experiences to the scientists of his time, she wanted him to have the benefit of whatever skill she could give him.

It was a fantastic story, fantastic in the most literal sense of the word. Perhaps it wouldn't seem quite as fantastic in Cal's time. How would his people react to him when he returned, when he told his tale? The accidental explorer, she thought with a smile. Well, Columbus had been looking for India when he'd discovered the New World.

She liked to think that he would be treated as a kind of hero, that he was a man whose name would be in history books.

He had the look of a hero, she mused, daydreaming a little as her glasses slipped down her nose. Tall and tough. The bandage over his brow added a rakish look—as the week's growth of beard had before he'd shaved it. For her, she remembered, and felt the deep glow of pleasure.

He was, perhaps, an ordinary man in his time. A man, she supposed, who did his job as others did, who groaned over getting up in the morning, one who occasionally drank too much or forgot to pay bills. He wasn't wealthy or brilliant or wildly successful. He was simply Caleb Hornblower, a man who had taken a wrong turn and become extraordinary.

To her, he would never be just a man. He would always be *the* man.

Would she love again? No, Libby thought with the calm of absolute certainty. She would be content, somehow, with her work and her family, with her memories. But to love again would be impossible. She had, even as a child, believed that there would be only one man for her. Perhaps that was why it had always been so easy for her to concentrate on studies and career while her contemporaries had drifted in and out of relationships and fallen in and out of love.

She hated making mistakes. Libby smiled a little reluctantly at the admission. It was a flaw, certainly, one of pride, but she had always detested the idea of taking a misstep, personally or professionally. That was why she studied harder than most, researched more thoroughly, considered more carefully.

It had paid off, she reflected as she pushed a few buttons and had her dissertation flashing onto the screen. She was young for the degree of success she'd achieved. And she intended to achieve a great deal more.

She was old, perhaps, to be having her first love affair. But caution and care hadn't led her astray. Loving Cal would never be a mistake.

Content, she pushed her glasses more securely on her nose, leaned forward and went to work.

He found her there hours later, her posture long forgotten, absorbed in a culture as different from hers as hers was to Cal. She'd switched on the desk lamp at dusk, and the light slanted across her hands.

Strong, capable hands, Cal thought. Probably inherited from her artist mother. The nails were short and unpainted, at the ends of long fingers. There was a scar, a faint one he'd noticed before, along the base of her thumb. He'd meant to ask her how she'd come by it.

He thought he'd been tired when he'd come in— not physically, but mentally, with the burden of figures and calculations weighing on his mind. But now, seeing her, fatigue was forgotten.

He'd managed, somehow, to stop thinking about her while he'd worked. It had been a deliberate effort to stop thinking, stop wanting, stop needing. Because of it, he'd managed to make some progress. He was all but sure of what he had to do to get home. He knew the odds and the risks. Now, watching her, he knew the sacrifice.

He'd only known her briefly. It was necessary, very necessary, to remind himself of that. His life wasn't here, with her. He had a home, an identity. He had a family, he realized now, that he loved more than he had once comprehended.

But he stood and watched her as the minutes ticked away, absorbing every breath, every careless gesture. The way her hair swept over her neck, the way her stockinged foot tapped impatiently when her fingers paused. Now and then she would drag a hand through her hair or cup her chin in her palms and stare owlishly at the screen. He found every movement endearing. When he finally said her name, his voice was strained.

"Libby."

She jolted and spun in her chair to stare at him. The hallway was dark behind him. He was just a silhouette, propped casually against the doorframe. Love nearly smothered her.

"Oh. I didn't hear you come in."

"You were pretty deep in your work."

"I guess." When he stepped into the room, the intensity in his eyes had her drawing her brows together. "What about yours? Did it go well?"

"Yes."

"You look upset. Is something wrong?"

"No." He reached down to touch her face, and his eyes softened. "No."

"Your calculations?"

"Coming along." Her skin felt like silk, he thought, and it warmed under his touch. "In fact, I made more progress than I'd expected."

"Oh." He thought he saw a shadow flicker in her eyes, but her voice was bright and encouraging. "That's good. Did you ride the cycle back?"

"Yeah. I left it behind the shed."

It had been a stupid question, she thought. He would hardly have hiked all the way. She wanted to ask him to take her up again, now, while the moon was rising. The wind was already picking up, warning of rain. It would be wonderful. But he looked tired, and troubled.

"Well, after all that you must be hungry." She glanced around as if noticing the dark for the first time. "I hadn't realized it was so late. Why don't I go down and toss something together?"

"It can wait." Taking her hand, he drew her to her feet. The machine continued to hum, forgotten by both of them. "We can go down later and both throw something together. I like the way you look in glasses."

With a quick laugh, she reached for them. He caught her hand so that both of hers were trapped in his.

"No, don't take them off." He tilted his head to kiss her, as if experimenting. Her taste was the same. Thank God. Most of the tension dissolved. "They make you look…smart and serious."

Though her heart was already thumping, she smiled. "I am smart and serious."

"Yes, I suppose you are." He ran his thumbs over the inside of her wrists and felt her pulse scramble. "The way you look right now makes me want to see just how unintellectual I can make you." With their hands still joined, he bent to kiss her, holding himself back, teasing and nibbling her lips until her breath was a shudder.

"Libby?"

"Yes."

"What can you tell me about the mudmen of New Guinea?"

"Nothing." She strained against him, moaning a bit when his lips continued to brush, featherlight, over hers. "Nothing at all. Kiss me, Caleb."

"I am." His lips cruised over her face, skimming here, lingering there. She was like a volcano, awakened after eons of sleep, ready to burst free, hot and molten.

"Touch me."

"I will."

It was never what she expected. He had her teetering on the edge with only a stroke of his hands. Then, as she trembled back to earth, he began to undress her, peeling off her flannel shirt, tugging off her jeans, while they stood beside the bed. She wore a narrow white undershirt in plain cotton. It seemed to fascinate him as he toyed with the straps, skimmed his finger along the low scooped neck, before he slipped it up and over her head. His lips were never still, nor were his hands, which roamed to exploit all the secrets he'd already discovered.

Delighted, delirious, she yanked his sweater over his head. It amazed her that the need could have sharpened and grown, outracing what she had felt for him the first time. Now she knew where he would take her and had already traveled some of the routes he navigated so expertly.

His skin was soft, smooth. It pleased her to run her hands up and over his back to feel it and the hard

muscle beneath. The contrast, the peculiarly mascu-
line contrast, made her knees weak. She heard his
breath quicken as she stroked her hands from shoulder
to waist.

To be wanted this…desperately. She could feel it
in the way he touched her, in the way his mouth came
back to hers again and again for longer, deeper, hun-
grier kisses. His tongue tangled with hers, enticing,
erotic, and she felt as well as heard him suck in his
breath as her knuckles grazed his stomach.

She had learned, Cal thought dizzily. And she had
learned quickly. Her hands, and the gentle movements
of her body against his, were driving him beyond reason. He wanted to tell her to give him a moment, to
give him the time he needed to gain a firm, lasting
grip on control. But it was already too late. Much too
late.

He dragged her to the bed. Her gasp of surprise
ended in a dark moan of pleasure. She reached for
him, only to find herself gripping the bedclothes as
he whipped her over the first raw edge.

She'd thought she knew what loving was. Even a
night steeped in it hadn't prepared her for this. He
was crazed, and in a moment her madness matched
his.

No gentle touch, no easy persuasion. It was all hot,
ripe need and a desperate race for satisfaction. Like
two lost souls, they rolled over the sheets and
drowned in each other.

A desperate demand. A fervent answer. Murmured
requests were for the sane. Tonight there were only
breathless moans and shuddering sighs. Her skin was
so slick with the heat passion pumped into her that it

slid sleekly over his. Each time his mouth found hers she tasted the rich, musky flavor of desire.

There were no velvet clouds now, but a storm breaking. Exciting. Electric. She could almost hear the air singing with it. Drums seemed to pound inside her head, inside her heart, beating in an ever-increasing rhythm. Gulping in air, she rolled over him to press her open mouth to his throat, his chest, knowing only that his flavor was dark, rich and wonderful.

He couldn't get enough. No matter how much she gave, he needed more and still more. He was unaware that his fingers were digging hard into her skin, bruising, even as his lips followed the trail. He could see her in the dim lamplight, the way her damp skin glowed, the way her head fell back each time pleasure overtook her. Her eyes were gold, like some dark, ancient coin. Tribute for a goddess. He thought of her as one now, as she rose over him, her body curved back like a bow, the light casting an aura around her hair.

He thought he would die for her, thought he would die without her. Then she was taking him into her, deeply, fully. He reached blindly, as she did, and their hands linked.

Then there was no thought at all.

He held her close long after the tremors had subsided in both of them. He tried to remember what he had done, what she had done, but it was all a blur of torrential sensations and emotions that had bordered on the violent. He was afraid he had hurt her, that now that her mind and body had cooled she would pull away from him and what was inside him.

"Libby?"

Her only answer was a slight shifting of her head against his chest. One of her greatest pleasures was feeling his heart race under her cheek.

"I'm sorry." He stroked her hair, wondering if it was too late for tenderness.

Her eyes opened. Even that effort was almost more than she could manage. There was a flicker of doubt she struggled to ignore. "You are?"

"Yes. I don't know what happened. I've never treated another woman like that."

"You haven't?" He couldn't see the smile that curved her lips.

"No." Cautious, ready to release her if she jerked away, he lifted her head. "I'd like to make it up to you," he began. Then saw that the glint in her eyes was not tears but laughter. "You're smiling."

"How," she said, kissing the bandage on his forehead, "would you like to make it up to me?"

"I thought I'd hurt you." He rolled her over on her back, then took a good long look. She was still smiling, and her eyes were dark with centuries of secrets only women fully understood. "I guess not."

"You haven't answered my question." She stretched, not because she meant to entice, but because she felt as contented as a cat in a sunbeam. "How are you going to make it up to me?"

"Well…" He glanced around the rumpled bed, then shimmied up to look down at the floor. Reaching down, he plucked up her fallen glasses. He twirled them once by the sidepiece, then grinned. "Why don't you put these on, and I'll show you?"

Chapter 9

Libby was lingering over a second cup of coffee, wondering if being in love was directly connected to the difficulty she was having facing a day cooped up with her computer. She recognized the signs of procrastination in Cal, as well. He sat across from her, poking at the remains of her breakfast. He'd already eaten his own.

More than procrastination, she mused. He looked troubled again, as he had when he'd come back the night before. As he had seemed, she thought, when they'd fallen asleep. More than once during the night, and the morning, she'd been certain he was about to tell her something. Something she was afraid she would hate to hear.

She wanted to find a way to encourage him, to smooth the way to his leaving her. Love, she thought with a sigh, had made her crazy.

The rain had come, in a long, quiet shower that had

lasted almost until morning. Now, with the sun, the light was soft, ethereal, and there were pockets of mist hugging the ground.

It was a good day for making excuses, for taking aimless walks in the woods, for making lazy love under a quilt. But thinking like that, Libby reminded herself, wouldn't help Cal find his way home.

"You'd better get started." It was a gentle nudge, offered without enthusiasm.

"Yeah." He would rather have sat where he was, ignoring reality. Instead, he stood and, giving her a quick kiss, walked to the back door. When he opened it, the kitchen filled with birdsong. "I was thinking I'd take a break during the afternoon. Maybe come back for lunch. I'm getting so I can't stomach the stores on the ship." It was more that he couldn't stand being away from her, but she smiled, taking him at his word.

"Okay." Already the day seemed brighter. "If I'm not slaving over a hot stove, I'll be upstairs working."

It seemed so normal, Libby thought when he closed the door behind him, to part in the morning with an easy kiss and plans to meet for lunch. That was probably best, she decided after she topped off her cup and took it upstairs with her. There was certainly little else about their relationship that anyone would have called normal.

She worked well into the afternoon, blaming her edginess on the caffeine. She didn't want to dwell on the fact that Cal had seemed too quiet, too thoughtful, that morning. They both had a lot on their minds. And, she reminded herself, he would be back soon. Since it would be a habit soon broken, she decided to cut her own work short to go down and fix him something special for lunch. When she reached the base of the stairs, she heard the sound of a car.

Visitors weren't just rare at the cabin, they were nonexistent. Feeling equal parts surprise and annoyance, she opened the front door.

"Oh, my God." Now it was all surprise, with a healthy dose of trepidation. "Mom! Dad!" Then it was love, waves of it, as she rushed out to greet her parents. They stepped out from either side of a small, battered pickup.

"Liberty." Caroline Stone welcomed her daughter with a throaty laugh and a theatrical spread of her arms. She was dressed almost identically to Libby, in faded jeans and a chunky, hip-grazing sweater. But, unlike Libby's plain red wool, Caroline's was a symphony of hues and tones she had woven herself. She wore two jet-black drop earrings—in the same ear—and a necklace of tourmaline that glittered in the light.

Libby kissed Caroline's smooth, unpowdered cheek. "Mom! What are you doing here?"

"I used to live here," she reminded Libby, then kissed her again while William stood back and grinned. They were two of the three most important women in his life. Though they were a generation apart, he noted with pride that his wife looked hardly older than his daughter. Their coloring and build was so similar that more often than not they were mistaken for sisters.

"What am I?" he demanded. "Part of the scenery?" He spun Libby around for one of his hard, swaying hugs. "My baby," he said, and gave her a loud, smacking kiss. "The scientist."

"My daddy," she responded in kind, "the executive."

He winced just a little. "Don't let it get around. So, let me get a look at you."

Grinning, Libby took her own survey. He still wore his hair too long to be conservative, though there was a sprinkle of silver in the dark blond waves, and a bit more dashed through his beard. Both were trimmed now by a barber with a French accent, but little else about William Stone had changed. He was still the man she remembered, the man who had carried her papoose-style through the forest.

He was tall, and at best he would be considered stringy. Long legs and arms gave him a gangly look. His face was gaunt, his cheekbones sunken. His eyes were a deep, pure gray that promised honesty.

"So?" Libby turned in a saucy circle. "What do you think?"

"Not too bad." He slipped an arm around Caroline's shoulders. Together they looked as they always had. United. "We did a pretty good job on the first two, Caro."

"You did an excellent job," Libby corrected. Then she stopped. "First two?"

"You and Sunbeam, love." With an easy smile, Caroline reached in the back of the pickup. "Why don't we get the groceries inside?"

"But I— Groceries." Biting her lip, Libby watched her parents pull out bags. Several bags. She had to tell them...something. "I'm so happy to see both of you." She grunted a bit when her father set two heavy brown sacks in her arms. "And I'd like to...that is, I should tell you that I'm not...alone."

"That's nice." Absently William pulled out another sack. He wondered if his wife had noticed the bag of barbecued potato chips he'd stashed inside. Of course she had, he thought. She never missed anything. "We always like to meet your friends, baby."

"Yes, I know, but this one—"

"Caro, take that one along inside. One's enough for you to carry."

"Dad." Seeing no other way, Libby blocked her father's progress. She snagged her lip again when she heard the door swing open and shut behind her mother. "I really should explain." Explain what, she wondered? And how?

"I'm listening, Libby, but these bags are getting heavy." He shifted them. "Must be all the tofu."

"It's about Caleb."

That caught his attention. "Caleb who?"

"Hornblower. Caleb Hornblower. He's…here," she managed weakly. "With me."

William cocked one gently arched brow. "Oh, really?"

The man in question parked his cycle behind the shed and, lecturing himself, strode toward the house. There was nothing wrong in taking an afternoon break. In any case, the computer was hard at work even in his absence. He'd completed most of the major repairs to the ship, and in another day, two at the most, it would be ready for flight.

If he wanted to spend an extra hour or so with a beautiful, exciting woman, he was entitled. He wasn't dragging his heels. He wasn't in love with her.

And the sun revolved around the planets.

Swearing under his breath, he walked through the open back door. Just seeing her made him smile. Even if he could only see her small, nicely rounded bottom as she rummaged in the bottom of the refrigerator.

His mood lifting, he walked quietly over to grab her firmly, intimately, by the hips.

"Babe, I can never make up my mind which side of you I like best."

"Caleb!"

The astonished exclamation came not from the woman he'd only just turned into his arms but from the kitchen doorway. His head whipped around, and he stared at Libby, who was gaping, wide-eyed, from across the room, her arms full of brown bags. Beside her stood a tall, thin man who was eyeing him with obvious dislike.

Slowly Caleb turned back to see that he was embracing an equally attractive, if somewhat older, woman than the one he'd expected.

"Hello," she said, and smiled quite beautifully. "You must be Libby's friend."

"Yes." He managed to clear his throat. "I must be."

"You might want to let go of my wife," William told him. "So that she can close the refrigerator."

"I beg your pardon." He took a long and very hasty step back. "I thought you were Libby."

"Are you in the habit of grabbing my daughter by the—"

"Dad." Libby cut him off as she dumped the bags on the table. As beginnings went, she thought, this one was hardly auspicious. "This is Caleb Hornblower. He's…staying with me for a while. Cal, these are my parents, William and Caroline Stone."

Terrific. Since he didn't think he could manage to have his molecules reappear in a different location, he figured he'd better face the music. "Nice to meet you." He found that the best place for his hands was his pockets. "Libby looks a great deal like you."

"So I've been told." Caroline beamed another smile at him. "Though never quite in that way." Wanting to let him off the hook, she offered him a hand. "Will, why don't you put those bags down and say hello to Libby's friend?"

He took his time about it. William wanted to size the man up. Good-looking enough, he supposed. Strong features, steady eyes. Time would tell. "Hornblower, is it?" William was pleased that Cal's grip was cool and firm.

"Yes." It was the first time he'd been weighed and measured so thoroughly since he'd enlisted in the ISF. "Should I apologize again?"

"Once was probably enough." But William held his opinion on the rest in reserve.

"I was just about to make lunch." She had to do something, Libby thought, to keep everyone busy until she'd worked out a solution.

"Good idea." Caroline pulled fresh cauliflower out of a bag. She'd found the chips, and a jar of pickled hot sausages William had smuggled in. "But I'll make it. Why don't you give me a hand, William?"

"But I—"

"Brew some tea," she suggested.

"I'd love some tea," Libby said, knowing it was a sure way to her father's heart. She took Cal by the hand. "We'll be right back." The moment they were in the living room, she turned on him. "What are we going to do?"

"About what?"

With a sound of disgust, Libby paced toward the fireplace. "I've got to tell them something, and it can

hardly be that you've just dropped in from the twenty-
third century."

"No, I'd just as soon you didn't."

"But I never lie to them." Torn, Libby poked a
charred log with her toe. "I can't."

He walked over to cup her chin in his hand. "Leaving out a few small details isn't lying."

"Small details? Like the fact that you came visiting
in a spaceship?"

"For one."

She closed her eyes. It should be funny. Maybe it
would be in five or ten years. "Hornblower, this situation would be awkward enough without the added
bonus of you being from where—make that *when*—
you are."

"What situation?"

She tried not to grind her teeth. "They're my parents, this is their house, and you and I are—" She
made a circling gesture with her hand.

"Lovers," he supplied.

"Will you keep your voice down?"

Patient, he laid his hands on her shoulders, gently
kneading. "Libby, they probably figured that out
when I almost kissed your mother in the refrigerator."

"About that—"

"I thought she was you."

"I know. Still—"

"Libby, I realize it wasn't the most traditional way
to meet your parents, but I think that of the four of
us I was the most surprised."

She couldn't help chuckling. "Maybe."

"Absolutely. So I think we should just get on to
the next step."

"Which is?"

"Lunch."

"Hornblower." With a sigh, she dropped her forehead on his chest. It was a pity this was one of the things she loved about him—his ability to appreciate the simple things. "I wish you'd get it through your head that this is a sensitive situation. What are we going to do about it?" She waited one beat. "If you ask me about what, I'm going to smack you."

"You talk tough." Framing her face with his hands, he lifted it. "Let's see some action."

Libby didn't make even a token protest as his mouth lowered to hers. It was all some sort of a dream anyway, she told herself. Surely she could make everything come out all right in her own dream.

There was a loud, annoyed cough from behind her. Jerking away from Cal, she looked at her father. "Ah…"

"Your mother says lunch is ready." Though he hated acting so predictably, he gave Cal one last measuring look before he went back into the kitchen.

"I think he's warming up to me," Cal mused.

In the kitchen, William scowled at his wife. "That man always has his hands on one of my women."

"One of your women." Caroline let out a long, robust laugh. "Really, Will." She tossed her head so that both of her earrings danced. "He does have very nice hands."

"Looking for trouble?" With one arm, he scooped her up against him.

"Always." She gave him a warm and very provocative kiss before turning toward the doorway. "Come sit down," she said, sharing her radiant smile with Cal. "I just threw a salad together."

She had four bowls set out on her own woven mats.

In the center of the table was a concoction of vegetables and herbs, with the surprising addition of green bananas, sprinkled with whole-wheat croutons and ready to be mixed with a yogurt dressing. Libby gave one wistful thought to the BLTs she'd planned on before she sat down.

"So, Cal…" Caroline passed him the bowl. "Are you an anthropologist?"

"No, I'm a pilot," he said, just as Libby announced, "Cal's a truck driver."

Libby muttered under her breath as Cal calmly dished up salad. "Cargo," he explained, pleased that he could honor Libby's wish to stick with the truth. "I deal primarily with cargo. Libby figures that makes me an airborne truck driver."

"You fly?" William drummed his long, skinny fingers on the table.

"Yes. That's all I ever really wanted to do."

"It must be exciting." Caroline leaned forward, always willing to be fascinated. "Sunbeam, our other daughter, is taking flying lessons. Maybe you can give her some pointers."

"Sunny's always taking lessons." There was both amusement and affection in Libby's voice as she passed the salad on to her mother. "She's good at everything. She took up parachuting and figured the next step was to learn how to fly the plane herself."

"Makes sense." He glanced over at Caroline. Caroline Stone, he thought, not for the first time. The twentieth-century genius. Cal would have found it no more incredible to be sharing a meal with Vincent Van Gogh or Voltaire. "This is a wonderful salad, Mrs. Stone."

"Caroline. Thanks." She slanted a look at her husband, knowing he would have preferred his sausages and chips and a cold beer. After more than twenty years, she hadn't quite converted him. That never stopped her from trying.

"I feel very strongly that proper nutrition is what keeps the mind clear and open," she began. "I recently read a study where proper diet and exercise was directly linked to longer life spans. If we cared for ourselves better, we could live well over a hundred years."

Noting the expression on Cal's face, Libby gave his ankle a kick under the table. She had a feeling he'd been about to inform her mother that people did live over the century mark, and regularly.

"What's the use of living that long if you have to eat leaves and twigs?" William began, but then he noted his wife's narrowed look. "Not that these aren't great leaves."

"You can have something sweet for dessert." She leaned over to kiss his cheek. Six rings glittered on her hands as she offered the bowl to Cal again. "Have some more?"

"Yes, thanks." He took a second serving. His appetite continued to amaze Libby. "I admire your work, Mrs. Stone."

"Really?" It still pleased her when anyone referred to her weaving as her "work." "Do you have a piece?"

"No, it's…out of my reach," he told her, remembering the display he'd seen behind glass at the Smithsonian.

"Where are you from, Hornblower?"

Cal switched his attention to Libby's father. "Philadelphia."

"Your work must involve a lot of traveling."

Cal didn't bother to suppress the grin. "More than you can imagine."

"Do you have a family?"

"My parents and my younger brother are still back...back east."

Despite himself, William thawed a bit. There had been something in Cal's eyes, in his voice, when he'd spoken of his family.

Enough, Libby decided, was enough. She pushed her bowl aside, picked up her tea with both hands, then leaned back, her eyes on her father. "If you have an application form handy, I'm sure Cal could fill it out. Then you'd have his date of birth and Social Security number, as well."

"A little snotty, aren't you?" Will commented over a forkful of salad.

"I'm snotty?"

"Don't apologize." Will patted her hand. "We are what we are. Tell me, Cal, what's your party affiliation?"

"Dad!"

"Just kidding." With a lopsided grin, he reached over to pull Libby onto his lap. "She was born here, you know."

"Yes, she told me." Cal watched Libby hook an arm around her father's neck.

"Used to play naked right out that door while I was gardening."

Despite herself, Libby laughed, even as she closed a hand over her father's throat. "Monster."

"Can I ask him what he thinks of Dylan?"

She gave his head a shake. "No."

"Bob Dylan or Dylan Thomas?" Cal asked, earn-

ing a narrowed look from William and one of surprise
from Libby before she remembered his affection for
poetry.

"Either," Will decided.

"Dylan Thomas was brilliant but depressing. I'd
rather read Bob Dylan."

"Read?"

"The lyrics, Dad. Now that that's settled, why
don't you tell me what you're doing here instead of
driving your board of directors crazy?"

"I wanted to see my little girl."

She kissed him, just above the beard, because she
knew it was partially true. "I saw you when I got
back from the South Pacific. Try again."

"And I wanted Caro to have the fresh air." He
sent his wife a smug look over his daughter's shoulder. "We both figured the air around here worked
well the first two times, so we'd try it again."

"What are you talking about?"

"I'm talking about this place being good for your
mother's condition."

"Condition? You're sick?" Libby was up and
grabbing her mother's hands. "What's wrong?"

"Will, you never could come to the point. What
he's trying to say is I'm pregnant."

"Pregnant?" Libby felt her knees go weak. "But
how?"

"And you call yourself a scientist," Cal murmured,
and earned his first laugh from Will.

"But—" Too dazed to be annoyed by the comment, she looked back and forth between her parents.
They were young, hardly more than forty, and vital.
She knew there was nothing unusual about couples in
their forties having babies. But they were her *parents*.

"You're going to have a baby. I don't know what to say."

"Try congratulations," Will suggested.

"No. Yes, I mean. I need to sit down." She did, on the floor between their chairs. She discovered sitting wasn't enough and took three long breaths.

"How do you feel?" Caroline asked.

"Dazed." She looked up, studying her mother's face. "How do you feel?"

"Eighteen...though I have talked Will out of delivering this one himself here at the cabin, the way he did with you and Sunny."

"The woman's lost her sixties values," Will muttered, though he had been tremendously relieved when Caroline had insisted on an obstetrician and a hospital. "So what do you think, Libby?"

She rose to her knees so that she could hug each of them. "I think we should celebrate."

"I'm one step ahead of you." Rising, William went to the refrigerator, then held a bottle aloft. "Sparkling apple juice."

The cork popped with a sound as festive as champagne. They toasted each other, the baby, the absent Sunny, the past and the future. Cal joined them, drawn in by their pleasure in each other. Here was one more thing that time hadn't changed, he thought. The giddy delight a coming baby brought to people who wanted it.

He'd never thought very seriously about starting a family. He'd known that when the time, and the woman, were right the rest would fall into place. Now he caught himself imagining what it would be like if he and Libby were toasting their own expected child.

Dangerous thoughts. Impossible thoughts. He had

only a matter of days left with her—hours, really—
and families required a lifetime.

Even as he yearned for one life, watching Libby's
parents together reminded him of his own family.
Were they watching the sky, wondering where he
was, how he was? If only he could let them know he
was safe.

''Cal?''

''Hmm? What?'' He blinked and saw Libby staring
at him. ''I'm sorry.''

''I was just saying we should build a fire.''

''Sure.''

''One of my favorite spots here is in front of the
fire.'' Caroline hooked her arm through William's.
''I'm so glad we stopped by for the night.''

''For the night?'' Libby repeated.

''We're on our way to Carmel,'' Caroline decided
on the spot, and gave William's hand a vicious
squeeze before he could speak. ''I craved a ride along
the Coast.''

''What she craved was a cheeseburger under her
alfalfa sprouts,'' William said. ''That's when I knew
she was pregnant.''

''And being pregnant entitles me to an afternoon
nap.'' Caroline sent her husband a slow smile. ''Why
don't you tuck me in?''

''I could use a nap myself.'' With his arm around
her shoulders, they started out. ''Carmel? Last I heard
we were spending a week here. Since when are we
going to Carmel?''

''Since four's a crowd, dummy.''

''That may be, but I haven't decided if I like the
idea of Libby being with him.''

''She likes it.'' Caroline walked into the bedroom

and was flooded with memories. The nights they'd shared, and the mornings. They'd made love in that bed, argued politics, planned ways to save the world from itself. She'd laughed there, cried there and given birth there. She sat on the edge and let her hands run over the spread. She could almost feel the murmur of memories.

Will, his hands tucked in the back pocket of his jeans, paced to the window.

She smiled at his back, remembering how he had been at eighteen. Even thinner, she recalled, even more idealistic, and just as wonderful. They had always loved this place, being children there, having children there. Even when things had changed, they had never lost that cocksure certainty of who and what they were. She understood him, heard his thoughts as if they were in her own head.

"A cargo pilot," Will muttered. "And what the hell kind of name is Hornblower? There's something about him, Caro, I don't know what, but something I'm not sure rings true."

"Don't you trust Liberty?"

"Of course I do." He looked back, insulted. "It's him I don't trust."

"Ah, the echo of time." She cupped a hand to her ear. "The exact words my father once spoke when referring to you."

"He was a poor judge of character," Will muttered, and turned back to the window.

"Most men are when it comes to the choices their daughters make. I remember you telling my father that I knew my own mind. Let's see, was that the first or second time he threw you out of the house?"

"Both." He had to grin. "He said you'd be back

in six months and that I'd end up selling daisies on a street corner. Fooled him, didn't we?''

''That was nearly twenty-five years ago.''

''Don't rub it in.'' He fingered his beard. ''Doesn't it bother you that they're here—together?''

''You mean that they're lovers?''

''Yes.'' He dug his hands in his pockets again. ''She's our baby.''

''I remember you telling me once that making love was the most natural expression of trust and affection between two people. That hang-ups about sex needed to be eradicated if the world was ever to experience true peace and goodwill.''

''I did not.''

''You certainly did. We were crammed into the back seat of your VW, steaming up the windows, at the time.''

He had to grin. ''It must have worked.''

''It did, mostly because I'd already decided you were the one I wanted. You were the first man I'd ever loved, Will, so I knew it was right.'' She held out a hand and waited until he'd clasped it. ''That man downstairs is the first Libby's ever loved. She knows what's right.'' He started to object, but she tightened her grip. ''We raised them to follow their hearts. Did we make a mistake?''

''No.'' He laid a palm on the gentle slope of her belly. ''We'll do the same for this one.''

''He has kind eyes,'' she said softly. ''When he looks at her, his heart's in them.''

''You always were overly romantic. That's how I caught you.''

''And kept me,'' she murmured against his lips.

''Right.'' He toyed with the hem of her sweater,

knowing how easy it would be to slip it over her head, and exactly what he would find beneath. "You don't really want to sleep, do you?"

With a laugh, she overbalanced so that they both tumbled onto the bed.

"It's so strange." Libby dropped down on the grass beside the stream. "Thinking that my parents are going to have another child. They looked happy, didn't they?"

"Very." Cal settled beside her. "Except when your father was scowling at me."

She laughed a little as she rested her head on his shoulder. "Sorry. He's really a very friendly man, most of the time."

"I'll take your word for it." He plucked at a blade of grass. It hardly mattered if he had her father's approval or not. Soon Cal would be out of his life, and out of Libby's.

She loved it here beside the water, which ran fresh and cold over the rocks. The grass was long and soft, dotted along the bank with small blue flowers. There would be foxglove in the summer, growing as tall as a man and bending over the stream with its purple or white bells. There would be lilies and columbine. At dusk deer would come to drink, and sometimes a lumbering bear would come fishing.

She didn't want to think of summer, but of now, when the air was as fresh as the water, with a clear, clean taste to it. Chipmunks raced in the forest beyond. She and Sunny had hand-fed the friendlier ones.

Wherever she went, to remote islands, to desert outposts, she would remember those early years of her life. And be grateful for them.

"That's going to be a very lucky baby," she murmured. Then she smiled as a thought struck her. "To think, after all these years, I might have a brother."

He thought of his own, Jacob, with his flaring temper and his sharp, impatient mind. "I always wanted a sister."

"There's something to be said for them, too. But they always seem to be prettier than you are."

He rolled her onto the grass. "I wish I could meet your Sunbeam. Ow." He rubbed a hand over his side where she'd pinched him.

"Concentrate on me."

"That's all I seem to do." He braced his arm beside her head as he studied her face. "I have to go back to the ship for a little while."

She tried valiantly to keep the sorrow out of her eyes. It had been easy to pretend there was no ship, and no tomorrow. "I didn't have a chance to ask you how it was going."

Quickly, he thought. Too quickly. "I'll know more when I check the computer. Can you make an excuse to your parents if I'm not back when they get up?"

"I'll tell them you're off meditating. My father will love it."

"Okay. Then tonight..." He lowered his head for a gentle kiss. "I'll concentrate on you."

"Concentrating's all you'll do." She linked her arms around his neck. "You're sleeping on the couch."

"I am."

"Definitely."

"In that case..." He slid down to her.

Later, during the night, when the fire was burning low and the house was quiet, Cal sat alone, fully dressed. He knew how to get back. At least he knew how he had gotten where and when he was and how to reverse the process.

With a few more repairs, basically unnecessary ones, he would be ready to go. Technically he would be ready. But emotionally… Nothing had ever torn him quite so neatly in two.

If she asked him to stay… God, he was afraid if she did, it would swing the balance of the tug-of-war he was waging. But she wouldn't ask him to stay. He couldn't ask her to go.

Perhaps when he made it back and offered the data to the world of science a new, less dangerous way would be created to conquer time. Perhaps he could come back.

Turning his head, he looked into the fire. More fantasies. Libby was facing the facts, and so would he.

He thought he heard her on the stairs. But when he looked it was William.

"Trouble sleeping?" he asked Cal.

"Some. You?"

"I always loved this place at night." Because he loved his daughter, as well, he was determined to make an effort to be civil, if not exactly friendly. "The quiet, the dark." He stooped to add another log to the fire. Sparks flew, then winked out. "I never pictured myself living anywhere else."

"I never imagined living in a place like this or realized how hard it would be to leave."

"A long way from Philadelphia."

"A very long way."

He recognized gloom when he heard it. William had courted it early in his youth, mistaking it for romance. Unbending a little, he dug out the brandy and two snifters. "Want a drink?"

"Yeah. Thanks."

William settled in the winged chair and stretched out his long legs. "I used to sit here at night and ponder the meaning of life."

"Did you ever figure it out?"

"Sometimes I did, sometimes I didn't."

It had been simpler, somehow, when his main concerns had been world peace and social reform. Now, God help him, he was nearing middle age—that area that had always seemed so gray and distant. It reminded him that he had once been a young man, much younger than the one facing him now, with his head in the clouds and his mind on a woman. The times they are a-changing, he thought wryly, and swirled his brandy.

"Are you in love with Libby?"

"I was just asking myself that same question."

William sipped his brandy. He preferred the traces of doubt and frustration he heard to a glib response. He'd always been glib. No wonder Caroline's father had detested him. "Come up with an answer?"

"Not a comfortable one."

Nodding, William lifted his glass. "Before I met Caro, I was planning to join the Peace Corps or a Tibetan monastery. She was fresh out of high school. Her father wanted to shoot me."

Cal grinned. He was beginning to enjoy the brandy. "I had a minute to be grateful you didn't have a weapon this afternoon."

"Being a pacifist by nature, I only gave it a passing thought," William assured him. "Caro's father thrived on the idea. I can't wait to tell him I got her pregnant again.'' Relaxed now, he savored the idea.

"Libby's hoping for a brother.''

"Did she say that?'' Now he grinned, lingering over the idea of a son. "She was my first. Every child's a miracle, but the first…I guess you never get over it.''

"She is a miracle. She changed my life.''

William's look sharpened. Hornblower might not realize he was in love, he thought, but there was little doubt about it. "Caro likes you,'' he commented. "She has a way of seeing into the heart of people. I only want to say that Libby isn't as sturdy as she seems. Be careful with her.''

He rose then, afraid he might start to pontificate. "Get some sleep,'' he advised. "Caro's bound to be up at dawn fixing whole-wheat pancakes or yogurt-and-kiwi surprise.'' He winced a little. He was a man who would always yearn in his heart for bacon and eggs. "You won points by the way you dug into that tofu amandine casserole.''

"It was great.''

"No wonder she likes you.'' He paused at the foot of the steps. "You know, I have a sweater just like that.''

"Really?'' Cal couldn't suppress the grin. "Small world.''

Chapter 10

"I knew you'd be up early." Libby slipped out the back door to join her mother.

"Not so early." Caroline sighed, annoyed with herself for missing the sunrise. "I've found myself getting a slower start the last couple of months."

"Morning sickness?"

"No." Smiling, Caroline hooked an arm around Libby's waist. "It seems all three of my children decided to spare me that. Did I ever tell you I appreciated it?"

"No."

"Well, I do." She gave Libby's cheek a quick kiss and noted the faint shadows under her eyes. Biding her time, she nodded toward the trees. "Like to walk?"

"Yes, I would."

They started off at a meandering pace, the bells Caroline wore at her wrists and ears jingling cheerfully. So much was the same, Libby thought. The trees, the sky, the quiet cabin behind them. And so much had changed. She leaned her head against her mother's shoulder for a moment.

"Do you remember when we used to walk like this, you and Sunny and I?"

"I remember walking with you." Caroline laughed as the branches arched overhead in a cool, green tunnel. "Sunny never walked anywhere. The moment she could stand she was off at a dash. You and I would poke along, just as we're doing now."

And what would this child be like? Caroline wondered, feeling a fresh thrill of anticipation.

"Then we'd pick some flowers or berries so that Dad would think we'd been doing something productive."

"It seems both our men are sleeping in today." When Libby didn't respond, Caroline waited until the silence between them was comfortable again. The forest was alive with sounds, the rustling of small game in the brush, the call of birds in flight. "I like your friend, Libby."

"I'm glad you do. I wanted you to." She bent to pick up a twig, then broke small pieces off as she walked. It was a nervous gesture Caroline knew very well. Sunny would let any and all feeling burst straight out, but Libby, her quiet, sensible Libby, would hold them in.

"It's more important that you do."

"I do, very much." Suddenly aware of what she was doing, Libby tossed the rest of the twig aside. "He's kind and funny and strong. This time I've had here with him, it's been wonderful for me. I never really thought I'd find someone who would make me feel the way Caleb makes me feel.''

"But you don't smile when you say that." Caroline reached up to touch her daughter's face. "Why?"

"This…time we have…it's only temporary."

"I don't understand. Why temporary? If you're in love with him—"

"I am," Libby murmured. "Very much in love with him."

"Then?"

Libby drew a long breath. It was impossible to explain, she thought. "He has to go back, to his family."

"To Philadelphia?" Caroline prompted her, at a loss.

"Yes…" There was a smile now, faint and wistful. "To Philadelphia."

"I don't see why that should make a difference," she began. Then stopped and put a hand on Libby's arm. "Oh, baby, is he married?"

"No." She might have laughed then, but she noted the deep and genuine concern in her mother's eyes. "No, it's nothing like that. Caleb could never be dishonest. It's very hard to explain, but I can tell you that right from the start we both knew that Cal would have to go back where he belonged, and I…I would have to stay."

"A few thousand miles shouldn't matter if two people want to be together."

"Sometimes distance is, well, longer than it looks. Don't worry." Leaning over, she kissed Caroline's cheek. "I can honestly say that I wouldn't trade the time I've had with Cal for anything. There was a poster in the cabin when I was little. Do you remem-

ber? It said something about…if you had something,
let it go. If it didn't come back to you, it was never
yours.''

"I never liked that poster," Caroline muttered.

This time Libby did laugh. "Let's pick some flowers.''

Libby watched them go a few hours later, her father
behind the wheel of the rumbling pickup, her
mother's earrings dancing as she leaned out of the
window to wave until she was out of sight.

"I like your parents.''

Libby turned to Cal, linking her hands around his
neck. "They liked you, too.''

He leaned down for a brief kiss. "Your mother,
maybe.''

"My father, too.''

"If I had a year or two to win him over he might
almost like me.''

"He wasn't scowling at you today.''

"No.'' He rubbed his cheek against hers as he considered. "It was down to a sneer. What are you going
to tell them?''

"About what?''

"About why I'm not here, with you?''

"I'll tell them that you went home.'' Because she
made the effort, her answer sounded casual and easy.
So easy that he nearly swore.

"Just like that?''

Her voice was a little brittle now, she knew, with
a tone that could easily be taken as callous. "They
won't pry if I don't want them to. It will be simpler
for everyone if I tell them the truth.''

"Which is?''

Was he determined to make it difficult? She moved her shoulders restlessly. "Things didn't work out, and you went on with your life. I went on with mine."

"Yeah, I guess that's best. No mess, no regrets."

Irritable, she thrust her fists in her pockets. "You have a better idea?"

"No. Yours is just dandy." He pulled away, annoyed with himself, annoyed with her. "I've got to get to the ship."

"I know. I thought I'd run into town and pick up the camera and some other things. If I get back early enough I'll ride out, check on your progress."

"Fine." He was damned if it was going to be so easy for her when he was being torn in two. Before he could regret it, he yanked her against him and crushed his mouth down on hers.

Hot, edgy, tasting of anger and frustration, the kiss spun out. Libby hung on, to maintain her physical, as well as her emotional, balance. She couldn't, wouldn't, give him what he seemed to need. Total capitulation. He'd never asked for that before, nor had she known she would so firmly withhold it. Trapped, she couldn't soothe, couldn't demand, as he devoured.

In one long, possessive stroke, his hands ran up her body, then down again with no lessening of force. She might have protested. There was something here that frightened her, that left her weak—not meltingly, but with an open-ended vulnerability that made her struggle to find her feet again. There was no gentleness here, nor was there the sense of urgent desire he had once shown her. Instead, the kiss was like a punishment, and a brutally effective one.

"Caleb—" She began, hitching in a shallow breath, when he released her.

''That should give you something to think about,'' he said, then turned abruptly to stalk away.

Stunned, she stared after him. One unsteady hand reached up to press against lips still tender from his assault. When her breathing steadied, her temper took hold. She'd think about it, all right. She stormed inside, slamming the door behind her. Moments later she stormed out again to climb into the Land Rover.

It was all going perfectly. And he was mad as hell. Technically he could take off within twenty-four hours. The major repairs were done, the calculations as finely tuned as he and the computer could make them in the time allotted. His ship was ready. He wasn't. That was what it came down to.

She was certainly ready to see him off, Cal thought as he fused a tear in the inner shell with his spot laser. Damned anxious, if it came to that. She was probably in town right now buying a camera so that she could take a few souvenir pictures before she waved goodbye. He shut off the laser and checked the seam.

Why did she have to be so practical about it?

Because she was practical, he reminded himself as he yanked off his protective goggles. That was one of the things he most admired about her. She was practical, warm, intelligent, shy. He could still see the way her eyes had looked the first time he'd told her he wanted her. They'd gone from big and tawny to big and confused.

And when he'd touched her. She'd gotten hot and trembly. She was soft, so incredibly soft. Cursing himself, he stowed the laser in the tool compartment, then tossed the goggles in beside them before he slammed the door. He couldn't imagine a man in the universe being able to resist those eyes, or that skin, or that wide, sexy mouth.

That was part of the problem, he admitted as he prowled the ship. Men wouldn't. Maybe she hadn't paid attention before. Maybe she'd been too wrapped up in her books and her work and her theories on the societal tendencies of man as a species. One day she was going to slip those glasses off her nose and look around—and realize that there were men, flesh-and-blood men, looking back at her. Men who could make promises, he thought in disgust. Even if they didn't mean to keep them.

Perhaps she hadn't realized how much passion, how much heat, how much power, she held. But he'd opened those doors for her. Opened, hell—he'd smashed them. Once he was gone, other men would tend the fire he'd lit.

The thought made him insane. Cal admitted it as he dragged his hands through his hair. Stark, raving crazy. He belonged in one of those padded cells Libby had spoken of. He couldn't stand it—the thought of someone else touching her, kissing her. Undressing her.

With an oath, he wheeled into his cabin and began to put it in order. That is, he tossed things around.

He was being selfish and unfair. And he didn't care. It was true that he would have to accept the fact that Libby would go on with her life, and that her life would include a lover—or lovers, he thought, grinding his teeth. A husband, perhaps, and children. He had to accept that. But he was damned if he had to like it.

After kicking a shoe into a corner, he dug his hands into his pockets and stared at the picture of his family.

His parents, he mused, going over each feature of their faces as he had never bothered to before. It had been three...no, four months sincc hc'd seen them. If you didn't count the centuries.

They were attractive, strong-looking people, despite his father's slightly hangdog expression. They had always seemed so content to him, so sure of their lives and what they wanted. He liked to picture them at home, with his mother laboring over some thick technical book and his father whistling between his teeth as he played with his flowers.

He had his mother's nose. Intrigued, Cal leaned down to peer closer. Strange, he'd never noticed that before. Apparently she'd been satisfied with the one she'd been born with and had passed it on to him.

And to Jacob, he realized as he studied his brother's image. But to Jacob she'd passed along brilliance, as well. Brilliance wasn't always a gift, Caleb thought with a grin. It seemed to make Jacob hotheaded, questioning and impatient. He remembered his mother saying that J.T., as his family called him, was more fond of arguing than breathing.

Cal decided he'd probably inherited his father's more even temperament. Except he didn't feel very even-tempered at the moment.

With a sigh, he sat on the bed. "You'd like her," he murmured to the images. "I wish you could meet her." That was a first, he thought. He'd never had the urge to bring any of his companions home for family approval. It was probably the result of spending the day with Libby's parents.

He was stalling. Rubbing his hands over his face, Cal admitted he was wasting his time with busywork and self-indulgent analysis. He should already be gone. But he'd promised himself another day. There was Libby's time capsule to do…that is, if she was still speaking to him.

She was bound to be angry about the little number he'd pulled on her before he'd left that morning. That was fine, he decided as he stretched out. He'd rather have her angry than smilingly urging him on his way. Lazily he checked his watch. She should be back in a couple hours.

Right now he was going to have a nap to make up for the long, frustrating and sleepless night he'd spent on her couch. Switching on the sleep tape beside the bed, he closed his eyes and tuned out.

Idiot, Libby thought, gripping the wheel tightly as she maneuvered the Land Rover along the winding switchback toward home. Conceited idiot, she clarified. He'd better have an explanation when she saw him again. No matter how she racked her brain, she could come up with no reason why he had kissed her in that furious, mean-spirited way.

Something to think about.

Well, she had thought about it, Libby reminded herself while she navigated the narrowing dirt road. It still made her furious. And it still didn't make any sense. Then again, she had a twice-married neighbor in Portland who claimed men never made sense.

They always had to her—as a species, anyway, Libby thought grimly. And on paper. Now, for the first time, she was involved in a one-on-one with a flesh-and-blood member of the male genus, and she was baffled.

Libby bumped over rocks as she tried once again to solve the mystery of Caleb Hornblower.

Perhaps it had had something to do with the visit by her parents. But then, he'd been moody the morning before they had arrived. Moody, but not angry, she remembered, and they had made slow, quiet love by the stream during the afternoon. He'd seemed cheerful enough at dinner, perhaps a little withdrawn, but that was only natural. It must be very difficult for him to be around people when he had to concentrate on not saying anything that might give him away.

She felt a tug of sympathy and stubbornly ignored it.

That was no reason for him to take his frustration out on her. Wasn't she trying to help him? It was killing her inside, but she was doing everything in her power to see that he got back to where he wanted to be.

She had her own life, as well. That fact soothed only a little as she barreled up a slope. She should be working on her dissertation and making the preliminary plans for her next field study. There was an offer of a lecture tour she had yet to fully consider. Instead, she was running errands—buying cameras and oatmeal cookies. For the last time, she decided huffily, but then she realized that it would indeed be the last time.

She stopped the Land Rover when the trail narrowed to a footpath. She hadn't really meant to come out to Caleb. During the entire trip she'd told herself she would go back to the cabin and get to work. Yet here she was, letting herself be pulled back. At least there was something she could do for herself.

On impulse, she grabbed the new Polaroid from the shopping bag. After unboxing it, she skimmed over the directions, then loaded it with the first of the packs of film she'd bought. As an afterthought, she grabbed the bag of chunky oatmeal cookies.

From the top of the slope she studied the ship. It lay huge and silent on the rocks and the downed trees, like some strange sleeping animal. Deliberately she blocked out thoughts of the man inside and concentrated on the ship itself.

The sixteen-wheeler of the future, she decided, carefully framing it. The Greyhound bus or power van. All aboard for Mars, Mercury and Venus. Express trips to Pluto and Orion available. With what was more a sigh than a snicker, she took two pictures. Sitting on the edge of the slope, she watched them develop. Fifty years ago, she mused, the idea of instant pictures had been science fiction. She glanced back at the ship. Man worked fast. Very fast.

Wanting a few more moments to herself, she ripped open the bag of cookies and began to nibble.

Of course, she'd never be able to show the picture that was already taking shape in her hand to anyone. One was for the capsule, but the other was for her personal files. She wanted to believe it was the scientist who had taken it, who would label and file it along with other pictures she would take and the hard copy of the report she was writing on this isolated experience.

But it had nothing to do with science, and everything to do with the heart. She didn't want to rely on her memory.

She slipped the pictures into her pocket, swung the camera over her shoulder and started down.

When she reached the hatch, she lifted her fist, then started to laugh. Did one knock on the door of a spacecraft? Feeling foolish with the ship looming over her, she rapped twice. A chipmunk scurried over the ground, scrambled onto the trunk of a fallen tree and stared at her.

"I know it's odd," Libby told him. "Just remember to keep it under your hat." She tossed half a cookie in his direction, then turned back to knock again. "All right, Hornblower, open up. I feel like an idiot out here."

She tried knocking, pounding, shouting. Once she gave in to temper and slammed the hull with a good kick. Favoring her sore toes, she stepped back. Furious with him, she'd nearly decided to turn back when it occurred to her he might not be able to hear her.

Stepping closer, she began to search for the device he had used to open the hatch. It took her ten minutes. When the hatch opened, she stormed inside, ready for a fight.

"Listen, Hornblower, I—"

He wasn't on the bridge. Frustrated, Libby dragged back her hair. Couldn't he even make himself available when she wanted to yell at him?

The shield was up. She hadn't been able to see in from the outside, but now she had a stunning panoramic view. Drawn, she crossed over to the controls. How would it feel, she wondered as she sat in his chair, to pilot something so huge, so powerful? She scanned the buttons and switches spread out before her. Was it any wonder he loved it? Even a woman who had always been firmly rooted to the ground could imagine the wild, limitless freedom of traveling through space. There would be planets, balls of color and light. The glimmer of distant stars, the glow of orbiting moons.

She liked to think of him that way, weaving

through the stars the way he had woven through the trees with her on the cycle.

Libby took a last scan of the controls, then studied the computer. A little ill at ease, she glanced around the empty bridge before she leaned forward.

"Computer?"

Working.

She jolted, then swallowed a nervous laugh. There were two questions she wanted to ask, but only one she truly wanted the answer to. Because she believed in facing facts, Libby inhaled, exhaled, then plunged.

"Computer, what is the status on the calculations for the return journey to the twenty-third century?"

Calculations complete. Probability index formulated. Risk factors, trajectory, thrust, degree of orbit, velocity and success factors locked in. Is report desired?

"No."

So he was finished. She'd known it, even when she'd tried to tell herself she had a few more days with him. He hadn't told her, but she thought she understood why. Cal wouldn't want to hurt her, and he would know, would have to know, how she felt. No matter how hard she tried to treat their relationship as a single moment in time, one based on passion and affection and mutual need, he had seen through her. He was trying to be kind.

She wanted to be glad for him. She had to be glad for him.

She took a minute to adjust, then asked what she had asked once before.

"Computer."

Working.

"Who is Caleb Hornblower?"

*Hornblower, Caleb, Captain ISF, retired. Born 2
February, to Katrina Hardesty Hornblower and By-
ram Edward Hornblower. Place of birth Philadelphia, Pennsylvania. Graduate Wilson Freemont Me-
morial Academy. Attended Princeton University,
withdrew after sixteen months without degree. Enlisted ISF. Served six years, seven months. Military
record as follows...*

With her lips pursed, Libby listened to the readout
of Cal's military career. There was citation after citation—just as there was reprimand after reprimand.
His record as a pilot was flawless. His disciplinary
record was an entirely different matter. She couldn't
help but smile.

She thought of her father and his ingrained distrust
of the military system. Yes, given a bit of time, she
thought, he would have grown very fond of Cal.

Credit rating 5.8, the computer continued.

"Stop." Libby heaved a sigh. She wasn't interested
in Cal's credit rating. She'd pried far enough into his
personal life as it was. Any other answers she wanted
would have to come from him. And quickly.

Rising, she began to wander through the ship, looking for him.

It was the music that tipped her off. She heard it
first, distant and lovely, with a vague curiosity. Something classical, with a kind of swelling passion. As
she followed it, she tried to identify the composer.

She found Cal asleep in his cabin. The music filled
the room, every corner of it, yet it was soft, soothing,
seductive. She felt the tug, the almost irresistible urge
to slip into the bed beside him, snuggling close until
he woke and made slow, sweet love to her.

She shook it off. The music, she decided. Somehow

it was comforting and erotic at the same time. Exactly the way his kisses could be. She wouldn't let it influence her or let herself forget that she was angry with him.

Still, she took a picture of him as he slept, then slipped it, almost guiltily, into her pocket.

After leaning against the doorway, she lifted her chin. It was a deliberately defiant pose, and she enjoyed it.

"So this is how you work."

Though she'd pitched her voice above the music, he went on sleeping. She considered going over and giving his shoulder a shove, then came up with a better idea. She slipped two fingers of her left hand into her mouth, inhaled, then blew out a sharp, shrill whistle, just as Sunny had taught her.

He came up in the bed like a rocket. "Red alert!" he shouted before he saw her smirking at him from the doorway. After leaning back against the cushioned headboard, he ran a hand over his eyes.

He'd been dreaming. Out in space, whipping through the galaxy, with the controls at his fingertips and worlds racing by hundreds of thousands of miles beneath him. She'd been there, right beside him, an arm wrapped around his waist, all the fascination, all the thrill of flying glowing on her face.

Until something had gone wrong. And the ship had shaken, the gauges had blinked, the bells had sounded. He'd heard her scream as they'd gone into a dive. He hadn't known what to do. Quite suddenly his mind had gone blank. He hadn't been able to save her.

Here she was now, while his heart was still sprinting from the dream, looking cocky and ready to spar.

"What the hell was that for?"

He looked as though he'd had a scare. She certainly hoped so. "It seemed the most efficient way to wake you up. I tell you, Hornblower, you keep working like this, you'll wear yourself right out."

"I was taking a break." He wished he'd taken a good long slug of potent, electric-blue Antellis liquor. "I didn't sleep much last night."

"Too bad." As sympathy went, it left a lot to be desired. Still studying him, she dug for a cookie.

"That couch is lumpy."

"I'll make a note of it. Maybe that's why you woke up on the wrong side of it." She took her time, nipping off tiny bite after tiny bite. It was an attempt to make him hungry, and she succeeded, though not in the way she'd intended.

He could feel his muscles tightening, each separate one. "I don't know what you mean."

"It's an expression."

"I've heard it." He knew he snapped the words out, but he couldn't help it. She flicked out her tongue to catch a crumb at the corner of her mouth. He nearly groaned. "I didn't wake up on the wrong side of anything."

"Well, I suppose it could be your nature to be surly and you've managed to repress it lately."

"I'm not surly." He all but growled it.

"No? Arrogant, then. Is that better?" Her slow half smile was meant to annoy, but it provoked a different emotion.

Trying to ignore her and what was going on inside his own rebellious body, he looked at his watch. "You took a long time in town."

"My time's my own, Hornblower."

His brows arched. If she hadn't been so smug about her own control, she might have noticed that the eyes beneath them had darkened. "You want to fight?"

"Me?" Her lips turned up again. She was the very picture of innocence. "Why, Caleb, after meeting my parents you should know I'm a born pacifist. I was rocked to sleep with folk songs."

He muttered an opinion, a single two-syllable word that Libby had always thought belonged to the slang of the twentieth century. Intrigued, she cocked her head.

"So, that's still the response when someone doesn't have a clever or intelligent answer. It's such a comfort to know some traditions survive."

He threw his legs off the edge of the bed and, his eyes on hers, slowly unfolded himself. He didn't step toward her, not yet. Not until he could trust himself not to plant a good clean jab on her outthrust chin. Strange, he'd never noticed the stubborn set of it before. Or that I-dare-you look in her eyes.

The worst of it was, the arrogance was every bit as arousing as the warmth.

"You're pushing, babe. I figure it's only fair to warn you that I don't come from a particularly peaceful family."

"Well..." Carefully she chose another cookie. "That certainly puts the fear of God into me." After rolling up the bag, she tossed it at him so that his defensive catch crumbled half the contents. "I don't know what's gotten under your skin, Hornblower, but I've got better things to do than worry about it. You can stay here and sulk if you like, but I'm going back to work."

She barely managed to turn around. He grabbed her

arms and had her pressed into the wall, his fingers digging in. Later she would wonder why she had been surprised that he could move that quickly, or that beneath the easy disposition there lurked a fierce, raw-edged temper.

"You want to know what's wrong with me?" His eyes, so close to hers, were the color that edged lightning bolts. "Is that what all this button-pushing's about, Libby?"

"I don't care what's wrong with you." She kept her chin up, though her mouth had gone dry. Libby knew that for her offering an apology would always be easier than sticking with a fight. Sometimes it wasn't pacifism but cowardice. She straightened her spine and drew in a deep breath. She was sticking.

"I don't give a damn what's wrong with you. Now let me go."

"You should." He wrapped her hair around his hand to pull her head back, slowly exposing her throat. "Do you think that every emotion a man has toward a woman is gentle, kind, loving?"

"I'm not a fool." She began to struggle, and she was more annoyed than afraid when he didn't release her.

"No, you're not." Her eyes were on his, fury matching fury. He thought he felt something break inside him, the last bolt that had caged the uncivilized. "Maybe it's time I taught you the rest."

"I don't need you to teach me anything."

"That's right, there'll be others to teach you, won't there?" Jealousy clawed deep, drawing thick, hot blood. "Damn you. And damn them, every one of them. Think of this. Whenever anyone else touches you, tomorrow, ten years from tomorrow, you'll wish it was me. I'll see to it.''

With his words still hanging in the air, he pulled her to the bed.

Chapter 11

She fought him. She refused to be taken in anger, no matter how deep her love. The bed sank beneath their combined weights, molding to them like a cocoon. The music drifted, calm and beautiful. His hands were rough as they dragged at the buttons of her shirt.

She didn't speak. It never occurred to her to beg him to stop, or to give in to the tears that would surely have snapped him back to his senses. Instead she struggled, trying to roll away from his ruthlessly seeking hands. She fought, furiously bucking, pushing against him, waging a private war against the traitorous response of her body, which would betray her heart.

She would hate him for this. The knowledge nearly broke her. If he succeeded in what he set out to do, it would wash away other memories and leave this one, this violent, distorted one, dominant. Unable to bear it, she fought now for both of them.

He knew her too well. Every curve, every dip, every pulse. On a wave of fury, he locked her wrists in one hand and dragged her arms over her head. His mouth savaged her neck while his free hand slid down, unerringly, to find one of those secret, vulnerable places. He heard her moan as the unwanted, unavoidable pleasure tore into her. Her body tensed, a wire ready to snap. It arched, a bow pulled taut. He felt the burst of release as it shuddered through her, heard her choked-off cry. He saw her lips quiver before she pressed them hard together.

Regret burned through him. He had no right, no one did, to take something beautiful and use it as a weapon. He'd wanted to hurt her for something beyond her control. And he had. No more, he realized, than he had hurt himself.

"Libby."

She only shook her head, her eyes tightly closed. Wishing for words that weren't there, Cal rolled over and stared at the ceiling.

"I have no excuse...there is no excuse for treating you that way."

She managed to swallow the tears. It relieved her, made it possible for her to steady her breathing and open her eyes. "Maybe not, but there's usually a reason. I'd like to hear it."

He didn't answer for a long time. They lay close and tense, not quite touching. There were dozens of reasons he could give her—lack of sleep, overwork, the anxiety over the possible failure of his flight. They would all be accurate, to a point. But they wouldn't be the truth. Libby, he knew, set great store by honesty.

"I care for you," he said slowly. "It isn't easy knowing I won't see you again. I realize we both have our own lives," he added before she could speak. "Our own place. Maybe we're both doing what has to be done, but I don't like the idea that it's easy for you."

"It isn't."

He knew it was selfish, but it relieved him to hear it. Reaching over, he linked his hand with hers. "I'm jealous."

"Of what?"

"Of the men you'll meet, the ones you'll love. The one's who'll love you."

"But—"

"No, don't say anything. Let me get it all out and over with. It doesn't seem to matter that I know it's wrong, intellectually. It's a gut reaction, Libby, and I'm used to going with them. Every time I imagine another man touching you the way I've touched you, seeing you the way I've seen you, I go a little crazy."

"And that's why you've been angry with me?" She turned her head to study his profile. "Over my imagined future affairs?"

"I guess you've got a right to make me sound like an idiot."

"I'm not trying to."

He moved his shoulders in what might have been a shrug. "I can even see him. He's about six-four and built like one of those Greek gods."

"Adonis," she suggested, smiling. "He gets my vote."

"Shut up." But she noted that his lips curved slightly. "He's got blond hair, streaked, kind of wind-swept, and this strong, rock-hard jaw with one of those clefts in it."

"Like Kirk Douglas?"

He shot her a suspicious look. "You know a guy like this?"

"Only by reputation." Because she sensed that the storm was over, she kissed Cal's shoulder.

"Anyway, he's got brains, too, which is another reason I really hate him. He's a doctor, not medical but philosophy. He can discuss the traditional mating habits of obscure tribes with you for hours. And he plays piano."

"Wow. I'm impressed."

"He's rich," Cal went on, almost viciously. "A 9.2 credit rating. He takes you to Paris and makes love to you in a room overlooking the Seine. Then he gives you a diamond as big as a fist."

"Well, well." She gave it some thought. "Can he quote poetry?"

"He even writes it."

"Oh, my God." She put a hand to her heart. "I don't suppose you could tell me where I'm going to meet him? I want to be ready."

He rolled over just enough to look at her. Her eyes were bright, but with amusement, not tears. "You're getting a real charge out of this, aren't you?"

"Yes." She lifted a hand to his face. "I suppose

it might make you feel better if I promised I'd join a convent.''

''Okay.'' He took her wrist to bring her palm against his mouth. ''Can I get it in writing?''

''I'll think about it.'' His eyes were clear again, deep and clear. He was Cal now, the man she could love and understand. ''Are we finished fighting?''

''Looks like it. I'm sorry, Libby. I've been acting like a lupz.''

''I'm not sure what that means, but you're probably right.''

''Friends?'' He bent down to brush her lips with his.

''Friends.'' Before he could draw back, she cupped his head in her hand and held him against her for a longer, deeper and much less friendly kiss. ''Cal?''

''Hmm?'' He traced her lips with his tongue, memorizing their shape and texture.

''Did this guy have a name? Ouch!'' Torn between laughter and pain, she jerked back. ''You bit me.''

''Damn right.''

''It was your fantasy,'' she reminded him primly, ''not mine.''

''And let's keep it that way.'' But he was grinning as he ran his hand up the smooth skin where her shirt had parted. ''I can give you others, if you're willing to settle.''

''Yes.'' His palm rounded over her breast, working magic. ''Oh, yes.''

''If I took you to Paris, we'd spend the first three days in that hotel suite and never get out of bed.'' He continued to tease, nipping here, stroking there, stopping just short of possession. "We'd drink champagne, bottle after bottle, and eat small dishes with exotic names and tastes. I'd know every inch of your body, every pore of your skin. We'd stay in that big, soft bed and go places no one else had ever been."

"Cal." She trembled as he circled her breasts with slow, openmouthed kisses.

"Then we'd get dressed. I can see you in something thin and white, something that skims off your shoulders, dips down your back. Something that makes every man who sees you want to murder me."

"I don't even see them." With a sigh, she traced her hands down him, lingering over every plane and angle. "I only see you."

"The stars are out. Millions of them. You can smell Paris. It's rich…water and flowers. We'd walk for miles so you could see all those incredible lights and wonderful ancient buildings. We'd stop and drink wine in a café at a table with an umbrella. Then we'd go back and make love again, for hours and hours."

His lips came back to hers, drugging her. "We don't need Paris for that."

"No." He braced himself over her, bracketing her head between his hands. Her face was already glowing, her eyes were half closed, that soft smile was on her lips. He wanted to remember this, this one instant when there was nothing and no one but her.

"Oh, God, Libby, I need you."

It was all she needed to hear, all she would ever ask to hear. She reached up to enfold him.

There was urgency here. She could taste it as his tongue plunged deep into her mouth, demanding. Impatient, his hands molded her body. Because his feelings mirrored her own, her response was explosive. Her blood was molten, throbbing as it flowed close under her skin. The heat was unbearable. Delicious. It grew only more intense as he stripped her.

A primitive sound hummed deep in her throat. With a speed and fury that rocked him, she was yanking off his shirt, dragging his jeans over his hips. Desperate, she rolled, reversing their positions, making a fast, hot journey over him. She heard his breath catch, and the sound sent her excitement soaring to new heights.

Power. It was indeed the ultimate aphrodisiac. She could make him tremble and ache and whisper her name. She'd never known that with such little effort she could make him helpless.

And he was beautiful. The feel of him under her hands, the taste of him that lingered on her tongue. And strong. There were ridges of muscles, firm, tight. But they trembled under the delicate dance of her fingertips.

He'd wanted to make her remember. Cal groaned under the weight of the sensations she was bringing to him. It was he who would remember, always. The music that he had always loved, the simple eloquence of it, filled his head. He knew it would remind him of her from now to forever.

He could feel the heat radiate from her as she moved her body up his, searching, finding his mouth. Her kiss was slow, sultry, something he could drown in. Then she was laughing, evading his questing hands as she drove him toward madness again.

He couldn't bear it. His heart was pounding against his ribs, echoed by dozens of frantic pulses throughout his body. The rhythm seemed to call out her name, again and again, until he was filled with it.

"Libby." The word was hoarse, as raw as his need. "For God's sake."

Then she closed over him like hot velvet. The sound she made was hardly more than a moan, but it vibrated with triumph. Lost in her own pleasure, she set a wild pace, feeling her strength bound high, then higher, as her need swelled.

A free-fall through space, a springboard through time. He'd experienced both, but they were nothing compared with this. Blindly he reached for her, and his hands slid down her slick skin. Just as their palms met, they leaped over the top together.

Perfection. Lazily content, Libby cuddled closer, resting her cheek just over Cal's heart, all but purring as he stroked her hair.

Soothed. Every part of her was content. Body, mind, heart. She wondered how long it was possible for two people to lie curled in bed without food or water. Forever. She smiled to herself. She could almost believe it.

"My parents have a cat," she murmured. "A fat yellow cat named Marigold. He doesn't have an ounce of ambition."

"A male cat named Marigold?"

Still smiling, she ran a hand down his arm. "You met my parents."

"Right."

"Anyway, he lies on the windowsill every afternoon. All afternoon. Right this minute I know exactly how he feels." She stretched, only a little, because even that seemed to require too much effort. "I like your bed, Hornblower."

"I've grown fond of it myself."

They were silent for a while, drifting. "That music." It was playing in her head now, sweet, almost unbearably romantic. "I keep thinking I should recognize it."

"Salvadore Simeon."

"Is he a new composer?"

"Depends on your point of view. Late twenty-first century."

"Oh." Her bubble burst. Sometimes forever was a very short time. Holding on one last moment, she turned her head to press her lips to his chest. His heart beat there, strong and steady. "Poetry, classical music and aircycles. An interesting combination."

"Is it?"

"Yes, very. I also know you're hooked on soaps and game shows."

"That's research." He grinned as she pushed herself to a sitting position beside him. "I want to be able to speak intelligently on all popular forms of twentieth-century entertainment." He paused a moment, thinking. "Do you suppose they kept archives? I really want to know if Blake and Eva work things out in spite of Dorian's conniving. Then there's the problem of who's framing Justin for the murder of the evil and despicable Carlton Slade. I vote for the sweet-faced but hard-hearted Vanessa."

"Hooked," she said again, and drew her knees up to her chest to grin at him. "Don't you have soaps?"

"Sure. Never took the time to watch. I always figured they were for homeworkers."

"Homeworkers." She repeated it, liking the precise, genderless phrase. "I haven't asked you all those questions." Libby settled her chin on her knees. "When we get back we should finish writing up everything that's happened to you."

He flicked a finger down her arm. "Everything?"

"Everything that applies. While we're doing that, and putting the capsule together, you can fill me in on the future."

"All right." He climbed out of bed. Maybe it would be best if they stayed busy for the next few hours. He started to reach for his pants, then noticed the Polaroid, which had fallen to the floor. "What's this?"

"A camera. Self-developing. You can have a picture in about ten seconds."

"Is that so?" Amused, he turned it over in his hands. He'd been given one for his tenth birthday that could do precisely the same thing—and it had fitted into the palm of his hand. It had also kept the time, reported the temperature and played his favorite music.

"You've got that superior smirk on your face again, Hornblower."

"Sorry. What do you do? Push this button?"

"That's right— No!" But she was too late. He'd already framed her and shot. "Men have been murdered for less."

"I thought you wanted pictures," he said reasonably as he held the developing image in his hand.

"I'm not dressed."

"Yeah." He smiled. "It's not bad," he decided. "One-dimensional, but it gets the point across. A very sexy point across."

Snatching at the sheet, she scrambled to the foot of the bed and made a grab.

"You want to see?" He held the print tantalizingly out of reach but turned it so that Libby saw herself, her arms hooked around her bare legs, her hair tousled, her eyes heavy. "God, I love it when you blush, Libby."

"I'm not blushing." She told herself she wasn't laughing, either, as she tugged on her clothes. Cal set the camera aside and tugged them off her again.

When they left the ship, the shadows were long. After a brief discussion they decided to strap Cal's cycle to the back of the Land Rover and drive back together.

"It's a good idea," Libby allowed. "If we had some rope."

"What for?" Turning a knob under the seat of the cycle, Cal pulled out two thick, hooked straps.

Libby shrugged. "Well, I suppose if you want to do it the easy way." She bent over the back wheel, planted her feet and braced herself.

"What are you doing?"

"I'm going to help you lift it." She took a firm grip and blew the hair out of her eyes. "Well, come on."

Cal tucked his tongue into his cheek. "Okay, but don't strain yourself."

"Do you have any idea how much equipment we lug around on digs?"

He smiled at her. "No."

"Plenty. On three. One, two, three!" She let out an astonished breath as they lifted the cycle shoulder-high. It couldn't have weighed more than thirty pounds. "You're a riot, Hornblower."

"Thanks." He secured the cycle quickly. "You going to let me drive this time?" When she dug the keys out of her pocket and jiggled them, he went into his pitch. "Come on, Libby, there's no one around."

"Be that as it may, you never showed me a driver's license."

"If we're talking technicalities, I don't think it would apply. Libby, if I can pilot that—" he jerked his thumb in the direction of the ship "—I sure as hell can drive this. I want to see what it's like."

She tossed him the keys. "Just remember, this vehicle stays on the ground."

"Got it." As pleased as a kid with a new toy, he settled behind the wheel. "It works with gears, right?"

"I believe so."

"Fascinating. This pedal here?"

"The clutch," she said, and wondered if she'd just taken her life in her hands.

"The clutch, right. That's what disengages the system so that you can change gears. Higher gears for higher speeds. That's the idea, isn't it?"

"The other pedal? The one beside it? That's the

brake. Pay attention to the brake, Hornblower. Pay very close attention.''

''Don't worry about a thing.'' He sent her a cocky grin, then turned the key. ''See?'' They went in reverse for two fast feet before they came to a jarring stop. ''Just a minute. I think I've got it now.''

''You've got to put it in off-road.''

''Off what?''

Though her palms were slightly damp, she showed him. ''Take it easy, will you? And try to go forward.''

''No problem.'' The Land Rover bucked the first few feet, causing Libby to grip the dash with both hands and pray. Cal was having the time of his life, and he was a little disappointed when the ride smoothed out. ''Nothing to it.'' He sent her a cocky grin.

''Just watch where you're going. Oh, God!'' She tossed her hands in front of her face so that she wouldn't see the tree they were about to ram.

''Are you always a nervous passenger?'' he asked conversationally as he maneuvered around the tree.

''I could grow to hate you. I'm sure of it.''

''Loosen up, babe. Let's take a little detour.''

''Cal, we should—''

''Run for the gusto,'' he finished. ''Isn't that the phrase?''

''I think it's 'Go for the gusto,' but this isn't a beer commercial.'' She bit her lip and clung to her safety belt. ''Anyway, you can keep it. I think I'd rather live a long, dull life.''

He plunged down a rocky slope, driving as if he'd been born behind the wheel. ''This is the next best thing to flying.'' He shot her a look. ''Well, maybe not the next best, but it's close.''

''I think several of my vital organs have jarred loose. Cal, you're going to go right through that—'' The water swooshed up, two glittering curtains on either side of the Land Rover. Libby was drenched when he shot up the opposite bank. ''Stream,'' she muttered, dragging her soaked hair out of her eyes.

As wet as she was, he gave a delighted whoop and swung around to go through the stream again. She heard her own laughter as the water slapped over her a second time.

''You're crazy.'' They left the ground briefly, then jolted down with a thud. ''But you're not dull.''

''You know, with a few modifications, this would go over big at home. I can't figure out why they don't make them anymore. If I came up with a prototype I could send my credit rating through the ozone.''

''You're not taking it with you. I still have fourteen payments to make.''

''Just a thought.'' He could have driven for hours. But the air was chill and she was beginning to shiver. Cal circled back.

''Do you know where we are?''

''Sure, about twenty degrees northeast of the ship.'' He tugged on her wet hair. ''I told you I could navigate. Tell you what, when we get back we'll take a hot shower. Then we can build a fire and have some of that brandy. Then we can—'' He swore and hit the brakes hard. A group of four in hiking gear was a few feet ahead.

''Damn,'' Libby muttered. ''We hardly ever get

anyone this close in so early in the season." It took
only a glance for her to determine that the price tags
had hardly been removed from the packs and boots.

"If they hike much farther in that direction, they'll
be on top of the ship."

Libby swallowed a bubble of panic and smiled as
the group approached. "Hello."

"Well, hi there." The man, big, solid and fortyish,
leaned on the Land Rover. "You're the first people
we've seen since morning."

"We don't get many hikers up this way."

"That's why we picked it. Right, Susie?" He patted a pretty, exhausted-looking woman on the shoulder. Her only answer was a very weary nod. "Rankin.
Jim Rankin." He took Cal's hand and pumped it.
"My wife, Susie and our boys, Scott and Joe."

"Nice meeting you. Cal Hornblower. Libby
Stone."

"Out four-wheeling it, huh?"

Noting Cal's blank look, Libby said, "Yes, we
were about to head in."

"Backpacking's for us." Jim grinned broadly.

It took less than ten seconds to see that only Jim
was enthusiastic about tackling the mountains on foot.
That might be an advantage. "How far have you
come?"

"Started off from Big Vista. Nice little campground, but too crowded. I wanted to show the wife
and boys nature in the rough."

Libby judged the boys to be about thirteen and fifteen, and both looked as if they were on the edge of
whining. Calculating the distance to the Big Vista

campground, she could hardly blame them. "That's quite a hike."

"We're tough. Right, boys?" Both sent him miserable looks.

"You weren't planning to go up this path?" Libby asked, gesturing.

"Matter of fact, we were. Thought we'd try for the ridge before nightfall."

Susie groaned and bent over to massage an aching calf muscle.

"You won't be able to reach it this way. Up ahead's a logging and reforesting area. Did you see the break in the trees?"

"Yeah, I did." He fiddled with the pedometer at his waist. "Wondered about it."

"Harvesting," she said without a blink. "Hiking and camping are off-limits. There's a five-hundred-dollar fine," she added for good measure.

"Well, I sure do appreciate you letting us know."

"Dad, can't we go to a hotel?" one of the boys asked.

"One with a pool," the other chimed in. "And a video arcade."

"And a bed," his wife murmured. "A real bed."

Jim offered Cal and Libby a wink. "Family gets a little cranky this time of day. Wait till you see that sun come up tomorrow, gang. It'll all be worth it."

"There's an easy trail to the west." Libby rose out of her seat to rest her hip on the side of the Land Rover. "Do you see it?"

"Yeah." Jim didn't like adjusting his itinerary, but the five hundred had done the trick.

She was glad she could give them one with a grad-
ual incline. "Another, oh, three-four miles, and
there's a clearing, makes a good campsite. The view's
fabulous. You shouldn't have any trouble making it
before sundown."

"We could give you a lift." Cal had noted the
tired, sulky look on the younger boy's face. The moment the offer was out, it lifted into an engaging grin.

"Oh, no, no, thanks all the same." Jim beamed.
"That would be cheating, wouldn't it?"

"Maybe." Susie shifted her pack on her aching
back. "But it might just save your life." She nudged
her husband aside and leaned toward Cal. "Mr. Hornblower, if you drive us to that campsite, you can name
your price."

"Now, Susie—"

"Shut up, Jim." She grabbed a hunk of Cal's damp
shirt. "Please. I've got four hundred and fifty-eight
dollars worth of gear on my back. It's yours."

With a hearty laugh, Jim put a hand on his wife's
arm. "Now, Susie. We agreed—"

"All bets are off." Her voice rose shrilly. In an
obvious effort to control it, she drew a deep breath.
"I'm dying here, Jim. I think the boys might be trau-
matized for life. You don't want to be responsible for
that, do you?" Because she wasn't entirely sure of
his answer, she jerked away to tuck each boy under
her arms. "You hike it," she said. "But I've got blis-
ters, and I don't think I'll ever regain the feeling in
my left leg."

"Suze, if I'd known you felt this way—"

"Fine." She wasn't willing to give him time to

finish a single sentence. "Now you do. Come on, guys."

They crammed into the back of the Land Rover. After a moment, Jim settled sadly in with them, his youngest on his lap.

"It's, ah, beautiful country," Libby began as she directed Cal along the trail. "You'll probably appreciate it more after you've rested and eaten." And a great deal more than that, she was sure, when Susie discovered they had circled a couple of miles closer to Big Vista.

"It's certainly full of trees." Susie sighed at the luxury of moving without effort. Because she knew Jim was sulking, she patted his knee. "Are you from around here?"

"Originally." Confident that Cal would find the way now, she shifted to face their passengers. "Cal's from Philadelphia."

"Really?" Susie debated flexing her foot, then decided not to risk it. "So are we. Is this your first time out here, Mr. Hornblower?"

"Yes, I guess you could say it's my first time here."

"Ours, too. We wanted to show our sons a part of the country that was still unspoiled. And we have." She gave her husband's knee another squeeze.

Resilient, Jim swung an arm over the back of the seat. "This is one trip they won't forget."

The boys exchanged looks and rolled their eyes but wisely kept silent. There was still a chance for that hotel.

"So, you're from Philadelphia. What do you think of the Phillies' chances this year?"

Cautious, Cal tried to be noncommittal. "I'm always hopeful."

"That's the ticket." Jim slapped Cal on the shoulder. "If they tighten up the infield and beef up the pitching staff they might have a shot."

Baseball, Cal realized with a grin. At least that was something he could relate to. "It's hard to say about this season, but I figure we'll take our share of pennants in the next couple hundred years."

Jim gave a bark of laughter. "That's taking the long view."

When they reached the clearing, their passengers were all in a more cheerful state of mind. The boys leaped out to chase after a rabbit. Susie stepped out more slowly, still favoring her legs.

"It is beautiful." She looked out over the layers of mountains, where the sun was hanging low. "I can't thank you enough, both of you." She glanced over to where her husband was already yelling at the boys to get busy and gather some firewood. "You saved my husband's life."

"He looked in pretty good shape, actually," Cal commented.

"No. I was going to kill him in his sleep." She smiled as she eased the pack from her back. "Now I won't have to, at least for a couple of days."

Jovial, Jim walked back to give his wife a hug. She winced as he squeezed tender muscles. "I tell you, Suze, a man can really breathe up here."

"For the time being," Susie murmured.

"Not like Philadelphia, bless it. Why don't you two stay for supper? Nothing like eating under the sky."

"You're very welcome to," Susie added. "On tonight's menu are the ever-popular beans, with the addition of hot dogs if the cold pack worked, and for dessert some delicious dehydrated apricots."

"Sounds great." And part of him was tempted to stay, just to sit and listen. He thought the Rankin family as entertaining as any daytime drama. "But we've got to get back."

Libby offered her hand to Susie and added a sympathetic pat. "If you follow the trail to the right it'll take you back to Big Vista. It's a long hike, but a pretty one." And one that would take them in the opposite direction from the ship.

"Can't thank you enough." Jim dug into his backpack and pulled out a business card. The gesture had Libby smothering a chuckle. You could take a boy out of the smog, but... "Give me a ring when you get back, Hornblower. I'm sales manager at Bison Motors. Cut you and the little woman a good deal, new or used."

"I'll keep it in mind." They climbed back into the Land Rover, offered a wave, then left the Rankins behind. "New or used what?" Cal asked Libby.

Chapter 12

Cal thought quite a bit about the Rankins. He had asked Libby if they were an average American family. Her response had been amused. If there was such a phenomenon, she'd told him, they probably fit it.

They interested him perhaps because he saw several parallels between them and his own family. His father, though no one would ever have confused him with big, beaming Jim Rankin, had always had a love of nature, unspoiled land and family trips. Like the other boys, Cal and Jacob had spent a good deal of time sulking, whining and rolling their eyes. And when the chips were down and the limit was reached, it had always been Cal's mother who had laid down the law.

Families, it seemed, were consistent over time. It was a comforting thought.

They had had their fire and brandy when they had

returned to the cabin. Then, because Libby was always one to organize, they had gone up to her machine to finish the report.

They would need three copies. The first for the capsule, the second for the ship—and Cal—and the third for Libby.

He'd had to admire her style when he'd read over what she'd done. There was no doubt in his mind that the scientists of his time would find Libby's report both concise and fascinating. The rest was largely technical, and though he knew she couldn't understand the calculations he was feeding her, she typed them out.

They'd spent hours over it, refining, perfecting, taking long periods when she would question him on the social, the political, the cultural climate of his time. She made him think about things he had taken for granted, about others he had casually ignored.

Yes, there was still poverty, but shelters and programs provided the very poor with a roof and a meal. There was still conflict, but all-out war had been avoided for more than 120 years. Politics were still argued over, babies were still cuddled. People complained that the skyways were too crowded. As far as Cal remembered there had been four, or it might have been five, women who had held the office of president.

The more questions he answered, the more she thought of. They fell asleep tangled together in bed in the middle of one of his answers.

They finished the time capsule late the next morning, filling the airtight steel box Libby had bought in town with what seemed most pertinent. One copy of the report was wrapped in plastic before they set it inside. Libby added one of her mother's woven mats and a clay bowl her father had made when she'd been a baby. They added a newspaper, a popular weekly magazine and, at Cal's insistence, a wooden spoon from the kitchen drawer. She added one of the two pictures she'd taken of his ship.

"We need more," Libby muttered.

"I wanted this." He held up a tube of toothpaste. "And I was hoping for some of your underwear."

"Yes to the first, no to the second."

"It's for science," he reminded her.

"Not a chance. We need a tool. We're always very pleased when we find a tool on a dig." She rummaged through a drawer and came up with a screwdriver, a small ball peen hammer and a pipe wrench. "Take your pick."

He took the wrench. "How about a book?"

"Terrific." She dashed into the living room and began combing the shelves. "I want popular fiction, something written in this era. Ah…Stephen King."

"I've read him. Terrifying."

"Horror transcends time, as well." She brought it into the kitchen and placed it in the box. "If they do any tests, they'll be able to date all of this material. It will back up your story. Come on outside, we'll take some pictures."

Because he got to the camera before her, Cal claimed his right to take the first shots. He snapped the cabin, Libby and the cabin, Libby beside the Land

Rover, in the Land Rover. Libby laughing at him. And yelling at him.

"Do you know how much film you've used?" Blowing out a breath, she ripped open another pack. "This stuff averages a dollar a shot. Anthropology's a fascinating field, but the pay's lousy."

"Sorry." He moved to the front of the cabin when she waved with the back of her hand. "I never thought to ask. What's your credit rating?"

"I have no idea." She took a shot of him standing, thumbs hooked in the pockets of his borrowed jeans. "We don't do things that way now. At least I think credit rating means something else. Now it's a matter of what you're worth, or what you make. Annual salary and that sort of thing." She was enough her parents' child that she rarely gave it much thought. "Why don't you unstrap your cycle and sit on it in front of the cabin? A now-and-then sort of thing."

He obliged. "Libby, I don't have any way to pay you back, in your currency, for all of this."

"Don't be silly. It was only a joke."

"There's a great deal more I can't pay you back for."

"There's nothing to pay back." She lowered the camera and weighed each word carefully. "Don't think of it as an obligation. Please. And don't look at me like that. I'm not ready to be serious."

"We don't have much time left."

"I know." She hadn't understood everything he'd dictated to her the night before, but she knew he would be gone before the sun rose the next day. "Let's not spoil what we have." She looked away to give herself a moment to regain her balance. "It's a shame this model doesn't have a timer. It would be nice to get a couple of pictures with both of us in them."

"Hold on." He walked around the side of the building, returning a few moments later with a garden hoe. "Sit on the steps," he told her, then proceeded to strap the camera to the seat of his cycle. He leaned over, checking and adjusting until he had Libby in frame. "Got it." Pleased with himself, he jogged over to sit beside her. He wrapped an arm around her shoulders. "Smile."

She already was.

He used the staff of the hoe to press the button, grinning when he heard the shutter click. The print slid out.

"Very inventive, Hornblower."

"Don't move."

He retrieved the first print, settled back beside her and pressed again.

"One for you, one for the box." He set both prints aside. "And one for me." He tipped her face up to his with his finger and kissed her.

"You forgot to take the picture," she murmured many moments later.

"Oh, yeah." His lips curved against hers as he poked with the hoe.

She took the first print in her hand and studied it. They looked happy, she thought. Happy, ordinary people. It meant a great deal to her now, and would mean even more to her later. She continued to hold it as she rose. "We'd better go bury the capsule."

They strapped it on the back of the cycle so that Libby was sandwiched between it and Cal's back. When they reached the stream, he slipped off and frowned at the shovel she handed him.

"This tool is very primitive. Are you sure there's no easier way?"

"Not in this century, Hornblower." She pointed down. "Dig."

"You can have the first turn."

"That's all right." She sat on the ground and tucked up her legs. "I wouldn't want to deprive you."

She watched him put his back into it. What would he use, she wondered, to dig it up again? How would he feel when he opened it? He would be thinking of her, she knew that. And he would miss her. She hoped he would sit in this same spot and read the letter she had tucked into the box. She'd made certain he hadn't seen her put it in.

It was only a page, but she'd put her heart on it.

She cupped her chin in her hand, listened to the water's music and remembered every word.

Cal. When you read this, you'll be home. I want you to know how happy I am for you. I can't claim to understand what it was like for you to find yourself here, away from everything familiar, separated from your family and friends. But I wanted you to know that in my heart I wanted you to be where you belonged.

I don't know if I can make you understand what the time I've had with you has meant to me. I love you so much, Caleb. It overwhelms me. There won't be a day that goes by that I won't think of you. But I won't be unhappy. Please don't think of me, or remember me that way. What you gave to me in these few days is more than I ever imagined, all I ever needed. Whenever I look at the sky, I'll picture you.

I'll still study the past to try to understand why man is what he is. Now, having known you, I'll always have hope for what he can become.

Be happy. I want to know you are. Don't forget me. I wanted to put a sprig of rosemary in the capsule, but I was afraid it would only turn to dust. Find some, and think of me. "Pray, love, remember."

Libby.

"Libby?" Cal leaned against the shovel, watching her.

"Yes?"

"Where were you?"

"Oh, not very far away." Glancing down, she lifted a brow. "Well, I knew a big strong man like you could dig a hole."

"I think I have a blister."

"Aw." She rose to kiss the tender skin between his thumb and forefinger. "Let's put it in. Then you can watch while I cover it up."

"Good idea." The moment the box was in, he handed her the shovel. Libby eyed it, then the pile of dirt that had to be replaced.

"Four women presidents?"

He stretched his tired back. "Might have been five."

With a nod, Libby began to shovel. "Cal?"

"Hmm?" He was giving serious consideration to a nice, lazy nap.

"The questions I asked before, those were the big ones, the sweeping ones. I wondered if I could ask you something more personal."

"Probably."

"Would you tell me about your family?"

"What would you like to know?"

"Who they are, what they're like." She tossed dirt into the hole in a steady rhythm that Cal enjoyed. "I'd like to imagine I knew them a little."

"My father's a research and development technician. Lab work, all indoors and confining. He's very dedicated, dependable. At home he likes to garden, plants flowers from seed and works them all by hand."

As he drew in the scent of the freshly turned earth that Libby worked, Cal could almost see his father cultivating his garden.

"Sometimes he paints. Really, *really* bad landscapes and still lifes. He even knows they're bad, but he claims art doesn't have to be good to be art. He's always threatening to hang one of them in the house. He's...I don't know, steady. I doubt I've heard him raise his voice more than a dozen times in my life. But you listen to him. He's like the adhesive that kept the family centered."

He stretched out on the grass to watch the sky as he continued. "My mother is...what was that term you used once? Wired? She's packed with energy and a blazing intellect that's almost scary. She intimidates a lot of people. She's always amused by that. I guess because inside she's soft as butter. She raised her voice plenty, but she always felt guilty about it. Jacob and I gave her a hell of a time.

"In her free time she likes to read—flashy novels or impossibly technical books. She's chief counsel for the United Ministry of Nations, so she's always poring over some six-inch pile of legal documents."

"The United Ministry of Nations?"

"I guess you'd call it an extension of the UN. It had to be expanded in...hell, I don't know when. I think it was expanded because of the colonies and settlements."

"It sounds like a very prestigious position." Libby discovered she was already intimidated.

"Yes. She thrives on it. On the work and the worry. She's got a great laugh—one of those big fill-the-room kind of laughs. They met in Dublin. She was practicing law there, and my father went over for a vacation. They matched and ended up in Philadelphia."

Libby tamped down the dirt. It had been impossible not to hear the affection in his voice, impossible not to understand it. "What about your brother?"

"Jacob. He's...intense is a good word. He gets his brain from my mother, and his temperament, she claims, from her grandfather. You're never quite sure with J.T. whether he's going to grin at you or throw a punch. He studied law and then, when he'd had his fill of it, dived into astrophysics. He collects problems so that he can pick them apart. He's a sonofabitch,"

Cal said affectionately, "but he has my father's unswerving, immeasurable sense of loyalty."

"Do you like them?" When Cal looked up, she elaborated. "What I mean is, most people love their family, but they aren't necessarily friends with them. I wondered if you liked them."

"Yes, I do." He watched as she strapped the shovel back on the cycle. "They'd like you."

"I could meet them if you took me with you." She bit her lip the moment the words were out. She couldn't turn around to look at him. She couldn't have said just when the thought had hatched in her mind.

"Libby—" He was up and standing behind her, his hands hovering over her shoulders.

"I've studied the past," she said quickly, turning and gripping his forearms. "If you let me come with you, it would give me the chance to study the future."

He framed her face with his hands. There was a glint of tears in her eyes. "And your family?"

"They'd understand. I'd leave them a letter, try to explain."

"They'd never believe you," he said quietly. "They'd spend years looking for you, wondering if you were still alive. Libby, can't you see that's what's tearing me apart about my own? They don't know where I am or what's happened to me. I know by now they're waiting to hear if I'm dead or alive."

"I'll make them understand." She heard the desperation in her own voice and fought to steady it. "If they know I'm happy, that I'm doing what I want to do, they'll be satisfied with that."

"Maybe. Yes, if they were sure. But I can't take you, Libby."

She made her hands drop away and stepped back. "No, of course not. I don't know what I was thinking of. I got caught up—"

"Damn it, don't." Grabbing her arms, he hauled her against him. "Don't think I don't want you, because I do. It's not a choice of right or wrong, Libby. If I could be sure, if there were no risks involved, I might toss you on the damn ship whether you wanted to go with me or not."

"Risks?" She'd stiffened at the word, and now she drew back. "What risks?"

"Nothing's foolproof."

"Don't treat me like a fool. What risks?"

He let out a long breath. There was a calculation he hadn't given her the night before. "The probability factor for a successful time warp is 76.4."

"76.4," she repeated. "It doesn't take a genius to figure out that leaves 23.6 as the factor for failure. What happens if you fail?"

"I don't know." But he could make a good guess. Frying in the sun's gravitational pull was one of the less painful possibilities. "And I won't take chances with you, no matter how much I want you with me."

She wasn't going to panic, because panic wouldn't help. Taking three deep breaths, she felt some balance return. "Caleb, if you gave yourself a little more time, do you think you could narrow the odds?"

"Maybe. Probably," he conceded. "Libby, I'm running out of time. The ship's already been in the open for two weeks. It was blind luck that we headed off the Rankins yesterday. What do you think would happen to me, to us, if it were found? If I were found?''

''The real season doesn't start for weeks. We hardly get more than a dozen hikers in a year.''

''It only takes one.''

He was right, and she knew it. They'd been living on borrowed time right from the start. ''I'll never know, will I?'' She traced a finger under the fading wound on his brow. ''Whether you made it.''

''I'm a good pilot. Trust me.'' He kissed her fingers. ''And it'll be easier for me to concentrate if I'm not worried about you.''

''It's hard to argue with common sense.'' She worked up a smile. ''I know you said you had a few last details to see to at the ship. I'm just going to walk back to the cabin.''

''I won't be long.''

''Take your time.'' She needed some of her own. ''I'll fix a bon voyage supper.'' She started off at an easy gait, then called over her shoulder, ''Oh, Hornblower, pick me some flowers.''

He picked an armful. It wasn't easy balancing them as he flew the cycle. The path beneath him was strewn with white and pink and pale blue blossoms. He thought they smelled like her—fresh, earthy, exotic.

In the hours he'd worked aboard ship one thought had run continually through his mind. She'd been willing to go with him. To leave her home. Not just her home, he corrected. Her life.

Perhaps it had been impulse, something that had been born of the moment.

Reasons didn't matter. He needed to hold on to that one sweet thought. She'd been willing to go with him.

He saw only the faintest light through the kitchen window. That had him frowning as he stored his bike and retrieved a few of the fallen flowers. Perhaps she'd decided to take a nap or was waiting for him in the front of the cabin by the fire.

He liked the idea of seeing her there, curled up on the couch under one of her mother's exquisite throws. She'd be reading, her eyes a little sleepy behind her glasses.

Pleased with the image, he opened the door and found a completely different, and even more alluring, one.

She was waiting for him. But it was candlelight. She was still lighting them, dozens of them, all pure white. The table was set for two, and a bottle of champagne sat nestled in a clear bucket. The room smelled of candles, of the spices she'd used for cooking, and of her.

She turned to smile at him, and he felt the breath quite simply leave his body.

Her hair was swept up off her neck so that he could see the long, delicate curve. She wore a dress the color of moonlight that glittered at the bodice as she moved. It left her shoulders bare, then slipped like a lover down her hips and thighs.

"You remembered." She crossed to him, holding out her arms for the flowers. He didn't move a muscle. "Are they for me?"

"What? Yes." Like a man in a trance, he offered them to her. "There were more when I started out."

"This is more than enough." She had a vase waiting, and she filled it. "Dinner's almost ready. I hope you like it."

"You dazzle me, Liberty."

She turned back, electrified by what she saw in his eyes. "I wanted to, just once." When he just continued to stare, her shyness rose up and had her twisting her fingers. "I bought the champagne and the dress while I was in town yesterday. I thought it would be nice to do something a little special tonight."

"I'm afraid if I move you'll vanish."

"No." She offered her hand and gripped hard when he took it. "I'll stay right here. Why don't you open the bottle?"

"I want to kiss you first."

Her heart went into her smile as she wound her arms around his neck. "All right. Just once."

They ate. But the trouble she had gone to over the meal was wasted. They didn't know what they were tasting. Champagne was superfluous. They were already drunk on each other. The candles burned down low while they lingered.

They carried some up to the bedroom, filling the room with the soft, flickering light so that they could watch each other as they loved.

There was sweetness, slow, savoring sweetness. There was urgency, fevered, racing urgency. There was power and tenderness, demand and generosity.

Hour melted into hour, but they never drew apart. Each tremble, each sigh, each heartbeat would be remembered. The candles guttered out, but they were still wrapped together.

Then, though the words were never spoken, they knew it was the last time. His hands seemed that much more gentle, her lips that much softer.

When it was over, the beauty left her weak and weepy. In defense, she curled against him and prayed for sleep. She couldn't bear to watch him go.

He lay still, wakeful until the first faint hints of light crept into the room. He was grateful she slept; he would never have been able to say goodbye. When he rose it hurt, a sharp, sweet ache that rocked him. Moving quickly, struggling to keep his mind blank, he pulled on the jumpsuit she'd set out for him.

Afraid of waking her, he touched only her hair, then moved quietly out of the room. Libby opened her eyes only when she heard the soft click of the cabin door. Turning her face into the pillow, she let the tears come.

The ship was secured, and the calculations were plotted. Cal sat on the bridge and watched night fade. It was important that he take off before sunrise. He had the timing down to a millisecond. There was little room for error. His life depended on it.

But his thoughts kept drifting back to Libby. Why hadn't he known it would hurt this badly to leave? Yet he had to leave. His life, his time, weren't here with hers. There was no use going over again what he had already agonized over a dozen times.

Still, he sat while precious moments clicked away.
Prepare for standard orbital flight.

''Yes,'' he told the computer absently. Instruments began to hum. In a way that was second nature to him, Cal prepared for take off. He paused again, staring at the viewscreen.

All systems ready. Ignition at your discretion.

''Right. Commence countdown.''

Commencing. Ten, nine, eight, seven...

From the kitchen doorway, Libby heard the rumble. Impatient, she rubbed tears from her eyes and strained to see. There was a flash. She thought she caught a quick glint of metal streaking across the lightening sky. Then it was gone. The woods were quiet again.

She shivered. She wished she could convince herself it was because the air was chill and she was wearing only her short blue robe.

''Be safe,'' she murmured. Then gave in and allowed herself the luxury of a few more tears.

Life went on, she lectured herself. The birds were beginning to sing. The sun was nearly up.

She wanted to die.

That was nonsense. Shaking herself, she set the kettle on to boil. She was going to have a cup of tea, wash the dishes they'd been too careless to notice the night before. Then she was going back to work.

She would work until she couldn't keep her eyes open, and then she would sleep. She would get up again and work again until her dissertation was complete. It would be the best damn paper her colleagues had ever read. And then she'd travel.

And she would miss him until the day she died.

When the kettle boiled, she poured her tea, then sat

with it at the kitchen table. After a moment, she shoved it aside, laid her head on her folded hands and wept again.

"Libby."

She knocked the chair over as she rose. He was there, standing in the doorway, fatigue all over his face and something, something much more powerful, in his eyes. She rubbed hers. He couldn't be there.

"Caleb?"

"Why are you crying?"

She heard him. Dazed, she pressed a hand against her ear. "Caleb." She repeated. "But how—I heard, I saw— You're gone."

"Have you been crying since I left?" He stepped toward her but only touched a fingertip to her damp cheek.

His touch was real. If she was mad, she accepted it. "I don't understand. How can you be here?"

"I have a question to ask you first." He dropped his hands to his sides. "Just one question. Are you in love with me?"

"I—I need to sit down."

"No." He caught her arm and held her still. "I want an answer. Are you in love with me?"

"Yes. Only an idiot would have to ask."

He smiled, but his grip held firm. "Why didn't you ever tell me?"

"Because I didn't want—I knew you had to go." Dizzy, she put a hand to her head. "Let me sit."

He released her, then watched her sink unsteadily into a chair.

"I haven't slept," she murmured, as if to herself. "I suppose I could be hallucinating."

He tilted her head back, then planted a hard, bruising kiss on her mouth. Before he could stop himself, he dragged her halfway out of the chair. "Is that real enough for you?"

"Yes," she said weakly. "Yes. But I don't understand. How can you be here?"

He let her go again. "I rode the cycle."

"No, I mean..." What did she mean? "I was standing at the door. I heard you take off. I even saw, just a glimpse, but I saw the ship in the sky."

"I sent it back. The computer's at the helm."

"You sent it back," she repeated slowly. "Oh, my God, Caleb, why?"

"Only an idiot would have to ask."

Her eyes filled and spilled over. "No, not for me. I can't bear it. Your family—"

"I left a disk for them. I told them everything, a great deal more than what's in the report I left on board. Where I was, why I had to stay. If the ship makes it back, and it has as good a chance without me as it did with me, they'll understand."

"I can't ask you to do this."

"You didn't." He took her hand before she could turn away again. "You would have gone with me, wouldn't you, Libby?"

"Yes."

"I might have taken you up on that if I'd been sure we would have lived through it. Listen to me." He drew her to her feet. "I'd started countdown. I'd convinced myself that my life was back there where I'd

left it. There were a dozen logical reasons why I had
to go. And there was one, only one, reason I had to
stay. I love you. My life is here.'' He tightened his
grip, brought her close. ''I came through time for you,
Libby. Don't ever, ever think I made a mistake.''

She shook her head. ''I'm afraid you'll think so.''

'' 'Time is… Time was… Time is past,' '' he murmured. ''My time is in the past, Libby. With you.''

Her eyes filmed over again. ''I love you so much,
Caleb. I'll make you happy.''

''I'm counting on it.'' He picked her up, pausing
to capture her mouth in a long, long kiss. ''You need
sleep,'' he told her. ''Real sleep.''

''No, I don't.''

He laughed, and the last vestige of tension fled. He
was exactly where he belonged. ''We'll see. Later
we'll talk about how we're going to handle the rest
of this.''

''Rest?''

''The marriage-and-family part I can handle.''

''You haven't asked me yet.''

''I'll get around to it. Anyway, I'm going to need
new ID. Then I've got to get a job. Something with
a—an annual salary, right?''

''Something you enjoy,'' she corrected. ''That's
more important than salary and group hospitaliza-
tion.''

''Group what?''

''Don't worry about it.'' She nuzzled into his neck.
''I suppose Dad could give you some kind of position
until you figure it all out.''

''I don't think I want to make tea.'' Suddenly inspired, he stopped by the side of the bed. ''Tell me, how do you go about getting a pilot's license around here?''

* * * * *

TIMES CHANGE

For Isabel,
Who's always been ahead of her time

Chapter 1

He knew the risks. He was a man who was willing to take them. One misstep, one bad call, and it would all be over, essentially before it had begun. But he had always considered life a gamble. Often—perhaps too often—he had allowed his impulses to rule and plunged recklessly into potentially dangerous situations. In this case, he had figured the odds painstakingly.

Two years of his life had been spent calculating, simulating, constructing. The most minute details had been considered, computed and analyzed. He was a very patient man—when it came to his work. He knew what *could* happen. Now it was time to discover what would.

More than a few of his associates believed he had crossed the line between genius and madness. Even those who were enthusiastic about his theories worried that he'd gone too far. Popular opinion didn't concern him. Results did. And results of this, the greatest experience of his life, would be personal. Very personal.

Seated behind the wide curve of the control panel, he looked more like a buccaneer at the helm of a ship than a scientist on the verge of discovery. But science was his life, and that made him as true an explorer as the ancient Columbus and Magellan.

He believed in chance, in the purest sense of the word—the unpredictable possibility of existence.

He was here now to prove it. In addition to his calculations, the technology at his command, his knowledge and his computations, he needed one element that any explorer required for success.

Luck.

He was alone now in the vast, silent sea of space, beyond the traffic patterns, beyond the last charted quadrant. There was an intimacy here between man and his dreams that could never be achieved in a laboratory. For the first time since his voyage had begun, he smiled. He had been in his laboratory too long.

The solitude was soothing, even tempting. He'd almost forgotten what it was like to be truly alone, with only his own thoughts for company. If he'd chosen, he could have cruised along, easing back on the throttle and taking the aloneness to heart for as long as it suited him.

Up here, at the edge of man's domain, with his own planet a bright ball shrinking in the distance, he had time. And time was the key.

Resisting temptation, he logged his coordinates—speed, trajectory, distance—all meticulously calculated. His long, agile fingers moved over dials and switches. The control panel glowed green, casting a mystic aura over his sharp-featured face.

It was concentration rather than fear that narrowed his eyes and firmed his lips as he hurtled toward the sun. He knew exactly what the results would be if his calculations were off by even the slightest margin. The bright star's gravity would suck him in. It would take only a heartbeat for his ship and its occupant to be vaporized.

The ultimate failure, he thought as he stared at the luminous star that filled his viewing screen. Or the ultimate achievement. It was a gorgeous sight, this glowing, swirling light that filled the cabin and dazzled his eyes. Even at this distance, the sun held the power of life and death. Like a hot, hungry woman, it bewitched.

Deliberately he lowered the shield on the viewing screen. He pushed for more speed, watching the dials as he neared the maximum the ship could handle. A check of gauges showed him that the outside temperature was rising dramatically. He waited, knowing that beyond the protective screen the intensity of light would have seared his corneas. A man shooting toward the sun risked blindness and destruction—risked never achieving his destiny.

He waited while the first warning bell sounded, waited as the ship bucked and danced under the demands of velocity and gravity. The calm voice of the computer droned on, giving him speed, position and, most important, time.

Though he could hear his own blood pounding in his ears, his hand was steady as it urged more speed from the laboring engines.

He streaked toward the sun, faster than any man

had ever been known to fly. Jaw clenched, he shoved
a lever home. His ship shuddered, rocked, then tilted.
End over end it tumbled—once, twice, a third time—
before he could right it. His fingers gripped the controls as the force slapped him back in the chair. The
cabin exploded with sound and light as he fought to
hold his course.

For an instant his vision grayed and he thought
fatalistically that instead of being burned up in the
sun's heat he would simply be crushed by her gravity.
Then his ship sprang free, like an arrow from a bow.
Fighting for breath, he adjusted the controls and hurtled toward his fate.

What impressed Jacob most about the Northwest
was the space. As far as he could see in any direction,
there was rock and wood and sky. It was quiet, not
silent but quiet, with small animals rustling in the
underbrush and birds calling as they wheeled overhead. Tracks dimpling the blanket of snow around his
ship told him that larger animals roamed here. More
importantly, the snow itself told him that his calculations were off by at least a matter of months.

For the moment, he had to be satisfied with being
approximately where he wanted to be. And with being
alive.

Always meticulous, he returned to his ship to record the facts and his impressions. He had seen pictures and videos of this place and time. For the past
year he had studied every scrap of information he
could find on the late twentieth century. Clothes, language, sociopolitical atmosphere. As a scientist he'd
been fascinated. As a man he'd been appalled and
amused by turns. And baffled when he'd remembered

that his brother had chosen to live here, in this primitive time and place. Because of a woman.

Jacob opened a compartment and took out a picture. An example of twentieth-century technology, he mused, as he turned the Polaroid snapshot over in his hand. He studied his brother first. Caleb's easy grin was in place. And he looked comfortable sitting on the steps of a small wooden structure, dressed in baggy jeans and a sweater. He had his arm around a woman. The woman called Libby, Jacob thought now. She was unquestionably attractive, as females went. Not as flashy as Cal's usual type, but certainly inoffensive.

Just what was there about her that had made Cal give up his home, his family and his freedom?

Because he was prepared to dislike her, Jacob tossed the picture back in its compartment. He would see this Libby for himself. Judge for himself. Then he would give Cal a swift kick and take him home.

First there were some precautions to take.

Moving from the flight deck to his personal quarters, Jacob stripped off his flight suit. The denim jeans and cotton sweater that had cost him more than he cared to remember were still in their plastic holder. Excellent reproductions, he thought as he tugged the jeans over his long legs. And, to give the devil his due, extremely comfortable.

When he was dressed, he studied himself in the mirror. If he ran into any inhabitants during his stay— a brief one, he hoped—he wanted to blend in. He had neither the time nor the inclination to attempt to explain himself to a people who were most assuredly slow-witted. Nor did he want any of the media coverage that was so popular in this time.

Though he hated to admit it, the gray sweater and the blue jeans suited him. The fit was excellent, and the material was smooth against his skin. Most importantly, in them he looked like a twentieth century man.

His dark hair nearly skimmed his shoulders. It was thick, and it was always disheveled, as he paid more attention to his work than to hairstyles. Still, it was an excellent frame for his angular face. His brows were often drawn together over dark green eyes, and his mouth, usually grim when he was poring over calculations, had an unexpected and powerful charm when he relaxed enough to smile.

He wasn't smiling now. He slung his bag over his shoulder and left the ship.

Depending on the slant of the sun rather than on his watch, Jacob decided it was just past noon. The sky was miraculously empty. It was incredible to stand under the hard blue cup and see only the faint white trail of what he assumed was the vapor trail from an old continental transport. They called them planes, he remembered, watching the stream lengthen.

How patient they must be, he mused, to sit cheerfully, shoulder to shoulder with hundreds of other people, hanging in the sky for hours just to get from one coast to another or from New York to Paris.

Then again, they didn't know any better.

Switching his gaze from sky to earth, he began to walk.

It was fortunate that the sun was bright. His preparations hadn't included a coat or any heavy outerwear. The snow beneath his boots was soft, but there was just enough of a wind to make the air uncomfortable until the hike warmed his muscles.

He was a scientist by vocation, and he could lose himself for hours, even days, in equations and experiments. But it wouldn't have occurred to him to neglect his body, either—it was as well toned and as disciplined as his mind.

He used his wrist unit to give him the bearings. At least Cal's report had been fairly specific as to where his ship had gone down and where the cabin he had stayed in when he had met this Libby was situated.

Nearly three hundred years in the future, Jacob had visited the spot and had excavated the time capsule that his brother and the woman had buried.

Jacob had left home in the year 2255. He had traveled through time and through space to find his brother. And to take him home.

As he walked he saw no signs of man, or of the posh resorts that would populate this area in another century or two. There was simply space, acres of it, untrampled and untouched. The sun cast blue shadows on the snow, and the trees towered, silent giants overhead.

Despite the logic of what he had done, the months of precise calculations, the careful working of theory into fact, he found himself chilled. The enormity of what he had achieved, where he had gone, struck him. He was standing on the ground, beneath the sky, of a planet that was more foreign to him than the moon. He was filling his lungs with air. He could watch it expel in white streams. He could feel the cold on his face and his ungloved hands. He could smell the pine and taste the crisp, clear air as it blew around him.

And he had yet to be born.

Had it been the same for his brother? No, Jacob thought, there would have been no elation, not at first.

Cal had been lost, injured, confused. He hadn't set out to come here, but had been a victim of fate and circumstance. Then, vulnerable and alone, he had been bewitched by a woman. Expression grim, Jacob continued to hike.

Pausing at the stream, he remembered. A little more than two years ago—and centuries in the future—he had stood here. It had been high summer, and though the stream had changed its course over time this spot had been very much the same.

There had been grass rather than snow under his feet. But the grass would grow again, year after year, summer after summer. He had proof of that. He *was* proof of that. The stream would run fast, where now it forced its way over rock and thick islands of ice.

A little dazed, he crouched down and took a handful of snow in his ungloved hand.

He had been alone then, too, though there had been the steady drone of air traffic overhead and a huddle of mountain hotels only a few kilometers to the east. When he had uncovered the box his brother had buried he had sat on the grass and wondered.

And now he stood and wondered. If he dug for it, he would come upon the same box. The box that he had left with his parents only days before. The box would exist here, beneath his feet, just as it existed in his own time. As he existed.

If he dug it up now and carried it back to his ship, it would not be there for him to find on that high summer day in the twenty-third century. And if that was true, how could he be here, in this time, to dig it up at all?

An interesting puzzle, Jacob mused. He left it to stew in his brain as he walked.

He saw the cabin and was fascinated. No matter how many pictures, how many films or simulations he had seen, this was real. There were patches of snow melting slowly on the roof. The wood was still dark, aged by mere decades. On the glass of the windows, sunlight sparkled as it streamed through the high trees. Smoke—he could see it, as well as smell it—puffed from the stone chimney and into the hard blue sky.

Amazing, he thought, and for the first time in many hours his lips curved. He felt like a child who had discovered a unique and wonderful present under the Christmas tree. It was his, for the moment, to explore, to analyze, to piece together and take apart until he understood it.

Shifting his bag, he walked up the snow-covered path to the steps. They creaked under his weight and turned his smile into a grin.

He didn't bother to knock. Manners were easily lost in the haze of discovery. Pushing the door open, he stepped into the cabin.

"Incredible. Absolutely incredible." His quiet voice hung in the air.

Wood, genuine and rich, gleamed around him. Stone, the kind that was chipped and dug out of the earth, merged with the wood in the form of a huge fireplace. There was a fire burning in it, crackling and hissing behind a mesh screen. The scent was wonderful. It was a small, cramped room, jammed with furniture, yet it was appealing in its cheeriness and its oddities.

Jacob could have spent hours in that room alone, examining every inch of it. But he wanted to see the rest. Muttering into his minirecorder, he started up the stairs.

Sunny yanked the wheel of the Land Rover and swore. How could she actually have believed she wanted to spend a couple of months in the cabin? Peace and quiet! Who needed it? She ground the gears as the Land Rover chugged up the hill. The idea that a few solitary weeks would give her the opportunity to sort out her life and finally decide what she wanted to do with it was ridiculous.

She knew what she wanted to do with it. Something big, something spectacular. Disgusted, she blew out a long breath that sent her blond bangs dancing. Just because she hadn't decided exactly what that something was didn't matter. She'd know it when she saw it.

Just as she always knew what it wasn't when she saw it.

It wasn't flying cargo planes—or jumping out of them. It wasn't ballet, and it wasn't touring with a rock band. It wasn't driving a truck, and it wasn't writing haiku.

Not everyone, at twenty-three, could be so specific about where his ambitions didn't lie, Sunny reminded herself as she spun the Land Rover to a halt in front of the cabin. Using the process of elimination, she should be well on her way to fame and success in another ten or twenty years.

Fingers drumming against the steering wheel, she studied the cabin. It was squat, and just homely enough not to be ugly. An old rocker stood on the porch that skirted the front. It had sat there year after year, summer and winter, for as long as she could remember. There was, she discovered, something comforting in continuity.

And yet with the comfort came a restlessness for the new, for the untouched and the unseen.

With a sigh, she sat back, ignoring the cold. What was it that she wanted that wasn't here, in this place? Or in any place she'd been? Still, when it had come time to question, when it had come time to think, she had come back here, to the cabin.

She had been born in it, had spent the first few years of her life inside it and running through the surrounding forest. Perhaps that was why she had come back when her life had seemed so pointless. Just to recapture some of that simplicity.

She loved it, really. Oh, not with the passion her sister, Libby, did. Not with the deep-rooted sentiment of their parents. But fondly, the way children often feel about an old, eccentric aunt.

Sunny couldn't imagine living there again, the way Libby and her new husband were. Day after day, night after night, without seeing another soul. Perhaps Sunny's roots were in the forest, but her heart belonged to the city, with its bright lights and its possibilities.

Just a vacation, she told herself, pulling off her woolen hat and running impatient fingers through her short hair. She was entitled to one. After all, she'd entered college at the tender age of sixteen. Too bright for her own good, her father had said more than once. After graduating just before her twentieth birthday, she had plunged into endeavor after endeavor, never finding satisfaction.

She tended to be good at whatever she did. Perhaps that was why she'd taken lessons in everything from tap dancing to tole painting. But being good at something didn't make it the right something. So she moved on, perennially restless, feeling perennially guilty for leaving things half-done.

Now it was time to settle down. So she had come here, to think, to decide, to consider. That was all. It wasn't as if she were hiding—just because she'd lost her last job. No, her last two jobs, she told herself viciously.

In any case, she had enough money to hold her for the rest of the winter—particularly since there was no place to spend any around here. If she went with her instincts and caught the next plane to Portland or Seattle—or anywhere something was happening—she'd be flat broke in a week. And she'd be damned if she'd go crawling back to her indulgent and exasperated parents.

"You said you were going to stay," she muttered as she pushed the door of the car open. "And you're going to stay until you figure out where Sunny Stone fits."

Hauling out the two bags of groceries she'd just purchased in town, she trudged through the snow. At the very least, she thought, a couple of months in the cabin would prove her self-sufficiency. If she didn't die of boredom first.

Inside, she glanced toward the fire first, satisfied that it was still burning well. Those few years in the Girl Scouts hadn't been wasted. She dumped both bags on the kitchen counter. She knew Libby would have immediately set about putting everything in its place. Sunny figured it was a waste of time to store something when you were only going to have to get it out again sooner or later.

With the same disregard, she tossed her coat over the back of a chair, then kicked her boots into a corner. Digging a candy bar out of a bag, she unwrapped it and wandered back into the living room. What she needed was a long afternoon of research. Lately she'd been toying with the idea of going back to school and trying for a law degree. The idea of arguing for a living had a certain appeal. Along with her clothes, her camera, her sketch pad, her tape recorder and her dance shoes she had packed two boxes of books on an assortment of professions.

During her first week in the cabin she had researched and discarded screenwriting as too unstable, medicine as too terrifying and running a retro clothing store as too trendy.

But law had possibilities. She could see herself as either the cold, hard-edged D.A. or the dedicated, overworked public defender.

It was worth looking into, she decided as she mounted the stairs. And the sooner she had her focus the sooner she could get back to where there was something more exciting to do than watch the melting snow run off the gutters.

The candy bar was halfway to her mouth when she stepped into the doorway and saw him. He was standing by the bed—her bed—obviously engrossed in the fashion magazine she'd tossed on the floor the night before. It was in his hands now, and his fingers seemed to stroke the glossy paper as if it were some exotic fabric.

Though his back was to her, she could see that he was tall. He had two or three inches on her willowy five-ten. His dark hair was long enough to fall over the collar of the sweater he wore, and it looked as if he'd ridden fast in an open car. Hardly daring to breathe, she took his measure.

If he was a wayward hiker, he was dressed neatly, and sparely. The jeans showed no signs of wear. The boots he wore were unmarked, expensive and, unless she missed her guess, custom-made. No, she didn't think he was a hiker, even a foolish one who would challenge the winter mountains.

He had a lean build, though she couldn't be sure what the baggy sweater hid in the way of muscle. If he was a thief, he was a stupid one, passing the time with a magazine rather than bundling up what passed for valuables in the cabin.

Her gaze shot over to the dresser and her jewelry case. Her collection wasn't extensive, but each piece had been selected with care and a disregard for expense. And it was hers, just as the cabin was hers, just as the room he'd invaded was hers.

Furious, she dropped the candy and snatched up the closest weapon, an empty pop bottle and, brandishing it, lunged forward.

Jacob heard the movement. Out of the corner of his eye he caught a red blur. Instinct had him turning, shifting, just as the bottle whizzed by his head and smashed against the nightstand. Glass exploded with a sound like a shot.

"What the—"

Before he could utter another word, his foot was kicked out from under him and he found himself flipped neatly and sprawled on his back. He stared up at a tall, slender woman with a shiny crop of blond hair and molten gray eyes. She was crouched, arms bent, hands flexed in an ancient fighting stance.

"Don't even think about it," she warned, in a voice

as smoky as her eyes. "I don't want to have to hurt you, so get up slow. Then get yourself downstairs and out. You've got thirty seconds."

Keeping his eyes on hers, he braced himself on one elbow. When dealing with a member of a primitive culture it was wise to go slowly. "Excuse me?"

"You heard me, pal. I'm a fourth-degree black belt. Mess with me and I'll crush your skull like a walnut."

She smiled when she said it. Otherwise he might have offered her excuses and explanations then and there. But she smiled, and a challenge was a challenge.

Without a word, he sprang up to land lightly on the balls of his feet in a stance that mirrored hers. He saw surprise in her eyes—not panic, surprise. He blocked her first blow, but he still felt it reverberate from his forearm to his shoulder. He shifted enough to prevent a well-aimed kick from connecting with his chin.

She was fast, he noted, fast and agile. He parried her offensive moves, staying on the defensive as he judged her. Fearless, he thought with pure admiration. A warrior in a world that still required them. And if Jacob had a weakness he would admit to, it was the love of a good fight.

He didn't toy with her. If he did, he knew, he'd end up on the floor with her foot on his throat. The kick that shot past his guard and into his rib cage was proof of that. It was an even match, he decided after five sweaty minutes, except for the fact that he had the advantage in reach and weight.

Deciding to put both to use, he feinted, blocked, then caught her in a throw that sent her flying onto the bed. Before she could recover, he spread himself over her, cautiously gripping her wrists over her head.

She was out of breath, but she wasn't out of fuel. Her eyes burning into his, she put all her strength into one last move. Just in time, he shifted his weight and avoided the knee to the groin.

"Some things never change," he muttered, and studied her while he waited for his labored breathing to slow.

She was stunning—or perhaps it was the fight that made her seem so. Her skin was flushed now, a rosy pink that enhanced the sunlight color of her hair. Its short, almost severe cut played up the elegance of her bone structure. She had sharp cheekbones. Warrior-like, he thought again. Like a Viking, or a Celt. Large, long-lidded gray eyes smoldered in frustration but not in defeat. Her nose was small and sharp, and her mouth was full, with the lower lip slightly prominent in a pout. She smelled like the forest—cool, exotic and foreign.

"You're very good," he said, and gave himself a moment to enjoy the way her body held firm and unyielding under his.

"Thanks." She bit the word off, but she didn't struggle. She knew when to fight and when to plot. He outweighed her and he had outfought her, but she wasn't ready to discuss terms of surrender. "I'd appreciate it if you got the hell off me."

"In a minute. Is it your custom to greet people by tossing them on the floor?"

She arched one pale brow. "Is it yours to break into people's homes and poke around in their bedrooms?"

"The door was unlocked," he pointed out. Then

he frowned. He was certain he was in the right place, but this was not the woman called Libby. "This is your home?"

"That's right. It's called private property." She struggled not to fidget while he studied her as though she were a particularly interesting specimen in a petri dish. "I've already called the police," she told him, though the closest telephone was ten miles away. "If I were you, I'd make tracks."

"If I wanted to avoid the police, it would be stupid to make tracks." He tilted his head, considering. "And you didn't call them."

"Maybe I did and maybe I didn't." The pout became more pronounced. "What do you want? There's nothing worth stealing in this place."

"I didn't come to steal."

A quick panic, purely feminine, fluttered just below her heart. Fury banked it. "I won't make it easy for you."

"All right." He didn't bother to ask her what she meant. "Who are you?"

"I think I'm entitled to ask you that question," she countered. "And I'm not really interested." Her heart was beginning to thud thickly, and she hoped he couldn't feel it. They were sprawled across the unmade bed, thigh to thigh, as intimately as lovers. His eyes, green and intense, stared into hers until she was breathless all over again.

He saw the panic now, just a flicker of it, and eased his grip on her wrists. Her pulse was beating rapidly there, causing an unexpected reaction to race through him. He could feel it singing through his blood as he shifted his gaze to her mouth.

What would it be like? he wondered. Just a touch,

an experiment. A mouth that soft, that full, was designed to tempt a man. Would she fight, or would she yield? Either would prove rewarding. Annoyed by the distraction, he looked into her eyes again. He had a purpose, one he didn't intend to detour from.

"I'm sorry if I startled you, or if I interfered with your privacy. I was looking for someone."

"There's no one here but—" She caught herself and swore under her breath. "Who? Who are you looking for?"

It was best to play it safe, Jacob decided. If he had somehow miscalculated the time, or if Cal's report had been faulty—as they had sometimes been before—it wouldn't be wise to be too specific. "A man. I thought he lived here, but perhaps my information is incorrect."

Sunny blew her bangs out of her eyes. "Who? What's his name?"

"Hornblower," Jacob said, and used his smile for the first time. "His name is Caleb Hornblower." The surprise in Sunny's eyes was all he needed. Instinctively his fingers tightened on her wrists. "You know him?"

Ideas about her sister's somewhat mysterious husband sprang into her mind. He was a spy, a fugitive, an eccentric millionaire on the run. Family loyalty ran deep, and she would rather have had bamboo slivers under her fingernails than betray a loved one.

"Why should I?"

"You know him," Jacob insisted. When her chin came up, he let out a frustrated sigh. "I've come a long way to see him." His lips curved at the understatement. "A very long way. Please, can you tell me where he is?"

When she felt herself softening, she jutted her chin out again. "Obviously he's not here."

"Is he all right?" Jacob released her hands and gripped her shoulders. "Has anything happened to him?"

"No." The very real concern she heard in his voice had her putting a hand over his. "No, of course not. I didn't mean to—" She caught herself again. If this was a trap, she was falling neatly into it. "If you want any information from me, you'll have to tell me who you are and why you want it."

"I'm his brother, Jacob."

Sunny's eyes widened as she let out a long breath. Cal's brother? It was possible, she supposed. The coloring was similar, and the shape of the face. There was certainly more family resemblance between this man and her brother-in-law than there was between herself and Libby.

"Well," she said after a brief debate with herself, "it really is a small world, isn't it?"

"Smaller than you can imagine. You do know Cal?"

"Yes. Since he married my sister, that makes you and me... I'm not exactly sure what that makes us, but I think we'd be better off discussing it vertically."

He nodded, but he didn't move. "Who are you?"

"Me?" She offered him a big, bright smile. "Oh, I'm Sunbeam." Still smiling, she wrapped her fingers around his thumb. "Now, if you don't want this dislocated, you'll get the hell off my bed."

Chapter 2

They moved apart warily, two boxers retreating to their corners at the sound of the bell. Jacob wasn't entirely sure how to handle her, much less the bombshell she had dropped. His brother was married.

Once they were standing a careful three feet apart, he dipped his hands in the pockets of the comfortable jeans. He noted that, though her stance was easy, she was still braced, ready to counter any move he might attempt. It would have been interesting to make one, just to see what she would do and how she would do it. But he had priorities.

"Where's Cal?"

"Borneo. I think it's Borneo. Might be Bora Bora. Libby's researching a paper." She had time to study him objectively now. Yes, there was a definite resemblance to Cal, in the way he stood, in the rhythm of his speech. But, even though she accepted that, she wasn't ready to trust him. "Cal must have told you she's a cultural anthropologist."

He hesitated, then brought out the smile again. He wasn't nearly as concerned now with what Cal had or had not told him in his report as with what his brother had told this woman named Sunbeam. Sunbeam, he thought distractedly. Was anyone really named Sunbeam?

"Of course." He lied smoothly and without compunction. "He didn't mention he'd be away. How long?"

"A few more weeks." She tugged the red sweater down over her hips. She could already feel bruises forming. It didn't annoy her. She had held her own—well, almost held her own—against him. And she hoped she'd get another shot. "It's funny he never said you were coming."

"He didn't know." Frustrated, he looked out the window at the snow and the trees. He'd come so close, so damn close, only to wait. "I wasn't sure I could make it."

"Yeah." With a lazy shrug, she rocked back on her heels. "Like you couldn't make it to the wedding. We all thought it was odd that none of Cal's family showed up for the big day."

He turned back at that. There was definite censoriousness in her voice. He didn't care for it—he rarely tolerated it—but in this case it was almost amusing. "Believe me, if we could have been here, we would have."

"Hmm. Well, since we've finished wrestling, we might as well go down and have some tea." She started toward the door, flicking a glance over him as she passed. "What degree black belt do you have?"

"Seventh." He cocked an eyebrow. "I didn't want to hurt you."

"Right." More than a little miffed, she started downstairs. "I didn't figure people like you would go in for martial arts."

"People like me?" He spoke absently as he ran his palm over the smooth wood of the railing.

"You're a physicist or something, right?"

"Or something." He spotted a woven throw over the back of a chair in striking colors that challenged rather than blended. Though the look of it tugged at his memory, he resisted the temptation to go over for a closer examination. "And you? What are you?"

"Nothing. I'm working on it."

When Sunny swung into the kitchen, she went directly to the stove. She didn't notice the blank astonishment on Jacob's face.

Like something out of an old video or reference book, he thought as he scanned the room. Only this was much, much better than any reproduction. Delightful, he thought, astonishment turning to pleasure. Absolutely delightful. His hands itched to try out every dial and knob.

"Jacob?"

"What?"

With her brows drawn together, Sunny stared at him. An oddball, she decided. Gorgeous, certainly, but an oddball. And for the time being she was stuck with him. "I said we're big on tea around here. Do you have a preference?"

"No." He couldn't resist. He simply couldn't. As she turned to put the kettle on to boil, he wandered over to the white enameled sink and turned a clunky chrome dial. Water hissed out of the wide-lipped faucet. Holding a finger under the running stream, he discovered it was ice-cold. When he touched the tip of his tongue to his damp finger he detected a faint metallic flavor.

Completely unprocessed water, he decided. Amazing. They drank it exactly as it came out of the ground. Forgettting Sunny, he stuck his finger under again and found that the water had heated enough to make him jolt. Satisfied for the moment, he turned the water off. When he turned back, he saw that Sunny was still standing by the stove. She was staring at him.

There was no use cursing himself, he decided. He was simply going to have to control his curiosity until he was alone.

"It's very nice," he offered.

"Thanks." Clearing her throat, she kept facing him as she reached behind for the mugs. "We call it a sink. They do have sinks in Philadelphia, don't they?"

"Yes." He took a chance, depending on his research. "I've never used one quite like this."

She relaxed a little. "Well, this place is a throwback."

"I was thinking exactly the same thing."

As the kettle began to sputter, she turned to make the tea. As she worked, she carelessly pushed her sweater up to her elbows. Long, limber arms, he noted. Deceptively fragile in appearance. He rubbed his own forearm. He'd already had a sample of their strength.

"Maybe Cal didn't tell you that my parents built this place in the sixties." She poured steaming water into cups.

"Built it?" he repeated. "Personally?"

"Every stone and log," she told him. "They were hippies. The genuine article."

"The 1960s, yes. I've read about that era. It was a counterculture movement. Youth against the establishment in a political and social revolution that involved a distrust of wealth, government and the military."

"Spoken like a true scientist." A weird one, she added silently as she brought the mugs to the table. "It's funny to hear someone who was born during that time talk about it as if it were as far removed as the Ming dynasty."

Following her lead, he sat down. "Times change."

"Yes." Frowning, she watched as he rubbed a fingertip over the table's surface. "It's called a table," she said helpfully.

He caught himself and picked up the mug. "I was admiring the wood."

"I'm pretty sure it's oak. My father built it, which is why there's a matchbook under one of the legs." At his blank look, she laughed. "He went through a carpentry phase. Almost everything he built in this place wobbles."

He could barely imagine it. Oak split from an actual tree and formed into a piece of furniture. Only those with the highest credit rating could afford the luxury. Even then they were limited by law to a single piece. And here he was, sitting in a house made entirely of wood. He would need samples. It might be difficult with her watching him, distrusting him, but it wasn't impossible.

Thinking it over, he sipped the tea, stopped, then sipped again.

"Herbal Delight."

Sunny lifted her mug in salute. "Right the first time. We could hardly drink anything else without risking a family crisis." With a shake of her head, she studied him over the rim of her mug. "It's my father's company. Didn't Cal tell you that, either?"

"No." Baffled, Jacob stared into the dark, golden tea in his mug. Herbal Delight. Stone. The company, one of the richest and most expansive in the federation, had been established by William Stone. The myths about his beginnings were as romanticized as those about the nineteenth-century president who had been born in a log cabin.

No, not a myth, Jacob thought as the fragrant steam rose from the cup. Reality.

"Just what did Cal tell you?"

Jacob sipped again and struggled for patience. He wanted to record all of this as soon as possible. "Just that he had…flown off course and crashed. Your sister took care of him, and they fell in love." The old resentment welled up in him, and he set down his mug. "And he chose to stay with her, here."

"You have a problem with that?" In a movement that mirrored his, Sunny set down her mug. When they eyed each other now, there was as much dislike as distrust in their looks. "Is that why you didn't bother to show up at the wedding? Because you were annoyed that he decided to get married without clearing it with you?"

His eyes, shades darker as anger grew, snapped to hers again. "No matter what or how I felt about his decision, I would have been here if it had been possible."

"That's big of you." She shot up to snag a bag of

cookies from the pile of groceries. "Let me tell you something, Hornblower. He's lucky to have my sister."

"I wouldn't know."

"I would." Sunny ripped the bag open and dug in. "She's beautiful and brilliant, kind and unselfish." She gestured with half a cookie. "And, if it's any of your business—which it isn't—they're happy together."

"I have no way of knowing that, either."

"Whose fault is that? You've had plenty of time to see them together—if it really mattered to you."

There was fury, rash and dark in his eyes now. "Time has been the problem." He rose. "All I know is that my brother made a rash decision, a life-altering one. And I intend to make certain it wasn't a mistake."

"You intend?" Sunny choked on a cookie and had to snatch up her mug and drink before she could speak again. "I don't know how things work in your family, pal, but in ours we don't make decisions by committee. We're each considered individuals with the right to choose for ourselves."

He didn't give a damn about her family. He only cared about his own. "My brother's decision affects a great number of people."

"Yeah, I'm sure his marrying Libby is going to change the course of history." Disgusted, she tossed the bag of cookies back on the counter. "If you're so worried, why the hell has it taken you over a year to put in an appearance?"

"That's my business."

"Oh, I see. That's your business. But my sister's

marriage is also your business. You're a real jerk, Hornblower.''

''I beg your pardon?''

''I said you're a jerk.'' She tugged a hand through her hair. ''Well, you go right ahead and talk to him when they get back. But there's one thing you haven't put in your calculations. Cal and Libby love each other, which means they belong together. Now, if you'll excuse me, I've got things to do. You can let yourself out.''

She stormed off. Moments later, Jacob heard what he imagined was the sound of a primitive wooden door slamming shut.

An exasperating woman, he thought. Interesting, of course, but exasperating. He was going to have to find a way to deal with her, since it was obvious he'd have to extend his stay until Cal's return.

As a scientist, he considered it a tremendous opportunity. To study a primitive culture firsthand, to talk face-to-face with an ancestor—of sorts. He glanced up at the ceiling. He doubted the volatile Sunbeam would appreciate being considered an ancestor.

Yes, it was a tremendous opportunity—scientifically. Personally, he already considered his association with the primitive woman a trial. She was rude, argumentative and aggressive. Perhaps he had the same traits, but he was, after all, superior, being older by several centuries.

The first thing he was going to do when he returned to the ship was open the computer banks and look up what the word *jerk* meant when applied to a man in the twentieth century.

Sunny would have been delighted to give him a concise definition. In fact, as she paced her room she thought of half a dozen more colorful descriptions of his character.

The nerve of the man. To waltz in here more than a year after his brother and her sister married. Not to congratulate them, she thought furiously. Not for a nice family reunion. But to offer his half-baked opinions as to whether Libby was worthy of his brother.

Creep. Jackass. Imbecile.

As she swung past the window, she spotted him down below. Her hand was already on the window sash, prepared to lift the glass so that she could shout the epithets at him. Her anger snapped off as quickly as it had ignited.

Why in the world was he walking into the forest? Without a coat? Narrowing her eyes, she watched him trudge through the snow toward the sheltering trees. Where the hell was he going? There was nothing in that direction but more trees.

A question sprang into her mind that she'd been too occupied to consider before. How had he gotten here? The cabin was miles from town, and a good two hours' drive from the nearest airport. How the devil had he managed to pop up in her bedroom, coatless, hatless, gloveless, in the middle of winter?

There was no car, no truck, not even a snowmobile, outside the cabin. The idea of him hitchhiking from the highway was ludicrous. A man didn't simply walk into the mountains in January. At least not if he was sane.

With a shudder, she stepped back from the window. Maybe that was the answer. Jacob Hornblower wasn't just a jerk. He was a deranged jerk.

That was an awfully big leap, she told herself. Just because she didn't like him wasn't a good enough reason to assume he was crazy. After all, he was Cal's brother, and over the past year Sunny had become very fond of Cal. Brother Jacob might be an annoying, interfering pain in the neck but that didn't mean he had loose screws.

And yet...

Hadn't she thought he was weird? Hadn't he acted weird? She looked out the window again, but the only sign of him was the fresh tracks in the snow.

Cal seemed normal enough, she mused, but what did any of them know about his family or his background? Next to nothing. It had always seemed to Sunny that her brother-in-law was strangely close-mouthed when it came to his family. She glanced back toward the window again. Maybe he had his reasons.

The man had acted odd right from the start, Sunny decided. The way he'd come into the house unannounced to stand in her bedroom and pore over a copy of *Vogue* as if it were the Dead Sea Scrolls.

Then there was his behavior in the kitchen. Playing with the faucet. And staring. It was as though he'd never seen a stove or refrigerator before. Or hadn't seen one in a very long time. Her mind was jumping like a rabbit. Because he'd been locked up, she thought. Put away where he wasn't a danger to society.

Catching her lip between her teeth, she began to pace again. Her foot connected with his flight bag. Jolting backward, Sunny stared at it. He'd forgotten it. That meant he would be coming back.

Well, she could handle it. She could take care of herself. Rubbing her palms against her thighs, she stared down at the bag. But it wouldn't do any harm to take a few precautions.

Going on impulse, she knelt down. Invasion of privacy or not, she was going to look through the bag. It was odd itself. No zipper or straps. The Velcro peeled apart almost soundlessly. Casting one guilty look over her shoulder, she began to dig.

A change of clothes. Another sweater, black this time. No label. The jeans were soft and obviously expensive, though there was no designer name on the back pocket. No label anywhere. And they were new. She would have sworn they had never been worn. Setting them aside, she pushed deeper. She found a vial marked fluoratyne that contained a clear liquid, and a pair of high-top sneakers in supple leather. No shaving gear, she mused, no mirror. Not even a toothbrush. Just a set of obviously new clothes and a vial that might very well contain some kind of drug.

Her last discovery was the most puzzling of all. An electronic device, no bigger than the palm of her hand, was tucked in the corner of the bag. Circular in shape, it was hinged back. When she opened it she saw a series of tiny buttons. After touching the first, she jumped back at the sound of Jacob's voice.

As clear as a bell, it came from the circle of metal in her hand. He was reciting equations, as far as she could tell. Neither the numbers nor the terms meant anything to her. But the fact that they were emitted by the little disk opened up new realms of possibility.

He was a spy. Probably for the other side. Whatever the other side was. And from his behavior it was natural to assume that he was an unbalanced spy. Imagination had never been Sunny's weak point. She could see it all perfectly.

He had been captured. Whatever techniques had been used to pull information from him had unhinged his mind. Cal had covered for him, making up a story about his brother being an astrophysicist, too deep in research to travel to the West Coast, when in reality he had been in some sort of federal institution. And now he'd escaped.

Sunny pushed buttons at random until Jacob's voice clicked off. She would have to treat him carefully. Whatever her personal feelings, he was family. She'd have to make absolutely certain he was a dangerous lunatic before she did anything about it.

A stupid, often annoying person. Jacob scowled at the puff of smoke he saw through the last line of trees. He didn't care for the definition of *jerk*. Being called annoying didn't bother him in the least. But stupid did. He would not tolerate some skinny woman who considered the combustion engine the height of technology calling him stupid.

He'd gotten quite a bit done overnight. His ship was well camouflaged, and his records had been brought up to date. Including his infuriating encounter with Sunbeam Stone. It hadn't been until sunrise that he'd remembered his flight bag.

If she hadn't made him lose his temper, he would never have left it behind. Not that it contained anything valuable. It was the principle of the thing. He was not absentminded by nature, and he only forgot minor details when his mind was absorbed with larger ones.

And he resented thinking of her. She had popped into his mind on and off as he'd worked through the night. A constant annoyance—like an itch on the shoulder blade that was just out of reach. How she'd crouched, ready to fight, chin up, body braced. How that body had felt under his, tensed, challenging. How her hair glowed, like her name.

Furious, he shook his head, as if to dislodge her from his thoughts. He didn't have time for women. It wasn't that he didn't appreciate them, but there was a time for pleasure. This wasn't it. And if it was pleasure he wanted, Sunbeam Stone was not where he should look for it.

The more he thought about where he was, when he was, the more he was certain that Cal needed to be brought to his senses and taken home.

Some sort of space fever, Jacob decided. His brother had suffered a shock, and the woman—as some women had throughout time—had taken advantage of him. When he approached Cal logically, they would get into the ship and go home.

In the meantime, he would take the opportunity to study and record at least this small section of the world.

At the edge of the forest, he paused. It was colder today, and he sincerely regretted the lack of warmer clothing. Gray clouds, plump with snow, had drifted in to cover the sun. In the gloomy light he watched Sunny lifting logs from the woodpile at the rear of the cabin. She was singing in a powerfully erotic voice about a man who had gotten away. She didn't hear his approach, and she continued to sing and stack wood in her arms.

"Excuse me."

With a yelp, she jumped back, sending the split logs flying. One landed hard on her booted foot, and she swore roundly and hopped up and down. "Damn

it! Damn, damn, damn! What's wrong with you?''
Clasping her wounded foot with one hand, she braced
the other on the cabin wall.

"Nothing." He couldn't help the grin. "I think
there's something wrong with you. Does it hurt?''

"No, it feels great. I live for pain." She gritted her
teeth as she set her foot gingerly back on the ground.
"Where did you come from?''

"Philadelphia." She narrowed her eyes. "Oh, you
mean now?'' With a jerk of his thumb, he said, "That
way." He paused to glance at the logs scattered in
the snow. "Want some help?''

"No." Favoring her foot, she crouched down to
retrieve the logs. All the while, she watched him carefully, braced for any move he might make. "Do you
know why I'm here, Hornblower? For peace and solitude." She blew the hair out of her eyes as she
looked up at him. "Do you understand the con-
cepts?''

"Yes."

"Good." Turning, she limped back into the cabin,
letting the door slam shut behind her. After dumping
the logs in the woodbox, she came back to the
kitchen. And swore. "What now?''

"I left my bag." He sniffed the air. "Is something
burning?''

With a sound of disgust, she darted to the toaster,
banging on it until the smoking, blackened bread
popped up. "This stupid thing sticks.''

To get a better look at the fascinating little device,
he leaned over her shoulder. "Doesn't look appetizing.''

"It's fine." To prove it, she bit into the toast.

Her scent drifted to him over the smoke. His instant

reaction annoyed him, but pride had him resisting the instinctive move away. "Are you always so stubborn?"

"Yes."

"And so unfriendly?"

"No."

She turned and was immediately made aware of the miscalculation. He didn't move aside, as she had expected. Instead, he leaned forward, resting his palms against the counter and casually caging her between his arms. There was nothing she detested more than being outmaneuvered.

"Back off, Hornblower."

"No." He did shift, but closer. As on their first meeting, their thighs rubbed, but there was nothing loverlike in the connection. "You interest me, Sunbeam."

"Sunny," she said automatically. "Don't call me Sunbeam."

"You interest me," he repeated. "Do you consider yourself an average woman of your time?"

Baffled, she shook her head. "What kind of a question is that?"

She had dozens of shades in her hair, from pale white to dark honey. He was sorry he had noticed. "One that requires a simple answer. Do you?"

"No. No one likes to be considered average. Now would you—"

"You're beautiful." His gaze skimmed over her face, deliberately, a test of himself and his endurance. "But that's merely physical. What do you think separates you from the average?"

"What are you doing, a thesis?" She lifted a hand

to shove him away and met the solid wall of his chest. She could feel his heartbeat there, slow and steady.

"More or less." He smiled. He was disturbing her at a very basic level, and he found it intensely satisfying.

It was his eyes, Sunny thought. Even if the man was unhinged, he had the most incredibly hypnotic eyes. "I thought you dealt with planets and stars, not with people."

"People live on planets."

"At least this one."

He smiled again. "At least. You could consider this a personal interest."

She wanted to shift but realized that would only make the contact more intimate. Cursing him, she kept her voice and her gaze level. "I don't want your personal interest, Jacob."

"J.T." He felt the quick tremor from her body into his. "The family usually calls me J.T."

"All right." She spoke slowly, all too aware that her brain had turned to mush. What she needed was some distance. "How about you get out of my way, J.T., and I put together some breakfast?"

If she didn't stop nibbling on her lip, he was going to have to stop her in the most effective way he knew. He hadn't realized that such a small, nervous habit could be seductive. "Is that an invitation?"

Her tongue slipped out to nurse her lip. "Sure."

He leaned closer, enjoying the way her eyes widened, darkened, steadied. It wasn't easy to resist. He was known for his brilliance, his tenacity, his temper. But not for his control. And he wanted to kiss her, not scientifically, not experimentally. Ruthlessly.

"Toast!" he murmured.

She let out a quick puff of air. "Froot Loops. They're great. My favorite."

He eased back, much more for his sake than for hers. If he was going to spend the next few weeks around her, he was going to have to work on that control. Because he had a plan.

"I could use some breakfast."

"Fine." Telling herself it was a change of strategy, not a retreat, she darted across the kitchen to pluck two bowls from the cupboard. With those and a colorful box in hand, she walked to the table. "We could never have these as kids. My mother was—is—a health fiend. Her idea of cold cereal is hunks of roots and tree bark."

"Why would she choose to eat tree bark?"

"Don't ask me." Sunny grabbed the milk from the fridge, then dumped it over the piles of colorful circles. "Anyway, ever since I moved out I've been on a binge of junk food. I figure since I ate healthy for the first twenty years I can poison myself for the next twenty."

"Poison," he repeated, giving the cereal a dubious look.

"To the health fiend, sugar's poison. Dig in," she added, offering him a spoon. "Burnt toast and cold cereal are my specialties." She smiled, charmingly. She, too, had a plan.

Because he wouldn't have put it past her to poison him, he waited until she had begun to eat before he sampled the cereal. Soggy candy, he decided. And fairly appealing. He considered the informal meal a good start if he wanted to ingratiate himself with her enough to pump her for information.

It was obvious that Cal had told no one except

Libby about where—and when—he had come from. Jacob gave him full marks for that. It was better all around if the matter was kept quiet. The repercussions would be…well, he had yet to calculate them. But Sunny might not have been far off when she had said that Cal's marrying her sister could change the course of history.

So he would play the game close, and cautious, and use the situation to his advantage. Use her to his advantage, he thought with only a twinge of guilt.

He intended to pick her brain, about her family, her sister in particular, her impressions of Cal. And he wanted her firsthand account of life in the twentieth century. With a little luck, he might be able to convince her to guide him into the nearest city, where he could add to his data.

It wouldn't do to lose her temper with him, Sunny thought. If she wanted to find out exactly who and what he was, she would have to employ more tact. It wasn't her strong point, but she could learn. She was as completely alone with him as it was possible to be. And, since she had no intention of packing up and leaving, she would just have to exercise some caution and some diplomacy. Particularly if he was as loony as she believed.

It was too bad that he was crazy, she thought, smiling at him. Anyone that attractive, that blatantly sexy, deserved a solid, working brain. Maybe it was only a temporary mental breakdown.

"So." She tapped her spoon against the side of her bowl. "What do you think of Oregon so far?"

"It's very big—and underpopulated."

"That's how we like it." She let the lull drag out. "Did you fly into Portland?"

He wavered between a lie and the truth. "No, my transportation brought me a bit closer. Do you live here with Cal and your sister?"

"No. I have a place in Portland, but I'm thinking of giving it up."

"To what?"

"Just giving it up." She shot him a puzzled look, then shrugged. "Actually, I'm toying with the idea of going east for a while. New York."

"To do what?"

"I haven't decided."

He set his spoon aside. "You have no work?"

Automatically her shoulders squared. "I'm in between jobs. I recently resigned from a managerial position in retail." She'd been fired from her job as assistant manager of the lingerie department of a mid-level department store. "I'm considering going back to school for a law degree."

"Law?" His eyes softened. There was something so appealing about the look that she nearly smiled at him and meant it. "My mother is in law."

"Really? I don't think Cal mentioned it. What kind of law does she practice?"

Because he thought it would be a bit difficult to explain his mother's position, he asked, "What kind did you have in mind?"

"I'm leaning toward criminal law." She started to elaborate, then stopped herself. She didn't want to talk about herself but about him. "It's funny, isn't it, that my sister should be a scientist and Cal's brother should be one? Just what does an astrophysicist do?"

"Theorizes. Experiments."

"About stuff like interplanetary travel?" She tried not to smirk but didn't quite succeed. "You don't really believe all that stuff—like people flying off to Venus the way they fly to Cleveland?''

It was fortunate he was a cool hand at poker. His face remained bland as he continued to eat. ''Yes.''

She laughed indulgently. ''I guess you have to, but isn't it frustrating to go into all that knowing that even if it becomes possible it won't happen in your lifetime?''

''Time's relative. In the early part of this century a flight to the moon was considered implausible. But it has been done.'' Clumsily, he thought, but it had been done. ''In the next century man goes to Mars and beyond.''

''Maybe.'' She got up to take two bottles of soda from the refrigerator. ''But it would be hard for me to devote my life to something I'd never see happen.'' As Jacob watched in fascination, she took a small metal object out of a drawer, applied it like a lever to the top of each bottle and dislodged the caps. ''I guess I like to see results, and see them now,'' she admitted as she set the first bottle in front of him. ''Instant gratification. Which is why I'm twenty-three and between jobs.''

The bottle was glass, Jacob mused. The same kind she had tried to strike him with the afternoon before. Lifting it, he sipped. He was pleasantly surprised by the familiar taste. He enjoyed the same soft drink at home, though it wasn't his habit to drink it for breakfast.

''Why did you decide to study space?''

He glanced back at her. He recognized a grilling when he heard one, and he thought it would be entertaining to both humor and annoy her. ''I like possibilities.''

"You must have studied a long time."

"Long enough." He sipped again.

"Where?"

"Where what?"

She managed to keep the pleasant smile intact. "Where did you study?"

He thought of the Kroliac Institute on Mars, the Birmington University in Houston and his brief and intense year in the L'Espace Space Laboratory in the Fordon Quadrant. "Here and there. At the moment I'm attached to a small private facility outside of Philadelphia."

She wondered if the staff of that private facility wore white coats. "I guess you find it fascinating."

"Only more so recently. Are you nervous?"

"Why?"

"You keep tapping your foot."

She placed a hand on her knee to stop the movement. "Restless. I get restless if I stay in one place too long." It was obvious, painfully so, that she wasn't going to get anywhere with him this way. "Listen, I really do have some things to..." Her words trailed off as she glanced out the window. She didn't know when the snow had begun, but it was coming down in sheets. "Terrific."

Following her gaze, Jacob studied the thick white flakes. "Looks like it means business."

"Yeah." She let out her breath in a sigh. Maybe he did make her nervous, but she wasn't a monster. "And it's not the kind of weather suitable for camping in the woods." Fighting with her conscience, she walked to the door, back to the table, then to the window. "Look, I know you don't have a place to stay. I saw you walk into the forest yesterday."

''I have…all I need.''

''Sure, but I can't have you go trudging into the hills in a blizzard to sleep in a tent or something. Libby would never forgive me if you died of exposure.'' Thrusting her hands in her pockets, she scowled at him. ''You can stay here.''

He considered the possibilities and smiled. ''I'd love to.''

Chapter 3

He stayed out of her way. It seemed the best method of handling the situation for the moment. She'd stationed herself on the sofa by the fire, books heaped beside her, and was busily taking notes. A portable radio sat on the table, crackling with static and music and the occasional weather report. Absorbed in her research, Sunny ignored him.

Taking advantage of the opportunity, Jacob explored his new quarters. She'd given him the room next to hers—larger by a couple of meters, with a pair of paned windows facing southeast. The bed was a big, boxy affair framed in wood, with a spring-type of mattress that creaked when he sat on the edge.

There was a shelf crowded with books, novels and poetry of the nineteenth and twentieth centuries. They were paperbacks, for the most part, with bright, eye-catching covers. He recognized one or two of the names. He flipped through them with an interest that was more scientific than literary. It was Cal, he thought, who read for pleasure, who had a talent for retaining little bits of prose and poetry. It was rare for Jacob to while away an hour of his time with fiction.

They were still using trees to make the pages of books, he remembered with a kind of dazed fascination. One side had cut them down to make room for housing and to make furniture and paper and fuel, while the other side had scurried to replant them. Never quite catching up.

It had been an odd sort of game, one of many that had led to incredible and complicated environmental problems.

Then, of course, they'd saturated the air with carbon dioxide, gleefully punching holes in the ozone, then fluttering their hands when faced with the consequences. He wondered what kind of people poisoned their own air. And water, he recalled with a shake of his head. Another game had been to throw whatever was no longer useful into the ocean, as if the seas were a bottomless dumping ground. It was fortunate that they had begun to get the picture before the damage had become irreparable.

Turning from the window, he wandered the room, running a fingertip along the walls, over the bedspread, the bedposts. Certainly the textures were interesting, and yet...

He paused when he spotted a picture framed in what appeared to be silver. The frame itself would have caught his attention, but it was the picture that drew him. His brother, smiling. He was wearing a tuxedo and looking very pleased with himself. His arm was around the woman called Libby. She had flowers in her hair and wore a white full-sleeved dress that laced to the throat.

A wedding dress, Jacob mused. In his own time the ceremony was coming back into style after having fallen into disfavor in the latter part of the previous century. Couples were finding a new pleasure in the old traditions. It had no basis in logic, of course. There was a contract to seal a marriage, and a contract to end one. Each was as easily forged as the other. But elaborate weddings were in fashion once more.

Churches were once again the favored atmosphere for the exchange of rings and vows. Designers were frantically copying gowns from museums and old videos. The gown Libby wore would have drawn moans of envy from those who admired the fuss and bother of marriage rites.

He couldn't imagine it. The entire business puzzled him, and it would have amused him if not for the fact that it involved his brother. Not Cal, who had always been enamored of women in general but never of one in particular. The idea of Cal being matched was illogical. And yet he was holding the proof in his hand.

It infuriated him.

To have left his family, his home, his world. And for a woman. Jacob slammed the picture down on the dresser and turned away. It had been madness. There was no other explanation. One woman couldn't change a life so drastically. And what else was there here to tempt a man? Oh, it was an interesting place, certainly. Fascinating enough to warrant a few weeks of study and research. He would undoubtedly write a series of papers on the experience when he returned to his own time. But…what was the ancient saying? A nice place to visit, but I wouldn't want to live there.

He would put Caleb in his right mind again. Whatever the woman had done to him he would undo. No one knew Caleb Hornblower better than his own brother.

They had been together not so long ago. Time was relative, he thought again, but without humor. The last evening they had spent together had been in Jacob's quarters at the university. They'd played poker and drank Venusian rum—a particularly potent liquor manufactured on the neighboring planet. Cal had commandeered an entire case from his last run.

As Jacob remembered, Cal had lost at cards, cheerfully and elaborately, as was his habit.

They had both gotten sloppy drunk.

"When I get back from this run," Cal had said, tipping back in his chair and yawning hugely, "I'm going to spend three weeks on the beach—south of France, I think—watching women and staying drunk."

"Three days," Jacob had told him. He'd swirled the coal-black liquor in his glass. "Then you'd go up again. In the last ten years you've been in the air more than on the ground."

"You don't fly enough." With a grin, Cal had taken Jacob's glass and downed the contents. "Stuck in your lab, little brother. I tell you it's a lot more fun to bounce around the planets than to study them."

"Point of view. If I didn't study them, you couldn't bounce around them." He had slid down in his chair, too lazy to pour himself more rum. "Besides, you're a better pilot than I am. It's the only thing you do better than I do."

Cal had grinned again. "Point of view," he had tossed back. "Ask Linsy McCellan."

Jacob had stirred himself enough to raise a brow. That particular woman, a dancer, had generously shared her attributes with both men—on separate occasions. "She's too easily entertained." His smile had turned wicked. "In any case, I'm here, on the ground, with her, a great deal more than you are."

"Even Linsy—" he lifted his glass "—bless her, can't compete with flying."

"With running cargo, Cal? If you'd stayed with the ISF you'd be a major by now."

Cal had only shrugged. "I'll leave the regimentation for you, Dr. Hornblower." Then he had sat up, sluggish from drink but still eager. "J.T., why don't you give this place the shake for a few weeks and come with me? There's this club in the Brigston Colony on Mars that needs to be seen to be believed. There's this mutant sax player— Anyhow, you've got to be there."

"I've got work."

"You've always got work," Cal had pointed out. "A couple of weeks, J.T. Fly up with me. I can make the transport, show you a few of the seedier parts of the colony, then I can call in to base before we watch those women on the beach. You just have to name the beach."

It had been tempting, so tempting that Jacob had nearly agreed. The impulse had been there, as always. But so had the responsibilities. "Can't." Heaving a sigh, he'd lunged for the bottle again. "I have to finish these equations before the first of the month."

He should have gone, Jacob thought now. He should have said the hell with the equations, with the responsibilities, and jumped ship with Cal. Maybe it wouldn't have happened if he'd been along. Or, if it had, at least he would have been there, with his brother.

The video report on Cal's wounded ship had shown exactly what Cal had been through. The black hole, the panic, the helplessness as he'd been sucked toward the void and battered by its gravitational field. That he had survived at all was a miracle, and a tribute to his skill as a pilot. But if he'd had a scientist on board he might have avoided the rest. And he would be home now. They would both be home. Where they belonged.

Calming himself, he turned from the window. In a few weeks, they would be. All he had to do was wait.

To pass the time, he began to toy with the clunky computer sitting on the desk in the corner. For an hour he amused himself with it, dismantling the keyboard and putting it together again, examining switches and circuits and chips. For his own entertainment he slipped one of Libby's disks into the drive.

It was a long, involved report on some remote tribe in the South Pacific. Despite himself, Jacob found himself caught up in the descriptions and theories. She had a way of turning dry facts about a culture into a testament to the people who made it. It was ironic that she had focused on the effects of modern tools and technology on what was to her a primitive society. He had spent a great deal of time over the last year wondering what effect the technology he had at his fingertips would have on her time and place.

She was intelligent, he admitted grudgingly. She was obviously thorough and precise when it came to her work. Those were qualities he could admire. But that didn't mean she could keep his brother.

Shutting the machine down, he went back downstairs.

Sunny didn't bother to look up when she heard him come down the stairs. She wanted to think she'd forgotten he was there at all as she'd pored over her law books. But she hadn't. She couldn't complain that he was noisy or made a nuisance of himself. Except that he did make a nuisance of himself just by being there.

Because she wanted to be alone, she told herself as she glanced up and watched him stroll into the kitchen. That wasn't true. She hated to be alone for long periods of time. She liked people and conversation, arguments and parties. But he bothered her. Tapping her pen against her pad, she studied the fire. Why? That was the big question.

Possibly loony, she wrote on her pad. Then she grinned to herself. Actually, it was more than possible that he'd had a clearance sale on the top floor. Popping out of nowhere, living in the forest, playing with faucets.

Possibly dangerous. That turned her grin into a scowl. There weren't many men who could get past her guard the way he had. But he hadn't hurt her, and she had to admit he'd had the opportunity. Still, there was a difference between dangerous and violent.

Forceful personality. There was an intensity about him that couldn't be ignored. Even when he was quiet, watchful in that strange way of his, he seemed to be charged. A live wire ready to shock. Then he would smile, unexpectedly, disarmingly, and you were willing to risk the jolt.

Wildly attractive. Sunny didn't like the phrase, but it suited him too well for her not to use it. There was something ruthless and untamed in his looks—the lean, almost predatory face and the mane of dark hair. And his eyes, that deep, dark green that seemed to look straight into you. The heavy lids didn't give them a sleepy look, but a brooding one.

Heathcliff, she thought, and laughed at herself. It was Libby who was the romantic one. Libby would always look into a person's heart. Sunny would always be compelled to dissect the brain.

Absently she sketched his face on a corner of the paper. There was something different about him, she mused as she penciled in the dark brows and the heavy lashes. It bothered her that she couldn't put her finger on it. He was evasive, secretive, eccentric. She could accept all that—once she discovered what he was evading. Was he in trouble? Had he done something that required him to pack up quickly and find a place, a quiet, remote place, to hide?

Or was it really as simple as he said? He had come to see his brother and to get a firsthand look at his brother's wife.

No. Scowling down at the impromptu portrait, Sunny shook her head. That might be the truth, but it was no more than half of it. J.T. Hornblower was up to something. And, sooner or later, she was going to find out what it was.

With a shrug, she set her pad aside. That was reason enough for her interest in Jacob Hornblower. She only wanted to know what made the man tick. With that in mind, she rose and went into the kitchen.

"What in the hell are you doing?"

Jacob glanced up. Spread all over the table in front of him were the various parts of the toaster and a carpet of crumbs. He'd found a screwdriver in a drawer and was having the time of his life.

"It needs to be fixed."

"Yes, but—"

"Do you like your bread burned?"

She narrowed her eyes. His fingers, long, lean and clever, skimmed over screws. "Do you know what you're doing?"

"Maybe." He smiled, wondering what she would say if he told her he could dismantle an X-25 primary unit in under an hour. "Don't you trust me?"

"No." She turned to put on the kettle. "But I don't suppose you can make it any worse than it already is." Friendly, she reminded herself. She would be friendly and casual, then move in for the kill. "Want some tea?"

"Sure." With the screwdriver in his hand, he watched her walk from stove to cupboard and back to stove. Grace, he thought, when combined with strength, was an appealing combination. She had a way of shifting her weight so that her whole body flowed into the movement. Yet there was a control about her, the kind of discipline seen in athletes and dancers. And it wasn't genderless, but innately and completely female.

When the nerves at the back of her neck began to prickle, she glanced over her shoulder. "Problem?"

"No. I like to watch you."

Because she didn't have a ready response for that, she poured the tea. "Want a cupcake?"

"Okay."

She tossed him a little chocolate cake wrapped in clear paper. "If you want something more elaborate for lunch, you're on your own." She brought the cups to the table, then sat across from him. "How are you with plumbing?"

"Excuse me?"

"The faucet in the tub leaks." Sunny tore the paper from her cupcake. "My solution's been to put a washrag on the drain to muffle the noise at night, but if you're handy there's probably a wrench around somewhere." She took the first bite, closing her eyes to better enjoy the taste. "We could consider it a trade-off for your meals."

"I can take a look." He was still holding the screwdriver, but he was more interested in the way she gently licked icing from the cake. It had never occurred to him that eating could be quite so sexy. "Do you live alone?"

She lifted a brow, then nipped at the cake again. "Obviously."

"When you're not here."

"Most of the time." She sucked chocolate from her finger and had his stomach clenching. "I like living alone, not having to check with anyone if I want to eat at ten or go dancing at midnight. Do you?"

"What?"

"Live alone?"

"Yes. My work takes up most of my time."

"Physics, right? Too bad." She settled back with her tea. The idea of him being a spy was beginning to sound absurd. And, to give him his due, she decided, he wasn't as crazy as she'd initially believed. Eccentric, she thought. If there was one thing Sunny understood, it was eccentricity. She'd lived with it all of her life. "So you really like splitting atoms, or whatever it is you guys do?"

"Something like that."

"What's your stand on nuclear reactors?"

He nearly laughed, but then he remembered where

he was. "Nuclear fission is like trying to dispose of a mouse with a rocket launcher. Dangerous and unnecessary."

"My mother would love you, but that doesn't sound very physicist-like."

"Not all scientists agree." Knowing he was on unsteady ground, he went back to the toaster. "Tell me about your sister."

"Libby? Why?"

"I have an interest in her, since she has my brother."

"She isn't exactly holding him for ransom," Sunny said dryly. "In fact, he rushed her down the aisle so fast, she barely had time to say 'I do.'"

"What aisle?"

"It's a figure of speech, J.T." She spoke slowly now, and with a sigh. "When people get married, they, you know, go down the aisle."

"Oh, right." He thought that over as he fiddled with the toaster. "You're saying that the marriage was Cal's idea."

"I don't know whose idea it was, if that matters, but he was certainly enthusiastic." Her fingers began to drum as her annoyance grew. "I get the impression you think Libby pushed Cal into something here, or that she, I don't know, used feminine wiles to trap him."

"Does she have them?"

After she finished choking on her tea, Sunny took a long breath. "This may be tough for you to understand, Hornblower, but Cal and Libby love each other. You've heard of love, haven't you? Or doesn't it compute?"

"I've heard of the concept," he said, mildly

enough. It was intriguing to watch her temper rise—as it did with very little provocation. Her eyes darkened, her skin flushed, her chin lifted. Attractive when composed, she was simply devastating when aroused. He wouldn't have been human if he hadn't considered how interesting it would be to arouse her in other, more rewarding ways. "I haven't experienced it myself, but I have an open mind."

"That's big of you," she muttered. Rising, she stuffed her hands in the back pockets of her jeans and stalked to the window. Lord, he was a prize. If she managed to keep from murdering him before Cal and Libby got back, it would be a miracle.

"Have you?"

"Have I what?"

"Been in love," he said, running the staff of the screwdriver through his fingers.

She sent him a particularly vicious look. "Keep out of my personal life."

"I'm sorry." He wasn't, not a bit. He was as determined to make her look like a fool as she was to make him sound like one. "It's just that you sounded so knowledgeable on the subject I assumed you'd had quite a bit of experience. Yet you're not matched—married—are you?"

Whether he'd aimed or just shot from the hip, he'd hit the target dead-on. She hadn't been in love, though she'd tried to be several times. Self-doubt only fanned the flames of anger.

"Just because a person hasn't been in love doesn't mean he or she can't appreciate its value." She whirled back, hating the fact that she'd been put on the defensive and determined to turn the conversation around. "The fact that I'm not married is purely a personal choice."

"I see."

The way he said it had her teeth snapping together. "And this has nothing to do with me. We're talking about Libby and Cal."

"I thought we were talking about love as a concept."

"Talking about love with a heartless clod is a waste of time, and I never waste mine." She balled a hand on her hip. "But we both have an interest in Libby and Cal, so we'll clear it up."

"All right." He tapped the screwdriver on the edge of the table. He didn't need a computer to tell him what a clod was. It was just one more thing she would have to pay for before this was over. "Clear it up."

"You automatically assume that my sister, being a woman, lured your brother, being only a man, into marriage. What an incredibly outdated theory."

His fingers paused in the act of reattaching the toaster's coil. "Is it?"

"Incredibly outdated, chauvinistic and stupid. The idea that all women want is marriage and a house with a picket fence went out with the poodle skirt."

Though he wondered who in his right mind would put skirts on poodles, there was something more important to touch on. "Stupid?" he repeated.

"Idiotic." Legs spread, jaw firm, she baited him. "Only a true idiot would be alive today with that kind of neanderthal attitude. Maybe the last few decades have passed you by, pal, but things have changed." She was on a roll now, a slender steamroller with right on her side. "Women have choices today, options, alternatives. An enlightened few even figure that, because they do, men benefit from the same expanding horizons. Except, of course, men like you, who are mired in their own self-importance.''

He stood at that, in a slow, deliberate manner that would have tipped her off if she hadn't been so angry. ''I'm not mired in anything.''

''You're up to your neck in it, Hornblower. From the minute you got here you've been trying to find some way to turn your brother's marriage into a set-up created by my sister.'' She took one long-legged stride toward him. ''I've got a flash for you. Only a fool gets tricked into marriage, and Cal doesn't strike me as a fool. That's where the family resemblance fades.''

A jerk, a clod, an idiot and now a fool. Yes, he thought, she was going to pay. ''Then why did he marry so quickly, without even attempting to come home and see his family first?''

''You'll just have to ask him,'' she shot back. ''It could be because he didn't want to be questioned or hounded or interrogated. In my family we don't pressure the people we love. And in the real world women get along just fine without setting snares for unwary men. The fact is, Hornblower, we don't need you.''

This time it was he who took the step. ''You don't?''

''No. Not for winning the bread or chopping the wood, running the country or taking out the garbage. Or—or fixing toasters,'' she added, with a wild gesture toward the mess on the table. ''We can do everything we need to do just dandy on our own.''

''You left out something.''

Her chin lifted a fraction higher. ''What?''

His hand clamped quickly around the back of her

neck. Sunny had time for a hiss of surprise before his mouth closed over hers. When a woman was expecting a left to the jaw, she had little defense against a heated embrace.

She murmured something. He felt her lips move beneath his. His name, he thought, as the whisper of sound and movement shuddered into him. He was angry—more than angry—but his hair-trigger temper had never taken him so deep into trouble before.

And she was trouble. He'd known it from the first glimpse.

Recklessly he ignored logic and consequences and dragged her closer. Her hands had shot out of her pockets, and now they were clenched taut as wire on his shoulders, neither resisting nor surrendering. He wanted, craved, one or the other. With an oath he nipped at her full, seductive lower lip until her gasp of pleasure shocked the air.

She'd been right about the high-powered voltage that ran through him. Her system was jolted again and again as he held her closer, tighter, harder. She didn't struggle. For, while her body was charged with the current that raced from him into her, her mind emptied, thoughts streaming away like colored chalk in the rain.

She felt his muscles tense under her fingers, heard his sharp intake of breath as she pressed herself more fully against him. She could taste the passion, riper, darker, than any she had ever known, but she couldn't be sure if it was his or her own.

It was as if she had come alive in his arms. He felt her go from rigid shock to molten aggression in the space of a heartbeat. Of all the women he had pleasured, or been pleasured by, he had never known one who matched him so perfectly. Passion to passion, demand to demand.

He ran his hands through her short cap of hair. Warm silk. Down the slender curve of her throat. Hot satin. With his tongue he sampled the potent flavors of her mouth, and then he groaned as she drew him deeper into her.

Never had need spun so quickly out of control, risen so high above the tolerable.

He hurt. And he had never hurt before, not from wanting. He reeled, the way a man might stagger from lack of food or sleep. And he knew fear—a sharp and sudden terror that his own destiny had been removed neatly from his hands.

It was that which had him yanking her away, his fingers biting into her arms as he held her back. His breath came fast and shallow, as if he had raced to the top of a cliff. Indeed, staring at her, he thought he could see the drop, spread below him like a vision of jagged rocks and boiling seas.

She said nothing, just stared with eyes that were huge and dark. In the milky winter light her skin was pale and clear. Like a statue, she stood utterly still, utterly silent. Then she began to tremble.

Jacob snatched his hands away as if he'd been burned.

"I suppose…" Because her voice was weak, Sunny took a long, cleansing breath. "I suppose that was your way of proving a point."

He pushed his hands into his pockets and felt exactly like what she had called him. A fool. "It was a choice between that and a left jab."

Either way, he'd scored a knockout. Steadier now,

she nodded. "If you're going to stay here for the time being, we're going to have to establish some rules."

She recovered quickly, he thought, with a bitterness that surprised him. "Yours, I suppose."

"Yes." She wanted to sit down, badly, but forced herself to face him eye-to-eye. "We can argue all you like. In fact, I enjoy a good argument."

"You're seductive when you argue."

She opened her mouth, then closed it again. No one had ever accused her of that. "I guess you'll just have to learn how to control yourself."

"It's not my strong suit."

"Or take a hike in what's already over a foot of snow."

He glanced toward the window. "I'll work on it."

"Fair enough." She took another long breath. "Though it's obvious we don't like each other very much, we can try to be civil as long as we're stuck with each other."

"Nicely put." He wanted to trace a finger down her cheek but wisely resisted the temptation. "Can I ask you a question?"

"All right."

"Do you usually respond so radically to men you don't like?"

"That's none of your business." Temper brought a flattering tinge of color to her cheeks.

"I thought it was a very civil question." Then he smiled and changed tactics. "But I'll retract it, because if we argue again so soon we'll just end up in bed."

"Of all the—"

"Are you willing to chance it?" he said quietly. He gave a slow, satisfied nod when she subsided. "I thought not. If it makes you feel any better, neither am I.'' So saying, he sat and picked up the tools again. ''Why don't we just cross the whole business off as poor judgment.''

''You were the one who—''

''Yes.'' He looked up, his gaze carefully neutral. ''I was.''

It was pride that had her stalking toward the table when she would have preferred to slink away and nurse her wounds. ''And I suppose it's asking too much to expect an apology.''

''I don't need one,'' he said easily.

She snatched up a toaster part and flung it. ''You're the one who did the manhandling, Hornblower.''

With difficulty, he checked himself. If he touched her again, now, they would both regret it. ''All right. I'm sorry I kissed you, Sunny.'' There was an edge to his voice as his eyes whipped up to hers. ''I can't begin to tell you how sorry.''

She spun around and stormed out of the room. The apology hadn't mollified her. In fact, it had only inflated an angry hurt. She picked up the heaviest book she could find and flung it across the room. She kicked the sofa, swore, then streaked up the steps.

It didn't help. None of it helped. The fury was still roiling inside her. And worse, much worse, was the need, the raw-edged need, that tangled with it. He'd done that, she thought, slamming the door. Deliberately, too. She was sure of it.

He'd managed to make her so angry, to push her so close to the edge, that she'd responded irrationally when he'd kissed her.

It wouldn't happen again—that she promised herself. Humiliation was nearly as bad as being outmaneuvered, and he'd managed to do both in a matter of hours. He was going to have to pay for it.

Throwing herself down on the bed, she decided to spend the rest of the afternoon devising ways to make Jacob Hornblower's life a living hell.

Chapter 4

He never should have touched her. Jacob cursed himself. Then he found that it was much more convenient, and much more satisfying, to curse her. She'd started it, after all. He'd known, right from the start, that she would make trouble for him.

There were some people in this world—in any world, he thought bitterly—who were just born to complicate other people's lives. Sunbeam Stone was one of them. In her looks, in her voice, in her gestures, in her personality, she had everything a woman needed to distract a man. To aggravate him to the edge of reason. And beyond.

She challenged him at every meeting. Those cool smiles, that hot temper. It was a combination he couldn't resist. And he was sure she knew it.

When he'd kissed her—and God knew he hadn't meant to—it had been like being shot into hyperspace without a ship. How could he have known that damn sulky mouth of hers would be so potent?

He'd never been attracted to passive women. But what difference did that make? He had no intention of being attracted to Sunny. He couldn't be. He damn well wouldn't be, no matter what tricks she pulled out of her twentieth-century hat.

What had happened was completely her fault, he decided. She'd taunted and tempted him. She'd wanted to confuse him. Gritting his teeth, he admitted that she'd done a brilliant job of it. After she had and he'd reacted as any normal man would, she'd looked at him with those big, gorgeous eyes full of panic and passion. Oh, she was a case, all right. His study of the twentieth century should have warned him that women had been much more bewildering back then. And craftier.

Hands in pockets, he paced to the window to watch the swirling snow. Oh, she was a bright one, he mused. Sharp as Venusian crystal, and twice as deadly. She knew something wasn't quite right about his story, and she was determined to find out just what he was holding back. And he was just as determined to keep her in the dark.

In a battle of wits, he had every confidence his would prevail. How much effort would it take to outwit a twentieth-century woman? After all, he was more than two hundred years ahead of her on the evolutionary scale. It was a pity she was so intriguing. And so primitively attractive. But he was a scientist, and he had already calculated that any kind of involvement with her would shoot his equations to hell.

Still, she was right about one thing, he decided. They were stuck with each other. The whole damn mountain was practically empty but for the two of them. The way the snow was falling, it was painfully obvious that they would be in each other's way for days. However irritating it might be, for the time being, he needed her.

He had to get around her, or through her, to get to his brother. Whatever it took, he would get to Cal.

Turning, he made a long, slow study of the kitchen. The first thing to be faced was that the cabin was too small for them to avoid each other. He could go back to his ship, but he preferred being here, recording firsthand observations. It would be easier to fight whatever attraction Cal felt for this time and place if he understood it. And his innate curiosity would never be satisfied on the ship.

So he would stay. And if that made the pretty Sunbeam uncomfortable, so much the better.

His own discomfort—and the kiss had caused him plenty—would just have to be dealt with. He was, after all, superior.

Feeling more calm, he went back to the table to reassemble the toaster.

As he worked, he could hear the ceiling creak and groan above his head. He smiled to himself when he realized that she was pacing on the second floor. He bothered her. And that was just fine. Maybe she would keep her distance—or at least stop daring him to do something they would both regret.

It was illogical to desire someone he didn't even like. To fantasize about someone he could barely tolerate. To ache for someone who annoyed him so consistently.

When the screwdriver slipped and mashed his thumb, he cursed her again.

* * *

He wasn't going to get away with it. She paced from wall to wall, from window to door, trying to work off steam. The nerve of the man, to grab her as if she were some mindless bimbo, then reject her just as callously. Did he think, did he really think, he could vent his…his sexual frustrations on her without compunction?

She had news for him.

No one, absolutely no one, treated her in that manner and lived to tell the tale. She'd been taking care of herself for too long. Men might pressure. She pushed them aside. They might seduce. She resisted, effortlessly. They might beg. She—

Her smile bloomed beautifully at the image of Jacob Hornblower begging. Oh, that would be a triumph, she thought. The enigmatic Dr. Hornblower on his knees, at her feet.

With a sigh, she began pacing again. It was a shame, a damn shame, that her standards didn't permit teasing or clichéd feminine ploys. No matter how much of a jerk he was, she had her ethics.

She was a modern woman, one who stood on her own, with or without a man. One who thought her own thoughts and fought her own fights. She was no Delilah to use sex as a weapon. But she wished, and how she wished, that once, just this once, she could ignore those ingrained principles and seduce him into a pitiful puddle of pleading.

He'd used sex, she thought, kicking a shoe out of her path. And wasn't that just like a man? They liked to claim that it was women who lured and teased and taunted. Incensed, she gave the hapless shoe a second, vicious kick. Men, the entire bloody species, preferred to play the innocent bystander entrapped by the femme fatale. Hah!

If anyone dared to call Sunny Stone a femme fatale she'd punch him right in the face.

He'd forced himself on *her*. Well, her stiff-necked honesty pushed her to admit that he hadn't used force for more than a fraction of a second—if at all. Before he'd kissed her senseless.

She hated that. The fact that she'd melted like some weak-kneed romantic heroine. She'd kissed him back, too. What was the word? Wantonly. It made her wince. One lousy kiss and she'd been plastered all over him. So, she owed him for that, as well.

The best way to pay him back, she realized, was to shoot straight for the ego. As far as she could tell, that was the biggest target a man offered a woman. Hiding in her room would only make him think he— and what had happened between them—mattered to her. So she would go about her business and act as though nothing had happened.

He was still in the kitchen when she came down. Sunny turned on the stereo and adjusted the volume. If it was loud enough, conversation would be difficult, if not impossible. After adding a log to the fire, she settled on the sofa with her books. Over an hour passed before he came out and went upstairs. She studiously ignored him.

More from boredom than from appetite, she went into the kitchen and fixed herself an enormous sandwich. Under other circumstances she would have offered to make one for her guest. But the idea of him going hungry just made her own meal that much more palatable.

Content, she bundled into coat and boots to go outside and fill the bird feeder. The short trip brought home to her the fact that her unwelcome company would be in her way for several days. The snow was blinding, falling in swirling sheets that covered her tracks almost as quickly as she made them. There was wind behind it, a nasty wind that raced keening through the trees and sent the pines roaring.

With snow up to the tops of her boots, she lugged the bag of feed back to the shed. Catching her breath, she let the storm blow around her. She could see nothing but the power of it, the anger of it. It was magnificent.

Annoyance faded. All dark thoughts vanished. As she stood with the wind battering her, the snow slapping wet on her cheeks, she felt the excitement and the peace that she rarely felt elsewhere.

Though she never stayed in the mountains long, though she always became restless and went off in search of noise and crowds, there was no place she would rather be in a storm. Winter snow or summer thunder. It was here, alone, that the force, the energy, the mystery, could be appreciated.

A city covered with snow would soon dig itself out. But the mountains were patient. They would wait for sun and time. As she stood with the wind wrapped around her like a wild, relentless lover she wished she could take some piece of this with her wherever she went.

From the window he watched her. She stood like some kind of winter goddess in the whirling snow. Hatless, her coat flapping open, she remained still, heedless, as the snow covered her hair. And she was smiling. Cold colored her cheeks. She seemed more than beautiful now. She seemed untouchable. And invincible.

He wondered as he looked down on her why he wanted her more at that moment than he had when she had been hot and passionate in his arms.

Then she looked up, as if she knew he was watching. Through the blowing curtain of snow, their eyes met. His hands balled into fists, fists identical to the one that clenched in his gut. She was no longer smiling. Despite the distance, he felt the power ricochet back to him, buckling his knees.

If he could have reached out for her then, he would have taken her, regardless of the consequences. In that one look, past, present and future merged into one. He saw his destiny.

Then she shifted, shaking the snow from her hair, and the spell shattered. He told himself she was only a woman, a foolish one, walking in a storm. She would have no lasting effect on him.

But it was a long time after he heard her come inside before he went downstairs again.

She was sleeping on the sofa, books piled at her feet and on the floor. One of the exquisite throws was tossed over her. Despite the volume of the stereo, she slept deeply. Nearby, the fire blazed.

She didn't look invincible now, Jacob decided. She looked disconcertingly serene. He supposed it was foolish to notice how long her lashes were as they shadowed her cheeks. How soft her mouth was when relaxed in sleep. How her hair, mussed from the wind, shone in the firelight.

They were only physical attributes, and in his time physical appearance could be altered simply and safely. It made life more pleasant, certainly, to look at a beautiful woman. But it was superficial. Totally superficial. Still, he looked for a long time.

Sunny woke like a shot when the music cut off. The abrupt silence had her leaping out of sleep with eyes wide and curses on her tongue. Disoriented and irritable, as she always was upon waking, she stared around the darkened room. The fire had burned down to a soft glow and shed little light. Though she didn't think she had slept long, night had fallen. And so, she realized, had a power line.

With a sigh, she pushed herself from the sofa and groped her way across the room looking for matches. With a candle in one hand and a pack of matches in the other, she turned and walked into Jacob.

At her quick squeal, he brought his hands to her arms, both to steady and to reassure. "It's only me."

"I know who it is," she snapped, infuriated that she'd jolted. "What are you doing?"

"Before or after the lights went out?"

She could see him well enough, silhouetted by the firelight, to make out the smile. "It's the storm."

"What about it?" The muscles in her arms were tensed. He had to resist the urge to slip his hands up the sleeves of her sweater and soothe them and stroke her skin.

"It knocked out the power."

He hadn't let her go. He'd told himself to, but his hands hadn't listened. "Would you like me to fix it?"

Her laugh was quick and a bit unsteady. She wished she could blame the power failure for her nerves, but she'd never been afraid of the dark. Until now. "It's a little more complicated than a toaster. The power company will get to it when they can."

He was sure he could jury-rig something, but he didn't mind the dark. "All right."

All right, she thought, letting out a long breath. In the meantime, she was alone with him. Added to the fact that she wasn't sure about his mental balance was the very real problem of being attracted to him. One thing at a time, she told herself, and took a deliberate step back.

"We have plenty of candles." To prove it, she lit the one she held in her hand. It helped her confidence when she saw the flame hold steady. "And plenty of wood. If you'll put a couple of logs on the fire, I'll deal with getting us more light."

He watched the way the small flame flickered in her eyes. She was nervous, he realized, and wished that didn't make her even more seductive. "Sure."

Sunny gathered every candle she could put her hands on. Too late she realized that one or two would have seemed rustic. The dozen she had scattered through the room only added an impossibly romantic atmosphere. Stuffing the matches in her pocket, she reminded herself that she wasn't affected by things like atmosphere.

"You wouldn't know what time it is, would you?" she asked him.

"Not exactly. Around six."

She sat on the arm of the sofa nearest the fire. "I slept longer than I thought." Now she was going to have to make the best of a bad situation. "So, did you entertain yourself this afternoon?"

"I fixed the faucet." It had taken more time and given him more trouble than he'd anticipated, but he'd managed.

"You're a regular Harry Homemaker, aren't you?"

Because it sounded sarcastic, she smiled. They really did only have each other at this point, and alienating him wouldn't be wise. "I could fix some sandwiches." She rose, willing to be gracious if it kept her busy. "Want a beer?"

"Yeah. Thanks."

Sunny took two of the candles into the kitchen and nearly relaxed before she realized he'd followed her in. "I can manage this by myself." She opened the refrigerator and swore when she remembered that the light wouldn't come on. Saying nothing, Jacob handed her a candle. She shoved two beers at him.

He remembered how she had dealt with the bottles that morning, and he was delighted when he found the same tool and popped the tops.

"Switch on the radio, will you?"

"What?"

"The radio," she repeated. "On the windowsill. We might get a weather report."

He found a small plastic box. He was grinning at it as he found the dial and turned on static.

"Mess with the tuner," she advised him.

He was contemplating *borrowing* it and taking it back home. "Mess with it?"

"You know…fool with it. See if you can come up with a station."

He stared at the little portable for a moment, wondering how one fooled an inanimate object. Making sure Sunny's back was to him, he took the radio off the windowsill and shook it. Because that seemed stupid, he began to turn dials. The static faded in and out.

"Mustard or mayo?"

"What?"

"On your sandwich," she said, striving for patience. "Do you want mustard or mayo?"

"It doesn't matter. Whatever you're having." He found some tinny music that was almost audible. How did people tolerate such unreliable equipment? he wondered. At home he had a portable unit that could give him the weather in Paris, a play-by-play of a ball game, a traffic report from Mars and a passable cup of coffee. Simultaneously. This antique child's toy wasn't coming up with anything more than what sounded like a banjo playing in a wind tunnel.

"Let me try." Setting the sandwiches aside, Sunny snatched the radio from him. In moments there was a blast of music. "It's temperamental," she explained.

"It's a machine," he reminded her, miffed.

"A temperamental one." Satisfied, she set it back on the counter, then carried her sandwich and her beer to the table. "Weather report's not much use anyway." She applied herself to the sandwich. "I already know it's snowing."

Jacob picked up one of the potato chips she had piled beside the bread. "More to the point is to know when it's going to stop."

"Speculation." She shrugged as he joined her. "No matter how many satellites they put up there, it's still guesswork."

He opened his mouth to contradict her but thought better of it and bit into his sandwich instead. "Does it bother you?"

"What?"

"Being..." What phrase would she use? "Being cut off."

"Not really—at least not for a day or two. After

that I start to go crazy." She winced, wondering if that was the best choice of words. "How about you?"

"I don't like being closed in," he said simply. He had to smile when he heard the light tap of her foot on the floor. He was making her nervous again. He took an experimental swig of beer. "This is good." He glanced around when a voice broke into the music to announce the weather. The cheerful, painfully breezy announcer carried on for several moments before getting to the mountains.

"And you people way up in the Klamath might as well snuggle up. Hope you've got your main squeeze with you, 'cause it looks like you're in for a big one. The white stuff's going to keep right on falling through tomorrow night. Expect about three feet, you hardy souls, with winds gusting up to thirty miles an hour. *Brrr!* Temperatures down to fifteen tonight, not counting old Mr. Wind Chill. Bundle up, baby, and let *looove* keep you warm."

"Not very scientific," Jacob murmured.

Sunny made a rude noise and scowled at the radio. "However it's presented, it means the same thing. I'd better bring in some more wood."

"I'll get it."

"I don't need—"

"You made the sandwiches," he pointed out, sipping more beer. "I'll get the wood when we're finished."

"Fine." She didn't want him to do her any favors. She ate in silence for a time, watching him. "You'd have been better off to wait until spring."

"For what?"

"To come to see Cal."

He took another bite of his sandwich. He wasn't

sure what it was, but it was terrific. "Apparently. Actually, I'd planned to be here…sooner." Almost a year sooner. "But it didn't work out."

"It's a shame your parents couldn't come with you…you know, to visit."

She saw something in his eyes then. Regret, frustration, anger? She couldn't be sure. "It wasn't possible."

She refused, absolutely, to feel sorry for him. "My parents couldn't stand not seeing Libby or me for so long."

The disapproval in her voice rubbed an already raw wound. "You have no conception of how the separation from Cal has affected my family."

"Sorry." But she moved her shoulders to show that she wasn't. "I'd just think if they were anxious to see him they'd have made the effort to do so."

"The choice was his." He pushed back from the table. "I'll get the wood."

Touchy, touchy, she thought as he started toward the door. "Hey."

He rounded on her, ready to fight. "What?"

"You can't go out without a coat. It's freezing."

"I don't have one with me."

"Are all scientists so softheaded?" she muttered. Rising, she went into a long cupboard. "I can't think of anything so stupid as to come into the mountains in January without a coat."

Jacob took a deep breath and then said calmly, "If you keep calling me stupid, I'm going to have to hit you."

She gave him a bland look. "I'm shaking. Here." She tossed him a worn pea coat. "Put that on. The last thing I want is to have to treat you for frostbite."

As an afterthought, she threw him a pair of gloves and a dark stocking cap. "You do have winters in Philadelphia, don't you?"

His teeth gritted, Jacob struggled into the coat. "It wasn't cold when I left home." He dragged the hat down over his ears.

"Oh, well, that certainly explains it." She gave a snort of laughter when he slammed the door behind him. He wasn't really crazy, she thought. A little dim, maybe, and so much fun to aggravate. And if she aggravated him enough, Sunny mused, she might just get some more information out of him.

She heard him cursing and didn't bother to muffle a laugh. Unless she missed her guess, he'd just dropped at least one log on his foot. Perhaps she should have offered him a flashlight, but...he deserved it.

Wiping the grin from her face, she went to the door to open it for him. He was already coated with snow. It was even clinging to his eyebrows, giving him a fiercely surprised expression. She bit down hard on her tongue and let him stomp across the kitchen, his arms loaded with wood. At the sound of logs crashing into the box, she cleared her throat, then calmly picked up her beer and his before joining him in the living room.

"I'll get the next load," she told him solicitously.

"You bet you will." His foot was throbbing, his fingers were numb, and his temper was already lost. "How does anybody live like this?"

"Like what?" she asked innocently.

"Here." He was at his wit's end. He threw out his arms in a gesture that encompassed not only the cabin but also the world at large. "You have no power, no conveniences, no decent transportation, no nothing. If you want heat, you have to burn wood. Wood, for God's sake! If you want light, you have to rely on unstable electricity. As for communication, it's a joke. A bad one.''

Sunny was a city girl at heart, but nobody insulted her family home. Her chin came up. "Listen, pal, if I hadn't taken you in you'd be up in the woods freezing like a Popsicle and no one would have found you until the spring thaw. So watch it.''

Overly sensitive, he decided, lifting a brow. "You can't tell me that you actually like it here.''

Her hands fisted and landed on her hips. "I like it here just fine. If you don't, we've got two doors. Take your pick.''

His little excursion to the woodpile had convinced him that he didn't care to brave the elements. Neither did he care to swallow his pride. He stood for a moment, considering his choices. Without a word, he picked up his beer, sat and drank.

Since Sunny considered it a victory, she joined him. But she wasn't ready to give him a break. "You're awfully finicky for a guy who pops up on the doorstep without so much as a toothbrush.''

"Excuse me?''

"I said you're awfully—''

"How do you know I don't have a toothbrush?'' He'd read about them. Now, with fire glinting in his eyes, he turned to her.

"It's an expression,'' Sunny said, evading his question. "I simply meant that I wouldn't think that a man who travels with one change of clothes should be complaining about the accommodations.''

"How would you know what I've got—unless you've been going through my things?"

"You haven't got any things," Sunny muttered, knowing that once again she'd opened her mouth before she'd fine-tuned her brain. She started to rise, but he clamped a hand on her shoulder. "Look, I only went through your bag to see—just to see, that's all." She turned, deciding a level look was the best defense. "How could I be sure you were who you said you were and not some maniac?"

He kept his grip painfully firm. "And are you sure now?" He caught the quick flicker in her eyes and decided to exploit it. "There wasn't anything in my bag to tell you one way or the other. Was there?"

"Maybe not." She tried to shrug his hand off. When it remained, she balled one of her own into a fist and waited.

"So, for all you know, I am a maniac." He leaned closer, until his face was an inch from hers, until her eyes saw only his eyes, until his breath mingled with her breath. "And there are all kinds of maniacs, aren't there, Sunny?"

"Yes." She had trouble getting the word past her lips. It wasn't fear. She wished it were. It was something much more complicated, much more dangerous, than fear. For a moment, with the firelight flickering beside them, the candles wavering, the wind beating soft fists on the window, she didn't care who he was. All that mattered was that he was going to kiss her. And more.

The fact that he would do more was in his eyes. The image of rolling on the floor with him sprang into her mind. A wild, willful tangle of bodies, a free, frantic burst of passion. It would be that way with him. The first time, and every time. Raging rivers, quaking earth, exploding planets. Such would love be with him.

And after the first time there would be no turning back. She was certain, as she had never been certain of anything, that if there was a first time, she would want him, she would crave him, as long as there was breath in her body.

His lips brushed hers. It could hardly be called a kiss, yet the potency of it sent shock waves streaking through her system. And had warning bells screaming in her head. She did the only thing a sensible woman could do under the circumstances. She drove her clenched hand into his stomach.

His breath pushed out in a huff of pained surprise. As he doubled over, nearly falling in her lap, she slipped to one side and sprang to her feet. She was braced and ready for his next move.

"You're the maniac," he managed after he'd wheezed some air into his lungs. "I have never in my life met anyone like you."

"Thanks." She was nibbling on her lip again, but she let her tensed arms drop to her sides. "You deserved that, J.T." She held her ground as he slowly lifted his head and sent her a long, killing look. "You were trying to intimidate me."

It had started out that way, he was forced to admit. But in the end, when he had leaned toward her, smelled her hair, felt the soft silk of her lips, it had had nothing to do with intimidation and everything to do with seduction. His. "It wouldn't be hard," he said after a moment, "to learn to detest you."

"No, I guess not." Because he was taking it better than she'd anticipated, she smiled at him. "I tell you what—since we are family, so to speak… I do believe you, by the way. That you're Cal's brother, I mean.''

"Thanks." Finally he managed to straighten up. "Thanks a lot."

"Don't mention it. As I was saying, since we're sort of family, why don't we call a truce? It's like this—if the weather keeps up, we're going to be trapped here together for several days."

"Now who's trying to intimidate whom?"

She laughed then and decided to be friendly. "Just laying my cards on the table. If we keep throwing punches at each other, we're only going to get bruised. I figure it's not worth it."

He had to think about that, and think hard. "I wouldn't mind going for two out of three."

"You're a tough nut, J.T."

Since he didn't know what to make of that description, he kept silent.

"I still vote for the truce, at least until the snow stops. I don't hit you anymore and you don't try to kiss me again. Deal?"

He liked the part about her not hitting him anymore. And he'd already decided he wouldn't *try* to kiss her again. He would damn well *do* it, whenever he chose to. He nodded. "Deal."

"Excellent. We'll celebrate the truce with another beer and some popcorn. We've got an old popper in the kitchen. We can make it over the fire."

"Sunny." She paused, candle in hand, in the doorway. He couldn't help but resent the way the flickering light flattered her. "I'm still not sure I like you."

"That's okay." She smiled. "I'm not sure I like you, either."

Chapter 5

She might have called it rustic. He might have called it primitive. But there was something soothing, peaceful and calming about popping corn over an open fire.

She seemed to have the hang of it, he thought, as she shook the long-handled box over the flames. The scent was enough to make his mouth water as the kernels began to pop and batter the screened metal lid. Though he could have explained scientifically how the hard seeds exploded into fluffy white pieces, it was more fun just to watch.

"We'd always make popcorn this way here," she murmured, watching the flames. "Even in the summer, when we were sweltering, Mom or Dad would build a fire and we'd fight over who got to hold the popper." Her lips curved at the memory.

"You were happy here."

"Sure. I probably would have gone on being happy

here, but I discovered the world. What do you think
of the world, J.T.?''

''Which one?''

With a laugh, she gave the popper an extra shake.
''I should have known better than to ask an astro-
whatever. Your mind's probably in space half the
time.''

''At least.''

She sat cross-legged on the floor, the firelight glowing on her face and hair. That face, he thought, with
its exquisite bones and angles, was perfectly relaxed.
She was obviously taking the truce seriously, ram-
bling on, as friendly as a longtime friend, about whatever came to mind.

He sipped his beer and listened, though he knew
next to nothing about the movies and music she spoke
of. Or the books. Some of the titles were vaguely
familiar, but he had spent very little of his time reading fiction.

He'd touched on some twentieth-century entertainment in his research, but not enough to make him an
expert in the areas Sunny seemed so well versed in.

''You don't like movies?'' she asked at length.

''I didn't say that.''

''You haven't seen any of the flicks I've mentioned
that have been popular in the last eighteen months.''

He wondered what she'd say if he told her that the
last video he'd seen had been produced in 2250. ''It's
just that I've been busy in the lab for quite a while.''

She felt a tug of sympathy for him. Sunny didn't
mind working, and working hard, but she expected
plenty of time for fun. ''Don't they ever give you a
break?''

''Who?''

"The people you work for." She switched hands and continued to shake the popper.

That made him smile a little, since for the past five years he had been in the position of calling his own shots and hiring his own people. "It's more a matter of me being obsessed with the project I've been working on."

"Which is?"

He waited a beat, then decided that the truth couldn't hurt. In fact, he wanted to see her reaction. "Time travel."

She laughed, but then she saw his face and cleared her throat. "You're not joking."

"No." He glanced at the popper. "I think you're burning it."

"Oh." She jerked it out of the flames and set it down on the hearth. "You really mean time travel, like H. G. Wells?"

"Not precisely." He stretched out his legs so that the fire warmed the soles of his feet. "Time and space are relative—in simple terms. It's a matter of finding the proper equations and implementing them."

"Sure. E equals MC squared, but really, J.T., bopping around through time?" She shook her head, obviously amused. "Like Mr. Peabody and Sherman in the Wayback machine."

"Who?"

"You obviously had a deprived childhood. It's a cartoon, you know? And this dog scientist—"

He held up a hand, his eyes narrowed to green slits. "A dog was a scientist?"

"In the cartoon," she said patiently. "And he had this boy, Sherman. Never mind," she added when she saw his expression. "It's just that they would set the dates on this big machine."

"The Wayback."

"Exactly. Then they would travel back, like to Nero's Rome or Arthur's Britain."

"Fascinating."

"Entertaining. It was a cartoon, J.T. You can't really believe it."

He sent her a slow, enigmatic smile. "Do you only believe what you can see?"

"No." She frowned, using a hot pad to remove the lid from the popper. "I guess not." Then she laughed and sampled the popcorn. "Maybe I do. I'm a realist. We really needed one in the family."

"Even a realist has to accept certain possibilities."

"I suppose." She took another handful and decided to get into the spirit of things. "Okay. So, we're in Mr. Peabody's Wayback machine. Where would you go—or when, I suppose I should say? When would you go, if you really could?"

He looked at her, sitting in the firelight, laughter still in her eyes. "The possibilities are endless. What about you?"

"I wonder." She held the beer loosely in her hand as she considered. "I imagine Libby would have a dozen places to go back to. The Aztecs, the Incas, the Mayans. Dad would probably want to see Tombstone or Dodge City. And my mother…well, she'd go where my father went, to keep an eye on him."

He dipped into the popcorn. "I asked about you."

"I'd go forward. I'd want to see what was coming."

He didn't speak, only stared into the fire.

"A hundred, maybe two hundred, years in the future. After all, you can read history books and get a pretty good idea of what things were like before. But after… It seems to me it would be much more exciting to see just what we've made out of things.'' The idea made her laugh up at him. ''Do they actually pay you to work on stuff like that? I mean, wouldn't it make more sense to figure out how to travel across town in, say, Manhattan in under forty minutes during rush hour?''

''I'm free to choose my own projects.''

''Must be nice.'' She was mellow now, relaxed and happy enough with his company. ''It seems I've spent most of my life trying to figure out what I wanted to do. I'm a terrible employee,'' she admitted with a sigh. ''It's something about rules and authority. I'm argumentative.''

''Really?''

She didn't mind his grin. ''Really. But I'm so often right, you see, that it's really hard to admit when I'm wrong. Sometimes I wish I was more…flexible.''

''Why? The world's full of people who give in.''

''Maybe they're happier,'' she murmured. ''It's a shame the word *compromise* is so hard to swallow. You don't like to be wrong, either.''

''I make sure I'm not.''

She laughed and stretched out on the rug. ''Maybe I do like you. We're going to have to tend this fire all night unless we want to freeze. We'll take shifts.'' She yawned and pillowed her head over her hands. ''Wake me up in a couple of hours and I'll take over.''

When he was certain she was asleep, Jacob covered her with the colorful blanket, then left her by the fire. Upstairs, it took him less than ten minutes to make some adjustments to the desktop computer and tie it in so that it would run off his mini unit. The mini didn't have the memory banks of his ship model, but it would be enough to make his report and answer the few questions he had.

"Engage, computer."

A quiet, neutral voice answered him. *Engaged.*

"Report. Hornblower, Jacob. Current date is January 20th. A winter storm has caused me to remain in the cabin. The structure runs off electric power, typically unreliable in this era. Apparently the power is transmitted through overhead lines that are vulnerable during storms. At approximately 1800 hours, the power was cut off. Estimated time of repair?"

Working... Incomplete data.

"I was afraid of that." He paused for a moment, thinking. "Sunbeam Stone is resourceful. Candles—wax candles—are used for light. Wood is burned for heat. It is, of course, insufficient, and only accommodates a small area. It is, however..." He searched for a word. "...pleasant. It creates a certain soothing ambiance." Annoyed, he cut himself off. He didn't want to think of the way she had looked in the firelight. "As reported earlier, Stone is a difficult and aggressive female, prone to bursts of temper. She is also disarmingly generous, sporadically friendly and—" The word *desirable* was on the tip of his tongue. Jacob bit it. "Intriguing," he decided. "Further study is necessary. However, I do not believe she is an average woman of this time." He paused again, drumming his fingers on the desk. "Computer, what are the typical attitudes of women toward mating in this era?"

Working.

As soon as he had asked, Jacob opened his mouth to disengage. But the computer was quick.

Most typically physical attraction, sometimes referred to as chemistry, is required. Emotional attachment, ranging from affection to love is preferred by 97.6 percent of females. Single encounters, often called one-night stands, were no longer fashionable in this part of the twentieth century. Subjects preferred commitment from sexual partners. Romance was widely accepted and desired.

"Define 'romance.'"

Working… To influence by personal attention, flattery or gifts. Also synonymous with love, love affair, an attachment between male and female. Typified by the atmosphere of dim lighting, quiet music, flowers. Accepted romantic gestures include—

"That's enough." Jacob rubbed his hands over his face and wondered if he was going crazy. He had no business wasting time asking the computer such unscientific questions. He had less business contemplating a totally unscientific relationship with Sunny Stone.

He had only two purposes for being where he was. The first and most important was to find his brother. The second was to gather as much data as possible about this era. Sunny Stone was data, and she couldn't be anything else.

But he wanted her. It was unscientific, but it was very real. It was also illogical. How could he want to be with a woman who annoyed him as much as she amused him? Why should he care about a woman he had so little in common with? Centuries separated them. Her world, while fascinating in a clinical sense, frustrated the hell out of him. *She* frustrated the hell out of him.

The best thing to do was to get back to his ship, program his computers and go home. If it weren't for Cal, he would do so. He wanted to think it was only Cal that stopped him.

Meticulously, he disengaged the computer and pocketed his mini. When he returned downstairs, she was still sleeping. Moving quietly, he put another log on the fire, then sat on the floor beside her.

Hours passed, but he didn't bother to wake her. He was used to functioning on little or no sleep. For more than a year his average workday had run eighteen hours. The closer he had come to the final equations for time travel, the more he had pushed. And he had succeeded, he thought as he watched the flames eat the wood. He was here. Of course, even with his meticulous computations, he had come several months too late.

Cal was married, of all things. And if Sunny was to be believed, he was happy and settled. It would be that much more difficult for Jacob to make him see reason. But he would make him see it.

He had to see it, Jacob told himself. It was as clear as glass. A man belonged in his own time. There were reasons, purposes. Beyond what science could do, there was a pattern. If a man chose to break that pattern, the ripple effects on the rest of the universe couldn't be calculated.

So he would take his brother back to where they both belonged. And Cal would soon forget the woman called Libby. Just as Jacob was determined to forget Sunbeam Stone.

She stirred then, with a soft, sighing sound that

tingled along his skin. Despite his better judgment, he looked down and watched her wake.

Her lashes fluttered open and closed, as exotic as butterfly wings in the shadowed light. Her eyes, dazed with sleep, were huge and dark. She didn't see him, but stared blindly into the flickering flame as she slowly stretched her long, lean body, muscle by muscle. The bulky purple sweater shifted over her curves.

His mouth went dry. His heartbeat accelerated. He would have cursed her, but he lacked the strength. At that moment she was so outrageously beautiful that he could only sit, tensed, and pray for sanity.

She let out a little moan. He winced. She shifted onto her back, lifting her arms over her head, then up to the ceiling. For the first time in his life he actively wished for a drink.

At last she turned her head and focused on him. "Why didn't you wake me?"

Her voice was low, throaty. Jacob was certain he could feel his blood drain to the soles of his feet. "I—" It was ridiculous, but he could barely speak. "I wasn't tired."

"That's not the point." She sat up and said crankily, "We're in this together, so—"

He didn't think. Later, when he had time to analyze, he would tell himself it was reflex—the same involuntary reflex that makes a man swallow when water is poured down his throat. It was not deliberate. It was not planned. It was certainly not wise.

He pulled her against him, dragging one hand through her hair before closing his mouth over hers. She bucked, both surprise and anger giving her strength. But he only tightened his hold. It was desperation this time, a sensation he could not remember ever having felt for a woman. It was taste her or die.

She struggled to cling to her anger as dozens of sensations fought for control of her. Delight, desire, delirium. She tried to curse him, but managed only a moan of pleasure. Then her hands were in his hair, clenching, and her heart was pounding. In one quick movement he drew her onto his lap and drove her beyond.

His breath was ragged, as was hers. His mouth frantic, his hands quick. Left without choice, she answered, as insistent, as insatiable, as he. A log broke apart, sparks flew to dance on stone. The wind gusted, pushing a puff of smoke into the room. She heard only the urgent groan that slipped from his mouth into hers.

Was this what she had been searching for? The excitement, the challenge, the glory? Heedlessly she gave herself to it, let the power swamp her.

The taste of her seemed to explode inside him, over and over. Hot, pungent, lusty. It wasn't enough. The more he took, the more he needed. Dragging her head back, he found her throat, the long, slender line of it enticing him, the warm, seductive flavor of it bewitching him. He skimmed his lips over the curve of it, letting his tongue and his teeth toy with her skin. It was still not enough.

As the firelight played over her face, he slipped his hands under the bulky sweater to find her. Her skin brought him images of rose petals, of heated satin. There was trembling as his hand closed over her breast. From her, from him.

With his eyes on hers, and shadows dancing between them, he lowered his mouth once more.

It was like sinking into a dream. Not a soft, misty one, but one full of sound and color. And, as he sank deeper, she wrapped herself around him. Her hands searched as his did, under his sweater, along the ridges of muscles.

As his lips began to roam over her face, she let her eyes close once again. And her heart, always so strong and valiant, was lost.

Love poured into her like a revelation. It left her gasping and clinging. It had her lips heating against his, her body liquefying. Her hands, always capable, slid helplessly down his arms.

Helplessly.

It was that which had her stiffening against him, pulling back, resisting. This couldn't be love. It was absurd, and dangerous, to think it could be.

"Jacob, stop."

"Stop?" He closed his teeth, none too gently, over her chin.

"Yes. Stop."

He could feel the change, the frustrating withdrawal of her while his body was still humming. "Why?"

"Because I…"

In a calculated movement, he skimmed his fingers down her spine, playing them over vulnerable nerves. He watched as her eyes glazed and her head fell back, limp. "I want you, Sunny. And you want me."

"Yes." What was he doing to her? She lifted a hand in protest, then dropped it weakly and let it rest against his chest. "No. Don't do that."

"Do what?"

"Whatever you're doing."

She was trembling now, shuddering. Completely

vulnerable. He cursed himself. It was a shock to realize that when she was defenseless he was hampered by ethics. "Fine." He grasped her hips and set her back on the floor.

Shaken, she hugged her knees to her chest. She felt as though she'd been plucked out of a furnace and tossed into ice. "This shouldn't be happening. And it certainly shouldn't be happening so fast."

"It is happening," he told her. "And it's foolish to pretend otherwise."

She glanced up as he rose to feed the fire. The heat still pumped out of the logs. A few of the candles they had left lit were guttering out. Outside the window there was a lessening of the darkness, so dawn had to be breaking beyond the storm. The wind still whooshed at the windows.

She had forgotten all that. All that and more. When she had been in his arms there had been no storm except the one raging inside her. There had been no fire but her own passions. The one promise she had made herself, never to lose control over a man, had been broken.

"It's easy for you, isn't it?" she said, with a bitterness that surprised her.

He looked back to study her. No, it wasn't easy for him. It should be, but it wasn't. And he was baffled by it. "Why should it be complicated?" The question was as much for himself as for her.

"I don't make love with strangers." She sprang to her feet with a fierce wish for coffee and solitude. Leaving him, she marched into the kitchen and plucked a soft drink from the refrigerator. She'd take her caffeine cold.

He waited a moment, going over what the computer had told him. The physical attraction was certainly there. And, as much as he detested the idea, his emotions were involved. It did no good to be angry. She was obviously reacting normally, given the situation. And it was he who was out of step. It was a sobering thought, but one that had to be faced.

But he still wanted her. And now he intended to pursue her. Logically, his success factor would increase if he pursued her in a manner she would expect from a typical twentieth-century man.

Jacob blew out a long breath. He didn't know precisely what that might entail, but he thought he understood the first step. It was doubtful that much had changed in any millennium.

When he walked into the kitchen, she was staring out the window at the monotonously falling snow. "Sunny." Oh, it went against the grain. "I apologize."

"I don't want your apology."

Jacob cast his eyes at the ceiling and prayed for patience. "What do you want?"

"Nothing." It amazed her that she was on the brink of tears. She never cried. She hated it, considered it a weak, embarrassing experience. Sunny always preferred a screaming rage to tears. But she felt tears burning behind her eyes now and stubbornly fought them back. "Just forget it."

"Forget what happened, or forget the fact that I'm attracted to you?"

"Either or both." She turned then. Though her eyes were dry, they were overbright, and they made him acutely uncomfortable. "It doesn't matter."

"Obviously it does." It shouldn't, but there seemed to be nothing he could do to change it. If she kept looking at him like that, he would have to touch her again. In self-defense he stuffed his hands in his pockets. "Maybe we've gotten our codes mixed."

Hurt was temporarily blocked by bafflement. "I don't—do you mean we got our signals crossed?"

"I suppose."

Tired all over again, she dragged a hand through her hair. "I doubt it. We'll just call it a temporary lapse."

"And do what?"

She wished she knew. "Look, J.T., we're both adults. All we have to do is act like it."

"I thought we were." He tried a smile. "I'm sorry I upset you."

"It wasn't completely your fault." She managed to smile back at him. "Circumstances. We're alone here, the power's out. Candle and firelight." She shrugged and felt miserable. "Anybody could get carried away."

"If you say so." He took a step forward. She took a step back. The pursuit, Jacob decided, was going to require strategy. "But I am attracted to you, even without candlelight."

She started to speak, discovered she didn't know what she wanted to say and dragged her hands through her hair again. "You should get some sleep. I'm going for more wood."

"All right. Sunbeam?"

She turned back, shooting him a look of amusement and exasperation at his use of her full name.

"I enjoyed kissing you," he told her. "Very much."

Muttering under her breath, she bundled into her coat and escaped outside.

* * *

The day passed slowly. Sunny might have wished he would sleep longer, but it hardly mattered. Awake or asleep, he was there. As long as he was, he intruded. At times, though she tried to bury herself in her books, she was so painfully aware of him that she nearly groaned.

He read—voraciously, Sunny thought—novel after novel from the bookshelf. Activity was almost completely confined to the living room and the warmth of the fire, which they took turns feeding.

At lunchtime they fell back on cold sandwiches, though she did manage to boil water over the fire for tea. They spoke to each other only when it was impossible not to.

By evening they were both wildly restless, edgy from confinement and from the fact that both of them wondered what the day would have been like if they had spent it under a blanket, together, rather than at opposite ends of the room.

He paced to one window. She paced to another. She poked at the fire. He leafed through yet another book. She went for a bag of cookies. He went for fresh candles.

"Have you ever read this?"

Sunny glanced over. It was the first word they had spoken to each other in an hour. "What?"

"Jane Eyre."

"Oh, sure." It was a relief to have a conversation again. She handed him the bag of cookies as a peace offering.

"What did you think of it?"

"I always like reading about the mannerisms of an earlier century. They were so stringent and puritanical back then, with all that passion boiling underneath the civilized veneer.''

He had to smile. ''Do you think so?''

''Sure. And of course it's beautifully written, and wonderfully romantic.'' She sat with her legs hooked over the arm of a chair, her eyes a little sleepy and her scent—damn her—everywhere. ''The plain, penniless girl capturing the heart of the bold, brooding hero.''

He gave her a puzzled look. ''That's romantic?''

''Of course. Then there's windswept moors and painful tragedy, sacrifice. They did a terrific production of it on PBS a few years ago. Did you see it?''

''No.'' He set the book aside, still puzzled. ''My mother has a copy at home. She loves to read novels.''

''That's probably because she needs to relax after being in court all day.''

''Probably.''

''What does your father do?''

''This and that.'' Suddenly his family seemed incredibly far away. ''He likes to garden.''

''So does mine. Herbs, naturally.'' She gestured toward her empty tea cup. ''But he putters around with flowers, too. When we were little he grew vegetables right outside the kitchen. It's practically all we ate, which is why I avoid them now.''

He tried to imagine it and simply couldn't. ''What was it like growing up here?''

''It seemed natural.'' She rose idly to poke at the fire, then sat on the couch beside him, forgetting for a moment how restless the storm was making her. ''I guess I thought everyone lived like we did, until we went to the city and I saw the lights, the crowds, the buildings. For me, it was as if someone had broken open a kaleidoscope and handed me all the colors. We would always come back here, and that was fine." With a half yawn, she sank back into the cushions. "But I always wanted to get back to all that noise. Nothing changes much here, and that's nice, because you can always depend on it. But there's always something new in the city. I guess I like progress."

"But you're here now."

"A self-imposed penance, in a way."

"For what?"

She moved her shoulders. "It's a long story. What about you? Are you a city boy yearning for the peace of the country?"

He glanced deliberately out the window. "No."

She laughed and patted his hand. "So here we are, two city dwellers stuck in the wilds of the Northwest. Want to play cards?"

His mood brightened instantly. "Poker?"

"You're on."

They rose at the same time, bumped, brushed. He took her arm automatically, then held on. He tensed, as she did. It wasn't possible to do otherwise. It was possible, barely, to prevent himself from lifting his other hand to her face. She'd done nothing to enhance it today. There was no trace of cosmetics. Her mouth, full, pouty, exciting, was naked. With an effort, he brought his eyes from it, and to hers.

"You're very beautiful, Sunbeam."

It hurt to breathe. She was terrified to move. "I told you not to call me that."

"Sometimes it fits. I've always thought beauty was

just an accident of genes or something accomplished through skill. You make me wonder.''

"You're a very strange man, Hornblower."

He smiled a little. "You don't know the half of it." He stepped back. "We'd better play cards."

"Good idea." She let out a quiet, relieved breath as she took the deck from a drawer. If she had a little time, alone, she might just figure out what it was about him that jolted her system. "Poker by firelight." She dropped onto the floor. "Now that's romance."

He sat opposite her. "Is it?"

"Prepare to lose."

But he won, consistently, continually, until she began to watch him through narrowed eyes. For lack of anything else, they were playing for cookies, and his pile of chocolate chips kept growing.

"You eat all those you're going to get fat."

He merely smiled. "No, I won't. I have an excellent metabolism."

"Yeah, I just bet you do." With a body like that, he'd have to. "Two pair, queens and fours."

"Mmm." He set his cards down. "Full house, tens over fives."

"Sonofa—" She broke off, scowling, as he raked in the chips. "Look, I don't want to sound like a sore loser, but you've won ten out of twelve hands."

"Must be my lucky night." He picked up the cards and riffled them.

"Or something."

He merely lifted a brow at her tone. "Poker is as much a science as physics."

She snatched up a cookie. "Just deal, Hornblower."

"Are you going to eat your ante?"

Miffed, she tossed it into the pot. "If I don't eat several times a day I get cranky."

"Is that what's wrong with you?"

"I'm basically a very nice person."

"No, you're not." He grinned as he dealt the cards. "But I like you anyway."

"I am nice," she insisted, keeping her face carefully bland when she spotted two aces in her hand. "Ask anybody—except my last two supervisors. Open for two."

Jacob obliged her by adding his two cookies to the pot. He liked her this way—warily friendly, competitive, relaxed, but ready to pounce on any infraction. He supposed it didn't hurt that the firelight painted interesting shadows that played over those fabulous cheekbones. He checked himself—and his hand. This seemed as good a time as any to find out more about her.

"What did you do, before you came here to decide to be a lawyer?"

She made a face, then drew three cards. "I sold underwear. Ladies' lingerie, to be specific." She glanced up, waiting for the disdain, and was mollified when she didn't see it. "I have a drawerful of great stuff I got on discount."

"Oh, really?" He thought about that for a moment, wondering just what her idea of great stuff consisted of.

"Yeah." She was delighted to see that she'd drawn another ace, but she kept her voice even. "The problem was, this particular supervisor wanted you to take the money, box the silks and keep your mouth shut—

even when the customer was making an obvious mistake.''

He tried to imagine her keeping her mouth shut. He couldn't. ''Such as?''

''Such as the pleasantly plump lady who was going to torture herself in a size eight merry widow. Bet three.''

''And raise it two. What happened?''

''Well, you open your mouth to make a gentle suggestion and before you know it you've got a pink slip.''

''You'd look nice in pink.''

She giggled and raised him two more. ''No...a pink slip, the boot, the ax. Canned.'' When he still looked puzzled, she elaborated. ''Your services are no longer required.''

''Oh. Terminated.''

''Right.'' His term seemed to describe the injustice of it perfectly. ''Who needs it?''

''You don't.''

She smiled at him. ''Thanks. Three aces, pal. Read 'em and weep.''

''Straight flush,'' he countered, and had her sputtering while he piled up more cookies. ''You don't have the temperament to work for someone else.''

''So I've been told,'' she muttered. ''Several times.'' She was down to her last five cookies. Her luck, Sunny thought, had been on the down side too long. ''But if it's a matter of learning how to adjust or learning how not to eat I'm going to have to go with the first. I don't like being poor.''

''I imagine you could do whatever you wanted to do, if you really wanted to do it.''

''Maybe.'' And that had always been the problem.

She had no idea what she wanted. She dealt the hand and, deciding to be reckless, went for an inside straight. And ended up with trash. A bluff was always better than a fold, she thought, pushing her miserly pile of cookies into the pot.

He cleaned her out with a pair of deuces.

"Here." Because winning always put him in a good mood, he offered her a cookie. "Have one on me."

"Thanks a lot." She bit into it. "Your luck seems to be on tonight."

"Apparently." He was feeling a bit reckless himself. She looked a great deal more appetizing than the cookies. "We could play one more hand."

"For what?"

"If I win, you make love with me."

Surprised, but determined to keep her poker face intact, she swallowed the bite of cookie. "And if I win?"

"I make love with you."

Popping the rest of the cookie into her mouth, she studied him as she chewed. It would almost be worth it, she mused, to see his face if she took him up on it. Almost worth it, she reminded herself. Either way, she would win. And she would lose.

"I think I'll pass," she said lightly. Rising, she walked over to the sofa, spread herself out on it and went to sleep.

Chapter 6

A blast of music ripped Sunny out of a dead sleep and had her rearing up. When lights blinded her, she groaned and tossed a hand over her eyes in self-defense.

"Who ordered the party?" she asked as Tina Turner roared out rock at top volume.

Jacob, who had dozed off in front of the fire, simply pulled the blanket over his head. Whenever he slept, he preferred to do it like the dead.

Swearing, she pushed herself up off the couch. She had stumbled halfway to the stereo before it dawned on her. "Power!" she shouted, then immediately raced over to sit on Jacob. She heard a muffled grunt from under the blanket and bounced gleefully up and down. "We've got power, J.T. Lights, music, hot food!" When he only grunted again, she poked him. "Wake up, you slug. Don't you know you can be shot for sleeping on sentry duty?"

"I wasn't sleeping. I was bored into catatonia."

"Well, snap out of it, pal. We're back on the circuit." She yanked the cover off his face and grinned when he scowled at her. "You need a shave," she observed. Then, in her delight, she gave him a loud, smacking kiss between the eyes. "How about a hamburger?"

He got a bleary look at her face, all smiles and mussed hair. To his disgust, he felt his body responding. "It can't be more than six in the morning."

"So what? I'm starving."

"Make mine rare." He pulled the blanket over his face again.

"Uh-uh. You have to help." Ruthlessly she ripped the blanket off him again. "Up and at 'em, soldier."

This time he opened only one eye. "Up and at what?"

"It's an expression, Hornblower." She shook her head. "Just how long were you in that lab?"

"Not long enough." Or entirely too long, if all it took to arouse him was a skinny woman sitting on his chest. "I can't get up when you're sitting on me. Besides, I think you broke my ribs."

"Nonsense. I'm ten pounds underweight."

"You wouldn't think so from here."

Too cheerful to be annoyed, she scrambled up, took a firm grip on his forearm and, after some pulling and tugging, dragged him to his feet. "You can make the french fries."

"I can?"

"Sure." To demonstrate her confidence in him, she kept her hand in his and pulled him into the kitchen. "Everything's in the freezer. God, it's cold in here." She rubbed the bottom of one stockinged foot on the top of the other. "Here." She tossed him a bag of frozen fries over her shoulder. "You just dump some on a cookie sheet and stick them in the oven."

"Right." He thought he could figure out the workings of the oven, but he hadn't a clue as to what a cookie sheet might look like.

"Pans are...down there." She gestured vaguely in the direction of a cabinet while she contemplated the package of hamburger.

"The meat's frozen," he pointed out.

"Yeah. Well, we'll have sloppy joes."

"Which are?"

"Delicious," she assured him. Whistling along with the music, she began to rattle pots. Cooking was far down on her list of favorite pastimes, but when push came to shove she was willing to give it her best shot. "Here, use this." She handed him a long, thin piece of metal blackened by heat.

The cookie sheet, Jacob surmised. He went to work. "I don't suppose there's a possibility of coffee."

"Sure. I keep a stash." Still whistling, she dumped the chunk of frozen meat in a pot and set it on low. In moments she had water on to boil and cups waiting. "Heat, hot water, real food." She did a quick little tap dance before digging into a bag of potato chips. "You don't appreciate the little things until you can't have them," she said with her mouth full. "I don't know how people managed before electricity. Imagine having to heat water over an open fire. It must have taken forever."

Jacob was watching the electric ring slowly turn red under the kettle. "Amazing," he agreed, and contemplated just eating the coffee grounds dry.

"Those fries won't cook unless you put them in the oven."

"Yeah." He wished she wouldn't watch him as he studied the dials. The Bake setting seemed safe enough—unless they were supposed to be broiled. He would have given a year of his life for the nutritional center in his lab.

"Spend much time in the kitchen?" Sunny asked from behind him.

"No."

"Who would have guessed?" With a cluck of her tongue, she turned the oven on, then popped the tray inside. "Takes about ten, maybe fifteen."

"Seconds?"

"I love an optimist. Minutes." Because she understood what it was like to wake up ready to chew glass, she patted his cheek. "Why don't you go have a shower? You'll feel better. Most of this should come together by the time you're finished."

"Thanks." As he made his way upstairs he figured it was the nicest thing she'd done for him so far.

He spent a great deal of time cursing the ridiculously archaic workings of her shower. But she was right. He did feel better when he'd accomplished it. Using his ultrasound, he rid himself of his beard. Then he took his daily dose of fluoratyne for his teeth and, curious, poked inside the mirrored cabinet over the sink.

It was a scientific treasure trove. Lotions, potions, creams, powders. A glance at the safety razor made him shudder. The toothbrush made him grin. He saw little puffs of white that appeared to be cotton, thin brushes, tiny pots filled with vividly colored powder.

There was a cream with an exotic name. When he

opened the top and sniffed, it was as if Sunny had joined him in the small, steamy room. He made quick work of putting it back on the shelf.

There were pills. A cursory glance showed him that she had them for headaches, body aches, head colds, chest colds. He would make a note to take back a few samples. There was a small plastic case that held a circle of tiny pills that weren't marked at all. Since they were half gone, he assumed they were something she took regularly. That concerned him. He didn't like to think that she was ill. Replacing them, he wondered how he might ask her about her medication.

He started downstairs, then simply followed the scents. He didn't know what she could have done with the hunk of frozen meat, but it smelled like heaven. And there was coffee. No perfume could have been sweeter. She handed him a cup as he walked in the door.

"Thanks."

"It's okay. I know how it feels."

He sipped, giving her a clinical study over the rim. Her eyes were clear, and her color was good. She looked perfectly healthy. In fact, he couldn't remember ever having seen anyone healthier. Or more alluring.

"When you look at me like that I feel like a germ under a microscope."

"Sorry. I was just going to ask how you felt."

"A little stiff, a lot hungry, but basically okay." She tilted her head. "How about you?"

"Fine. I had a headache," he said, suddenly inspired. "I took some of your pills."

"Okay."

"The ones in the little blue case weren't marked."

Her eyes widened, rolled, then filled with laughter. "I don't think they'd do you much good."

"But you need them?"

This time she closed her eyes and shook her head. "And he calls himself a scientist. Yeah, you could say I need them. Better safe than sorry, right?"

Baffled, but losing ground, he nodded. "Right."

"Then let's eat."

She had plates by the range with buns open on them. Using a generous hand, she scooped the saucy meat into them, tossed a heap of fries beside it and was done. She didn't speak again until she'd worked her way through half the meal.

He watched her dump a stream of white crystal from a pottery tube on her potatoes. He shook some on his own experimentally. Salt, he discovered. The real thing. Though the taste was wonderful, he resisted the temptation to use more and wondered about her blood pressure. If he could have figured a way, he would have popped her into the medilab on the ship for a checkup.

"I guess we're going to live."

He wasn't sure what he was eating, but she was right again. It was delicious. "It stopped snowing."

"Yeah, I noticed. Listen, I hate to say it, but I'm glad you were here. I'd have hated to be here alone the last couple of days."

"You're pretty self-sufficient."

"But it's better when you have somebody to fight with. I never asked...do you plan to hang around until Cal and Libby get back? It could be weeks."

"I came to see him. I'll wait."

She nodded, wishing his answer hadn't relieved her. She was getting entirely too used to his company.

"I guess you must be in a position to take as much time off as you like."

"You could say that time is exactly what I do have. How long are you staying?"

"I'm not sure. It's too late to get into school this semester. I thought I might write to some colleges. Maybe I'll try the East Coast. It would be a change." She sent him a quick, hesitant smile. "How would I like Philadelphia?"

"I think you would." He wondered how to describe it to her so that she would understand. "It's beautiful. The historic district is very well preserved."

"The Liberty Bell, Ben Franklin, all that."

"Yes. Some things last, no matter what else changes." Though it had never mattered much to him before. "The parks are very green and shady. In the summer they're full of children and students. The traffic's miserable, but that's all part of it. From the top of some of the buildings you can see the entire city, the movement, the old and the new."

"You miss it."

"Yes. More than I'd imagined." But he was looking at her, seeing only her. "I'd like to show it to you."

"I'd like that, too. Maybe we can talk Cal and Libby into flying out. You could have a real family reunion." She saw his expression change and instinctively laid a hand over his. "Did I say something wrong?"

"No."

"You're angry with him," Sunny murmured.

"It's personal."

But she wasn't going to be put off. He wasn't the

snarling idiot she had first assumed him to be. He was just confused. If there was one trait she shared equally with her sister, it was the inability to turn away a stray.

"J.T., you must see how unfair it is to resent Cal for falling in love and getting married, for starting a life here."

"It's not that simple."

"Of course it is." This time, she promised herself, she would not lose her temper. "They're both adults, and they're certainly able to make up their own minds. Besides, well, they're wonderful together." He sent her a silent, cynical look that infuriated her. "They are. I've seen them with each other. You haven't."

"No." He nodded. "I haven't."

"That's nobody's fault but—" She caught herself, ground her teeth and went on, more calmly. "What I'm trying to say is that I might not have known Cal before he became part of the family, but I know when someone's happy. And he is. As for Libby—he does something for her no one else ever has. She's always been so shy, so easily pushed into the background. But with Cal she just glows. Maybe it's not the easiest thing to accept that someone else is the best thing that ever happened to a person you love—but you have to accept it when it's true."

"I don't have anything against your sister." Or, if he did, he intended to keep it to himself for the time being. "But I intend to talk to Cal about the change he's made in his life."

"You really are bullheaded."

He considered the description and decided it was apt enough. "Yes." He smiled at her, delighted by the sulky mouth, the lifted chin. "I'd say we both are."

"At least I don't go around poking my nose into other people's affairs."

"Not even pleasantly plump women who want to torture themselves into…what was it—a Merry Widow?"

"That was entirely different." With a sniff, she pushed her plate away. "I may be cynical, but even I believe in love."

"I never said I didn't."

"Oh, really?" Her lips curved, because she was sure she had backed him into a corner. "Then you won't interfere if you see that Cal and Libby are in love."

"If they are, I hardly could, could I? And if they're not—" he gestured, palm up, "—then we'll see."

She steepled her fingers, measured him. "I could always send you back into the forest, let you freeze in your sleeping bag."

"But you won't." He toasted her with his coffee cup. "Because, underneath the prickly hide, you're basically kindhearted."

"I could change."

"No, you couldn't. People don't, as a rule." Abruptly intense, he leaned forward to take her hand. It was a gesture he didn't make often, and one that he couldn't resist at that moment. "Sunny, I don't want to hurt your sister. Or you."

"But you will. If we're in your way."

"Yes." He turned her hand over thoughtfully. It was narrow, and surprisingly soft and delicate for one that packed such a punch. "You have strong family feelings. So do I. My parents…they've tried to understand Cal's decision, but it's difficult for them. Very difficult.''

''But they've only to see him for themselves to understand.''

''I can't explain.'' He shifted his eyes from their joined hands to hers. ''I wish I could. More than I can tell you.''

''Are you in trouble?'' she blurted out.

''What?''

''Are you in trouble?'' she repeated, tightening her fingers on his. ''With the law, or something.''

Interested, he kept his hand in hers. Her eyes were huge and drenched with concern. For him. He couldn't remember ever being more touched. ''Why would you think so?''

''The way you've come here… I guess the way you haven't come before. And you act… I don't know how to explain. You just seem so out of place.''

''Maybe I am.'' It should have been amusing, but he didn't smile. If he hadn't been so sure he would regret it, he would have pulled her into his arms and just held on. ''I'm not in trouble, Sunny. Not the way you mean.''

''And you haven't been—'' she searched for the most delicate way to approach the subject ''—ill?''

''Ill?'' Baffled, he studied her. The light dawned, slowly. ''You think I've been—'' Now he did smile, and surprised them both by bringing her hand to his lips. ''No, I haven't been ill, physically or otherwise. I've just been busy.'' When she tried to draw her hand away, he held on. ''Are you afraid of me?''

Pride had always been her strongest suit. ''Why should I be?''

''Good question. You wondered if I was—'' he

gestured again ''—unbalanced. But you let me stay. You even fed me.''

The uncharacteristic gentleness in his voice made her uncomfortable. ''I'd probably have done the same for a sick dog. It's no big deal.''

''I think it is.'' When she pushed away from the table, he rose with her. ''Sunbeam.''

''I told you not to—''

''There are times when it's irresistible. Thank you.''

She was more than uncomfortable now. She was unnerved. ''It's okay. Forget it.''

''I don't think so.'' Gently his thumb stroked over her knuckles. ''Tell me, if I had said I was in trouble, would you have helped?''

She tossed her head carelessly. ''I don't know. It would depend.''

''I think you would.'' He took both her hands and held them until she was still. ''Simple kindness, especially to someone away from home, is very precious and very rare. I won't forget.''

She didn't want to feel close to him. To be drawn to him. But when he looked at her like this, with such quiet tenderness, she went weak. There was nothing more frightening than weakness.

''Fine.'' Fighting panic, she shook her hands free. ''Then you can return the favor and do the dishes. I'm going for a walk.''

''I'll go with you.''

''I don't—''

''You said you weren't afraid of me.''

''I'm not.'' She let out a long-suffering breath. ''All right, then, come on.''

The moment she opened the door, the cold stole

her breath. The wind had died down and the sun was fighting through the layers of high clouds, but the air was like brittle ice.

It would clear her head, Sunny told herself. For a moment in the kitchen, with him looking so intently into her eyes, she'd felt as though… She didn't know what she'd felt. She didn't want to.

It was enough to be free to walk, though the snow was up to her knees. Another hour of confinement and she'd have gone mad. Perhaps that was what had happened to her in there, with him. A moment of madness.

"It's wild, isn't it?"

She stood in what had been the backyard and looked out on acres of solid white. The dying wind moaned through the trees and sent powdery snow drifting.

"I've always liked it best in the winter. Because if you're going to be alone you might as well be completely alone. I forgot the bird food. Hang on."

She turned, wading through the snow. He thought she moved more like a dancer now than an athlete. Graceful despite the encumbrances. It worried him to realize that he'd been content to watch her for hours. In a moment she was trudging back, dragging an enormous burlap sack.

"What are you doing?"

"Going to feed the birds." She was out of breath but still moving. "This time of year they need all the help they can get."

He shook his head. "Let me do it."

"I'm very strong."

"Yes, I know. Let me do it anyway."

He took the sack, braced, put his back into it and

began to haul it across the snow. It gathered snow—
and weight—with every step.

"I thought you weren't a nature lover."

"That doesn't mean I'd let them starve." And
she'd promised Libby.

He hauled the bag another foot. "Couldn't you just
dump it out?"

"If a thing's worth doing—"

"It's worth doing well. Yeah, I've heard that one."

She stopped by a tree and, standing on a stump,
began to fill a big wood-and-glass house with seed
from the sack. "There we go." She brushed seed
from her hands. "Want me to carry it back?"

"I'll do it. Why any self-respecting bird would
want to hang around here in the middle of nowhere I
can't understand."

"We're here," she called out as he hauled the sack
across the snow.

"I can't understand that, either."

She grinned at his back, and then, not being one to
waste an opportunity, she began to ball snow. She had
a good-size pile of ammunition when he came out
again, and she sent the first one sailing smack into
his forehead.

"Bull's-eye."

He wiped snow out of his eyes. "You've already
lost at one game."

"That was poker." She picked up another ball,
weighed it. "This is war. And war takes skill, not
luck."

He dodged the next throw, swearing when he
nearly overbalanced, then caught the next one in the
chest. Dead center.

"I should tell you I was the top pitcher on my

softball team in college. I still hold the record for strikeouts.''

The next one smacked into his shoulder, but he was prepared. In a move she had to admire, he came up with a stinging fastball that zoomed in right on the letters. He'd pitched a few himself, but he didn't think he would mention that he'd been captain of the intergalactic softball team three years running.

''Not bad, Hornblower.'' She sent out two, catching him with the second on the dodge. She had a mean curve, and she was pleased to note that she hadn't lost her touch. Snow splattered all over his coat. One particularly well-thrown ball nearly took off his hat.

Before her pile began to dwindle, she had him at eight hits to two and was getting cocky. It didn't occur to her that he had closed half the distance between them.

When he took one full in the face, she doubled over with laughter. Then she shrieked when he caught her under the arms and lifted her off her feet.

''Good aim, bad strategy,'' he commented before he dropped her face first in the snow.

She rolled over, spitting out snow. ''I still won.''

''Not from where I'm standing.''

With a good-natured shrug, she held out a hand. He hesitated. She smiled. The moment he clasped her hand, she threw her weight back and had him flying into the drift beside her.

''What does it look like now?''

''Hand-to-hand.''

He grasped her by the shoulders. They only sank deeper. Snow worked its way, cold and wet, down the collar of his borrowed coat. He found it, and the way her body twisted and turned against his, impossibly stimulating. She was laughing, kicking up snow as she tried to pin him on the icy mat. Breathless, she managed a half nelson, and she nearly had the call when she felt herself flying over his shoulder.

She landed with a thump, half buried, and lay there for a second, dragging in air. "Nice move," she panted. Then she dived at him again. She scissored, dipped and managed to slither out of his hold. Working fast, she twisted until she was half-sitting, half-lying on his back. Using her weight, she dunked his face in the snow.

"Say uncle."

He said something a great deal ruder, and she laughed so hard she nearly lost her grip.

"Come on, J.T., a real man admits it when he's licked."

He could have beaten her, he thought in disgust as his face numbed. But twice when he'd tried for a hold his hand had skimmed over particularly interesting curves. It had broken his concentration.

"Two out of three," he mumbled.

"If we try for two out of three, we'll freeze to death." Taking his grunt for agreement, she helped him turn over. "Not bad for a scientist."

"If we took it indoors, you wouldn't have a chance." But he was winded.

"The point is, I came out on top."

He lifted a brow. "In a manner of speaking."

She only grinned. "I wish you could see your face. Even your eyelashes are white."

"So are yours." He lifted a gloved hand that was already coated with snow and rubbed it on her face.

"Cheat."

"Whatever works." Exhausted, he let his hand drop again. He didn't know the last time he'd been taken—or when he'd enjoyed it so much.

"We'd better get some more wood." She braced a hand to get up, slipped and landed with a thump on his chest. "Sorry."

"It's all right. I've got a few ribs left."

His arms had come around her. His face was close. It was a mistake, she knew, to stay this way, even for a moment. But she didn't move. And then she didn't think. It was the most natural thing in the world for her to lower her lips to his.

They were cool, and firm, and everything she wanted. Kissing him was like diving headfirst into a cold mountain lake. Thrilling, exhilarating. And risky. She heard her own sound of pleasure, quick and quiet, before she threw what was left of caution to the winds and deepened the kiss.

She winded him. Weakened him. Loss of control meant nothing. Control was meant to be given up in passion. But this…this was different. As her lips heated his, he felt both will and strength drain away. There was a mist in his brain as thick and as white as the snow they lay in. And he could think of nothing and no one but her.

The women who had come before her were nothing. Shadows. Phantoms. When her mouth slid agilely over his he understood that there would be no women after her. She had, in one heady instant, taken over his life. Surrounded it, invaded it. Consumed it.

Shaken, he brought his hands to her shoulders, prepared, determined, to hurl her aside. But his fingers only tightened, and his need only grew.

It was like a rage in him. She could feel it. It was

building in her, as well. A fury. A driving hunger. And his mouth, his mouth alone, was dragging her over the rocky border between heaven and hell. So close, she thought, that she could feel the flames licking at her skin, tempting her to tumble recklessly into the fire. For it would be all brimstone and heat with him. And she was afraid, very afraid, that she would never be satisfied with less.

She lifted her head, an inch, then two. She was amazed to find her mind spinning and her breath uneven. It had only been a kiss, she reminded herself. A kiss, however passionate, didn't alter lives. Still, she wanted distance, and quickly, so that she could convince herself she was the same person she had been before it.

"We really have to get that wood," she managed. Suddenly she was terrified that she wouldn't be able to stand. It wouldn't do her ego a bit of good to have to crawl back to the house. Cautiously she rolled away from him. Then, using every ounce of will she possessed, she dragged herself to her feet. She made a production out of brushing the snow from her coat and wished he would say something. Anything.

"Look."

Wary, she turned. But he was only pointing to the feeder, where a few hardy birds were enjoying breakfast. It helped her relax a little. "Well, I've done my duty by them." Because she was suddenly and brutally aware of the cold, she gave herself a quick shake. "I'm going in."

She waded across the snow. They didn't speak again as they gathered wood, as they tromped snow from their boots or as they carried the logs to the woodbox. Sunny banked down an urge for a steaming cup of tea. She wanted to be alone. She wanted to think.

"I'm going up for a shower." Feeling miserably awkward, she watched him toss logs on the fire.

"Fine."

She made a face at his back. "Fine."

He waited until he heard her climb the stairs before he straightened. The woman was scrambling his brain, he decided. It was highly probable that he was still disoriented from the trip. That was why she was having such a profound effect on him. All he needed was a little more time to adjust. Data or no data, it would be best if he took that time aboard ship.

He took a long, thoughtful look at the cabin. Still, he'd promised to do the dishes. It would be an interesting experience to try his hand at it.

Upstairs, Sunny stripped off layers of clothes, letting each item fall carelessly to the floor. Naked, she turned the shower on, letting it run until the hot water was steaming. She winced as she stepped under it, then let out a long, lazy sigh.

Better, she told herself. It was certainly a better way of getting her blood moving than kissing Jacob. No, it wasn't.

She laid her forehead against the wall of the shower and with her eyes closed let the water rain over her.

Maybe she'd been a little crazy when she'd kissed him, but she'd never felt more alive. She couldn't blame him, not this time. She had made the move. She had looked into his eyes and known he was the one.

Yet how could he be? She barely knew him, was far from convinced she trusted him. Half the time she was sure she disliked him. But... But, she thought again. The other half of the time she was afraid she was falling in love with him.

It was completely irrational, undeniably foolish and totally genuine. All she had to do was figure out what to do about it.

Pouring shampoo into her palm, she tried to think. She was a practical woman. As far back as her memory took her, she had been able to take care of herself. Problems, even emotional ones, were meant to be surmounted. If she was falling in love, she would deal with it. The trick was not to do anything rash.

Caution, common sense and control, Sunny decided. She lathered her skin lavishly. She would keep a practical distance from Jacob until she got to know him better, until she was more certain of her feelings. It made perfect sense. More confident now, she turned under the spray and let the water sluice the suds from her.

Once she had determined her own feelings, she would work on his. There was no denying he was a strange sort of man. Interesting, certainly, but different in ways she had yet to fully figure out.

She could handle him. After turning off the water, she slicked a hand down her hair. She had always been able to handle men very satisfactorily. In this case, she just had to handle herself first.

Satisfied, she kicked her clothes out of the way. Dry, she wrapped a towel around her and stepped out into the hall.

He'd enjoyed doing the dishes. It was just the sort of mindless chore he'd needed to relax his mind. And his body. The plastic squeeze bottle marked dishwashing liquid claimed to contain real lemon juice.

He took a sniff of his hands and found the lingering scent pleasant. As soon as he got back to the ship he was going to make a report on it.

And the task had given him time to put his reaction to Sunny in perspective. Being attracted to her was natural, even elemental. But he was intelligent enough to control certain primal urges. Particularly when acting on them would cause incredible complications.

She was beautiful, desirable, but she was also impossible. The idea of pursuit had been a bad one. He was well aware now that a physical encounter with her would not be simple. It could only be problematic. He would solve the problem for both of them by gathering up his things and spending the bulk of his time on his ship. When Cal came back he would convince his brother that he had made a mistake. Then they would go home, where they belonged. And that would be the end of it.

It should have been. Perhaps it would have been. But he came to the top of the stairs just as Sunny stepped out of the bath. She held a towel at her breasts with both hands. He gripped the rail so hard that he wondered the wood didn't crumble under his fingers.

Bad timing. The thought went through both of their heads. Or perhaps it was perfect timing.

Chapter 7

He crossed to her slowly, soundlessly. Inevitably. In his eyes she saw mirrored her own needs. A reflection of desires, raw and ready, that she had refused to acknowledge. Even now, faced with them, she wanted to deny that they existed. Not with this power. Not with this potency.

She could have held up a hand, said one simple word. *No.*

Perhaps it would have stopped him. Perhaps not. But her hands remained clutched on the towel. And she said nothing. At all.

At her back she could feel the steam from the shower still rising. Or was it anticipation that heated her skin? Her fingers were balled tight, lodged in the subtle valley between her breasts. Her eyes were steady on his. But her pulse scrambled erratically, as if she had just crossed the finish line of a long, arduous race.

He didn't touch her. Not at first. He already knew that once he did, the time to turn back would be lost for both of them. A part of him wished desperately that he could simply walk back, turn away and continue on the route he already had mapped out. She was a detour, a dangerous combination of curves that would only lead him astray.

But, looking at her, his eyes dark and intent on her face, he knew that his bridges were already smoking behind him.

He touched her face…took it in his hands. Cupped it, molding his fingers to the angles, as if to mold the shape of it in his mind. To remember her, always, as she was in this one instant, to remember her through all the centuries that would keep them apart.

He heard her breath catch, then release, felt the faint, almost delicate, tremblings of passion still restrained. All the while he watched her, measuring that look in her eyes. Part panic, part challenge. Resisting her would be as impossible as stopping his own heartbeat at will.

Slowly, deliberately, he spread his fingers, skimming them up so that his palms slid over her jawline, her cheekbones, her temples, until his hands were caught in her wet, sleek hair. He took one fistful of it, then two.

Her gaze never faltered from his. She wouldn't permit it to. But she couldn't prevent a quick, soft gasp as he drew her head back. Her lips parted, in both invitation and acceptance, as he leaned closer. Only the thinning mist from the bath wound between them.

With his mouth a breath away from hers, he stopped, waited. It had nothing to do with hesitation. There was as much challenge in his eyes as in hers.

To meet it, she moved forward, the slight sway of her body closing the narrow distance between them.

"Yes," she said, and lifted her mouth to his.

No single word could have lit the fires so quickly. No practiced seduction could have broken the last chains on his control. His fingers tightened in her hair, and his mouth swooped down on hers.

The glory of it. He felt hunger answer hunger, desperation ply desperation. Her mouth was like an oasis, offering the last cool drop of life to a dying man who knew he must stumble back into the sun. She appeased even as she incited, promised even as she demanded. There was honey for the taking, rich and thick, but always at the risk of being stung. The risk made the reward all the sweeter.

He had never known a woman could make him suffer, and make him relish the pain, all from a meeting of lips.

Her hands were trapped between their bodies. They flexed, impatient, not for release but to take as he was taking. She spread them flat on his chest, fretting for freedom. But her murmur of protest was lost in his assault on her mouth before it merged with a groan of pleasure.

His teeth nipped and nibbled, and then his tongue plunged deep, greedily. Deaf and blind to all else, she dived in, as recklessly as he.

Her hands were free for an instant. Before she could clutch at him, her world seemed to tilt, and she was swept up in his arms. Swept off her feet, she thought giddily. No man before him had ever dared to attempt it. No man before him would have succeeded. With muscles like iron, he caught her hard against him, closing the distance to the bedroom in a few long-legged strides. Even as she tugged at his sweater, they were tumbling onto the bed.

With one frantic stroke, he ripped the towel from her, then gripped her seeking hands in his, fingers interlacing, locking, so that he could look his fill. The thin winter light seeped through the window to lie loverlike on her skin.

Her struggle to free her hands stopped. For a moment, she thought her breathing had, as well.

He knew his had. It wasn't air that rushed through him, but a desire so acute it left him reeling.

She was pale as moonlight, long limbed, with the fine-toned muscles of a dancer or an athlete. The strength was there, and the femininity. As he looked, and looked, and looked, she began to tremble.

Her hair was dark, wet and slicked back from her face. Now, as they had earlier with anger, her eyes had deepened to smoke. And they watched him.

With her hands still caught in his, he lowered his mouth. She arched, as greedy as he for the contact. Even as the kiss pumped through her like a drug, she tried to tug her hands free. But he was relentless, as if he knew that once he released her the power would be taken from him. Not to dominate, but only to pleasure, he kept her prisoner.

She moaned as the soft cotton of his sweater brushed her skin. She wanted his flesh against hers. She wanted her hands on him, and his on her. But he used his mouth, only his mouth, to drive her to the edge of reason.

Rapidly, almost savagely, he moved his lips over her—her face, her neck, her shoulders. She spoke his name, writhing frantically beneath him, but he moved restlessly on.

With openmouthed kisses he circled her breasts, tormenting himself as much as her. Then he drew the point into his mouth to nip, to suck, to stroke with the rough edge of his tongue.

He had known the flavor of women, but hers was new, so exclusively hers that he knew that if he supped of ten times ten thousand others, he would never be satisfied. Never had he known so keen or so perfect a match. The ache to claim all of her sprinted inside him.

"Jacob." His name was like a prayer that was transformed into a frantic moan. "Let me—"

But the words ended on a stunned, suffocated cry as he shot her over a towering, airless peak. She flew, thoughts and feelings tangling and breaking apart. Still his hands were locked with hers. Gasping, giddy, she closed her eyes as her tensed muscles went lax.

If this was pleasure, she had never tasted it before. If this was passion, she understood for the first time why a woman would die for it.

Dazed, she opened her eyes. The fierce triumph in his had her heart pounding against her ribs again. "I can't—I haven't—"

"You can, and you will. Again." And he watched, ravenous, as he sent her soaring.

Shudders racked her. Each movement of her body beneath his pushed her closer to the edge of reason. Freed, her hands slid bonelessly to the rumpled sheets. There was a mist in front of her eyes. As his hands joined his mouth in plundering her, she wondered that she didn't simply float up and away into it.

Touch me.

She wasn't certain if he spoke the words or if his

need merely echoed in her head. Through layers of drugged pleasure she lifted her arms, brought him close. And found his mouth with hers.

Strength raced back into her, edgier, more potent, from the weakness. A new level of desperation had her dragging his sweater over his head. Twin gasps of pleasure speared the quiet as her hands found him.

Warm, firm. Hers. She stroked and explored as thoroughly, as mercilessly, as he. Catapulted by a hunger grown insatiable, she rolled with him on the bed, her mouth fused to his, tearing at his jeans with frantic fingers until heated flesh met heated flesh.

He had thought he knew what delights a woman could bring when she touched a man. But *she* had never touched him before. All he had known, all he had experienced before, paled. And meant nothing.

He was filled with her body, mind and soul. She was everything he'd dreamed of without knowing he was dreaming, everything he'd wished for without knowing he was wishing. As her lips ran over him, small, hungry sounds rising in her throat, desire built to a rage.

Over and over they rolled on the bed, legs tangling as they pushed each other from brink to brink. The war they fought was punctuated by searing kisses, bruising strokes. Driven beyond reason, he gripped her hips. But she was already rising to meet him, to take him in.

Sheathed inside her, he felt the first shudders, hers, his, rip through them. Her legs locked around him. His fingers dug into the sheets. Reason shattered. Rhythms matched.

And he was rocketing through space, through time. All he knew was that she was with him.

* * *

She lay crossways on the bed, one arm flung out,
the other hand still clutched in Jacob's hair. His body
was as limp as hers as he sprawled over her, his head
resting between her breasts. His first thought was that
her heart, thudding under his ear, matched the pace
of his own. Before reason could set in, he slid a hand
over the warm tangle of sheets and covered hers. He
knew he would never be able to describe the sensation
that rippled through him as her fingers curled against
his.

He was heavy. She didn't care. It seemed perfectly
feasible that she could spend the rest of her life lying
just so, listening to his breathing and to the quiet
sound of snow melting from the eaves in the sun.

So this was what it was to love, she mused. She
hadn't known she'd waited all her life to feel like this.
It had always seemed possible to her to live her life
alone, independent, content with the freedom to do as
she pleased when she pleased.

The idea of sharing a bed with a man you cared
for, respected, understood, had seemed practical and
certainly human enough. But the idea of sharing a
life—or needing to share it because you couldn't
imagine living without one person—had always
struck her as romantic nonsense.

No more.

And he was such a beautiful man. Strong and
smart. Stubborn and opinionated. Exactly, she realized, the kind of man she needed. Without any one
of those qualities, her personality would have driven
her to run right over him, making both of them miserable. Because he had them, she would run into him
often, bruising them both. And she'd be wildly happy.

Smiling, she caught herself stroking his hair. After

letting out a careful breath, she made herself stop. What did a woman like her do with these tender feelings? She understood passion. At least she understood it now. But what about this soft, yielding sensation, this dependence, this need to nurture and cherish and simply love? How would a man like Jacob Hornblower react to this sudden gush of emotion?

He'd sneer at her. Closing her eyes, she admitted that she would have sneered herself only hours before.

But everything had changed. For her, Sunny reminded herself. If she was honest she would accept the fact that she'd started falling the moment she'd faced him, ready to fight, in this very same room.

But Jacob... She herself had called him a tough nut. Cracking him, discovering whether there was indeed a soft center capable of gentler emotions, would be a difficult task. It would take effort, she thought. That was no problem. It would take patience. That was.

Oblivious of where her thoughts were headed, he turned his head enough to brush a kiss to the curve of her breast.

"Your taste," he murmured.

"Hmm?"

"It keeps me hungry." He scraped his teeth along her skin, then smiled when he felt her heart skip a beat. "I like you here best." He propped himself up to study her face lazily. "Naked and in bed."

"A typical male attitude." Deliberately she danced her fingers down his hip and watched his eyes darken. "But then, I think I prefer you in the same state."

"It's convenient that we finally agree about something." He shifted so that he could trace her lips with the tip of his tongue. "I like your mouth, Sunbeam. It's stubborn and sexy."

"I could say the same about yours."

"We agree again."

"A new record." She caught his lower lip between her teeth. "We could push our luck. What else do you like?"

"Your..." His smile spread slowly. "...energy."

"Another winner."

With a laugh, he deepened the kiss. She was just as sweet, and just as potent, as the first time. "Your body," he decided. "I definitely like your body."

She sighed into his mouth. "We're on a roll, J.T. Don't stop now."

He shifted his attention to her earlobe. "This is a nice spot," he murmured, nuzzling until they were both dizzy. "But I suppose, under the circumstances, I can confess that I find your mind...intriguing."

"Intriguing," she repeated, as shudder after delicious shudder passed through her. "An interesting choice of words."

"It seemed more apt than infuriating at the moment. And I..." His words trailed off when he spotted a line of faint bruises on her shoulder. He placed the tips of his fingers on them experimentally. "I've marked your skin," he said, surprised and a bit appalled. If he had bruised her during a fight, he wouldn't have given it a second thought. But in bed, while loving...that was a different matter. "I'm sorry."

She twisted her head to glance at them. She certainly hadn't felt them. "Are you?"

He looked back to see her lips curved in what he

considered a typically female smile. "No, I suppose I'm not."

"Under the circumstances," she supplied.

"Right." He started to speak again, to make some joke, but found himself suddenly and totally at a loss for words. Something in her smile, in her half-hooded eyes, in the tilt of that damn-you chin, turned his brain to mush.

Ridiculous, he told himself as he continued to stare at her. Absolutely and completely ridiculous. Whatever he was feeling, it couldn't be love—not the kind of love that caused men to make foolish and life-altering decisions. It was affection, he told himself. Attraction, desire and passion, tempered with a certain amount of caring, perhaps. But love. He had no room for it. And no time.

Time. Reality struck him like a blow. Time was the biggest obstacle of all.

He started to push himself away, to put some distance between them until he could think clearly again. Still smiling, she wrapped arms and legs around him. "Going somewhere?"

"I must be heavy."

"You are." She continued to smile, then traced her lips with her tongue. Her hips moved gently, sinuously, against his. Thrilled, she watched his eyes cloud as he grew inside her. "I was hoping we could do a little experiment."

He shook his head but failed to clear it. "Experiment?"

"Physics." She trailed a single fingertip down his back. "You know about physics, don't you, J.T.?"

He used to. "That's Dr. Hornblower to you," he muttered, and buried his face in her throat.

"Well, Doc…isn't there this theory about an object in motion remaining in motion?"

His breath was ragged in her ear. "Let me show you."

She ached all over. And she'd never felt better in her life. Bleary eyed, she winced at the intruding sunlight. Morning. Again, she realized.

She wouldn't have believed it was possible to spend the better part of a day and all of a night in bed. With only snatches of sleep. With a grumbling sigh, she tried to roll over and met the solid wall of Jacob's body.

He'd been busy since dawn, she mused. Busy working her over to the edge of the bed. Now he took up ninety percent of the mattress, along with all of the sheets and blankets. The only thing saving her from sliding onto the floor was the weight of the leg he had hooked around her hips. And the arm stretched carelessly, and certainly not amorously, over her throat.

She shifted again, met the unmoving line of resistance and narrowed her eyes. "Okay, pal," she said under her breath, "we're going to begin as I mean to go on, and I don't mean to roll onto the floor every night for the rest of my life."

She gave him an unloverlike nudge in the stomach with her elbow. He swore and shoved her another inch toward the edge.

Tactics, Sunny decided. She changed hers by sliding a hand intimately over his hip and thigh. "J.T.," she whispered, trailing a line of kisses down his cheek. "Honey."

"Hmm?"

She nibbled delicately at his ear. "Jacob? Sweetheart?"

He made another vague sound and cupped her breast. Sunny's brow lifted. His movement had cost her another precious fraction of an inch.

"Baby," she added, figuring she was running out of endearments. "Wake up, sugar. There's something I want to do." Gently, seductively, she brushed her lips down to his shoulder. "Something I really need."

As his lips curved, she bit him. Hard.

"Ow." His eyes flew open, temper and bafflement warring in them. "What the hell was that for?"

"So I could get back my share of the bed." Satisfied, she snuggled into the pillow he'd just vacated. She opened one eye and was gratified to see that he was scowling at her. "Anyone ever tell you you're a bed hog? And a blanket thief." She snatched the loose cover and rolled into it.

"You're the first one to complain."

She only smiled. She was counting on being the last. Frowning, he rubbed the wound on his shoulder. There were shadows under her eyes. They made her look vulnerable. The faint throbbing where her teeth had connected reminded him that she was anything but.

Inside that angular body was a whirlwind of energy. All wells of passion that he was sure—even with the marathon they'd put each other through— had yet to be tapped. She'd taken him places he hadn't believed existed. Places he was already yearning to return to. In the deepest part of the night she had been insatiable, and impossibly generous. He'd had only to touch her to have her respond. She'd had only to touch him to cause the need to churn.

Now, in the full light of morning, she was wrapped in the blankets, with only her tousled cap of hair and half of her face in view. And he wanted her.

What was he going to do about her? With her? For her? He hadn't a clue.

He wondered how she would react if he told her everything. She'd go back to thinking he was unbalanced. He could prove it to her. And once he had they would both have to face the fact that whatever had happened between them during the last spin of the earth on its axis was transient. He wasn't ready for that.

For once in his life he wanted to delude himself. To pretend. They would have only a few weeks together at best. More than other men, he had firsthand knowledge of how fickle time could be. So now he would use it, and take what he had with her.

But how could he? Sitting up, he rubbed his hands over his face. It wasn't fair to her. It was grossly unfair, particularly if his instincts were correct and her feelings were involved. Not telling her would hurt her when it ended. Telling her would hurt her before it had really begun. And maybe that was best.

"Going somewhere?" she asked him.

He was reminded of when she had used the same phrase before, and where it had ended. Now he thought of how he could tell her just how far away he was going. She was an intelligent woman. He had only to give her the facts.

"Sunny."

"Yes?" She ran a hand up his arm. Then, feeling repentant, she rose long enough to kiss his shoulder where she had bitten it.

"Maybe this shouldn't have happened." He saw by the way her smile faded that he'd begun badly.

"I see."

"No, you don't." Annoyed with himself, he made a grab for her before she could roll out of bed.

"Don't worry about it," she said stiffly. "When you've been fired as often as I have you get used to rejection. If you're sorry about what happened—"

"I'm not." He cut her off with a brisk shake that turned the glazed hurt in her eyes to smoke.

"Don't ever do that again."

"I'm not sorry," he said, struggling for calm. "I damn well should be, but I'm not. I can't be, because all I can think about is making love with you again."

She blew her hair out of her eyes and swore to herself that she would be calm. "I don't know what you're trying to say."

"Neither do I." He released her to tug his fingers through his hair. "It mattered," he blurted out. It wasn't what he'd meant to say, but it, too, was a fact. "Being with you mattered to me. I didn't think it would."

The ice she had deliberately formed around her heart melted a little. "Are you upset because it was more than sex?"

"I'm upset because it was a hell of a lot more than sex." And he was a coward, he realized, because he couldn't tell her that what they had now would end before either of them was ready. "I don't know how to handle it."

She was silent for a moment. He looked so angry—with himself. And as confused as she was by what had grown—no, by what had exploded into life—between them. "How about one day at a time?"

He shifted his gaze to hers. He wanted to believe it could be that simple. Needed to. "And what happens when I leave?"

The ice had definitely melted, because she felt the first slash in her heart. "Then we'll deal with it." She chose her words carefully. "Jacob, I don't think either of us wanted to get involved. But it happened. I wouldn't want to take it back."

"Be sure."

She lifted a hand to his cheek. "I am." Afraid she would say too much too soon, she bundled back under the covers. "Now that that's settled, it's your turn to make breakfast. You can yell up the stairs when it's ready."

He said nothing. The thought of what might tumble from his heart to his lips unnerved him. If it was a choice between saying too much and saying too little, he had to choose the latter. He rose, tugged on what clothes came to hand, and left her.

Alone, she turned her face into the pillow. It smelled of him. Letting out a long, weary sigh, she willed her body to relax. She had lied. Rejections wounded her deeply, left her miserable and aching and full of self-loathing. A rejection from him would hurt so much more than the loss of a job.

Rubbing her cheek on the pillowcase, she watched the slant of sunlight. What would she do if he ended it? She would recover. She needed to believe that. But she knew that if he turned away from her, recovery would take a lifetime.

So she couldn't let him turn away.

It was important not to push. Sunny was very aware that she demanded too much from the people close to her. Too much love, too much attention, too much patience, too much faith. This time it would be different. She would be patient. She would have faith.

It would be easier, she knew, because he was as unsteady as she. Who wouldn't be, with the velocity and force with which they had come together? If they could progress so far in such a short time, how much further could they go in the weeks ahead?

All they needed was a little time, to get to know each other better, to work on those rough edges. Forget the rough edges, she thought, gazing at the ceiling. Those would take a couple of lifetimes, at least. In any case, she rather liked them.

But time…she was certain she had that right. Time was what they needed to get used to what had happened, to accept that it was going to keep right on happening.

She smiled at that, her confidence building again. And if that didn't work she'd browbeat him into it. She knew exactly what she wanted. And that was a first. She wanted Jacob T. Hornblower. If, after he had seen and spoken with Cal, he packed his pitiful little bag and headed back east, she would just go after him.

What was a few thousand miles between friends? Or lovers.

Oh, no, he wasn't going to shake her off without a fight. And fighting was what she did best. If she wanted him—and she was certain she did—then he didn't have a chance. She had as much right to call things off as he did, and she was far from ready. Maybe, if he was lucky, she'd let him off the hook in fifty or sixty years. In the meantime, he was just going to have to deal with it, and with her.

"Sunny! This stuff is in the bowls, and I can't find the damn coffee."

She grinned. Ah, the sweet sound of her lover's voice carrying on the morning air. Like music, like the trilling of birds—

"I said, I can't find the damn coffee."

Like the roar of a wounded mule.

Madly in love, she tossed the heap of blankets aside.

"It's in the cupboard over the stove, dummy. I'll be right down."

Chapter 8

Another week of quiet, serenity and nature in the rough would drive Sunny mad. She'd already accepted that. Even love wasn't enough of a buffer against hour after hour of solitude, punctuated only by the occasional call of a hardy bird and the monotonous drip, drip, drip of snow melting from the roof.

For variety she could always listen to the wind blow through the trees. When she had stooped that low she realized that she would gladly trade all of her worldly possessions for the good grinding noise of rush-hour traffic in any major city.

A girl might be born in the woods, she thought, but that didn't mean you could keep her there.

Jacob was certainly a distraction, an exciting one. But as the days passed it became clear that being snowbound in a log cabin in the middle of nowhere was no more his definition of a good time than it was hers. The fact that she found that a relief didn't ease the boredom.

They managed to occupy their time. Arguing, in bed and out. Two restless personalities stuck in the same space were bound to strike sparks. But their minds were as restless as their bodies and needed stimulation.

Sunny compensated by hibernating. Her reasoning was, she couldn't be bored if she was asleep. So she developed the habit of taking long naps at odd hours. When he was certain she was asleep, Jacob would slip out, taking advantage of the bonus he'd found in the shed. Cal's aircycle. With that he would make a quick trip to his ship and input new data into the main computer.

He told himself that he wasn't deceiving her, he was simply performing part of the task he had come to her time to accomplish. And if it was deceit, it couldn't be helped. He'd nearly convinced himself that what she didn't know couldn't hurt her. At least for the time being.

Though he was as restless as she, he found himself storing up memories, images, moments. The way she looked when she woke—sleepy-eyed and irritable as a child. The way she'd laughed, the sun shining on her hair, when they'd built a house of snow under the pine trees. The way she felt, passion humming under her skin, when they made love in front of the fire.

He would need them. Those memories, those re-membrances of each conversation or spat. Each time he returned to the ship he was reminded of just how much he would need them. He told himself he was only preparing to go on with his life. And so was she.

She had written inquiries to the handful of universities she'd selected. But the weather had so far prevented her from venturing out as far as Medford to mail them. She had read, lost to Jacob at poker, even dragged out her sketchbook in desperation. When she tired of drawing the view of snow and pine trees from the windows, she sketched the interior of the cabin. Bored, she resorted to drawing caricatures.

Jacob read incessantly, and he'd taken to scribbling in a spiral notebook he'd dug out of some drawer. When Sunny asked him if he was preparing for an experiment, he made noncommittal noises. When she pressed him, he simply pulled her into his lap and made her forget to ask questions.

They lost power twice, and they made love as frequently as they argued. Which was often.

Sunny was certain, when she caught herself making the bed for lack of anything better to occupy her time, that if they didn't *do* something they would both find themselves in a home for the gently deranged.

Leaving the bed half-made, she sprinted to the top of the stairs. "J.T."

He was currently trying to keep himself sane by building a city of cards. "What?"

"Let's drive to Portland."

Jacob's attention was fixed on a particularly intricate arrangement. He thought the structure was beginning to resemble the skyline on Omega II.

"J.T."

"Yeah." With fingers that were rock-steady, he added another card.

"I guess it's too late," Sunny murmured, and sat down to the west of the city. "He's already gone around the bend."

"Do we have any more of these?"

She sighed at his dwindling stack of cards. "Nope."

"I was thinking of a bridge."

"Think shock therapy."

"Or maybe a skybelt."

"A what?"

He caught himself and put another card in place. "Nothing. My mind was wandering."

She snickered. "What's left of it."

"You were saying?"

"I was saying let's get out of Dodge."

"I thought Medford was the closest town."

She opened her mouth, closed it again. "Sometimes," she said at last, "I'm not sure if you belong on the same planet with the rest of us."

"It's the right planet." A portion of his pasteboard roof fluttered. "Breathe the other way, will you?"

"Jacob. If you could spare a moment of your valuable time."

He glanced up then, and he had to smile. "You have the sexiest pout I've ever seen."

"I don't pout." When she caught herself doing just that, she hissed between her teeth and blew down a building.

"You've just murdered thousands of innocent people."

"There's only one person I'm going to murder." Desperate, she grabbed a handful of his sweater. "J.T., if I don't get out of here I'm going to start bouncing off the walls."

"Can you do that?"

"Just watch me." She leaned closer. "Portland. People, traffic, restaurants."

"When do you want to leave?"

With a huff, she sat back again. "You *were* listening."

"Of course I was listening. I always listen. When do you want to leave?"

"A week ago. Now. I can be ready in ten minutes."

She sprang up. Though Jacob winced when his city collapsed, he rose with her. "What about the snow?"

"It hasn't snowed for three days. Besides, we have four-wheel drive. If we can get to Route 5, we're home free."

The thought of getting out nearly made him forget his priorities. "And if Cal comes back?"

She was all but dancing with impatience. "They're not due back for a couple of weeks. Anyway, they live here." Carelessly she stepped on his demolished city. "J.T., think carefully. Do you really want to see a grown woman turn into a raving lunatic?"

"Maybe." Taking her by the hips, he pulled her intimately close. "I like it when you rave."

"Then prepare to enjoy yourself."

"I am." He dragged her to the floor.

She argued—briefly. "I'm going," she said, undoing the buttons of her flannel shirt.

"Okay."

"I mean it."

"Right." He tugged the plain white undershirt over her head.

She struggled but couldn't prevent her lips from curving. Giving up, she helped him off with his sweater. "And so are you."

"As soon as you're finished raving," he promised, then closed his mouth over hers.

* * *

Sunny threw a small bag into the back of the Land Rover. She'd taken time to grab a toothbrush, a hairbrush, her favorite camisole and a lipstick. "In case we have to stop on the way," she explained.

"Why would we?"

"I don't know how long it's going to take us to get out of the mountains." She settled in the driver's seat. "It's about five hours after that."

Five hours. It took them five hours to get from one part of a single state to another. For the past few days he'd nearly forgotten how different things were.

She shot him a look, eyes bright, lips curved. "Ready?"

"Sure."

It was difficult not to stare as she turned a small key and sent the combustion engine roaring. He could feel the vibration through the floorboards. A few small adjustments, he mused, and even an archaic vehicle could be made to run smoothly and quietly.

Jacob was on the brink of pointing this out to her when she shoved the Land Rover in gear and sent snow spitting out from under the tires.

"All right!"

"Is it?"

"This baby rides like a tank," she said happily as they lumbered away from the cabin.

"Apparently." He braced himself, finding it incongruous that he should worry about life and limb here, when he had taken countless trips at warp speed. "I suppose you know what you're doing."

"Of course I know what I'm doing. I learned how to drive in a Jeep." They labored up an incline where snow had melted and refrozen into a slick surface.

Jacob judged the height and breadth of the trees. He could only trust that she knew how to avoid them.

"You look a little green." She had to chuckle as they plowed, then fishtailed, then plowed again, making erratic but definite progress. "Haven't you ever ridden in one of these?"

He had an image of driving his own LSA vehicle—Land, Sea or Air. It was smooth and quiet and as fast as a comet. "No, actually, I haven't."

"Then you're in for a treat."

The Land Rover bumped over rocks hidden under the snow. "I bet."

They forged through the drifts. He nearly relaxed. By all indications, she knew how to handle the vehicle. Such as it was. After the first twenty minutes, the heater began to hum.

"How about some tunes?"

His brow creased. "Fine," he said cautiously.

"You're in charge."

"Of what?"

"Of the tunes." She navigated carefully down an incline. "The radio."

He eyed a particularly large tree. At their current rate and angle, he estimated thirty seconds to impact. "We didn't bring it."

"The car radio, J.T." She missed the tree by six or eight inches. "Pick a station."

She'd taken her hand from the wheel for an instant to gesture at the dashboard. Eyes narrowed, Jacob studied it. Trusting luck, he turned a dial.

"It works better if you turn it on before you try to tune in a station."

Biting back an oath, he tried another dial and was greeted by a blast of ear-popping static. After adjusting the volume, he applied himself to the tuner. His first stop was an instrumental melody, loaded with strings, that made him cringe. Still, he glanced over at Sunny.

"If that's your choice, we'll have to reassess our relationship immediately."

Sound faded in and out as he played with the tuner. He hit on some gritty rock, not too dissimiliar from what might have sounded over the airwaves in his own time.

"Good choice." She turned her head briefly to smile at him. "Who's your favorite musician?"

"Mozart," he answered, because it was partially true and undeniably safe.

"You're going to like my mother. When I was a kid, she used to weave to his *Clarinet Concerto in A Minor*." With the radio still rocking, she hummed a few bars. "For the purity of sound, she'd always say. Mom's always been big on pure—no additives, no preservatives."

"How did you keep food fresh without preservatives?"

"That's what I say. What's life without a little MSG? Anyway, then Dad would switch on Bob Dylan." She laughed, more relieved than she wanted to admit when they turned onto the first plowed road. "One of my earliest memories of him is watching him weed his garden, with his hair down to his shoulders and this scratchy Dylan record playing on a little portable turntable. 'Come gather 'round, people, wherever you roam.' All he was wearing—Dad, not Dylan—was bell-bottoms and love beads."

Jacob got an uncomfortable flash of his own father, dressed in his tidy gardening clothes, blue shirt, blue slacks, his hair carefully trimmed under a stiff peaked cap, his face quiet as he hand-pruned his roses and listened to Brahms on his personal entertainment unit.

And of his mother, sitting in the shade of a tree on a lazy Sunday afternoon, reading a novel while he and Cal had tossed a baseball and argued over strike zones.

"I think you'll like him."

Dragged back, Jacob blinked at her. "What?"

"My father," she repeated. "I think you'll like him."

He battled down the anger that had risen up inside him. It was simple enough to put two and two together. "Your parents live in Portland?"

"That's right. About twenty minutes from my place." She let out a quiet, satisfied breath as they turned onto Route 5 and headed north. "They'll be glad to meet you, especially since Cal's family has been so shrouded in mystery."

The friendly smile she offered him faded when she saw his expression. When her hands clenched on the wheel it had nothing to do with anger and everything to do with despair.

"Meeting my parents is not synonymous with a lifetime commitment."

Her voice was stiff and cold. If he hadn't been so lost in his own unhappiness, he would have heard the hurt beneath it.

"You didn't mention visiting your parents." The fact was, he didn't want to meet them, or to think of them as people.

"I didn't think it was necessary." Her clutch foot began to tap on the floorboards. "I realize your idea of family differs from mine, but I wouldn't think of coming back to town and not seeing them."

Bitterness rose like bile in his throat. "You have no idea what family means to me."

"No?" She gave a quick, moody shrug. "Let's just say I can surmise that you don't have a problem cutting certain members of it out of your life for extended periods. Your business," she said before he could retort. "And you're certainly not obligated to come with me when I go to see my family." Her fingers began to tap in time with her foot. "In fact, I'll be happy not to even mention your name."

He was careful not to speak again. If he did, too much of what he was feeling would pour out, leaving too much to be explained.

She didn't know how he felt. It was all so easy, so straightforward, for her. All she had to do was hop into this excuse for transportation and spend a few hours on what passed for a roadway. And she could see her family. By using the current system of communication she could speak with them over relatively long distances. Even if she decided to travel to the other side of the planet, some element of twentieth-century technology would provide a link.

She knew nothing of separation, of losing a part of yourself and not knowing why. How would she react if she found herself faced with the possibility of never seeing her sister again?

She wouldn't be so damn smug then.

For the next hour or so, Jacob amused himself by sneering at the other vehicles on the road. Ridiculously clumsy, slow and absurdly inefficient. Carbon monoxide pumping into the atmosphere. Gleefully poisoning their own air. They had no respect, he thought. For themselves, their resources, their descendants.

And she thought he was insensitive.

He wondered what would happen if he strolled into what passed for a research lab in this age and showed them the procedure for fusion.

They'd probably sacrifice a lamb and make him a god.

He sat back, arms crossed. They'd just have to figure it out for themselves. Right now, his biggest problem was keeping warm, with all the cold air blowing off of Sunny.

He frowned when she pulled out onto a ramp. He hadn't been paying close attention, but he was certain they hadn't driven for five hours. "What are you doing?"

"I'm going to get something to eat and put gas in the car." She snapped the words off without a glance at him.

Hugging her resentment to her, she pulled into a gas station, got out and slammed the door behind her. As she reset the self-service pump, she muttered under her breath.

She'd forgotten how his mind worked. Obviously he was deluding himself into believing that she was luring him into some sort of trap. *I want you to meet my parents. How do you feel about a double-ring ceremony?* Sunny ground her teeth. It was insulting.

Maybe she was in love with him—and that was a situation she dearly hoped could be reversed—but she hadn't done one single thing to pressure him. Or to lead him to believe that her heart was all aflutter at waiting for him to get down on one knee.

If he thought she'd intended to flaunt him in front

of her parents like so much matrimonial beefcake, he
had another think coming. The jerk.

Jacob sat a moment, then decided to get out to
stretch his legs. And get a look at his surroundings.

So this was a refueling station, he mused, studying
the gas pumps. Sunny had stuck the nozzle end of a
hose into a compartment on the side of the Land
Rover. From her expression, she didn't look too
happy about standing out in the cold with her hand
on the switch. Behind her, the pump—the gasoline
pump, he elaborated—clicked as numbers turned
over. The odor of fuel was strong.

Other cars crowded the pump islands. Some waited
in their vehicles for a man in a cap to come out and
go through the procedure Sunny was doing for herself. Others did as she was, and shivered in the cold.

He watched a woman bundle a trio of children
around the side of a building that was set farther off
the road. The children were arguing and whining, and
the woman was snatching at arms. He had to grin. At
least that much hadn't changed over time.

On the road, cars chugged by. Jacob wrinkled his
nose at the stench of exhaust. A sixteen-wheeler
roared by, leaving a stream of displaced air in its
wake.

There were plenty of buildings, such as they were.
Tall ones, squat ones, all huddled together as if they
were afraid to leave too much room between them.
He found the style uninspired. Then, less than a block
down the street, he spotted something that brought
him a pang of homesickness. A pair of high golden
arches. At least they weren't completely uncivilized,
he thought. He was grinning when he turned back to
Sunny.

She didn't respond.

Ignoring him, she screwed the gas cap in place and hung up the hose. Silent treatment or not, he told himself, he would not apologize for something that was so clearly her fault. Still, he followed her into the building and was distracted by rows of candy bars, shelves of soft drinks and the prevalent scent of crude oil.

When she took out paper money, Jacob had to stick his hands in his pockets to keep himself from reaching out to touch it. The man in the cap ran grimy fingers over the keys of a machine. Red numbers appeared in a viewbox. The paper was exchanged, and Sunny was given metal disks.

That was money, too, Jacob reminded himself. Coins, they were called. He was frustrated when she dumped them in her bag before he could get a close look. He wondered how he could approach her for some samples.

The woman he'd seen earlier herded the three children inside, and the room was immediately filled with noise. All three fell greedily on the rows of candy bars.

"Just one," the woman said, an edge to her voice. "I mean it." She was digging in her purse as she spoke.

The children, bundled in coats and hats, set up an arguing din that ended in a shoving match. The smallest went down on her bottom with a thump and a wail. Jacob bent automatically to set her on her feet, then handed her the smashed candy bar. Her bottom lip was quivering, and her eyes, big and round and blue, were filled to overflowing.

"He's always pushing me," she complained.

"You'll be as big as they are pretty soon," he told her. "Then they won't be able to push you around."

"Sorry." Sighing, the woman picked her daughter up. "It's been a long trip. Scotty, you're going to sit on your hands for the next ten miles."

When Jacob turned to leave, the little girl was smiling at him. And so, he noted, was Sunny.

"Are you talking to me again?" he asked as they walked back to the car.

"No." She tugged on her gloves as she sat in the driver's seat. It would have been easier to go on hating him if he hadn't been so sweet with the little girl. "I'm a great deal harder to charm than a three-year-old."

"We could try a neutral subject."

She turned on the engine. "We don't have any neutral subjects."

She had him there. He lapsed into silence again as she merged with traffic. But he could have kissed her when she turned into those golden arches.

She followed a sign that said *Drive-thru* and stopped at a board that listed the restaurant's delicacies. "What do you want?"

He started to ask for a McGalaxy Burger and a large order of laser rings, but he didn't see either on the menu. Once again he put his fate in her hands. "Two of whatever you're having." Because he couldn't resist, he toyed with the hair at the back of her neck.

Annoyed, she shook his fingers off. She spoke into the intercom, listened for the total, then joined the line of cars waiting to be served. "We'll make better time if we eat while we drive."

They inched forward. "Are we in a hurry?"

"I don't like to waste time."

Neither did he, and he wasn't sure how much more they had together. "Sunny?"

No response.

"I love you."

Her foot slipped off the clutch. Her other slammed the brake pedal when the Land Rover stalled. The car was still rocking as she turned to gape at him. "What?"

"I said I love you." It didn't hurt as much as he'd thought it would. In fact, it felt good. Very good. "I figured we might as well have it out in the open."

"Oh." As responses went, it wasn't her best. But she was staring straight ahead into the rear window of the car in front. There was a stuffed cat suction-cupped to the glass. It was grinning at her. The car behind her gave an impatient beep of the horn and had her fumbling with the ignition key. Rattled, she pulled up to the service window.

"Is that all you can say?" Annoyance colored his tone as she turned to blink at him. "Just 'Oh'?"

"I...I'm not sure what..."

"That'll be $12.75," the boy shouted through the window as he held out white paper bags.

"What?"

He rolled his eyes. "It's $12.75. Come on, lady."

"Sorry." She took the bags, dumped them in Jacob's lap. Even as he swore at her, she dug out a twenty and passed it to the boy. Without waiting for her change, she pulled into the first available parking space and stopped the car.

"I think you singed my—"

"Sorry," she snapped, cutting him off. Because she felt like a fool, she rounded on him. "It's your own fault, Mr. Romance, dropping something like that on me while I'm stuck in a line of cars at a fast-food drive-in. What did you expect me to do, throw myself in your arms while they were adding on the pickles?''

"I never know what the hell to expect from you.'' He reached into the bag, brought out a foil-wrapped burger and tossed it to her.

"From me?'' She unwrapped the burger and took a huge bite. It did nothing to ease the fluttering of her stomach. "From me? You're the one who started this, Hornblower. One minute you're snapping my head off, the next you're telling me you love me, and then you're throwing me a cheeseburger.''

"Just shut up and eat.'' He shoved a paper cup into her hand.

He'd bite off his tongue before he'd say it to her again. He didn't know what had come over him. Gasoline fumes, undoubtedly. No man in his right mind could fall in love with such an obstinate woman. And—no help from her—he was still in his right mind.

"A few minutes ago you were begging me to talk to you,'' she pointed out, sucking on her straw.

"I never beg.''

She turned then, eyes smoky. "You would if I wanted you to.''

He could have strangled her then, for saying what he realized was no more than the truth. "I thought we were going to drive while we ate.''

"I changed my mind,'' she said tightly. The way her insides were shaking, she wasn't sure she could navigate ten feet. She'd be damned if she'd let him know it. Since it wasn't possible to kick him, due to their position, she simply turned and stared through the windshield.

She continued eating mechanically and cursed him for spoiling her appetite.

Imagine, telling her that he loved her while they were waiting for hamburgers. What style, what finesse. She tapped her fingers on the wheel and bit back a sigh. How incredibly sweet.

Cautious, she cast a sidelong look at him. His profile was set, his eyes were steely. She had seen him angrier, she supposed, but it was a close call. Something about the way he fumed in frustrated silence made her feel incredibly sentimental. Twenty years from now she would look back and smile over the way he had said those magic words the very first time.

She scrambled onto her knees and threw her arms around him. He gasped as cold liquid splashed on his knees. "Damn it, Sunny, you've spilled it all over me."

He squirmed, then stilled when her mouth found his. He tasted her laughter on the tip of her tongue. Hampered by the gearshift, he struggled to drag her closer.

"Did you mean it?" she demanded, shoving what was left of their lunch aside.

No way was he going to let her off that easily. "Mean what?"

"What you said."

He settled her awkwardly in his lap, making sure her bottom came in direct contact with his wet knees. "Which time?"

Her breath came out in a huff, but she curled her arms around his neck. "You said you loved me. Did you mean it?"

"I might have." He worked his hands up under her coat but had to be content with the flannel of her shirt. "Or I might have been trying to start a conversation."

She bit his lip. "Last chance, Hornblower. Did you mean it?"

"Yes." God help them both. "Want to fight about it again?"

"No." She rested her cheek against his. "No, I don't want to fight. Not right now." He felt her sigh move through her body. "It scared me."

"That makes two of us."

After pressing a kiss to his throat, she drew back. "It gets even scarier. I love you, too."

He'd known it, and yet— And yet, hearing her say it, seeing her eyes as she spoke, watching her lips form the words, nothing could have prepared him for the force of feeling that poured into him. A waterfall of emotion. Tumbling through it, he pulled her mouth to his.

He couldn't bring her close enough. It didn't seem odd that they were huddled inside a car in a parking lot beside a busy street in broad daylight. Much odder was the fact that he was here at all, that he had found her, despite the centuries.

When he lived, she couldn't go. When she lived, he couldn't stay. And yet, in this small space of time, they were together.

Time was passing.

"I don't know what we're going to do about this," he murmured. There had to be a way, some equation, some theory. But what computer could analyze data that was so purely emotional?

"One day at a time, remember?" She drew back, smiling. "We've got plenty of time." She hugged him close, and she didn't see the trouble come into his eyes. "Speaking of which, we've got almost two hours before Portland."

"Too long."

She chuckled, then squirmed back into her seat. "I was thinking the same thing."

She zoomed out of the lot, keeping her eyes peeled. With a grin of satisfaction, she pulled into the first motel she spotted. "I think we can use a break." After snatching up her bag, she strolled into the office to register.

This time she used a plastic card—something much less foreign to him. With little trouble and less conversation, she secured a key from the clerk.

"How long have we got?" Jacob asked as he swung an arm over her shoulder.

She shot him a look. "It may be a motel," she said, steering them toward a door marked '9', "but I don't think this particular chain rents rooms by the hour. So…" She turned the key in the lock. "We've got the rest of the day—and all night—if we want."

"We want." He caught her the moment she stepped inside. Then, wheeling her around, he used their joined bodies to slam the door closed. Because his hands were already occupied, Sunny reached behind her to secure the chain.

"J.T., wait."

"Why?"

"I'd really prefer it if we drew the drapes first."

He ran the palm of one hand over the wall, searching for a button while he tugged at her coat with the other.

"What are you doing?"

"Looking for the switch.'

She chuckled into his throat. "At thirty-five a night you have to close the curtains by hand." She wiggled away to deal with it. "I'd love to see the kind of motels you're used to."

The light became dim and soft, with a thin, bright slit in the center, where the drapes met. She was standing just there, with the light like a spear behind her. And she enchanted him.

"There's this place on an island off Maine." He shrugged out of the borrowed coat, then sat down to pry off his boots. "The rooms are built on a promontory so that they hang over the sea. Waves crash up beneath, beside, in front. The windows are..." How to explain it? "They're made out of a special material so that you can see out as far as the horizon but no one can see in—so that beyond one entire wall there's nothing but rock and ocean. The tubs are huge and sunken, and the water steams with perfume."

He rose slowly, picturing it. Picturing her there, with him. "You can have music, just by wishing for it. If you want moonlight, or the sound of rain, you've only to touch a switch. The beds are big and soft, so that when a man reaches for his woman she all but floats to him over it. While you're there, time stops for as long as you believe it."

Aroused, she let out a shaky breath. "You're making this up."

He shook his head. "I'd take you there, if I could."

"I have a good imagination," she said as he pushed the coat from her shoulders. She shuddered when he ran his hands down her. "We'll pretend we're there. But I don't think there's moonlight."

Smiling, he eased her down and pulled off her boots one by one. "What then?"

''Thunder.'' Her breath shivered out when he trailed his fingers up her calf. ''And lightning. That's what I feel when you touch me.''

There was a storm in him. He saw the power of it reflected in her eyes. She rose so that her body skimmed up his, inch by tormenting inch. Before he could take her lips, she was pressing them, already hot, to his throat. The pulse that hammered there excited her, the taste inflamed her. Wanting more freedom, she pushed his sweater up and up, then let it fall to the floor in a heap.

With a lingering sound of pleasure, she traced her lips over his chest, absorbing the texture, the intimate flavor, of his skin. It was soft, dreamily soft, over the hard ridges of muscles. His scent, earthy and male, delighted her.

There was thunder. She could feel it when she let her mouth loiter over his heart. It beat for her. There was lightning. She saw the flash of power when she looked into his eyes.

He was surprised he could still stand. What she was doing was making him dizzy and desperate. Those long, lovely fingers already knew his body well. But every time they explored they found new secrets.

And her mouth… He gripped her shoulders as she took her lips on a lazy journey down his chest, over the quivering muscles of his stomach. Her tongue left a moist trail. Her throaty laugh echoed in his head.

He felt her fingers on the snap of his jeans, and the denim as it slid from waist to hipbone. Pleasure arrowed into him, its point jagged.

Time didn't stand still. It reeled backward until he was as primitive as the men who had forged weapons from stone. With an oath, he dragged her up into his arms, his mouth branding hers, all fire and force.

Then she was under him on the bed, her body as taut as wire. Her breath heaved, seemed to tear out of her lungs, as his hands raced over her. Possessed. She could hear him speak, but the roaring in her head masked the words. Driven, he ripped her shirt down the front, sending buttons flying. Wild to touch her, he hooked his fingers in the collar of the thin cotton beneath it and tore it aside.

She called out his name, stunned, elated, terrified by the violence she had brought out in him. Then she could only gasp, fighting for air, for sanity, as the first climax rocketed through her. But there was no weakness this time.

Energized, she reared up, enfolding him so that they were half sprawled, half kneeling, on the bed. Torso to torso, hip to hip. With her head thrown back, she let him take his mouth over her, pleasuring, receiving pleasure.

Like a madman, he tore, pulled, dragged at her jeans, until her body was as naked as his. Her hands slid off his slick skin as she tried to draw him to her. It was then that she realized that he was shuddering, his body vibrating with a need even she hadn't guessed at.

She started to speak his name, but he was inside her, filling her, firing her. His muscles were taut as he braced her against him, letting her frenzy drive them both.

Faster, deeper, as she soared over wave after wave. Passion became abandonment as her body bowed back, tempting his eager mouth to feast on her. Sensation layered over sensation until they were all one torrid maze of light and color and sound. As he pulled her back, his body thrust inside hers, she no longer knew where she began and he stopped. She forgot to care.

Chapter 9

Sunny unlocked the door to her apartment, ignoring the faint creak behind her that meant Mrs. Morgenstern had cracked her own door to watch the comings and goings on the third floor.

She had chosen the third floor, despite the vagaries of the elevator and the nosiness of the neighbors, because the tiny apartment boasted what passed for a balcony. On it there was just room enough for a chair, if she angled it so that she sat with her ankles resting on the rail. It overlooked the parking lot.

It was good enough for her.

"This is it," she announced, a bit surprised by the surge of nostalgia that filled her at the sight of her own things.

Jacob stepped in behind her. Sunlight poured through the skinny terrace doors to his right. Pictures marched along the walls—photographs, sketches, oil paintings and posters. Even in her own rooms, Sunny preferred company.

Piles of vibrantly colored pillows were heaped on a sagging, sun-faded sofa. In front of it was a table piled with magazines, books and mail—opened and unopened. In the corner, a waist-high urn held dusty peacock feathers.

Across the room was another table that Jacob recognized as a product of expert workmanship from an even earlier century. There was a fine film of dust on it, along with a pair of ballet shoes, a scattering of blue ribbons and a broken teapot. A collection of record albums were stuffed into a wooden crate, and on a high wicker stool stood a shiny china parrot.

"Interesting."

"Well, it's home. Most of the time." She shoved the paper bag she was carrying into his arms. It contained the fresh supply of cookies and soft drinks they'd picked up along the way. "Put these in the kitchen, will you? I want to check my machine."

"Right. Where?"

"Through there." She gestured, then disappeared through another door.

He had another moment's pause in the kitchen. It wasn't just the appliances this time. He was growing used to them. It was the teapots.

They were everywhere, covering every available surface, lining a trio of shelves on the walls, sitting cheek by jowl on top of the refrigerator. Every color, every shape, from the tacky to the elegant, was represented.

It had never occurred to him that she was a collector, of anything. She'd always seemed too restless and unrooted to take the time to clutter her life with things. Strangely, he found it endearing to realize that she had pockets of sentimentality.

Curious, he studied one of her teapots, a particularly florid example of late twentieth-century— He couldn't bring himself to call it art. It was squat, fashioned out of inferior china, with a bird of some kind on the lid and huge, ugly daisies painted all over the bowl. As a collector's item, he decided, it had a long way to go.

He set it aside and went to explore.

The blue ribbons were prizes, he discovered. For swimming, fencing, riding. It seemed Sunny had spent a lifetime scattering her talents. Her name was signed—scrawled, really—on some of the pictures on the walls. Sketches of cities, paintings of crowded beaches. He imagined many of the photographs were hers, as well.

There was more talent there, showing a clear eye and a sharp wit. If she ever settled on any one thing, she was bound to shoot right to the top. Oddly enough, he preferred her just as she was, scattering those talents, experimenting, digging for new knowledge. He didn't want her to change.

But she had changed him. It wasn't easy to accept it, but being with her, caring for her, had altered some of his basic beliefs. He could be content with one person. Compromises didn't always mean surrender. Love didn't mean losing part of yourself, it meant gaining that much more.

And she had made him wonder how he was going to face the rest of his life without her.

Turning toward the bedroom, he went to find her.

She was standing in what he first took for a closet. Then when he saw the bed, he realized it was the entire room. Though it was no more than eight by eight, she had crammed something into every nook and cranny. More books, a stuffed bear in a virulent orange, ice skates. A set of skis hung on the wall like sabers.

The dresser was crowded with bottles, at least twenty different brands of scent and lotion. There was also a photograph of her family.

He found it difficult to concentrate on it, as she was standing by the bed, stripped to the waist. She had taken off his sweater. He'd been forced to loan it to her for the remainder of the trip, as he'd destroyed her shirt. With one ear cocked toward the unit by her bed that served as radio, alarm clock and message machine, she rooted through her closet for another top.

"Hey, babe." The voice on the machine was cajoling and very male. The moment he heard it, Jacob despised it. "It's Pete. You're not still steamed, are you, doll? Come on, Sunny, forgive and forget, right? Give me a call and we'll go dancing. I miss that pretty face of yours."

Sunny gave a quick snort and dragged out a sweatshirt.

"Who's Pete?"

"Whoa." She put a hand between her breasts. "You scared me."

"Who's Pete?" he repeated.

"Just a guy." She tugged the sweatshirt on. "I was hoping you'd bring in one of those sodas." She sat on the bed to pull off her boots.

"Sunny." This time the voice on the phone was smooth and feminine. "We got a postcard from Libby and Cal. Let us know when you get back in town."

"My mother," Sunny explained, wriggling her toes. Grinning, she passed him the sweater. "You can have this back now."

Not entirely sure what he was feeling, he took off his coat. Beneath it, his chest was bare. As he started to pull the sweater over his head, the machine announced the next message.

"Hey, Sunny, it's Marco. Where the hell are you, sweet thing? I've been calling for a week. Give me a buzz when you get back." There was a sound, like a big, smacking kiss before the beep.

"Who's Marco?" Jacob asked, deadly calm.

"Another guy." Her brows rose when he took her arm and pulled her to her feet.

"How many are there?"

"Messages?"

"Men."

"Sunny...Bob here. I thought you might like to—"

Deliberately Sunny shut off the machine. "I haven't kept track," she said evenly. "Do you want to compare past lives, J.T.?"

He didn't answer, because he found he couldn't. Releasing her, he walked away.

Jealousy. It filled him. And how he detested it. He didn't consider himself a reasonable man, but he was certainly an intelligent one. He knew she hadn't begun to live the moment he had walked into her life. A woman like her, beautiful, bright, fascinating, would attract men. Many men. And if it had been possible he would have murdered each and every one of them for touching what was his.

And not his.

He swore and spun around to see her watching him from the doorway.

"Are we going to fight?"

He ached. Just looking at her, he ached, for what was, and for what could never be. "No."

"Okay."

"I don't want them near you," he blurted out.

"Don't be a jerk."

He reached her in three strides. "I mean it."

She tugged her arms free and glared at him. "So do I. Damn it, do you think any of them could mean anything to me after you?"

"If you don't—" Her words sunk in and stopped him. Lifting his hands, palms out, he stepped back. She stepped forward.

"If I don't what? If you think you can give me orders, pal, you've got another thing coming. I don't have to—"

"No, you don't." He cut her off, taking her balled fist in his hand. Not his, he reminded himself. He was going to have to start getting used to that. "I'm not handling this well. I've never been in love before."

The fighting light died from her eyes. "Neither have I. Not like this."

"No, not like this." He brought her fingertips to his lips. "Just review the rest of your communications later, will you?"

Amused by his phrasing, she grinned. "Sure. Listen, help yourself to whatever's in the kitchen. The TV's in the bedroom, the stereo's out here. I'll be back in a couple of hours."

"Where are you going?"

She picked up a pair of discarded sneakers and tugged them on. "I'm going to go see my parents. If you're up to it later, maybe we can have a real dinner out and go dancing or something.''

"Sunny." He took her hand as she picked up her coat. "I'd like to go with you."

Solemn eyed, she studied him. "You don't have to, Jacob. Really."

"I know. I'd like to."

She kissed his cheek. "Go get your coat."

William Stone stalked to the door of his elegant Tudor home in bare feet. His sweatshirt bagged on his long, skinny frame. The knees of his jeans had worn through, but he refused to give them up. In one hand he carried a portable phone, in the other a banana.

"Look, Preston, I want the new ad campaign to be subtle. No dancing tea bags, no heavy-metal music, no talking teddy bears." On a sound of frustration he yanked the door open. "Yes, that includes waltzing rabbits, for God's sake. I want—" He spotted his daughter and grinned from ear to ear. "Deal with it, Preston," he ordered, and broke the connection. "Hi, brat." He spread his arms and caught her on a leap.

Sunny gave him a noisy kiss, then stole his banana. "The tycoon speaks."

William grimaced at the portable phone. Such pretensions embarrassed him. "I was just…" His words trailed off when he spotted Jacob on the threshold. He searched his mind for a name. Sunny often brought men to the house—friends and companions. William refused to think of his little girl having lovers. Though this one looked familiar, he couldn't place the name.

"This is J.T.," Sunny said between bites of banana. She had her arm around her father's waist.

Two peas in a pod, Jacob thought, pleased that he'd been able to dig up the expression. The same coloring, the same bone structure, the same frank, measuring looks. Taking the initiative, Jacob stepped forward and offered a hand.

"Mr. Stone."

Since one arm was still holding his daughter—a bit possessively—William stuck the phone in the back pocket of his jeans before he shook Jacob's hand.

"Hornblower," Sunny continued, enjoying herself. "Jacob Hornblower. Cal's brother."

"No kidding." The handshake became more enthusiastic, the smile more friendly. "Well, it's nice to see you. We were beginning to think Cal had made up his family. Come on in. Caro's around somewhere."

He released Jacob but kept a firm hold on Sunny as he led the way through the foyer into the living room. Jacob got the impression of bold colors mixed with pastels. And, again, elegant. A simple, timeless elegance.

A few pieces of glittery crystal, gleaming antiques and, of course, what he now realized was Caroline Stone's stunning art. If Jacob was surprised to find her woven masterpieces so casually displayed on the walls, he was speechless to see another spread on the floor as a rug.

"Have a seat," William was saying as he walked thoughtlessly over what Jacob considered a priceless work of art. "How about a drink?"

"No, nothing. Thank you." He was staring at an

ornamental lemon tree in the window. His own father nurtured the same type of plant.

"You'll have to have tea," Sunny said, patting Jacob's hand as she sat on the sofa beside him. "If you don't, you'll hurt Daddy's feelings."

"Of course." He glanced up at William again and caught his narrowed-eyed, speculative look.

The phone in William's back pocket rang. He ignored it. Recognizing the gleam in her father's eye and wanting to delay the questions for the time being, Sunny dropped the banana peel in his hand. "I'd just love some, Daddy. How about Oriental Ecstasy?"

"Fine. I'll take care of it."

He disappeared through a doorway, the phone still shrilling in his pocket.

Sunny chuckled and put her hand on Jacob's again. "I suppose I should warn you…" She tilted her head, curious. Jacob was gawking—she couldn't think of another word for his expression—at one of her mother's wall hangings. "J.T.? Would you like to tune in?"

"Yes. What?"

"I was going to warn you, my father's nosy. He'll ask you all kinds of questions, most of them personal. He can't help it."

"All right." He couldn't resist. Rising, he walked over to the rectangle of cloth and ran his fingers over the soft material and bleeding colors.

"Beautiful, isn't it?"

"Yes, it's very beautiful."

She got up to stand beside him. "She's become a very well respected artist."

Respected was a mild word for Caroline Stone. Her work was found behind glass in museums. It was studied and revered by art students throughout the settled universe. And he was here, running his fingers over an exquisite piece of it.

"She used to sell blankets and things for grocery money."

"That's a myth."

"I beg your pardon?"

"Nothing." He dropped his hand, shoved it into his pocket. For the first time since he had stepped off the ship he felt totally disoriented. These were people he had learned about from study disks. Historical figures. Yet he was here, in their home. He was in love with their daughter. How could he be in love with a woman who had lived, and died, centuries before he had been born?

Panic. He tasted it. Turning, he gripped her arms. Reality, solid and warm. He was holding it in his hands. "Sunny."

"What's wrong?" He was so pale, and his eyes were so dark. "What is it?"

He just shook his head. There was nothing he could say. No words he knew to explain it. Instead, he brought his mouth down on hers and let her flavor chase away the fear.

"I love you."

"I know." Moved by the desperation in his voice, she lifted a hand to his cheek. The urge to soothe and ease was still new to her. "We'll both get used to it eventually."

"Hello."

They drew apart to see Caroline standing in the doorway. Her dark, straight hair skimmed her shoulders. Beaded columns swung at her ears. There was a small smile on her face, a quietly lovely face that was animated by large, amused eyes. She was wearing a baggy man's shirt, trim denim pants and beaded moccasins. In her arms she held a gurgling baby.

"Mom." Sunny dashed across the room to hug both woman and child. She was taller than Caroline and had to bend slightly to give her the same enthusiastic kiss she had given her father. Laughing, she took the baby. Then, holding him above her head, she began to turn in a circle. "Hi, Sam! How's it going? Oh, you're getting so big!"

"He has his sister's appetite," Caroline pointed out.

Grinning, Sunny planted the giggling baby on her hip. "J.T., this is my mother, Caroline, and my brother, King Samuel."

"J.T." Caroline's artist's eyes had already seen the resemblance and made the connection. "You must be Cal's brother."

"Yes." The sense of unreality came back as she crossed the room. Rather than offering a hand, she kissed him.

"We were hoping we'd finally meet some of Cal's family. He's very proud of you."

"Is he?" A trace of resentment came through in his tone.

Caroline noticed it, let it pass. "Yes. Did your parents make the trip with you?"

"No. They weren't able to come."

"Oh." The disappointment in her eyes was brief but sincere. "Well, I hope we can get together one day. Where's Will?" she asked Sunny.

"Making tea."

"Of course. Please, sit down. You're an astrophysicist?"

"That's right." He settled back on the sofa, with Caroline Stone opposite him and Sunny on the floor with the baby.

"J.T.'s into time travel at the moment."

"Time travel?" Caroline smiled and crossed her slender legs. "Will'll go crazy. Though I think parallel universes are his current interest."

"What happened to reincarnation?"

"He's still a staunch disciple. He's convinced he was a member of the first Continental Congress."

"Always the revolutionary." Sunny tickled her brother's belly as she smiled up at Jacob. "My father likes to pick controversial subjects so he can argue about them. Oh, look! Sam's crawling!"

"A newly acquired skill." With two parts pride and one part wonder, Caroline watched her chubby, towheaded son pull himself across the rug. "Will's already taken a caseful of videos."

"I'm entitled," William said as he wheeled in a tea cart. "As I remember, Sunny went from crawl to walk to run so fast we hardly had time to blink."

"And you recorded it all on that secondhand movie camera." Caroline rose, stepped over her son, and kissed Will before she helped him with the tea.

"So…" William had already gone over his list of questions in the kitchen. "…did you just get into Portland?"

"This afternoon," Jacob told him, and accepted his cup of tea.

"You were looking for Cal when you tracked down Sunny."

"That's right." He sipped, trying to resolve himself to the fact that he was drinking Herbal Delight with the man who had invented it. "He'd given me the—'' coordinates nearly slipped out ''—directions to the cabin.''

''The cabin?'' The teacup paused on the way to William's lips. ''You've been to the cabin—with Sunny?''

''We had a hell of a snowstorm last week.'' Sunny laid a hand lightly on her father's knee. ''Lost power for a couple of days.''

''Together?''

She managed to keep her expression bland. ''It's hard to lose it separately in a space as small as the cabin.''

Amused, Caroline watched her son crawl over Jacob's feet. ''It's a shame you missed Cal and Libby. I hope you plan to wait until they get back.''

The baby was chewing on his pant leg. After setting his teacup aside, Jacob reached down to set Sam in his lap. ''I'll wait.''

''Where?'' William wanted to know. Sunny dug her fingers into her father's knee.

''Did you know that J.T.'s experimenting with time travel?''

''Time travel?'' Fascination warred with paternity. Paternity won. ''Just how long were you two together in the mountains?''

Jacob let Sam gnaw on his index finger. ''A couple of weeks.''

''Really?'' His eyes narrowed, and he laid a proprietary hand on Sunny's shoulder. ''I suppose the snow kept you from making more suitable arrangements?''

Sunny rolled her eyes. Caroline sighed. Jacob ran a hand over Sam's fine, pale hair.

''The arrangement suited me well enough.''

"I'll bet it did." William leaned forward, then hissed as Sunny dug again, shooting for the worn denim at his knees.

"Did you know, J.T., that my father absconded..." She liked the word, enjoyed rolling it off of her tongue. "...with my mother when she was sixteen?"

"Seventeen," William corrected.

"Not quite." This from Caroline as she sipped her tea.

He shot her a look. "You were only a couple months shy. And that was entirely different."

"Naturally," Sunny agreed.

"It was the times," William muttered. "It was the sixties."

Sunny kissed his sore knee. "That explains everything."

"You had to be there. Besides, we wouldn't have had to elope if Caro's father hadn't been so interfering and unreasonable."

"I'm sure you're right." Sunny fluttered her lashes at him. "There's nothing worse than a father who pokes his nose in where it doesn't belong."

He caught her nose between his two fingers and twisted. "Watch it."

She just grinned. "Tell me, is Granddad speaking to you yet?"

"Barely."

"Except when they make fools of themselves over Sam," Caroline put in. "He's almost forgiven us for the fact that you and Libby weren't around for him to spoil when you were babies. Would you like me to take Sam, J.T.?"

"No, he's fine." The baby was playing with Jacob's fingers, gurgling to them and sampling one occasionally. "He looks like you," he murmured, turning to Sunny.

Her lips curved. She couldn't have explained how it made her feel to watch him cuddle a baby on his lap. "I like to think so."

William drummed his fingers on the arm of his chair. The Hornblower boys seemed to have some kind of charm that worked on his daughters. Though he'd decided Cal was nearly good enough for Libby, he was reserving judgment on this one.

"So, you're a scientist." William had a great deal of respect for scientists, but that didn't mean he was ready to accept the picture of his daughter snuggled up with one. In his cabin. Without any electricity.

"Yes."

Talkative son of a gun, William thought, and prodded deeper. "Astrophysics?"

"That's right."

"Where did you study?"

"Maybe you'd like his grade point average," Sunny muttered.

"Shut up." William patted her head. "I've always been fascinated with space, you see." This time his smile was cautiously friendly. "So I'm interested."

If this was the game, Jacob decided, he could play it. "I got my law degree from Princeton."

"Law?" Sunny said. "You never told me—"

"You didn't ask." His eyes dipped to her, then zeroed in on her father again. "Physics started out as a hobby."

"An unusual one," William mused.

"Yes." Jacob smiled. "Like growing herbs."

William had to laugh. "About time travel—"

"Take a break, Will," Caroline advised him. "You

can grill the man more later. Your son needs to be changed.''

''And it's my turn.'' William unfolded his long legs. He crossed to Jacob, his heart turning to mush as Sam lifted up his chubby arms. ''There's my boy. Have some more tea,'' he told Jacob. ''We'll talk about those experiments of yours later.''

''I'll come with you.'' Sunny pushed herself up off the floor. ''You can show me all the toys you bought him since last month.''

''Wait till you see this train…'' he said as they walked out.

''Will likes to pretend the toys are for Sam.'' Caroline smiled as she rose to fill Jacob's cup again. ''I hope you're not too annoyed.''

''By what?''

''The Spanish Inquisition.'' She moved back to sit on the arm of her chair. She reminded him of Sunny. ''Actually, it was pretty mild, compared to what he put Cal through.''

''Apparently Cal passed.''

''We love him very much. Nothing would have made Will happier than to bring him into the business. But Cal has to fly, as I'm sure you know.''

''He never wanted anything else.''

''It shows. It was the same with Libby. She always knew what she wanted. It's more difficult for Sunny. I wonder sometimes if all that energy and intelligence hasn't given her too many choices. You'd understand that.'' At his questioning look, she continued. ''From a law degree from Princeton to astrophysics. That's quite a leap.''

With a brief turn at professional boxing in between.

He shrugged. "It takes some of us longer to make up our minds."

"And those kind of people usually jump in with both feet. Sunny does."

She was subtler than her husband, Jacob thought, and more difficult to put off. "She's the most fascinating woman I've ever met."

And he is in love with her, Caroline reflected. Not happy about it, but in love. "Sunny's like a tapestry, woven in bold colors. Some of the threads are incredibly strong and durable. Others are impossibly delicate. The result is admirable. But a work of art needs love, as well as admiration." She lifted her hands. "She'd hate to know I described her that way."

His gaze shifted to the vivid, blending colors of the wall hanging. "She wouldn't care for the delicate."

"No." Caroline felt a tug of regret, and of relief. So he knew her younger daughter, and he understood her. "It's old-fashioned, I suppose, but all Will and I really want is to know that she's happy."

"It's not old-fashioned." His mother had said almost the same words to him about Cal before he'd left home.

With a sigh, Caroline turned to glance at the wall hanging he was studying. "That's one of my older pieces. I made that while I was pregnant with Sunny. I sold most of my work back then, but for some reason I held on to this one."

"It's beautiful."

On impulse she rose to take it down from the wall. Her fingers slid over it. She remembered sitting at her handmade loom, watching the sunlight play on the colors as she chose them, blended them. With Will in the garden, Libby sleeping on a blanket spread on the grass and a child moving in her womb. The image was all the sweeter for the time that had passed between.

"I'd like you to have it."

If she had offered him a Rembrandt or an O'Keeffe, he would have been no more stunned. "I couldn't."

"Why not?"

"It's priceless."

She laughed at that. "Oh, my agent puts prices on my work. Ridiculous prices, for the most part. I'd hate to think that my pieces will only end up in art galleries or museums." She folded it. "It would mean a lot more if I knew some of them were being enjoyed by my family." When he said nothing, she held it out. "My daughter took your brother's name. That makes us family."

He didn't want to feel like family. He needed to hold on to his resentment, to go on thinking of Caroline and William Stone as names in history. But he found himself reaching out and taking the soft cloth.

"Thank you."

The nursery was painted a soft green. An antique iron crib in white was draped with a blanket Caroline had woven in pastels. The room was full of toys, many of which Sam would have no interest in for years. But there were dozens of stuffed animals, ranging from elephants to the traditional teddy bear.

Picking one up, Sunny waited until her father laid Sam on the changing table. "You're pathetic."

"Maybe you don't remember the punishment for

sass,'' Will said mildly as he unsnapped Sam's overalls.

"I'm a little too big for you to make me sit in a chair until I apologize."

He shot her a look. "Don't bet on it."

"Dad." Sighing, she set the bear aside. "From the time I turned thirteen you've interrogated every male I've brought into the house."

"I like to know who my daughter's seeing socially. There's no crime in that."

"There is the way you do it."

Sam gurgled and kicked his feet as Will freed him of his diaper. Will dusted powder on him, enjoying the scent. "I liked you better when you were this size."

"Tough." She walked over to rest her elbow on his shoulder. Even at her most rebellious, she'd never been able to do anything but love him. "I suppose you're going to grill the girls Sam brings home when he starts dating."

"Of course. I'm not sexist." Neither was he stupid. "Do you want to tell me that you and J.T. have been spending a few platonic days in the cabin?"

"No."

"I didn't think so." He fastened a fresh diaper on his son. Life had been so simple, he thought, when all he'd had to worry about was diaper rash and teething. "Sunny, you haven't known the man more than a few weeks."

She stuck her tongue in her cheek. "Does this mean you've changed your views on free love?"

"The sexual revolution is over." He snapped Sam's overalls again. "For several very good reasons."

She held up a hand. "Before you start listing them, why don't I tell you I agree with you?"

That took some of the wind out of his sails. Sunny had come by her argumentative nature honestly. "Good. Then we understand each other."

"That promiscuity is neither morally or ethically correct or physically wise? Absolutely. I've never been promiscuous."

"I'm relieved to hear it." Seeing Sam's eyes droop, Will took him to the crib. After winding up a mobile of circus animals, he laid his son down.

"I didn't say I was a virgin."

Will winced—he hated to think of himself as a fusty prude—then sighed. "I guess I suspected as much."

"Want to make me sit in a chair until I apologize?"

His lips quirked. "I don't think it would do much good at this point. It's not that I don't trust your judgment, Sunbeam."

She'd never been able to resist him. Moving closer, she took his face in her hands and kissed him. "But your judgment is so much better."

"Naturally." He grinned and patted her bottom. "It's one of the few advantages of hitting forty."

"You'll never be forty." She managed to keep her lips from curving. "Dad, I might as well confess. I have been with a man before."

"Not that weasely Carl Lommins."

She made a face. "Give me some credit. And don't interrupt—I'm making a point. When I was with someone it was because I was fond of him, because there was mutual respect and there was responsibility. You taught me that, you and Mom."

"So you're telling me I'm not supposed to worry about your relationship with J.T."

"No, I'm not telling you not to worry. But I am telling you I'm not fond of him."

"Well, then—"

"I'm in love with him."

He studied her eyes. When a man had been in love, passionately, with the same woman for most of his life, he recognized the signs. It was time to accept that he had seen those signs on his daughter's face the moment she had walked in the door.

"And?"

"And what?" she countered.

"What are you going to do about it?"

"I'm going to marry him." The statement surprised her enough to make her laugh. "He doesn't know it yet, because I just figured it out myself. When he goes back east, I'm going with him."

"And if he objects?"

Her chin came up. "He'll have to learn to live with it."

"I guess the problem is you're too much like me."

She put her arms around his neck to hug him close. "I won't like being so far away. But he's what I want."

"If he makes you happy." William drew her away. "He damn well better make you happy."

"I don't intend to give him a choice."

Chapter 10

"It'll be fun." Sunny navigated into a narrow parking space under a brightly lit sign that aggressively flashed Club Rendezvous. Jacob studied the winking colored lights with some doubt, and she patted his hand. "Trust me, pal, we need this."

"If you say so."

"I do. Besides, if I find out you can't dance, I want to be able to dump you now and save time." She just laughed when he twisted her ear. "And you owe me."

"Why is that?"

She flipped down the visor and gave what she could see of her face a quick check in the mirror. On impulse she pulled out a lipstick and painted her mouth a vivid red. "Because if I hadn't been so quick with the excuses you'd be eating dinner at my parents'."

"I liked your parents."

Touched, she leaned over to kiss his cheek. Seeing she'd left the imprint of her lips there, she rubbed at it with her thumb.

"Damn it."

"Hold still a minute," she complained when he backed away. "I've just about got it." Satisfied, she dropped the tube of lipstick back in her bag. "I know you like my parents. So do I. But you'd never have gotten nachos and margaritas at Will and Caro's." She lowered her voice. "My mother cooks."

Taking no chances, he rubbed at his cheek himself. "Is that a crime in this state?"

"She cooks things like alfalfa fondue."

"Oh." Once he'd managed to imagine it he'd decided he much preferred the spicy Mexican meal they had shared a short time before. "I guess I do owe you."

"Your very life," she agreed. Opening her door, she squeezed herself through the narrow opening between it and the neighboring car. The flashing lights danced over her, making her look exactly as she was—exciting and exotic. "And after a couple of weeks in nature's bosom I figure we could both use some live music—the louder the better—a rowdy crowd and some air clogged with cigarette smoke."

"Sounds like paradise." He managed, with some effort, to push himself out the other door. "Sunny, I don't feel right about you exchanging all your currency."

She lifted both brows, half-amused, half-puzzled, by his phrasing. "You exchange currency when you go into a foreign country. What I've been doing is called spending money."

"Whatever. I don't have any with me to spend."

She thought it was a pity that a man so obviously intelligent and dedicated should earn a small salary. "Don't worry about it." She'd only started counting pennies herself since she'd become self-supporting. So far, she hadn't shown much of a knack for it. "If I get to Philadelphia, you can pick up the tab."

"We'll talk about it later." He needed to change the subject, and he found the answer close at hand. "I wanted to ask you what you call that outfit you're wearing."

"This?" She glanced down at the snug, short and strapless red leather dress under her winter coat. "Sexy," she decided, running a tongue over her teeth. "What do you call it?"

"We'll talk about that later, too."

With her arm through his, she crossed the broken sidewalk. The swatch of formfitting leather didn't provide much protection against the wind, but it felt good to wear something other than jeans. It felt even better to note how often Jacob's gaze skimmed over her legs.

The cold was forgotten when she opened the door to a blast of heat and music.

"Ah...civilization."

He saw only a dim room dazzled by intermittent flashes of light. The music was every bit as loud as she'd promised, pulsing with bass, blaring with horns. He could smell smoke and liquor, sweat and perfume. Through it all was the constant din of voices and laughter.

While he took it in, she passed their coats to the checker on duty and slipped the stub in her bag.

She was right. He'd needed it—not just the sensory

stimulation, not just the anonymous crowd, but also the firsthand look at twentieth-century socializing.

Overall there was very little difference from what he might have found in his own time. People, then and then, tended to gather together for their entertainment. They wanted music and company, food and drink. Times might change, but people's needs were basically the same.

"Come on." She was dragging him through the crowd to where tables were crammed together on two levels. On the first was a long bar. There was a man rather than a synthetic behind it, serving drink and setting out bowls filled with some kind of finger food. People crowded there, hip to hip.

On the second level was a half circle of stage where the musicians performed. Jacob counted eight of them, in various kinds of dress, holding instruments that pitched a wall of sound that roared out of tall boxes on either corner of the stage.

In front of them, on a small square of floor, tangles of arms and legs and bodies twisted in various ways to the beat. He noted the costumes they chose and saw that there was no standard. Snug pants and baggy ones, long skirts and brief ones, vivid colors and unrelieved black. Women wore shoes flat to the floor or, like Sunny, shoes with slender spikes at the back.

He imagined this meant those particular women wanted to be taller. But it had the side effect of making it very pleasant to look at their legs.

He appreciated the style of nonconformity, the healthy expression of individual tastes. He knew there had been a space of time between this and his own when society in general had accepted a uniform. A brief period, Jacob mused, but it must have been a miserably dull one.

As he stood and observed, waitresses in short skirts bustled on both levels, balancing trays and scribbling the orders shouted at them.

Inefficient, he thought, but interesting. It was simpler to press a button on an order box and receive your requirements from a speedy droid. But it was a bit friendlier this way.

With her hand in his, Sunny led him up a short flight of curving stairs and began to scout around for an empty table. "I forgot it was Saturday night," she shouted at him. "It's always a madhouse on Saturdays."

"Why?"

"Date night, pal," she said, and laughed. "Don't worry, we'll squeeze in somewhere." But she abandoned her search to smile at him. "What do you think?"

He lifted a hand to toy with the trio of balls that hung from slender chains at her ears. "I like it."

"The Marauders are good. The band." She gestured as the sax player went into a screaming solo. "They're very hot out here."

"In here," he corrected. "It's hot in here."

"No, I mean... Never mind." Someone bumped her from behind. Taking it in stride, she wound her arms around Jacob's neck. "I guess this is our first date."

He ignored the crowd and kissed her. "How's it going so far?"

"Just dandy."

Taking that to mean "good," he kissed her again. Her satisfied sigh set off a chain reaction inside him.

"We could always just stand here," he said, directly in her ear. "I don't think anyone would notice."

"You were right," she said on another sigh. "It is hot in here. Maybe we should just—"

"Sunny!" Someone caught her by the waist, spun her around and, ending on a dip, pressed a hard, wet kiss to her mouth. "Baby, you're back."

"Marco."

"What's left of me. I've been pining away for weeks." He slung a friendly arm around her shoulders. "Where'd you disappear to?"

"The mountains." She smiled, pleased to see him. He was skinny, unpretentious and harmless. Despite the dramatic kiss, they had decided years before not to complicate their friendship with romance. "How's the real world?"

"Dog-eat-dog, love. Thank God." He glanced over her shoulder and found himself being burned alive by a pair of direct green eyes. "Ah...who's your friend?"

"J.T." She laid a hand on Jacob's arm. "This is Marco, an old poker buddy. You don't want to play with J.T., Marco. He's murder."

Marco didn't have to be told twice. "How ya doing?" He didn't offer his hand, because he wanted to keep it.

"All right." Jacob measured him. He figured if the man kissed Sunny again it would be simple enough to break his skinny neck.

"J.T. happens to be the brother of my sister's husband."

"Small world."

Jacob didn't bat an eye. "Smaller than you think."

"Right." If Marco had been wearing a tie he would

have loosened it. But with his collar already open he didn't have a clue how to ease the constriction in his throat. "Listen, do you guys need a table?"

"Absolutely."

"We pulled some together back there, if you want to climb in."

"Okay." She looked up at Jacob. "Okay?"

"Sure." He was already annoyed with himself. The jealousy had been an emotional rather than an intellectual reaction. He watched Sunny's long legs as she walked between the tables. And an entirely justified reaction. Maybe men had progressed, but they had always been, would always be, territorial.

Half a dozen people greeted Sunny by name as they stopped at the table. Because most of the introductions were lost in the roar of the music, Jacob only nodded as he took his seat.

"This round's on me," Marco announced when he finally managed to flag down a waitress. "Same thing," he told her. "Plus a glass of chardonnay for the lady and..." He lifted a brow at Jacob.

"A beer. Thanks."

"No problem. I sold three cars today."

"Good for you." Sunny leaned over a bit, easily pitching her voice above the noise as she elaborated for Jacob's benefit. "Marco's a car dealer."

Jacob got the image of Marco shuffling automobiles, then passing them around a poker table. "Congratulations" seemed the safest possible comment.

"I do okay. Just let me know if you're in the market. We got in a shipment of real honeys this week."

Jacob spared a glance at the brunette on his other side as she rubbed her arm against his. "I'll do that."

Relieved that Sunny's new friend no longer looked

as though he wanted to rearrange his face, Marco shifted his chair a little closer. "So what do you drive, J.T.?"

There was a universal moan around the table. Marco accepted it with a good-natured shrug and popped a handful of peanuts into his mouth.

"Hey, it's my job."

"Like taking little old ladies for test drives is a job," someone joked.

"It's a living." Marco grinned. "None of us are rocket scientists."

"J.T. is," Sunny said.

"Are you?" The brunette scooted her chair closer. She had big brown eyes, Jacob noted. Eyes that just brimmed with invitations. "In a manner of speaking."

"Oh, I just love brainy men."

Amused, Jacob picked up the beer the waitress set in front of him. He caught the look Sunny shot across the table. He recognized it. Jealousy, it appeared, was contagious. Nothing could have pleased him more. He took a long swig and tolerated the smoke the brunette blew in his direction. It was no use telling her that she was endangering her very attractively packaged lungs.

"Do you?"

She kept her eyes on his as she slowly crushed out the cigarette. "Oh, yes. I'm very attracted to intelligence."

"Let's dance." Sunny shoved back her chair and snagged Jacob's sleeve. "Nice try, Sheila," she muttered, and dragged Jacob onto the dance floor.

"Is that her name? Sheila?"

She turned to him, into him, and tilted her chin upward. "Who wants to know?"

"Don't you want me to be nice to your friends?" He settled his hands on her hips. With her heels, her eyes were level with his. And her body fit his perfectly.

"No." Her mouth moved into a pout as she twined her arms around his neck. "At least not the stacked ones."

Curious, he looked back at the table. "Is she stacked?"

"As if you didn't notice. Unfortunately, her I.Q. measures the same as her bustline."

"I like your...I.Q. better."

"Good thinking." Grinning, she brushed a kiss over his mouth. "I can't blame her for giving it her best shot. You're awfully cute."

"Small dogs are cute," he muttered. "Babies are cute."

"You like babies."

"Yes, why not?"

She toyed with the ends of his hair. "Just checking. Anyway, you are cute. And sexy." She took a playful nip at his bottom lip. "And brainy." She settled her cheek against his as he drew her closer. And mine, she thought. All mine. "What does the *T* stand for?" she murmured.

"Which *T*?"

"In J.T."

"Nothing."

"It has to stand for something." She let out a sound of pleasure. "You dance very well." The sax was playing again, crying the blues this time. Sunny's eyes dipped closed as Jacob molded her against him.

They were hardly moving in the press of bodies surrounding them. As his hands roamed over her back and his lips down her throat she didn't care if they ever moved again.

Her thighs brushed against his. The leather fitted her like a second skin, one he was already imagining peeling away from her. As he turned her in his arms, slowly, sinuously, he shifted to taste the bare flesh of her shoulder. Even over the echoing music he could hear her skin humming. Lazily he trailed his lips back to toy with hers.

"You smell incredible. Like spring in the desert, hot, with some lingering trace of flowers gone wild."

Unable to resist, she deepened the kiss until her head swam. "J.T.?"

"Yes?"

"I'm not sure, but I think we could get arrested for this."

"It would be worth it."

She opened her eyes, met his. "Let's go home. I don't like crowds the way I used to."

They stayed a week, so that she could drag him to movies, malls, more clubs. She attributed his constant fascination to the fact that he'd never been in the Northwest before. Each time they went out, it was as though he were seeing things for the first time. Because of that, she enjoyed the hours and the errands more than she ever had.

When they were alone, when she trembled in his arms, she realized that it didn't matter where they were. They were together. And if with each passing moment she fell more deeply in love, she did so freely and with absolute joy.

For the first time in her life she began to think of a future with a man, one man. She imagined passing through the years with him—not always content, but always satisfied. She thought of a home, and if white picket fences and car pools didn't enter the fantasy, children did. She could picture the arguments, the noise and the laughter.

Before much longer, she thought, they would talk about it. They would plan.

He allowed himself the week. A handful of days meant so little in the vastness of time. And meant so much to him. He recorded everything he could, and branded the rest on his memory. He didn't mean to forget, not an instant.

Yet he worried about how he could tell her where he had to travel when he left her so that it would hurt the least. More, he worried because he was no longer sure he had the courage to live without her.

When they left to go back to the cabin he told himself that it was the beginning of the end. If it had to end—and he saw no alternative—it would end honestly. He would tell her everything.

"You're so quiet," she said as they turned up the long, bumpy road that led to the cabin.

"I was thinking."

"Well, that's fine, but you haven't picked one fight in five hours. I'm worried about you."

"I don't want to fight with you."

"Now I'm really worried." She'd known that something was on his mind, something that caused her palms to sweat. Deliberately she made her voice light and cheerful. "We'll be back in a few minutes. Once you're trapped inside the cabin, hauling wood and eating out of a can, you'll be your old cranky self.''

"Sunny, we have to talk."

She moistened her lips. "All right." Her nerves began to hum as she stopped the car in front of the cabin. "Before or after we unload?"

"Now." It had to be now. He took her hand and said the first words that came to mind. "I love you so much."

The little fist of fear in her stomach unclenched. "We're never going to fight if you keep talking like that." She shifted closer to kiss his cheek. It was then that she noticed the smoke pumping out of the chimney. "Jacob, someone's here."

"What?"

"In the cabin." She saw the front door open. "Libby!" With a laugh, she shoved the car door open and bounded out. "Libby, you scared me to death." As Jacob watched, she threw her arms around a slim brunette. "Look at you! You're so tanned!"

"There's a lot of sun in Bora Bora." Libby kissed her sister's cheeks. "When we got back last night we thought you'd skipped out on us."

"Just a quick trip into the real world to recharge."

Libby's laugh was smooth and easy. She knew her sister very well. "That's what I told Cal. All your books were still here." Suddenly she gripped both of Sunny's hands. "Oh, Sunny, I'm so glad you're back. I can't wait to tell you. I—" A movement caught her eye. Glancing over, she saw Jacob as he climbed out of the Land Rover. As their eyes met, her half smile of greeting faded and her fingers tightened on Sunny's.

"What? What is it? Oh." Smiling, Sunny turned.

"Guess who dropped in? This is Jacob, Cal's brother."

"I know." Libby felt as though the ground had vanished from under her feet. She'd seen his face before, in the picture Cal had kept on his ship. But this was no picture. It was a flesh-and-blood man, a furious one. As they stared at each other in silence, the blood seeped slowly out of her face.

He's come for Cal, she thought, and had to bite back the scream of protest that rose into her throat.

She's terrified, he realized. Something moved inside him that he stubbornly ignored. He wouldn't feel for her. He wouldn't think of her as anything but the obstacle preventing his brother from returning home.

"J.T.?" Instinctively Sunny put a protective arm around Libby's shoulders. There was something here, she realized. And she was the only one not in on the secret. "Libby, you're shivering. You shouldn't be standing out here without a coat. Let's go inside." She tossed a look back over her shoulder. "Let's all go inside."

"I'm all right." Shaken, Libby walked inside to the fire and tried to warm her icy hands. No amount of heat could warm her trembling heart. She wouldn't look at him again, not until she had herself under some kind of control. In the back of her mind, the little germ of fear had lived. Someday they would come for him. But she hadn't believed it would be so soon. They'd had so little time.

Time, she thought bitterly. It was a word she could learn to hate.

Sunny stood between them, baffled. The tension was so thick in the small room that she could smell it as easily as the woodsmoke. "All right." She looked from Libby's rigid back to Jacob's stony face without any idea who she should go to. "Would either of you like to tell me what's going on?"

"Hey, Libby, if that was that sexy sister of yours, I want to tell her—"

Barefoot, his sweatshirt torn, Cal strode in from the kitchen. Everyone turned toward him. It was like a slow, deliberate ballet. His easy grin froze. All motion stopped.

"J.T." His voice was hardly more than a whisper as joy and disbelief flooded through him. "J.T.," he said again. Then, with a whoop, he was across the room, grabbing his brother in a hard hug. "Oh, God, Jacob! It's really you!"

Libby watched them until tears blurred her vision and she turned away.

Sunny beamed. The two brothers held each other in a fierce embrace. She could see the emotions run over Jacob's face and found them beautiful.

"I can't believe it," Cal murmured, pulling his brother back to study, to devour, his face. "You're really here. How?"

He kept his hands on Cal's arms, needing the simple and tangible contact. "The same way as you, but with more finesse. You look good." Somehow he'd expected to find Cal pale and thin and tired from coping with the twentieth century. Instead, his brother was tanned, alert and obviously happy.

"You, too." His smile faded a bit. "Mom? Dad?"

"They're fine."

Cal nodded. It was a hurt he had learned to live with. "You got my message. I couldn't be sure."

"We received it," Jacob said dully.

"You've met Libby, then." Regret vanished. Turning, he held a hand out for his wife. She didn't move.

"We've met." Jacob inclined his head and waited. She could take the first step.

"You'll both have a lot to talk about." Using every ounce of effort, she managed to keep her voice steady.

"Libby." Her name was a murmur as Cal crossed to her. He laid a hand on her cheek until she lifted her eyes to his. He saw the love and the fear in them. "Don't."

"I'm fine." Calling up more strength, she squeezed his hand. "I have some things to do upstairs. You two should catch up." She shifted her glance to Jacob. "I know you've missed each other."

Turning, she fled up the stairs.

Sunny shifted her gaze from her sister's retreating back to Cal's unsmiling face and then to Jacob's angry eyes. "What the hell is going on here?"

"Go up with her, will you?" Cal laid a hand on her shoulder but continued to look after his wife. "I don't want her to be alone."

"All right." She could already see, just by looking at the two of them, that she'd get no explanations here. She'd damn well get one from Libby.

Cal waited until Sunny had climbed the stairs. Facing his brother again, he recognized the fury, the passion, and the hurt in him. "We have to talk."

"Yes."

"Not here." He thought of his wife.

"No." Jacob thought of Sunny. "We'll go to my ship."

Sunny paused outside the bedroom door. Taking a deep breath, she pushed it open. Libby sat on the edge of the bed, hands folded. There were no tears. Tears would have been less heartbreaking than the despair on her face.

"Honey, what is it?"

Libby felt as though she were in a dream. Looking up, she focused on the reality of her sister. "How long has he been here?"

"About three weeks." Sunny sat on the bed to take Libby's hand in hers. "Talk to me. I thought you'd be happy to finally meet Cal's brother."

"I am—for him." Hoping that much was true, she pressed a hand to her jittery stomach. "Did he explain to you why he's here? Where he's from?"

"Of course." Puzzled, Sunny gave her a little shake. "Come on, Libby, snap out of it. J.T.'s a little rough around the edges, but he isn't a monster. He's just concerned about Cal, and maybe a little hurt that he chose you and settled here."

"Oh, God." Unable to sit, Libby rose to pace to the window. She heard the hum of an engine and saw the Land Rover disappear into the forest. "I would have let him go," she said quietly, and closed her eyes. "Back then I was prepared to. I couldn't have asked him to give up his family, his life. But now I can't let him go. I won't."

"Where would he go?"

Libby rested her head on the cool glass of the window. "Back." She laughed a little. "Forward. Jacob must have told you how impossibly complicated it all is."

Rising, Sunny walked over to lay her hands on Libby's shoulders. They were taut, like bundles of wire. Automatically she worked to relax them. "Cal's a grown man, Libby, and staying here was his choice. J.T.'s just going to have to accept that.''

"But will he?"

"When he first got here, J.T. was angry and resentful. He just wasn't able to understand Cal's feelings. But things have changed. For both of us.''

Slowly Libby turned. What was in her sister's heart was clearly written in her eyes. Libby felt a lurch of panic. "Oh, Sunny."

"Hey, don't look at me like that." She grinned. "I'm in love, not terminally ill."

"But what are you going to do?"

"I'm going to go back with him."

With an inarticulate cry, Libby threw her arms around Sunny's neck. She clung, rocking.

"For Lord's sake, Libby, you're as bad as Jacob. It's only Philadelphia. You're acting like I'm going to set up housekeeping on Pluto."

"There aren't any settled colonies on Pluto."

With a strangled laugh, Sunny pulled away. "Well, I guess that leaves that out. We'll have to make do with a condo in Philly."

Libby studied Sunny's face, and her expression gradually changed. The tears that had dampened her eyes dried. "You don't understand, do you?"

"I understand that I love J.T. and he loves me. We haven't talked about life commitments yet, but it's only a matter of time." She stopped, wary. "Libby, why are you looking at me as though you want to wring my neck?"

"Not yours." Libby's voice had firmed. She might be the quieter of the two, but when those she loved were threatened she could put an Amazon queen to shame. "The bastard."

"I beg your pardon?"

"I said he's a bastard."

Sisterly love notwithstanding, Sunny's hackles were rising. "Now look, Libby—"

She shook her head. She wasn't about to be stopped now. "Did he tell you he loved you?"

Nearly out of patience, Sunny snapped off an oath. Then: "Yes."

"And you've gone to bed with him."

Sunny's eyes narrowed. "Have you been taking lessons from Dad?"

"Of course you've gone to bed with him," Libby muttered, pacing the room. "He's made you fall in love with him, taken you to bed, and hasn't had the decency to tell you."

Sunny's foot was tapping a rapid tattoo. "Tell me what?"

"That he and Cal are from the twenty-third century."

Sunny's foot stopped. In the sudden silence, she gaped at Libby. All that sun, she thought. Her poor sister had had her brain fried in Bora Bora. Slowly she crossed the room.

"Lib, I want you to lie down while I get you a cold cloth."

"No." Still fueled by fury, Libby shook her head. "You sit down while I go get you a brandy. Trust me. You're going to need it."

When Cal stepped onto the bridge of the ship, the wave of nostalgia rolled over him like warm water. The cargo planes he piloted in the life he'd chosen satisfied his need to fly, but they weren't much of a challenge. Unable to resist, he ran his hands over the command console.

"She's a beauty, J.T. New model?"

"Yes, I thought it best to have it designed specifically for this trip. We made some adjustments for heat and maneuverability."

Cal couldn't prevent his hand from gripping the throttle. "I'd like to take her up, see what she can do."

"Be my guest."

Cal laughed. "We'd be spotted in the first thousand miles and find ourselves on the front page of the *National Enquirer*."

"Which is?"

"You have to see some things for yourself." Reluctantly he turned away from the console and temptation. Again he studied Jacob's face, feature by feature. "God, it's good to see you."

"How could you do it, Cal?"

Blowing out a long breath, he sat in the pilot's chair. "It's a long story."

"I read the report."

Cal gave him a long, steady look. "Some things don't come through in reports. You've seen her."

"Yes, I've seen her."

"I love her, J.T. I couldn't begin to tell you how much."

Jacob felt a spark of empathy and banked it down. He couldn't think of Sunny now. "We thought you were dead. Almost six months."

"I'm sorry."

"Are you?" Jacob swung to the viewscreen to stare out at the snow. "Five months and twenty-three days after you were reported lost, your ship crash landed about sixty kilometers from the McDowell base in the Baja. Empty. We had your reports.'' His gaze flashed back to his brother. ''And I had to watch Mom and Dad grieve all over again.''

''I wanted you to know where I was. And why. J.T., I didn't plan this. You saw the log.''

''I saw it.'' His jaw set. ''You should be dead. I calculated the probability factor of you pulling out of that void in one piece. There was none.'' For the first time he smiled. ''You've always been a hell of a pilot, Cal.''

''Yeah, but you can't input fate into computer banks.'' He'd thought about that long and hard over the past months. ''I was meant for Libby, J.T. You can calculate into the next millennium and that won't change. As much as I love you, I can't leave her and go back.''

In silence, J.T. studied him. He hated most of all that he understood. Weeks before, only weeks, he would have argued, shouted. He would have locked Cal in a cabin and taken off for home without giving him a choice. ''Does she love you as much?''

A ghost of a smile played on Cal's lips. ''She never asked me to stay. In fact, she did everything she could to help me prepare for the return trip. She even asked to go with me. She would have given up everything.''

''Instead, you stayed here. You gave up everything.''

''Do you think it was easy for me to make the choice?'' Cal demanded. He pushed himself out of the chair, driven by fury and frustration. ''It was the hardest thing I've ever done. Damn it, there was no choice. I didn't know if the ship would make it back, and I couldn't risk her life. I was prepared to risk my own, but not hers. If I had left her, I would have been right back in the void again. And I wouldn't have cared.''

Jacob didn't want to understand. But he did. ''I've spent two years working on perfecting this time-travel procedure, having this ship designed, fine-tuning all the equations. I'm not saying that more work, more study, isn't necessary, but I made it without any major problems. The success factor is 88.57. Come home, Cal, and bring her with you.''

Cal stared at the viewscreen. He'd learned a great deal over the past year. The most important lesson was that life was not simple. The choices to be made could not be made lightly.

''There's another piece of data you haven't considered, J.T. Libby's pregnant.''

Chapter 11

She didn't speak. In the past thirty minutes, Sunny had gone from believing her sister had a wicked case of sunstroke to wondering if she herself had gone quietly mad without noticing it.

The twenty-third century. Black holes. Spaceships. Sunny had finally lapsed into silence as Libby had recounted a story about a mission to Mars—dear Lord, Mars—and Cal's fateful encounter with an uncharted black hole, which, through a combination of luck, skill and the mysterious hand of destiny, had shot him backward from the middle of the twenty-third century to the spring of last year.

The confused Cal, an intergalactic cargo pilot with an affection for flying and poetry, had become a time traveler.

Time travel.

Oh, God, she thought. *Time travel.*

She remembered clearly the faint smile on Jacob's

face when he had told her of his current experiments. But that didn't mean— No. She took a steadying breath, determined to control her wandering imagination.

It had to be some sort of joke. People did not, accidentally or otherwise, zoom through time and fall in love. Jacob was from Philadelphia, she reminded herself as she gulped down brandy. He was a scientist with a bad attitude, and that was all.

"You don't believe me," Libby said with a sigh.

Care and patience, Sunny told herself as she dragged a hand through her hair. Her sister needed care and patience. "Honey, let's just take this slow."

"You think I'm making it up."

"I'm not sure what I think." She took a cleansing breath. "Okay, you're trying to tell me that Cal, a former captain in—what was it?"

"The International Space Force."

"Right. That he crashed his spaceship in the forest, after being sent through time by an encounter with a black hole."

She'd hoped that when she said it herself, when Libby heard it repeated, her sister would come out of whatever spell she was in. But Libby just nodded. "That's fairly accurate."

"Fairly accurate." Sunny tried again. "And now Jacob, going about it through more organized methods, followed the same route so he could visit with his brother."

"He wants to take him back. I could see it by the way he looked at me."

The misery on Libby's face had Sunny reaching out a hand. "Cal loves you. Nothing J.T. did or didn't do could change that."

"No, but…Sunny, can't you see? He didn't pop up here on impulse. He must have worked for months, even years, to find the way. If a man's obsessed with something—"

"All right," she interrupted. "He didn't pop up here on impulse. For reasons I've never fully understood, he's angry that Cal married you and decided to live in Oregon."

"Not just Oregon," Libby shot back. "Twentieth-century Oregon."

"Now, take it slow, honey. I know you're upset, but—"

"Upset?" Libby countered. "Damn right I'm upset. The man traveled over two hundred years, and he's not going to want to go back without Cal."

At a loss, Sunny flopped back on the bed. "Libby, you've got to get ahold of yourself. You're the sensible one, remember? You have to know this is all nonsense."

"Okay." Deciding on a different tack, she took a deep breath. "Can you tell me, honestly tell me, that you haven't noticed something odd about J.T.?" She held up a hand before Sunny could answer. "Not just eccentric, not just endearingly different, but downright odd?"

"Well, I…"

"Ah." Taking her sister's hesitation for agreement, she pressed on. "How did he get here?"

"I don't know what you mean."

"I mean…did he drive up in a car? I didn't notice one."

"No, he didn't come in a car. At least…" She rubbed her suddenly damp hands on her thighs. "He walked out of the woods."

"Walked out of the woods." Libby nodded grimly. "In the middle of winter."

"Lib, I'll concede that J.T.'s a little unusual."

"The way he seems fascinated or puzzled by ordinary objects?"

She remembered the kitchen faucet. "Well, yes."

"The way he doesn't always understand colloquialisms or phrases?"

"That, too, but—Libby, just because the man acts a little odd occasionally and has a hard time with slang doesn't mean he's an alien from outer space."

"Not an alien," Libby said patiently. "He's as human as you or I. He's just from the twenty-third century."

"Oh, is that all?"

"Maybe there's a simpler way to convince you." She rose and took Sunny's hand. "Whatever happens between Cal and me, we'll work it out together. But you have to understand it, all of it. I'm only doing this because you have a right to know what you're walking into."

She nodded. She didn't dare speak, because too much of what Libby had told her made a horrible kind of sense. And she was afraid, very afraid.

With competent movements, Libby took what seemed to be a watch from the deep drawer of her desk. While Sunny looked on, she attached a line of clear wire from the stem of the watch to the computer. After booting up the machine, she gestured.

"Come on over."

Cautious, Sunny joined her. "What is that thing?"

"It's Cal's wrist unit. Computer."

Working.

Sunny jumped back a foot at the sound of the mechanical voice and sent a chair tumbling. "How did you do that?"

"With a mix of twentieth-century and twenty-third-century technology."

"But…but…but…"

"You haven't seen anything yet," Libby warned, and faced the screen again. "Computer, relate file information on Jacob Hornblower."

Hornblower, Jacob, born Philadelphia, June 12, 2224. Astrophysicist, currently head of AP department at Durnam Science Laboratory, Philadelphia. Graduated Princeton University magna cum laude 2242, earned degree in law 2244. Status AAA. Doctorate in astrophysics from O'Bannion 2248. Named MVP Intergalactic Softball League 2247-49. Position: pitcher. ERA 1.28.

Sunny bit back a hysterical giggle. "Stop."

The computer went silent. On rubbery legs, Sunny stepped back until she collided with the bed.

"It's true, isn't it?"

"Yes. Take a few deep breaths," Libby advised her. "It takes a while to absorb it."

"He told me he was experimenting with time travel." She felt the laughter bubble up again, hot and uncontrollable. "That's a good one." She squeezed her eyes shut. It was a dream, she told herself, just a ridiculous dream. But when she opened her eyes again everything was the same. "Looks like the joke's on me." She heard the door slam on the floor below. Instantly she was on her feet. "I'm going to have this out with him, right now."

"Why don't you—" Libby cut herself off when Sunny rounded on her. "Never mind." She sunk back on the bed as Sunny charged down the stairs.

But it was Cal she ran into, not Jacob. "Where is he?" she demanded.

"He's, ah…out. Is Libby upstairs?"

"Yes." Feet spread, eyes challenging, she blocked the stairs. "She's upset."

"She needn't be."

Because what she saw in his eyes answered some of her questions, she relaxed. "I'm glad you realize what a lucky jerk you are, Caleb."

"I love you, too."

She relented enough to kiss him. Later, she decided. Later she would think all this through. And probably go insane. But for now she had a job to do.

"I want to know where your creep of a brother is. And don't try to put me off. Libby told me."

But he was still cautious. "Told you what?"

She tilted her head. "Is it too late to welcome you to the twentieth century?"

A new smile tugged at his mouth. "No. J.T.'s out in his ship. It's about five kilometers northeast. Just follow the tracks." He caught her arm before she could rush off. "He's going through a bad time, Sunny. I've hurt him."

"Not nearly as much as I'm going to."

He started to speak again, but he remembered that Jacob had always been able to take care of himself. He went upstairs to his wife.

She was still sitting on the bed, staring at, but not out of, the window. Her face was composed, her hands folded in her lap so that they pressed lightly against the life growing in her. Looking at her, Caleb felt a single stunning wave of love.

"Hi."

She jolted, struggled to smile. "Hi. Busy day." Before he could speak, she sprang up. "I've got a dozen things to do. I haven't finished unpacking, and I really ought to fix something special for dinner tonight."

"Wait a minute." He took her arms before she could walk by, then simply brought her into his. "I love you, Libby."

"I know." With her head on his shoulder, she held on.

"No, I don't think you do." Gently he pulled her away to study her face. "Even after all this time, I don't think you do. How could you think I would leave? Then or now?"

She just shook her head.

"Sit down," he murmured.

"Caleb, I don't know what to say to you." She sat, twining her nervous fingers together. "I can only imagine how you must feel, having your brother here when you thought you'd never see him again. Being reminded of everything you gave up, and the people you left behind."

"Are you finished?"

Her only answer was a miserable shrug.

"J.T. gave me a copy of a letter he found when he dug up our time capsule." He pulled her fingers apart to link them with his as he sat beside her. "He didn't read it," he continued "It was still in the envelope."

"How did he copy it if it was still in—" She caught herself and managed a small laugh. "Stupid question."

"You put it in the capsule so I'd be able to read it when I got back." He took it out of his pocket. Libby frowned at it. It looked precisely as it had when she'd slipped it into the box. And yet…the paper was different, she realized when she touched it. Thicker, stronger. And, she added to herself, probably not paper at all. At least not as she thought of paper.

"I stopped on the way back from the ship to read it." He spread the letter in his lap. "If I had been crazy enough to leave you, this would have brought me back. Somehow."

"It wasn't meant to do that."

"I know." He took her hand, kissed it. "What it means is a great deal to me. Do you remember what you wrote?"

"Some of it."

"This part." He looked down at the letter. "'I wanted you to know that in my heart I wanted you to be where you belonged.'" He set the letter aside. "Did you mean that?"

"Yes."

"Then you'll be happy to know that I'm exactly where I belong." With long, slow kisses, he eased her back on the bed. "And so are you."

Sunny didn't have any trouble finding the tracks. There were only two sets, both from the Land Rover. One leading away from the cabin and one leading back. Her face grim, she kept her hands firm on the wheel and her mind empty.

She wouldn't think, not yet. Once she had begun to think it would probably send her screaming off a cliff. True, she'd always had an affection for the unusual, but this...this was going a bit too far.

When she saw the ship, nestled comfortably on a blanket of snow, she hit the brakes too hard and sent the Land Rover skidding sideways. It looked as big as a house.

She imagined it was half the size of the cargo ship

Cal had piloted. Probably sleeker, jazzier. Its smooth white finish gleamed in the sunlight. She saw what appeared to be a window that banded around the bow. As she gaped, Jacob stepped up to it and looked out at her.

The sight of him inside it, inside of something that shouldn't even exist, turned her blank astonishment back into fury. Abandoning the Land Rover, she leaped out and stormed over to the ship.

He released the hatch. The door slid silently open, and a set of stairs flowed out. She mounted them, moving a little slower now. Going over the speech he'd planned, Jacob reached out to take her hand and help her through the entranceway.

"Sunny, I—" Whatever he had planned to say was interrupted when her fisted hand connected solidly with his jaw. Off balance and seeing stars, he stumbled back and landed hard on the deck.

She loomed over him, righteous fury glowing in her eyes. "Get up, you miserable coward, so I can hit you again."

He sat where he was for a moment, rubbing a hand over his jaw. He didn't mind the blow so much. He knew he'd had it coming. But he didn't care to be called a coward. Under the circumstances, though, it was best to let her get it all out of her system.

"You're upset."

"Upset?" The word hissed out between her teeth. "I'll show you upset." Because he obviously wasn't going to get up, she dived onto him.

She knocked the wind out of him with another punch as he grappled for her hands. "Damn it, Sunny, stop. I'm going to have to hurt you."

"Hurt me?" Blind with anger, she struck out as he

struggled to roll on top of her. This time her knee slipped by his guard and landed dead on. As the air whistled out of his lungs, he collapsed on top of her. "Get off me, you creep."

He couldn't have moved if his life had depended on it. The pain, deserved or not, was like a silvery shimmer from crotch to brain. His only defense was his weight as he sprawled breathlessly over her.

"Sunny..." He dragged air into his lungs and saw a new constellation. "Your match," he conceded.

The fight had drained out of her. She didn't want him to know how weak and helpless she felt. With her jaw tensed, she prayed her voice wouldn't tremble.

"I said get off me."

"As soon as I'm sure I'm still intact. If you let me get my wind back, we can go another round." He managed to lift his head.

She was crying. Huge, silent tears welled up in her eyes and slid down her cheeks. More stunned by them than by the blow, he shook his head. "Don't." He brushed the tears away, but more fell to replace them. "Damn it, Sunny, stop it."

"Let go of me."

He rolled aside, determined to leave her alone until she composed herself. Before he realized it, he was gathering her close, dragging her onto his lap, stroking her hair.

"Don't touch me." Her body was rigid. Anger and humiliation battled inside her. "I don't want you to touch me."

"I know. I have to."

"You lied to me."

"Yeah." He pressed his lips to her hair. "I'm sorry."

"You used me."

"No." His arms tightened. "No. You know better than that."

"I don't know you at all." She tried to arch away, but he only cradled her closer. Abruptly she threw her arms around him, burying her face against his throat. "I hate you. I'll hate you as long as I live."

The tears were no longer silent. They poured out in hard, racking sobs as she clung to him. He said nothing, had nothing to say. The woman who had knocked him flat with a right hook he understood. The one who clawed and spit and fought he knew how to handle. This one, this soft, weeping bundle in his arms, was a mystery. Defenseless, heartbroken, fragile.

And he fell in love with this Sunny, as well.

She clung to him, hating herself. She wanted to strike out, to make him pay for breaking her heart, but she could only hold on, taking the comfort he offered.

Carefully he rose with her in his arms. He needed to soothe, to protect, to love. He wanted to stroke her until her tears dried, hold her until her body calmed again. Most of all he wanted to show her that of all the things he'd done falling in love with her was the most important.

She couldn't stop, though she despised every tear. She couldn't fight him now, at her weakest point. Now she could only hold on to him, let the storm rage and find some small comfort in the gentle way he held her.

He took her into his cabin, where the light was dim.

The bed was water-soft, covered with pale blue sheets. The walls were blue, as well. A quiet, restful color. Still holding her, he lay with her on the bed while her tears dampened his cheek.

When her sobs began to lessen, he trailed his lips down her temple to her mouth. Her lips were wet, and they were still trembling. As his touched them, she pulled away to roll onto her side.

"Sunny." Feeling awkward, he touched her shoulder. "Please, talk to me."

She didn't bother to jerk his hand away. She just stared at the pale blue wall. "I feel like such a fool. Crying over you."

He didn't know if any woman had ever done that before. Certainly none had ever cried in his arms. "I never wanted to hurt you."

"Being lied to always hurts."

"I didn't lie. I just didn't tell you the truth." He could see the logic of it, needed to. But he doubted she could. "I was going to tell you everything today."

She nearly laughed. "Do they still use that old chestnut in the twenty-third century?" She had said it out loud. The twenty-third century. And she was in what could only be called a spaceship with a man who wouldn't be born until she was long dead. She'd have preferred to believe it was all a dream, but the pain was too real.

"I came for my brother," he told her. "I never planned to become involved with you, to fall in love with you. It happened too fast."

"I was there, remember?"

"Look at me."

She shook her head. "Let's just forget it, J.T. A

man like you probably thinks he's entitled to have a woman in every century."

"I said look at me." Patience gone, he pulled her back, holding her by the shoulders so that she was forced to meet his eyes. "I love you."

The words seeped into her and weakened her resolve. Her only defense was heat. "Apparently the definition of love has changed. Don't lose any sleep over it. I'll be fine."

"Will you listen to me?"

"It doesn't matter what you say."

"Then it won't hurt to listen."

She shook her head fiercely. Now that the tears were over, she was ready to lash out again. "You never intended to stay with me, to build a life with me. It was just a temporary arrangement for you. But I can't blame you for that. You never promised, you only implied. And you never used the old candlelight-and-wine routine to romance stars into my eyes."

But the stars had been there, she thought. She'd been blinded by them. "In any case, I'm responsible for my own feelings. But I can blame you, and I can detest you, for not being honest."

"It was too complicated. I didn't know how you would react."

"I thought scientists were supposed to experiment. You are a scientist, aren't you?"

"Yes. All right. The fact is, I just didn't want to think about anything but you when I was with you." When she struggled to turn away again, he held her still. "You wanted honesty, so listen to it. Whatever I did, it was because I couldn't stop myself. I didn't want to stop myself. If that was wrong, it was because I stopped thinking with my head. If I handled it badly, it was because I didn't know how to approach you here, now. I didn't feel I could tell you about all of this. And then I was falling in love and didn't know how to deal with it. Didn't know how you would expect me to.''

Frustrated, he stroked her cheek. ''Sunny, I didn't think it was possible to tell you the truth. And I didn't know how...'' He stopped, swore. ''If it had been possible, I would have shown you more romance, but I didn't have a gift for you.''

''A gift?'' She'd really believed she was too weary to become annoyed again. She'd been wrong. ''What the hell are you talking about?''

''Romance,'' he repeated, more than a little embarrassed. ''Attention, flattery, the giving of gifts.''

''That's the stupidest thing I've ever heard. Romance? Is that your superior species' definition of romance?'' She pushed his hands away. ''Idiot. Romance has nothing to do with presents or flattery. It has to do with caring and compassion, with sharing your hopes and your dreams. It means being honest.''

''This is honest.''

He lowered his mouth to hers. She prepared to resist, to hold him off with icy disdain. But for the first time his mouth wasn't hungry, it wasn't passionate, it wasn't desperate. It was, instead, infinitely tender. The beauty of it shimmered through her like liquid sunlight. Her defensive front of disinterest melted away like snow in the spring.

He looked at her. Was there confusion in his eyes? she wondered. It couldn't matter, she told herself. She couldn't allow herself to care so much a second time. But he laid a soothing hand on her cheek and touched his lips experimentally to hers.

He hadn't known being gentle could be so weakening. Or so fulfilling. There had always been power when he'd touched her. Bolts of power. Now there was only warmth, a quiet river of it, running through him. He wanted to share it with her, to show her how precious she was and would always be.

"I love you," he murmured. When she tried to shake her head, he only repeated the words again and again as his mouth whispered over hers.

She couldn't fight him like this. Not when the fog had rolled in over her brain and her body was sinking in some thick, syrupy darkness. Her breath shook as she tried to say his name. He covered her trembling lips with his own. Patient, so patient, as hers warmed and moved beneath his.

Time, he thought as he slowly deepened the kiss. They would take all they needed. And when the time had ended she would know that he would never love again as he had loved her.

He undressed her. Though his fingers shook from the pull of his own emotions, they didn't hurry. Button by button he loosened her shirt, pressing his lips lightly to each new opening. Softly, sweetly, he trailed his fingers over her flesh, parting the material.

There was no greed now, only an aching, bittersweet tenderness.

Surrendering, she eased his sweater up over his shoulders so that she could feel the warmth of his skin against hers. If she only had today, she would forget all the yesterdays, all the tomorrows. As his mouth met hers again, it was as though it were the first time they had kissed. The first time they had loved.

This she would remember. The heady flavor of his

lips, those quiet, lovely words he spoke against her mouth. Not promises. There could be no promises. But there was the depthless green of his eyes to drown in. There was the impossible gentleness of his hands to be lost in.

He slipped her jeans over her hips, following the route with his mouth, down her thigh, over her knee and her calf. In the dim, silent room, there was no day or night. And a heart so filled with love could not break.

She enchanted him, until he believed they would always be here together, alone, with only the soft sigh of the bed shifting, yielding beneath the pressure of their bodies. Alone, with only the soothing stroke of her fingers over his skin. With only her drifting, tenuous scent swimming in his brain.

And the love he felt pulsed through his blood, seeped into his bones, until he knew he would never be free of it. There was joy in that. She would be with him, despite all distances.

He slipped into her with a yearning that was deep. She enfolded him with an unquestioning generosity. As they moved together, time stood beautifully still.

She woke, blinking in the darkness and afraid. Beside her, the bed was cool. He was gone. Panic snatched at her throat and had her rearing up. She bit back the cry and steadied herself.

He wasn't gone—or at least he hadn't gone far, for she was still on the ship, in his bed. With her heart pounding, she lay back and tried to think.

The way he had loved her had been so sweet, so kind, so patient. And so much like goodbye. She couldn't cry again, Sunny promised herself as she squeezed back tears. Crying solved nothing. If she loved him, and she did, the only thing she could do for him was to be strong.

She dressed in the dark, then went to look for him.

The ship confused her. There was another cabin, smaller than Jacob's but painted in the same pale blues. She passed through another area she assumed was the galley only because there was an empty carton of some sort of drink on a smooth, narrow counter and a metal door built into the wall that after a critical study she decided was some sort of oven.

She found him on the flight deck, sitting at the command console. His wore only his jeans. The viewing screen showed a panorama of forest and the shadow of distant ridges. He was staring through it as he spoke to the computer.

"Set coordinates for 1500 hours."

Affirmative.

"Preferred destination as close as possible to original departure data, time and position."

Understood.

"Estimate approximate flight time from lift-off to time warp."

Working… Estimate three hours, twenty-two minutes from lift-off to orbit of sun. Is closer calculation desired?

"No."

"Jacob."

He spun in his chair, swore under his breath. "Disengage."

The computer screen went blank.

"I thought you were sleeping."

"I was." Accusations, threats, pleas, sprang to her

lips. She bit them back. She had promised herself she would be strong. "You're going back."

"I have to." He rose to cross to her. "Sunny, I've tried to find another way. There is none."

"But—"

"Do you love your parents?"

"Yes, of course."

"And I love mine." He took her hand, weighed it in his. "I can't begin to explain what we went through when we thought Cal was dead. My mother... She's very strong, but when the news came that he was lost, presumed dead, she was ill with grief. Days, weeks."

"I'm sorry," she said quietly. "I can only imagine how you must have felt."

He shook his head. Those days were still difficult to speak of. "And then, when we learned the truth, they both tried to accept. He was alive, and that meant everything. But to know that they would never see him again, never know." He broke off in frustration. "Maybe they can accept, especially when I explain to them that he's happy here. When I tell them about the child."

"What child?"

"Cal's—Libby's carrying a child. Didn't she tell you?"

"No." Shaken, Sunny pressed a hand to her temple. "Everything was so confused. And I... Libby's pregnant." With a little laugh, she dropped her hand. "How about that? We're going to have a niece or nephew." It seemed right, only right, that when her world was at its darkest there should be that tiny glimmer of life, and of hope, in the future.

Yet it was that same future she was losing him to.

"Having a baby only takes nine months," she began, trying to sound casual. "I don't suppose you'd consider hanging around to see whether we should buy blue or pink balloons."

It was so easy to see beyond her smile, into her eyes, where the sadness hovered. "I can't take a chance on leaving the ship here so long—and I've already overstayed my projected equations. Sunny, my parents have a right, a need, to know about Cal's life, about the child. Their grandchild."

"Of course."

"If I could stay… There's nothing there that means as much to me as what I've found with you. You have to believe that."

She struggled to remain calm while her world silently fell apart. "I believe that you love me."

"I do. But if I don't go back, if I don't give them that much, I could never live with myself."

She turned away, because she understood too well. "Once, when I was nine or ten, I wandered off. We were at the cabin for the summer and I wanted to explore. I thought I knew the forest so well. But I got lost. I spent a night under a tree. When Mom and Dad found me the next afternoon they were frantic. I've never seen my father cry, not like that."

"Then you know why I can't just turn my back on them."

"Yes, of course." She managed to smile as she faced him. "I'm sorry I caused such a scene before."

"Don't."

"No, really, I am. I didn't have any right to say the things I said." But, try as she might, she couldn't apologize for decking him. "I can't begin to understand what it must have been like for you all these weeks. Trying to fit in and bide your time until Cal came back.''

''It wasn't so hard. I had you.''

''Yes.'' She lifted a hand to his cheek, let it fall away. ''I'm glad you did. I want you to know that.''

''Sunny—''

''So when do you go?'' Deliberately she moved out of reach. If he touched her, however gently, she might shatter.

''Tomorrow.''

She had to lock her knees to keep them from buckling. ''So soon?''

''I thought it best, for everyone.''

She wondered that her smile didn't crack her face. ''I'm sure you're right. But you'll want to spend a little more time with Cal. You've come a long way.''

''I'll talk to him in the morning. And to Libby,'' he added. ''I want to set things right with her.''

Now the smile came more easily. ''They're good for each other. You see that, don't you?''

''I'd have to be blind not to.''

''Science and logic aside, sometimes emotions are the most accurate equations.'' Feeling stronger, she held out her hand. ''I'd like to stay the night, here with you.''

He brought her close, struggling not to crush her against him. ''I'll come back.'' When she shook her head, he pulled her away. The passion was in his eyes again, and the anger. ''I will. I swear it. I need a little more time, to test. I managed to work it out this far in only two years. With another two, I can make it smoother, until it's as basic as a shuttle to Mars.''

''A shuttle to Mars,'' she repeated.

''Just trust me,'' he told her, drawing her back.

''When I work it all out we'll have more time together.''

''More time,'' she murmured, and shut her eyes.

Chapter 12

She left before he awakened. It seemed the best way. She hadn't slept at all. She had lain awake during the night trying to find the best way.

He had put music on, something dreamy and beautiful by a composer she hadn't heard of. Because he had yet to be born. He had adjusted the lights so that the cabin had been washed with simulated moonbeams.

To add romance. She understood that now, loved him for it. He had wanted to give her everything it was possible for him to give her on that last night. And he had given her everything but what she wanted most. A future.

It occurred to her as she thought over the twist her life had taken that up until this point all her decisions had been black-and-white. A choice was either right or wrong. But this time, this most important time, there were dozens of shades in between.

She drove back to the cabin slowly. How could she have said goodbye again? Some pains could not be endured a second time. Sunny could only hope he would understand what she was doing. She hoped she understood it.

She parked in back of the cabin and sat for a little while, studying the way the glaze of ice on the tree limbs glittered in the morning sun. Listening to the sound, the sound of almost perfect silence. Tasting the hint of coming snow in the air.

Slowly, fighting back the grief, she walked to the cabin and entered the kitchen quietly.

Libby had left a light in the window. The sight of the old kerosene lamp burning dully in the morning light brought the hateful tears to her eyes again. She swallowed them, then sat at the table to run her fingers over the wood as Jacob had only weeks before.

"You're up early."

Sunny lifted her eyes and met her sister's. "Hi." Her lips curved. "Mom."

Instinctively Libby laid a hand on her stomach. "Jacob told you. I wanted to."

"Great news is great news whatever the source." She rose to gather her sister close. There was joy here, and she clung to it. "No morning sickness?"

"No. I've never felt better."

"Cal better be spoiling you."

"Rotten." Libby drew back to brush at Sunny's fringe of bangs. Her sister's eyes were shadowed and sad. "How are you?"

"I'm okay." Because her legs felt unsteady again, she turned back to sit at the table. "I'm sorry I ran out the way I did."

"That doesn't matter." Libby was dressed in a

baggy sweater and cords, her favored outfit for the mountains. Studying her, Sunny thought her sister had never been more beautiful. She wondered if she would ever carry a child, feel that love growing inside her.

"I flattened him."

"Good," Libby said, with a nod of approval. Movements automatic, she filled the teakettle with water, then set it on the burner. "Want some breakfast?"

"Later, maybe."

"Sunny, I'm so sorry."

"Don't be." Sunny reached behind her to close a hand over the one Libby had laid on her shoulder. "Really, it's all right."

"You really love him."

"Yes, I love him."

Wishing she could find a way to grant her sister the happiness she felt herself, Libby rested a cheek on Sunny's hair. "Cal says J.T.'s planning to do some more work on the equations for the time travel. To hone it down, to make it safer, and more practical, if that word can apply."

"Yes, he told me."

"He's brilliant, Sunny. Really brilliant. It's not just Cal's bragging. I read the rest of his file. And the fact that he was able to make this trip after only two years of work is proof of it. Once he finishes his testing, he'll come back."

"I hope he can." She closed her eyes. "I really hope he can." Then, with a laugh, she buried her face in her hands. "Listen to us. We're here talking about all of this as if it were the most natural thing in the world. I must still be in shock."

"After more than a year, I still wake up some mornings wondering if I imagined it all."

"But you have Cal," Sunny murmured, letting her hands fall into her lap. "He's right there to prove it's real."

"Sunny, if I—" She broke off when Cal walked into the room. She lifted her shoulders, let them fall. "Is there anything I can do?"

"No. I'm handling it, I promise you that."

"I'm going to get some fresh air," Libby announced. "Cal, take care of the tea, will you?"

A look passed between them. "Sure."

Sunny knew them both well enough to understand that they'd planned this little bit of business so that Cal could speak to her alone.

"What do you want?" he asked when Libby had shut the door behind her. "Froot Loops or burnt toast?"

"J.T. fixed the toaster."

"Oh yeah?" He gave it a casual glance. "He's always liked to fiddle with things." The kettle began to boil, giving him another moment to think through what he wanted to say. "Sunny...I think we'll get snow before nightfall."

"Cal, why don't you relax? As tempting as it was, I didn't murder him."

"I wasn't worried about that." He poured hot water into two cups. "Not too much, anyway. It's more a matter of wanting to explain."

"That your brother's a jerk? I know that."

"He's also sensitive."

She could still be amused. That was a relief. "Are we talking about the same man? Hornblower, Jacob?

Astrophysicist? The one with the bull head and the nasty temper?''

An apt description, he thought. ''Yeah. I don't mean like he cries at vid—movies,'' he remembered. ''Or that he takes it to heart when you call him names. He's sensitive where other people are concerned. Family.'' Not certain he was handling the situation correctly, he brought the tea to the table. ''Half the time when he'd get into fights it was because someone had said something about me. It used to annoy me, because I wanted to take care of it myself, but he'd always plow right in before I had the chance. And my parents...I can't think of a single time he'd forget a birthday or Mother's Day.''

''They still have Mother's Day?''

''Sure.''

''Cal.'' Absently she stirred sugar into her tea. ''How did you decide to stay?''

''I didn't decide,'' he told her. ''What I mean is, I don't think *decide* is the word. It implies choice. I couldn't leave Libby. I tried. But I've never stopped thinking about my family.''

''Whether you consider you had a choice or not, it had to be difficult.''

''For me it was pretty cut-and-dried. I couldn't even be sure if I'd make it back. I sent the ship and the reports because if there was a chance I could let them know I was alive, safe, I had to.'' He laid a hand over hers. ''With J.T., it's different. He knows he can make it back, and if he didn't go he'd be leaving them without hope. He couldn't do that.''

''No, he couldn't do that.'' She lifted her head. ''It's been hard for you.''

''This has been the best year of my life.''

"But the adjustments, the separation…"

"If I'd been tossed back another five hundred years it wouldn't have mattered. As long as I'd found Libby."

"She's lucky to have you."

"I like to think so." He grinned, then sobered. "He loves you, Sunny."

Something flickered in her eyes before she lowered them. "Did he tell you that?"

"Yes, but he didn't have to. I saw it the first time he said your name. I guess what I wanted to tell you was that he's never felt about anyone the way he feels about you."

"Will you help me, Cal? I left before he woke up." She pressed her lips together to keep them from trembling. "I can't say goodbye."

Libby stood by the stream watching the water fight its way around the ice. In her mind she saw it as it had been in the spring, when the water had gurgled lazily over the rocks and the song of birds had been everywhere. The grass had been soft and green.

It was there that she and Cal had buried the time capsule. And there they had made love, while her heart had broken at the picture of him unearthing it again in some springtime hundreds of years ahead.

Instead, he had stayed, and it was his brother who had taken out the box they had placed there. Now it was her sister's heart that was breaking.

Whatever comfort she offered Sunny wouldn't be enough.

It seemed wrong that she should have everything while Sunny lost. She had Cal, and the home they loved, the life they were building. She had the child.

With a soft smile, she pressed a hand to her stomach. The child who would come at summer's end and bind them even closer together.

Sunny would have only memories, and there was nothing Libby could do about it.

She turned her head slightly and saw Jacob.

He was only a few feet away. She hadn't heard his approach in the muffling snow. In the shadows cast by the trees she saw how much he resembled Cal. The same build, the same coloring, the same sharp facial bones. There was a measuring look in his eyes that made her wonder how long he had been standing and watching her in silence.

She didn't approach him. Though he posed no threat to her—and she admitted that she had been foolish and overemotional ever to believe he could—he had taken her sister's heart. And broken it.

"Cal's inside." Her voice was cool and clipped. She made no attempt to be friendly.

She showed her anger differently from Sunny, he mused. Sunny exploded with hers, went straight on the attack. Apparently Libby let hers bubble and brew inside. He wondered if she realized it was just as volatile.

"I wanted to talk to you."

She had never enjoyed confrontations, but she braced for this one. "There's nothing you can say to me that would make me influence Cal to leave with you. The choice is his, whether you believe it or not. Just as it was before."

"I know." He moved slowly across the snow until he stood beside her. "It isn't something I thought I would understand or accept, but I do. Our parents will... It will mean a great deal to them when I tell them about you. About the child.''

''He misses them.'' Her voice was thick as she battled the tide of emotion. ''They should know that.''

''They will.''

''Why didn't you tell her?'' she demanded. ''How could you have let her fall in love with you when you knew you were going to leave?''

His hands fisted as he plunged them into the pockets of his pea coat. ''I spent two years working, inching my way here. For one reason. Only one. To find my brother and take him home.''

Her eyes smoldered at that. ''You can't have him.''

''No.'' He nearly smiled. Perhaps she was more like Sunny than he had originally thought. ''And I can't have Sunny, either. I have to live with that. She isn't the only one who fell in love. She isn't the only one to lose.''

''But you knew what you were doing.''

Vibrating with frustration, he faced her. For the first time she saw that his eyes were haunted and miserable. ''You thought Cal would leave. Did it stop you from loving him, or him from loving you?''

''No.'' With a little sigh, she put a hand on his arm. ''No, it didn't.''

''She's strong,'' he said. His control had slipped a few notches when he'd heard the understanding in her voice. ''She won't allow herself to hurt for long. If I can't come back...'' The pain ripped through him, forcing him to take a slow, deep breath. ''If I can't come back, she'll go on.''

''Do you really believe that?''

''I have to.'' He dragged an unsteady hand through

his hair. With the ache rippling through him, he told her what he hadn't been able to tell Sunny. What he hadn't wanted to face himself. "I haven't perfected the procedure. This time I was months off. The next time, if there is one, I may be years off. She may have started a new life. I have to accept that."

She smiled at him. "I study people. When you make it a profession, you learn more than tradition and social mores. You learn that real love, lasting love, is very rare. It should never be simply accepted, J.T. It should be cherished."

He gazed across the white world he was just beginning to understand. "I'll think of her every day for the rest of my life."

"Have you never heard the word *compromise*?"

"I'm not very good at it. If I could find one, I'd learn to be good at it. I can only tell you that everything I do from the moment I get back will be geared toward finding a way to return here, within a day, within an hour, of the time I left."

Moved, she leaned up and kissed his cheek. It surprised her when his arms came around her, held her. Without hesitating, she returned the embrace.

"Take care of them. Both of them."

"I will." She tightened her hold briefly, then smiled when she saw Cal walking toward them. Kissing Jacob again, she released him before she held out a hand for Cal's. "Why don't I go make some breakfast?"

"Thanks." Cal's fingers squeezed hers. "I love you."

With a quick smile, she headed back to the cabin.

"Is Sunny inside?"

Cal turned back to his brother. "She came back

early.'' He put a hand on Jacob's arm to restrain him.
''J.T., she asked me to tell you that she wishes you
a safe trip but she can't say goodbye again.''

''The hell with that.''

''Jacob.'' Cal shifted to block his brother's path.
''She needs to do it this way. Believe me, it won't
help her if you try to see her again.''

''Just cut it off clean?'' Jacob pulled out of Cal's
hold. ''As simple as that?''

''I didn't say it was simple. There's no one who
knows better how you feel than I do. If you love her,''
he continued, ''let her have her way in this.''

Holding up his hands, Jacob whirled and strode a
few paces off. Pain roiled inside him, pain edged with
resentment. She wouldn't even see him one last time.
Already she was just a memory. Perhaps it was best,
he told himself, best that he could believe she was
already getting on with her life.

If he could do nothing else for her, he could honor
this last request.

''All right. Tell her...'' He trailed off, swearing.
He would never be able to find the words for what
he was feeling. Even if he'd had Cal's knack for poetry, the phrases would have fallen short.

''She knows,'' Cal told him. ''Come on inside.''

In the afternoon they drove him to the ship. He
wondered if Sunny was watching from a window as
they disapeared into the forest. But when he looked
back, searching, the sun was glaring on the glass and
he could see nothing.

Cal talked constantly, trying to fill the void with
chatter. Jacob saw that he reached for Libby's hand,
held it tight.

And he was denied even that, he thought. Even one last touch.

Cursing Sunny, he climbed out of the car. "I'll tell Mom and Dad everything."

Cal nodded. "Get back to the lab. I want to know that you'll come back and bring them for a visit."

"I'll be back." He embraced his brother.

"I love you, J.T."

Letting out a long breath, he broke away to turn to Libby. "Tell your sister I'm going to find a way."

"I'm counting on it." Libby blinked back tears as she handed him an envelope. "She asked me to give this to you, but to make you promise you won't open it until you get back to your own time."

He reached out, but she pulled it back. "Your word. Cal tells me you take promises seriously."

"I won't open it until I'm gone." He folded it carefully before slipping it in his pocket. He kissed her, one cheek, the other, then her mouth. "Keep well, sister."

The first tear overflowed. "And you." She turned her face into Cal's shoulder as Jacob stepped through the hatch.

"He'll be back, Libby." He lifted a hand in farewell, then let it fall. Smiling, he pressed a kiss to her hair as she wept. "It's only a matter of time."

Inside, Jacob cleared his mind and went to work. The procedure for lift-off was basic, but he went through the routine as meticulously as a first-year pilot. He didn't want to think. Couldn't afford to.

He had known it would hurt, but he had never imagined this kind of dull, gnawing pain. It made his fingers stiff on the switches.

The lights hummed as he set the controls for ignition. Through the viewscreen he saw that Cal had moved Libby back out of harm's way. For the last time he searched the forest for signs of Sunny. There was nothing. He threw the last switch.

The ship rose gently, almost silently. He knew he couldn't afford to linger, but he kept the speed down until his brother was only a speck in the sea of white and green. With an oath, he jammed the throttle and shot through the atmosphere.

Space was soothing, the dark silence of it. He didn't want to be soothed. It would be best if he held on to his anger, his frustration. His jaw set, he engaged his computer.

"Implement coordinates to sun."

Coordinates implemented.

Seen through the viewscreen, the world was only a pretty colored ball.

Mechanically he navigated, compensating for a small shower of meteors. It was very simple, really, he thought. Now there was no traffic, commercial or private. No route patrol ships to communicate with. No checkpoints.

He hit the switch and bulleted into hyperspace. As before, his eyes narrowed, his muscles tensed, as he hurtled toward the sun. He watched dispassionately as the gauges registered the increase in outside temperature. With the viewscreen lowered, he flew blind, expertly but without the passion that had fueled him on his last voyage.

Working with the computer, he increased the speed, adjusted the angle. Meticulous and mechanical, his fingers moved over the command console. Though he was prepared, the g's slammed him back in his chair. Holding course, he swore, filling the cockpit with his anger and his hopelessness.

Now, though his heart was thousands of miles below, there was no turning back.

Like a bullet from a gun, he shot through space and time and away from his heart.

He was breathless when the procedure was complete. A line of sweat rolled down his back. A glance at his gauges told him he had been successful.

Successful, he thought miserably, rubbing his hands over his eyes. Raising the viewscreen, he looked out on his own time.

It looked so similar, the stars, the planets, the inky darkness. There were more satellites, and in the distance he saw a blip of light he knew was a research lab. In less than thirty minutes he would join the traffic patterns. He would no longer be alone. Leaning back, he closed his eyes in quiet desperation.

She was gone.

Fate had brought him to her, then had torn him away. Fate, he thought, and his own intellect. He would use that intellect. If it took a lifetime, he would find a way to bring their lives together again.

Perhaps he would suffer over the months or years it took him to complete the necessary tests that would take him back, safely, close to the time of his lift-off. But he would get back, and he would calculate so minutely that she would barely realize he'd ever been gone.

Slowly he took the letter out of his pocket. It was all he had left of her. Some message, he thought. A few words of love and remembrance. It wouldn't be enough, he thought furiously, and ripped it open.

There was only one word.

Surprise.

Baffled, he stared at it.

Surprise? he thought. Just surprise. What kind of last message was that? So damn typical of her, he decided, balling the paper up in his fist. Then, relenting, willing to settle for even as little as this, he smoothed it out again.

At a faint sound, he whirled in the chair.

She was standing at the doorway to the flight deck. She was deathly pale, and her eyes were glassy. But as he watched, dumbfounded, her lips moved into a smile.

"So, you got my message."

"Sunny?" He whispered her name at first, wondering if he was hallucinating. It was only one of the potential side effects of time travel. He would have to remember to make a note of it.

But he could not only see her, hear her, he could smell her. He catapulted out of the chair to grab her close, to devour her mouth like a starving man.

Then it struck him. Terrified him.

"What are you doing here?" he demanded, shaking her. "What the hell have you done?"

"What had to be done." When she swayed, he cursed her again.

"Yell at me later," she said calmly. "I think I'm going to pass out."

"No, you're not." Though he was infuriated, he lifted her as though she were fragile glass and carried her to a chair. Then he was all business.

"You're light-headed?"

"Yes." She put her hand on her temple. "It was a hell of a trip."

"Nauseous?"

"Some."

He pressed a round black button, and a small compartment opened. He pulled out a square box. From it he took a tiny, paper-thin pill. "Let this dissolve on your tongue. Idiot," he said, even as she obeyed. "You aren't prepped for traveling at warp speed."

The relief was instant. She took a long breath, pleased that she wasn't going to disgrace herself. Ignoring him for the moment, she turned to the view-screen. The galaxy was spread out before her.

"Oh, my God." The color that had come back into her cheeks fled again. "It's incredible. Is that—is that Earth?"

"Yes." His palms were damp. If his stomach didn't settle, he'd have to resort to a pill himself. "Sunny, do you have any idea what you've done?"

"How fast are we going?"

"Damn it, Sunny."

"Yes, I know what I've done." She swiveled in the chair to rest her hands on his knees. Her eyes, when they met his, were dark and clear. "I've passed through time with you, Jacob."

"You have to be out of your mind." He wanted to shake her until her bones rattled. He wanted to hold her against him until they melted. "How could you have pulled off a ridiculous stunt like this?"

"Cal and Libby helped me."

"They helped you? They knew you'd planned this?"

"Yes." When she felt her hands begin to tremble, she sat back and folded them in her lap. She didn't want him to know how frightened she was. "I decided last night."

"You decided," he repeated.

"That's right." Her chin lifted, and she gave him a long, level look. "I talked to Cal this morning, told him what I wanted to do." Calmer now, she turned to the viewscreen again. There were lights in the sky. Stars. Instead of looking up at them, she looked out. As incredible as it was, she was hurtling through space with the only man she had ever loved. Would ever love.

Someone had to be sensible. Someone had to be calm. But he wasn't sure it could be him. "Sunny, I don't think you understand what you've done."

"I understand perfectly." She looked back at him. Yes, she was calm again, she realized. Calm, with her mind clear and her heart content. "Cal made a token protest—more for Libby's sake than mine, really. But when I spoke with her she understood. She brought me to the ship herself this afternoon, when you were busy with Cal."

"Your parents..."

"Would want me to be happy." There was a pang, a deep one, when she thought of them. "Libby and Cal will explain everything to them." Because she was sure her legs were steady again, she rose to walk around the flight deck. "I'm not saying they won't be sad, or that they won't miss me if it isn't possible to go back. But I think my father—particularly my father—will get a tremendous charge when he thinks of where I am." She laughed. "*When* I am."

She turned back, still smiling. "Neither of us is good at compromising, J.T. With us, it's all or nothing. That's why we'll get along so well."

"I would have come back." He covered his face with his hands, then dragged them back through his hair. "Damn it, Sunny, I told you I'd come back. A year, maybe two or three."

"I didn't want to wait that long."

"You idiot, if I had managed to perfect it I'd have been back five minutes after I'd left, in your time."

Her time. It struck him so hard, so deep, that he wasn't sure he could speak. "You had no right to make a decision like this without discussing it with me."

"It's my decision." Riled, she stalked back to him. "If you don't want me, then I'll just find some nice, appreciative companions. Maybe on Mars. I can take care of myself, pal. Just consider that I've hitched a ride."

"It has nothing to do with what I want. It's what's best for you."

"I know what's best for me." She rapped a fist on his chest. "I thought it was you, but I've made one or two mistakes before." She spun away and took two steps before he grabbed her.

"Where are you going to go?" he demanded. "There's still a few thousand kilometers before we hit breathable atmosphere."

"It's a big ship."

"Sit down."

"I don't—"

"I said sit down." He gave her a none-too-gentle shove that sent her sprawling into the chair. "And shut up. I have something to say to you." When she braced her hands on the arms of the chair, he lifted a fist. "If you get up, I swear I'm going to belt you."

Seething, she sat back. "That's one term that appears to have survived the centuries."

"If I'd known what you were planning I'd have

used that term before. There were risks involved here
that you have no conception of. If I'd made a mistake,
a miscalculation, even the slightest—''

''But you didn't.''

''That's not the point.''

''What is the point, Hornblower?''

''You shouldn't have done this.''

She let out an impatient breath. ''Well, it's no use
belaboring that point, because I have done it. Why
don't we move on to the next step?''

He found he had to sit himself. ''You may never
be able to get back.''

''I know. I've accepted that.''

''If you change your mind—''

''Jacob.'' Sighing, she rose, only to kneel beside
him. ''I can't change my mind unless I change my
heart. And that's just not possible.''

He reached out to touch her hair. ''I wouldn't have
asked this of you.''

''I know. And if I had asked to come with you you
would have given me half a dozen very logical reasons why I couldn't.'' She turned her face into his
palm. ''And you'd have been wrong. What I couldn't
do is live without you.''

''Sunny.''

''Look at it this way. I've always felt that I was
ahead of my time, kind of placed in the wrong era.
Maybe I'll do better in yours.''

''This was a stupid thing to do.'' Then he pulled
her up into his lap. ''Thank God you did it.''

''Then you're not mad?''

He showed her just how mad he was when his
mouth took hers. ''When you wouldn't see me today,

it was as if you'd cut out my heart. It didn't matter, because I'd wanted to leave it with you."

Tears rushed to her eyes, but she forced them back. She wanted only to smile at him. "That's almost poetic."

"Don't get used to it." Still holding her, he leaned forward to make some adjustments on the control panel.

"Can you teach me how to drive this?"

He slanted her a look. She was here, really here. And his. Forever. "I'm already terrified of the idea of you at the controls of a cruise rider."

"I'm a quick study."

"That's what I'm afraid of." He drew her back until she was settled in the curve of his arm. "I'm not sure even my world's ready for you."

"But you are."

He kissed her again, gently. "I've been ready all my life."

With a sigh, she teased his mouth until the passion simmered. "I don't suppose we could put this thing on automatic pilot or whatever."

"Not at this point."

"We did make it back, didn't we?"

He inclined his head toward the screen. "We've got a little way to go yet."

"No, I mean *back*. What year is it?"

He gestured toward the dials. "2254."

The enormity of it made her giddy. His arms made her trust. "So that makes me…287 years old." She cocked a brow. "How do you feel about older women?"

"I'm crazy about them."

"Remember that when I hit three hundred and

things start to sag.'' She kissed him lightly. ''I plan to frustrate you, annoy you and generally make your life chaos for a long time.''

''I'm counting on it.''

Together they watched the blue-green sphere that was home draw closer.

Epilogue

The sound of crashing waves seemed to fill the room. The clear wall opened the suite to the passion of the lightning-split sky and the boiling sea. The scent of jasmine, rich and sultry, rose on the air. Low, pulsing music echoed over the roar of waves and the violent boom of thunder.

"I was right," Sunny murmured.

Jacob shifted on the cloud bed to draw her closer. "About what—this time?"

"The storm." Her body still vibrated from passion just released. "I knew it wasn't a night for moonlight or tropical sunsets."

She had been right. But he hated to admit it. "The atmosphere didn't make that much difference."

She rolled, all but floated, to lie across him. "Is that why you brought me here? To the place you once described to me?"

"I brought you here for a few days of relaxation."

"So that's what you brought me here for. When are we going to relax?" She grinned before she bent down to press kisses on his chest. "See, you're already tensing up again."

He skimmed a hand over her hair. "How long have we been married?"

Lazily she touched a button on the side of the bed. The time flashed, the numbers suspended in the air, then blinked off. "Five hours and twenty minutes."

"I figure we'll relax in about fifty years." His hand wandered to her bare shoulder. "Do you like it?"

"Being married?"

"That, too. But I mean this place."

He was so sweet, she thought, the way he didn't want her to think he was too sentimental. "I love it, and since we're newlyweds and allowed to be mushy I'll tell you that bringing me here was the most romantic thing you've ever done."

"I thought you might prefer Paris, or the Intimacy Resort on Mars."

"We can always go to Mars," she said, and giggled. "I'm almost getting used to saying things like that. I told you I was a quick study."

"You've been here six months."

"You are a tough nut." She slid down him to rest her cheek on his chest. "Six months," she repeated. "It took you long enough to marry me."

"I'd have had it over with in six minutes if you and my father hadn't gotten together."

"Over with?" She raised her head, her eyes dangerous. "Income tax reports are things you want to get over with."

"Income tax reports?" he repeated, blankly.

"I forgot. Unpleasant tasks," she said. "That's

what you want to get over with. If marrying me was so unpleasant, why did you bother?''

"Because you would have nagged me.'' He winced when she pinched him. "Because I thought it was the least I could do.'' This time he laughed, rolling onto her as she dug her nails into his arms. "Because you're gorgeous.''

"Not good enough.''

"And marginally intelligent.''

"Keep trying.''

"Because loving you has scrambled my circuits.''

"I guess that'll do.'' Happy, she linked her arms around his neck. "Maybe it was a lot of fuss and bother, but it was a beautiful wedding. I'm glad your father talked us into something traditional.''

"It was all right, as ceremonies go.'' And when he'd seen her start down the aisle on his father's arm, draped in shimmering white, he'd been struck dumb.

"I like your parents. They've made me feel very much at home.'' With her tongue in her cheek, she looked at him again. "Especially when they let me in on deep, dark family secrets.''

"Such as?''

"The *T* in J.T.'' When he grimaced, she really began to enjoy herself. "It seems you were so rotten, so undisciplined, so…''

"I was just a curious child.''

"…so hardheaded,'' she continued, without missing a beat, "that your father used to say Trouble was your middle name. And the *T* stuck. Aptly.''

"You haven't seen trouble yet.''

She slid up again to nip his lip. "I'm hoping I will.''

After a quick kiss, he slid out of bed.

The silky sheets pooled at her waist as she sat up. "Where do you think you're going? I haven't finished with you yet."

"I forgot something." He hadn't forgotten at all. He'd been waiting for the right moment. He adjusted the lights so that they flickered like the flames of a dozen candles. Moments later, he returned with a box. "It's a gift."

"Why?"

"Because I've never given you one." He set it in her hands. "Are you going to open it or just stare at it?"

"I was enjoying the moment." With her tongue caught between her teeth, she opened the box. Inside was a teapot, squat, of cheap china, with a bird on the lid and huge, ugly daisies painted on the bowl. "Oh, God."

"I wanted you to have something from your time." He felt a little foolish, not ready to admit that he had spent months scouring antique shops. "When I saw this, it was...well, like fate. Don't cry."

"I have to." She sniffled, then raised her drenched eyes to his. "It survived. All this time."

"The best things do."

"Jacob." She made a helpless gesture, then hugged the pot. "There's nothing you could have given me that would have meant more."

"There's something else." He sat beside her. After taking the teapot, he set it aside. "Would you like to see your family for Christmas?"

For a moment, she couldn't speak. "Are you sure?"

"I'm nearly there, Sunbeam." He brushed away a

tear, let it shimmer on his fingertip. ''Just trust me a little while longer.''

Fighting tears, she put her arms around him. ''Take all the time you need. We've got forever.''

* * * * *

When California's most talked about dynasty is threatened, only family, privilege and the power of love can protect them!

THE COLTONS

Coming in September 2001

THE DOCTOR DELIVERS

by Judy Christenberry

The disappearance of her beloved foster cousin, Emily, and her stressful nationwide tour had finally taken their toll on the Colton dynasty diva, Liza Colton. But it seems the dashing doctor Nick Hathaway was working miracles on Liza's strained singing voice—and her aching heart!

Available at your favorite retail outlet.

Where love comes alive™

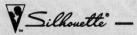